monsoonbooks

THAI GIRL

Andrew Hicks first came to Thailand in the late seventies and in more recent years has travelled extensively throughout the country with backpack and notebook, observing the interaction of Thais and foreign visitors.

In his various incarnations he has been a corporate lawyer in London and a lecturer in law at universities in Nigeria, Hong Kong, Singapore and England. When living in Hong Kong, his interest in and concern for migrant workers led him to write a bestselling self-help manual for Filipina domestic helpers. That concern is also a primary focus of this, his first novel.

The *Thai Girl* website, featuring a Readers Forum, an interview with the author, the author's acknowledgements and a picture gallery is at **www.thaigirl2004.com**.

The author welcomes your views about the book and the issues raised in it for publication on the site's Readers Forum. These should please be sent to **andrew@thaigirl2004.com**.

Andrew Hicks

thai girl

monsoon

monsoonbooks

Published in 2006
by Monsoon Books Pte Ltd
52 Telok Blangah Road
#03–05 Telok Blangah House
Singapore 098829
www.monsoonbooks.com.sg

First published in Thailand in 2004 by TYS Books,
a division of the TY Group of Companies

ISBN-10: 981-05-3918-5
ISBN-13: 978-981-05-3918-4

Printed in Singapore

10 09 08 07 06   2 3 4 5 6 7 8 9

Dedication

Thai Girl is dedicated to the migrant workers of Thailand who, through force of circumstance, leave their land and families in search of a livelihood elsewhere. In particular it is dedicated to those from Isaan, the arid North East region, who provide an endless supply of cheap labour for the modern economy and who in consequence are now losing a traditional way of life and values that are the essence of rural Thailand.

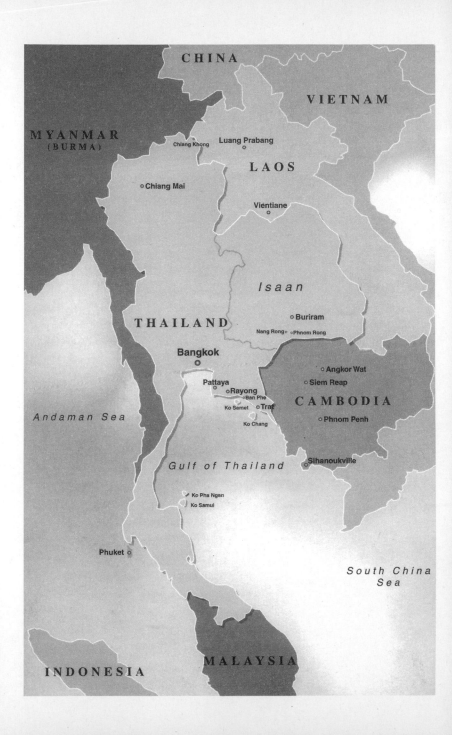

1

'Hey, Emm, where did the knickers go? They were in knickers just now,' yelled Ben over the music, keeping his eyes on the girls.

'Stuffed 'em down the boots,' Emma bellowed back.

'I must've blinked!' he hissed. 'And now they're all in their birthday suits.'

In the Bangkok go-go bar, a dozen or so Thai girls were gyrating mindlessly around chromium poles. Sitting a few feet away on pink plastic seats, Emma and Ben stared in disbelief. They were typical backpackers in tee shirts and loose trousers with leg pockets, Ben tall, fair and blue-eyed, Emma carefully made up, her dark hair tied in a neat bunch at the back. As new arrivals in Thailand their pallor contrasted with the golden skin of the dancers who now wore nothing more than thigh boots and glazed expressions.

'Must be weird for a nice lad like you, Ben ... all this flesh on display,' said Emma.

'Think I can get used to it, thanks,' he replied with a broad grin.

'Maybe that says something about you then. *You* wanted to come in here, not me. And now you've seen it all ... bums and tits to last a lifetime.'

'Well, it's certainly livelier than the bars on campus!' he said, his eyes out on stalks.

Emma's head was still spinning from twenty four hours of travel, from jetlag, a day of culture shock in a hot, steamy city, and now the deafening noise of the go-go bar.

After they were hustled inside by the touts at the door, a waitress dressed as a schoolgirl brought them cold beers and a bill that came as an unpleasant shock. To Emma's embarrassment, Ben refused to let it pass.

'The touts said there's no cover charge ... no wonder with beers at this price!' he shouted at the girl. 'What a rip-off.'

Looking hurt, she took his money and stalked off without a word.

'Rip-off or not, Ben, it's still cheaper than your snobby pubs back home. And you're getting loads to gawp at!' said Emma, glaring at him in disgust.

'Easy Emm, this is what everyone comes to see. Don't take it so seriously.'

'Not serious? Women for sale!' she retorted.

'But they look happy enough to me ... it's them chooses to be dancers.'

'Get real! Nobody does this unless they have to. And I tell you Ben, I just can't believe I'm in here!' she said, shifting uncomfortably on her seat.

'Well, I didn't force you, did I,' said Ben.

'You damn well did! You made me come with you to Thailand and now you drag me into this dreadful place.' She gave him a long, withering look.

Later that night in their grubby guesthouse room, Emma lay sobbing silently into the pillow, trying hard not to let her convulsions shake the bed. Beside her, Ben was sleeping soundly, oblivious to her distress. She lay awake for hours contemplating the rest of the holiday in Thailand with dread.

It was now a mystery to her why she had let herself be talked into travelling with him, though it was probably the romantic dream of Thailand that tipped the balance. She recalled her preconceptions of old Siam, of Anna and the King in soft focus, jumbled up with images of temples and mountains, tropical beaches, buffalo carts and rice farmers in conical hats. But she had quickly discovered that the reality was very different. Bangkok was modern and materialistic, and nothing could warn of the oppressive heat that made walking the crowded streets arduous and debilitating.

She remembered the arguments about going to Thailand together that started a few months earlier when she and Ben graduated from Sussex University on the English south coast and student life came to a sudden end. Ben was staying at his family home in Haywards Heath and she was living with her parents in Swindon, both of them working all hours to clear their student debts and save enough to go travelling. After three years in each others' pockets at university, she had quickly adapted to a more distant relationship by email and telephone; at least on the phone she could have a smoke without getting told off.

It was often Ben who picked up the phone and made the call.

'Hi Emm, how's it going?' he began, his telephone voice upbeat as always.

'Grim. Crappy work and hell with the wrinklies. What about you?'

'Friend of Dad's just got me a great job doing questionnaires in the high street.'

'Daddy would have a friend! I'm still stuck in Tescos all day, and night times pulling pints in a grotty pub round the corner,' she grumbled.

'So what's wrong at home then?'

'Well, everything. Soon as I get back from work Mum just starts. If plates are still dirty from breakfast, she goes ballistic … and when I spend too long on the phone or in the shower. It's that sort of stupid stuff.'

'Is that all?'

'No, they make me feel I've let them down because I can't find a proper job,' she said miserably.

'What's the hurry to get a job anyway? Come to Thailand with me instead … you always said you would.'

'I'm not sure I can, Ben. Jobs are so difficult to find and if I drift off, I won't get anything worth having.'

'Stuff careers! Live life first.'

'You mean run away?' Emma hugged the phone and chewed her lip.

'Remember us in third year, Emm? Thinking about the beaches was the only thing that kept us going. But anyway, if you don't come with me, what are you going to do with yourself?'

Emma had no answer which made her even more irritated by Ben's casual failure to look for a career. With his solid middle class background, his self-confidence and family contacts, he gave her the impression that the world owed him a living. As she lay on the bed in Bangkok unable to sleep, her smouldering resentment came back to her, the phone conversation always predictable.

'Emm, why did you want to work for M & S anyway? One step up from stacking shelves if you ask me. And that biscuit factory thing in Swindon was rubbish.'

'Well, I was going for something secure.'

'But why get a job you don't really like?'

'Got to do something.'

'And if you weren't that keen, why worry when you didn't get it?'

'Because Dad sees me as a failure … even worse if I bugger off to Thailand with you,' she complained.

'Travel first, and when you get back there's always law, accounting, investment banking.'

'Maybe for you … with your family opening doors.'

'That's crap, Emm and you know it!'

Feeling insecure and sorry for herself, Emma tried not to sound too feeble. 'Life's been on rails so far,' she said, 'but they don't help you any more … after graduating you're on your own. And they keep on saying, "Well, what sort of career d'you want, Emma?" But how do I know what I want to do with the rest of my life?'

'Keep working at it and the right thing'll turn up,' said Ben.

'Me with a Lower Second in Sociology? Awesome or what!'

'You've got to believe in yourself, Emm, you're not that useless.'

'Ben, I really hate you sometimes.'

'And I hate your moods and sulks.'

As she lay sweltering in the damp heat of the tropical night, Emma thought of the time Ben rang to tell her about taking his little sister into the local pub for the first time. There was something about Ben's cosiness with Megan that always infuriated her.

'Emm, she's still only sixteen,' said Ben, 'but the barman didn't even ask her age.'

'That's fine for you, isn't it … playing the big brother,' she said frowning into the phone. 'But me being a younger sister isn't that great, I can tell you. Now Kate's married and gone, it all falls on me.'

'What does?'

'Like mealtimes. Mum says, "When'll you be back for supper tonight?" Or, "What would you like to have?" And it drives me mad.'

'What's so wrong with that?'

'She does it to provoke me … control freak, sort of.'

'I don't get you,' he said, sounding surprised.

'She makes a fuss over every little job and expects me to fit in with her routine. It does my head in. Then she says, "Emma, when did you last cook or shop? You never put the rubbish out, Emma." And "What about the cat litter?"'

'Parents say stuff like that,' said Ben.

Emma ignored him and kept talking.

'It's what she doesn't say as well. My room's a mess, but she doesn't dare tell me to tidy up … just comes in and noses around, violating my personal space.'

'Come on Emm, it's not that bad being at home.'

'I hate it. I feel trapped.'

'Better come to Thailand with me then,' he said triumphantly.

'Shut up Ben and listen. Why aren't you shit-scared about what you're going to do when you get back?'

'Well, I'm going to enjoy travelling and think about a career after. One thing at a time.'

His glib answers annoyed her, especially as he was refusing to see that their relationship was at a crossroads.

'Look Ben,' she said, 'the problem with me coming to Thailand's not just about careers … it's about us as well.'

'Why's it about us?'

'Now we've finished uni, what are we going to do? Travel together or call it a day?'

'Hadn't really thought about it like that,' he said vaguely.

'Why not, you wally?' She flicked her lighter and lit a cigarette.

'Dunno, Emm. All I know's we promised ourselves a trip. You were as keen as me.'

'But it's more complicated now. You're no help ... and I get so much pressure from Mum and Dad not to go.'

'My folks are okay ... they think me travelling's a great idea.'

'They would! Mummy's blue-eyed boy!' She drew angrily on the cigarette.

'Oh sod off! Don't start that again,' said Ben.

'No, I'm just not sure I still want to go with you.'

'Why ever not?' he said, sounding hurt.

'Because I'm not sure about you any more ... sorry, but I had to say it.'

'Emm, please don't let me down now,' he begged. 'Maybe it'll bring us back together.'

'No, I've got to make a go of things here,' she said. 'Though if I can't find a decent job ... suppose I'll have to come with you to Thailand.'

Sleepless on Khao San Road listening to the sounds of the city, Emma knew that this had been decision-making by default; it was no decision at all. And the dream of Thailand that had finally persuaded her to travel with him was so far totally failing to materialise.

Emma had never liked flying, but she tried to be fatalistic. Once Ben had booked the flights, she was destined to converge at the airport with several hundred others, to present her ticket and passport and be herded onto the plane. She could be fated to die in a ghastly inferno or be seated next to someone who snores. She was to be catapulted across the globe to a world she had never before experienced, her ordered existence ending at Bangkok airport where another very different culture begins.

The long but comfortable Qantas flight passed surprisingly quickly as she and Ben were able to snatch some sleep before landing in Bangkok. The airport was still part of their own familiar world but, tired and bleary from more than twenty hours of travelling, both were subdued and anxious. They queued before a silent immigration officer who stamped visas into their passports; this was not yet the land of smiles. They waited by the carousel for their backpacks, then passed through customs and walked down the long arrivals hall. Confronting a dark sea of Thais, many holding up the names of arriving passengers, Emma longed to be met or to have a comfortable hotel already booked.

Walking out through the glass doors into the roar of the traffic, they were hit by the smell of diesel fumes and drains and by a blanket of hot, humid air. There were taxis parked in lines and Thai faces everywhere, the taxi touts milling about and talking loudly. Emma was feeling overwhelmed and disorientated. But everything happened fast and she soon found herself sitting in the back of a small green and red Nissan taxi, their rucksacks stowed safely in the boot. The driver was smiley and communicative.

'Okay, you go Khao San Road? First time in Thailand?'

'Yes,' said Ben, doing the talking.

'You married already?'

'No, we're students.'

'*Farang* have money, so why you not married?'

'What's *farang*?' asked Ben, ducking the question.

'*Farang* means European. *Farang* good for business ... so welcome to Thailand.' The cheerful taxi driver, their first Thai, was making a good impression.

The Bangkok traffic was a crazy roller-coaster ride, the taxi sitting gridlocked for ages, then surging forward aggressively before hitting the next blockage.

'*Rot dtit*,' said the taxi driver. 'Traffic jam every day.' Emma marvelled that it was possible to be a Bangkok taxi driver and stay sane.

Staring out as the urban landscape unfolded, she was struck by the sheer scale of the city, its high-rise tower blocks crowding on all sides, concrete grey as far as the eye could see. Speeding along the overhead expressway, she could look down on flat roofs cluttered with pot plants, washing lines and television aerials, human details in a harsh environment.

Massive hoardings stood next to the road: Mitsubishi Motors,

Quality in Motion; Cathay Pacific, the Heart of Asia; Bridgestone, a Grip on the Future; Volkswagen, Panasonic, Canon, Pepsi and Nissan, all familiar names in a globalised world. From the next hoardings they passed the glossy haired Sunsilk girls gazed serenely down on the traffic jams with global eyes, eyes that to Emma looked hardly Asian.

As they rushed towards the city centre, she silently admired the towers of Thai Airways, clad in gleaming blue glass and, to her surprise, lavish showrooms for Porsche and Jaguar cars. In front of her stood the tallest building she had ever seen, the seventy eight storeys of the Bayoke tower, on her right the roofs of a traditional Thai temple a bizarre contrast to the stark commercial phalluses of the city.

This seemed to be a city of extremes, the sleek modern buildings dwarfing older ones which were grimy and unmaintained. Its quirkiness was brought home to her when the taxi driver, passing a Buddhist shrine outside a luxury hotel, took both his hands off the wheel, held them together in prayer and bowed his head down low.

Exciting though it all seemed, Emma was already finding Bangkok more than a little scary. This ugly place in which she would have to survive on a shoe-string budget was alien and threatening. Though cocooned in the taxi and about to start the holiday of a lifetime, her butterflies were rampant; it was like teetering at the top of the high diving board, staring down at the water.

The dull ache in her stomach was even worse when at last she took the plunge, nervously emerging from the taxi onto the pavement in Khao San Road. Her first glance took in a street packed with guest houses, travel agents and cafés. On both sides were shops and stalls, selling everything backpackers might need. She could see colourful tee shirts and ethnic trinkets, food for sale off barrows, and everywhere busy crowds of cool-looking travellers.

Feeling very much the new girl in school, Emma shouldered her pack and apprehensively set off with Ben to find somewhere to stay. In three or four backstreet places they asked for a room but there were no vacancies. She was becoming overwhelmed by the heat, her back aching from hours on the plane and from carrying her heavy rucksack. Tiredness, dehydration, culture shock and the fear of not finding anywhere showed in her face.

'Look Emm, sit down with the bags and I'll go and look on my own,' said Ben.

'But what if I don't like it?'

'Oh stuff that. We can always move on tomorrow.'

She breathed a sigh of relief when Ben came back, having found a room in a dingy guesthouse. Damp and musty and with communal showers and toilets, at least it was well within their budget. 'What's wrong with cockroaches anyway,' he said as he opened the door.

Feeling thoroughly let down by Thailand, Emma was appalled at what she saw inside, though she dared not complain. Now she somehow had to get through the rest of the day and then face a long evening struggling to stay awake. She did not expect it to be fun, but her first night out with Ben in Bangkok was to be nothing short of a disaster.

2

Never one to opt for an early night even after an exhausting journey, it was Ben who suggested they take a look at Bangkok's famous nightlife. Emma had no better ideas and knew he would not be easily dissuaded, so she protested only weakly when he told the taxi driver to take them to the bar area off Sukhumvit Road.

The tropical night was exotic and steamy, just like the nightlife. Emma would have preferred a walk down one of the quieter *sois*, a side street of bars, travel agents and hotels, but Ben seemed to know where he wanted to go.

'So what's this evil-looking place then?' she asked him.

'It's Nana Plaza ... like Patpong but not as sleazy. Gotta see it now we're here.'

'Speak for yourself! Looks a hell-hole to me.'

With Emma trailing behind, Ben led the way past stalls selling food from fried insects and bamboo grubs to spicy Thai curries. In the open-air bars on the ground floor, they could see beer-swilling western men being minded by bar girls and beyond in a three-storeyed building, the air-conditioned go-go bars, their names flaunted in garish neon signs; 'Caligulas', 'San Francisco Strip.' 'Big show now on.'

'I wouldn't mind somewhere with aircon,' said Ben. 'And maybe with a show.'

'Aircon's fine but what sort of show?'

'No idea Emm, but we'll only find out if we give it a go.'

'Amazing Thailand, my arse ... none of this was in the brochures,' she said bitterly.

She followed Ben up the stairway to the open gallery on the first floor where they crossed to the balustrade and looked down onto the rubbish strewn roofs of the bars below. Rangy cats prowled nearby and stared at them with wary eyes.

'Come on Emm, let's have a look in the bars then,' said Ben.

'Do we really have to,' moaned Emma.

Walking down the gallery they passed a group of girls sitting on tin stools around folding tables, unselfconsciously doing each others' hair and make-up and eating rice from styrofoam takeaway boxes. At the first bar, the touts tried to stop them going past, throwing back the curtain across the open doorway for them to see inside.

'Welkaam, sir … take a look, sir. No cover charge.'

Through the curtain they got their first glimpse of a go-go bar. Lit with flickering purple lights and pulsating with music, it was almost empty of customers. Emma's eye was compelled by the girls in backless thongs, dancing around poles on a raised platform in the middle of the room, some of them flabby and overweight. Detesting the touts who were all over her, she backed away from the door, trying to make her escape.

'No Ben, I'm not going in there,' she said.

'Nor me … the girls look like you since you put on all that weight.' Emma bit her lip and pretended not to have heard him.

As they went further along the gallery, they were set upon by touts at each doorway, one a dwarf in a Mexican hat.

'Come inside sir … lovely girls, lesbian fucking show.'

A glance through the curtains confirmed that the bars were much the same, a place to drink and pick a girl.

Outside the last door, several bar girls were spread across the walkway, lounging around on stools. In tight G-strings and flouncey dresses, they were bizarre, almost witch-like. Suddenly Ben twigged and rushed past, afraid to make eye contact. This was the gay bar; these were the fabled ladyboys he had been reading about.

'Bugger me if I'd go anywhere near that lot,' he said over his shoulder.

'But what's the difference, Ben? It's just the same … sex for sale.'

They hastily made for the stairs up to the next floor, the air super-heated from the air conditioners that vented into the stairwell.

'Hey, this bar looks livelier,' said Ben. 'Let's have a quick beer.'

'Suppose I can't stop you!' complained Emma.

And so she found herself reluctantly sitting in the G-String bar on their first night in Bangkok, confronting a varied assortment of bare breasts. At first she sat awkwardly upright, while Ben leaned forward, his elbows on the seat backs in front for a better view. He was living out his ultimate fantasy.

As the girls clung to their poles, sometimes chatting and joking with each other, the music pounded incessantly; "It's my life … it's now or never, and I ain't gonna live forever!" A few danced vigorously, undulating their bodies up and down the pole in a sinuous rhythm, eyeing their reflections in the mirrors that lined the walls, but most looked terminally bored.

The customers were mainly tourists, including a number of couples. Emma guessed that like Ben, they claimed to be there because Bangkok's nightlife just has to be seen. Though as she glanced round she could also see several single men with girls draped over them who were clearly not there for spectator sport only.

When there was a break in the music, the girls sitting with customers got up and changed places with the dancers on stage, revealing to Ben the mystery of the disappearing knickers.

'Now I get it,' he said. 'They slip a leg out and shove their pants down the top of the other thigh boot! Cunning eh, Emm?'

Emma was not impressed.

As Ben watched in fascination, two girls in blue bikinis who had just finished dancing casually came and sat alongside him. The nearer one whispered something into his ear, took his hand and began to massage it firmly with both of hers. Emma, sitting the other side of him, was appalled.

'What you name?' asked the girl.

'I'm Ben,' he replied. 'And what's yours?'

'My name Porn.' Ben tried not to laugh.

As Porn then began to rub his thigh, Emma looked on in anger and disgust; she felt she had become invisible to both of them. Ben was now eye to eye with his temptress who was trying to say something to him about cola. Stirred by the spread of her thighs and the cleft of her bust he broke into a sweat. Porn picked up a drinks menu and started fanning him furiously.

'You buy lady drink? Cola for my friend,' she asked him sweetly. Emma was quick to figure out that as well as selling their bodies, their job was to sell drinks. Seething with barely contained indignation, she turned and dug Ben hard in the ribs. Porn, realising she was onto a loser, gave up on him and moved away.

'Christ Ben, I've had enough of this,' said Emma.

'Enough of what?'

'How could you let her do that right in front of me. You were just lapping it up.'

'Couldn't stop her,' he said feebly.

'Do you have absolutely no respect for me?'

'Course I have,' he said, with a grin on his face, still staring at the dancers.

'Like hell, you do! I've had it up to here!' Abruptly she jumped up from her seat and stormed off, disappearing into the crowded bar.

Baffled by her recent moodiness and reluctant to miss the show, Ben did not attempt to follow her.

Emma was thinking of dumping him and going straight back to the guesthouse, but first she had to make for the toilet at the far end of the bar. To her dismay she found it packed with men and go-go dancers waiting silently in line for the stalls, as disengaged as office workers queuing for the photocopier. When at last she closed the toilet door behind her there was a moment of relative calm, only spoiled by the sight of the wet seat and the open bucket into which used paper and other horrors were thrown.

As she fought for a washbasin, something snapped inside her; she had taken more than enough for one night. She was damned if she was going to take a taxi home on her own, leaving Ben to his own devices in the bar. Angrily pushing her way out, she found him still sitting engrossed, just as she had left him a few minutes before.

'Say something then,' she demanded, refusing to sit down.

'What's that?' he said half ignoring her.

'Right Ben, you've really done it now … we're going.'

'Hang on Emm, let's give it a bit longer. There's a new load of girls coming on.'

A group of three girls were now dancing directly in front of them. Young and fresh, they seemed to be enjoying themselves, laughing and joking with each other. One of them stood out because although she was topless, she was wearing long blue cargo pants. She kept rolling down the waistband of her trousers to show her bikini bottoms, the suggestion far more erotic for Ben than the full nudity of the others.

Emma was by now becoming more and more enraged.

'I told you Ben, we're going … right now. Look, don't get me wrong, I don't care what you do, but first you take me back to our flea-pit,' she shouted, giving his arm an angry pull. Slowly he got up and followed her to the door, conspicuously glancing backwards at the stage.

In the heat of the night, they ran the gauntlet of the touts outside the bars as they left Nana Plaza. Neither of them spoke, Emma seething silently. Back in the street, they walked in the direction of Sukhumvit Road looking for a taxi.

'That was exactly what you wanted to see, wasn't it,' she challenged him.

'We had to give it a go, Emm … we are in Bangkok!'

'Well, *I* didn't have to see it.'

'Then next time you'd better stay home. Swindon's safer,' said Ben sharply. Emma gritted her teeth and tried to ignore the provocation.

'So tell me Ben, did you like it?' she retaliated.

'It was okay,' he said flatly.

'Okay was it? So what was it you liked? Tell me that.'

'Oh sod off Emm … get off my back. It's only dancing girls.'

'Only dancing girls!' she shouted. 'But these girls are for sale, for pity's sake.'

'No, they're not,' said Ben, looking apprehensive.

'They damn well are. The men pay the bar to take them out, then screw'em for sixpence.'

'Maybe some of them do it for the dosh … but you can't blame them, Emm.'

'I'm not blaming the girls, idiot, I'm blaming the men! Like the bar owner and the tossers in there ogling their tits, just like you were, Ben,' she fumed.

'Yes, but you're a loser if you pay for sex. I'd never pay for it.'

'Because it offends your male ego I suppose … not because you're abusing the girl! Anyway Ben, you never pay because you fuck me for free … but not tonight you won't!' She looked daggers as he anxiously watched out for a taxi.

'Thought you'd like to see Nana Plaza, Emm,' he said, trying to sound conciliatory.

'You had it all planned, bringing me here, didn't you. Bet you wish I wasn't around … I'm really cramping your style!' Her fury came to a climax. 'And how *dare* you tell me I'm fat!'

Ben was beginning to realise that Emma was more angry than he had ever seen her.

'Easy Emm, cool it. What've I done to make you so mad?' He gave her a look of offended innocence.

'That's the point … you just don't get it, do you,' she snapped.

'Yes okay, so I liked the girlies … what normal bloke wouldn't.'

'All men are blokes and aren't answerable, is that it?' said Emma frostily.

'Well, some of 'em were drop-dead gorgeous … but Emm, you can't be jealous about bar girls.'

She kept her cool but was raging inside.

'So you tell me this then,' she said. 'Which girl did you like the best?'

'Tricky one,' he laughed. 'Spoiled for choice!'

'Maybe … but tell me which one you'd choose for yourself.'

Standing on the kerbside late at night looking for a taxi, the traffic pounding past, Ben then made his big mistake. He answered her question.

'I'll go for the one in long pants with the pert little tits. She's really something, Emm … you don't have to be a man to see that.'

'And you don't have to be a man to hit someone!'

The sound of the slap and his cry of surprise and pain made the Thais in the street briefly turn their heads, though they had become indifferent to the uncouth foreigners in their scruffy clothes.

After a silent taxi ride back to the guesthouse on Khao San Road, Emma found herself suffocating in their tiny room. She was repelled by the smelly grey bed sheet and the towelling bedspread which she guessed had covered a multitude of bodies since last being laundered. The stagnant air was hot and humid and showering in the washroom down the corridor did not clean the stickiness from her skin. Lying on the bed with Ben at arms length beside her in the semi-darkness, she could contain her feelings no longer.

'It was you pushed me into coming to Thailand, Ben,' she said. 'And now you do this to me!'

'Do what to you?' he said, sitting up in surprise.

'Walking all over me … treating me like shit.'

'That's rubbish, Emm!'

'No Ben, I still can't believe you slobbering over those girls right in front of me.'

'Look, we've been through this already … and I'm sorry,' he said in a low voice.

'It's no use saying sorry. You can't undo it now, you know.'

'Can't undo what?'

'I mean the next time we're together, I'll know you're fucking the Thai girl with the pert little tits … and not making love to me. If there is a next time that is!' She turned away from him and rolled herself into a ball, holding her knees tightly to her chest.

3

The morning after the late night out, Emma was awake far too early. She lay looking at the ceiling, Ben in his boxer shorts sprawled on his front next to her, still dead to the world. Mulling over their months apart since graduating, her mind awash with the strife in the girlie bar, she very much feared travelling with him could go terribly wrong. Hardly able to sleep under the wheezing fan and detesting the heat of the city, she longed to get out of Bangkok; the Thailand she had dreamed of must surely be elsewhere.

Ben woke up that morning determined to enjoy the day, having apparently forgotten the furious argument of the previous night. He was in buoyant but provocative mood as they got ready to visit their first Thai temple.

'Come on Emm, let's get going.'

'Just wait can't you.'

'While you get dolled up! Emm, you don't need lipstick.'

'Shut up, Ben,' she said pursing her crimson lips in the mirror.

'You're reinventing yourself again. Like those highlights ... hardly recognised you at Heathrow,' he said mercilessly.

'Bet you wish I hadn't come, now you don't fancy me anymore.'

'You used to have a great body, Emm, and you kept your hair natural.'

'Mousey hair, you called it,' she said resentfully.

'And do you really need that long skirt? You're trying too hard again.'

'You complain when I don't,' she said, almost inaudibly.

'Well, at least the skirt hides your bum!' Ben fingered the door handle impatiently.

'Piss off, Ben. You're just horrible!'

'But Emm, you used to love being teased,' he said more gently.

'No, I didn't! I always hated it,' she whispered, sitting down suddenly on the edge of the bed. 'The long skirt's for the temple … but I'll wear what the hell I like anyway.'

Ben had decided that their first trip out should be to the Grand Palace and Wat Phra Kaeo, the Temple of the Emerald Buddha. From Khao San Road to the temple, they had their first tuk tuk ride. The tuk tuk, a tiny three-wheeled taxi, was waiting by the side of the road, the driver looking for business.

'How much to the Grand Palace?' demanded Ben.

'Gran' Palace, fifty baht.'

'Not fifty baht! Twenty baht,' said Ben.

The driver furiously revved the engine, covering them in exhaust smoke and glanced over his shoulder for a gap in the traffic.

'Forty baht last price.'

'Okay, forty baht.'

Honour satisfied and an apparent discount won, Ben climbed in, followed by Emma. The tuk tuk had a bench seat behind the driver and was clearly not for those of a sensitive disposition. They were not strapped in and were open to the elements, except for a low plastic hood. The engine had a prodigious output of noise and fumes and propelled the little cyclops-eyed projectile at suicidal speeds through the heavy traffic. As they passed along the side of Sanam Luang, the dusty open space once used for executions and Royal cremations, they clung on for grim death, scared but exhilarated. Ben felt cheated of his forty baht when all too soon they screeched to a halt by a gateway through the palace walls.

The Grand Palace satisfied even Emma's lust for the exotic. This was the ultimate oriental fantasy, a maze of buildings in classical Thai style, of soaring roofs, spires and pinnacles in white, gold and many rich hues. Packed with visitors, they all had to take off their shoes at the door of the temple itself, Thai shoes going in one set of racks and foreign shoes in another, though the smell of feet was the same.

Inside the temple the wardens beckoned Emma and Ben to sit down like the Thais, the feet carefully pointed away from the Buddha image. High up on its tiny gilded throne, the Emerald Buddha presided over a scene of reverence and awe. It was clear to Emma that for the Thais, visiting the temple was of deep spiritual significance and that they were strongly imbued with the ritual of Buddhism. She watched as a group of elderly ladies made offerings of lotus flowers, candles and joss sticks at the altar. Thailand at last she thought.

The Grand Palace was unbearably hot and humid and even the locals were glowing and mopping their brows. Emma sat and wilted, but Ben was determined to go on to Wat Po, another temple nearby, to see the famous reclining Buddha. Back in the street he approached a young tuk tuk driver with a low opening bid.

'Twenty baht to Wat Po, okay?'

'Okay, okay, twenty baht.'

Ben was disappointed to be denied a haggle but as they shot away into the traffic, the driver turned and spoke to him over his shoulder.

'Wat Po closed already. Big soldier die, have cremation. Later go.'

'But you said you'd take us,' shouted Ben, not sure he'd taken it all in. Why accept the fare to Wat Po and then cry off?

The driver shouted back, swerving recklessly through the heavy traffic.

'Sorry, no probrem. I take you better temple, go shopping, then come back Wat Po two o'crock.'

'Come off it mate, this stinks. Wat Po, now, pronto.' Ben tapped him on the shoulder and pointed ahead down the road.

'Ben!' Emma chimed in as the driver angrily screeched to a halt at the side of the road. 'You've really upset him now.'

They got out onto the pavement in surprise as the driver refused to take them any further. Ben handed him ten baht and they headed off on foot, his curses sounding in their ears.

'Well, that wasn't very clever,' said Emma. 'It's bloody hot and we've no idea where we are.'

'Look, Emm, you're so naive. He was onto some sort of rip-off ... to take us to expensive shops and get commissions.'

'He was okay until you pissed him off.'

'He pissed *me* off! Anyway, we've got the map and it's not that far.'
They reached Wat Po on foot in ten minutes and it was open after all.

Emma found Wat Po less formal than the Grand Palace, a riot of
colourful temples, trees and sculpted bushes, the reclining Buddha, a vast
gilded figure peeping out from inside the temple building. She too was
feeling the need to recline when they came to a place in the grounds
where visitors can stop for a traditional Thai massage or to have their
fortunes told.

'So what's it to be, Emm?' asked Ben. 'A sweaty massage or
the fortune-teller? The sign says he can predict your love life after
marriage.'

'Don't want to think about the future, least of all my love life. Let's
get back to Khao San Road.'

Now wary of tuk tuks, they took an air-conditioned taxi which gave
them a chance to talk in relative cool and calm.

'Look, Ben, I'm not sure I can hack much more of Bangkok,' said
Emma, slumped exhausted in the back seat. 'I want to move on.'

'Okay then. We can try one of the travel agents next to our doss
house.'

'It's Chiang Mai I really fancy. Should be cooler in the mountains.'

'No Emm, I'm desperate for a beach,' said Ben insistently.

They pushed their way through tightly packed stalls selling clothes
and cheap jewellery to get to the travel agents in Khao San Road, its door
covered with hand written signs: 'Cambodia visa service, special island
visit, Koh Chang, Koh Samet.' Inside the tiny office Emma only cared
about the cool of the air conditioning and even ignored the cockroach
that skittered across the chaos of papers and files on the desk. Two male
travellers thumbing through a ring-binder of brochures, shifted their
chairs along to make room for them. The girl behind the desk, done up
like a china doll, gave them a synthetic smile but said nothing as they sat
down.

'We want to get out of Bangkok. Islands, beaches … Cambodia
maybe,' said Ben.

'Uh? You go Cambodia?' said the girl. Emma looked on, a little surprised.

'What about Angkor Wat?' he asked.

'No problem. Minibus to Aranyaprathet, then open truck to Siem Reap. Road no good but very cheap. Twenty people in the back, hot and dirty ... nine hours, maybe twelve. Better you fly aeroplane if you care your ass.'

'Have you ever been to Cambodia?'

'Why I go? I care my ass,' she said with a grimace.

'Can't afford to fly so it's got to be islands and beaches then.'

'Chiang Mai and mountains,' pleaded Emma.

One of the travellers sitting next to them leaned across.

'Couldn't help hearing you,' he said in a strong Australian accent. 'If it's an island you want, I can suggest the very thing. Not far, great scene.'

'Sure, we're interested,' replied Ben. 'What's it called?'

'The island's Koh Samet ... six kilometres long and only about three hours east of Bangkok. Chuck and me are getting a minibus there tomorrow morning.'

'What d'you think, Emm?' asked Ben.

'Sounds okay. Anything's better than Bangkok,' she said, collapsed in her chair.

'Right,' said Ben to the cupid's bow at the desk. 'We'll go for it.'

'Minibus tomorrow? Maybe full already,' she said.

There was a sharp intake of breath from Emma.

'But you told us no problem for seats,' Chuck, the American chipped in. The girl gave him a sour look, silently picked up the phone, and in ten minutes they all had tickets booked for the next day to Koh Samet.

'Minibus outside tomorrow morning eight thirty,' she said to Emma and Ben.

'But you told us nine o'clock,' said Maca.

'Better I say them eight thirty so come nine o'crock. Don't want late for bus.'

Ben was relieved at getting something settled and maybe to mollify Emma.

'So we'll all be going together then. Brilliant,' he said to the two traveller types.

'Yeah mate, good on yuh.' The Australian extended his hand. 'I'm Maca and this is Chuck. Think we should celebrate with a beer?'

'Great idea,' said Ben.

'Cool,' said Chuck vacantly as the girl looked on in amusement and picked at her bowl of greasy noodles.

After the chill of the shop, the noise and heat of the street again engulfed them. Khao San Road's chaos of stalls and eating places was crowded and lively. Maca and Chuck gravitated to their favourite bar, open-fronted with rattan seats, full of transients of every kind watching an English soccer match on a large TV screen. The four of them took a table and Maca ordered beers all round.

'So how long've you been in Thailand, Maca?' Ben asked him.

'Well, coming and going to Cambodia and Lao, been here about six months this time. But I've lived several years in Thailand altogether ... working on irrigation projects in the North East.'

'And where else have you been? Travelling I mean.'

'Don't get me yabbering on about that, mate ... I'd bore you silly.'

'No way, man! Maca's Africa story's wild,' said Chuck with rare animation.

'And how about you two?' asked Maca, tipping back his beer bottle.

'Well, we've hardly been anywhere,' said Ben. 'Emm and me just finished uni so we're chilling out for a bit.'

'Sweet,' drawled Chuck, gazing into the middle distance.

'Oh ... and we're Ben and Emm,' added Ben.

'Good to meet yuh, Ben,' said Maca, and to Emma, 'M as in Melbourne?'

'No, Emm as in Emma. So why are you "Maca"?' she asked him.

'Cos' I'm Andy Mackintosh. And you have to be British, right?'

'How did you know that!' said Emma innocently.

Well lubricated with beer, the preliminary chit chat was relaxed and easy. Maca and Chuck had clearly done it many times before, meeting fellow travellers and comparing experiences, while Ben and Emma were sizing up this new species for the first time. Emma characterised Maca as a typical outback Australian of about thirty. In saggy beige jeans and an old shirt with long sleeves half rolled up, his tangled mop of hair was tied in a bunch at the back. His skin looked dry and freckly and his face was creased into a slightly inane grin, the pale blue eyes constantly smiling. He wore his body awkwardly as if he was not fully coordinated; doped up perhaps, she thought. She took to him immediately though she did not exactly fancy him.

Chuck, the American, was the better-looking one. Deeply tanned with a strong physique, his soft brown eyes peered from behind rimless spectacles. In his mid-twenties, he wore long baggy shorts, a fresh tee shirt and fake Adidas sandals, his beard well-trimmed, a little Jewish. Emma was intrigued by his reserve and tried to bring him into the conversation.

'What do you do Chuck?'

He looked slightly startled at being spoken to.

'What do I do? When?'

'I mean your work.'

'Work? I travel … same as Maca.' There was a long pause. 'Have to get back to school and finish like you two, maybe.'

'But you must've worked sometime?'

'Yeah … got a computer business. Set it up back in the States designing web site solutions. It was cool, but I needed some space.'

'And Maca, how about you?' asked Ben.

'Electrical engineer. I work wherever there's a skills shortage … Jiddah, Dubai, Hong Kong, and of course Thailand. Good money, but travelling's best.'

'Well we're still amateurs at travelling,' said Ben, 'but it's been great so far.'

'Speak for yourself,' protested Emma testily.

'So what's bugging you about Bangkok, Emma?' asked Maca.

'Well, the obvious things I suppose. Bloody hot, overcrowded, just an ugly city and some of the people are so rude. Tuk tuk driver tried to rip us off and that girl in the travel agents wouldn't hold down a job at home … got no idea of customer service.'

'Okay Emm,' said Ben, 'but what about the taxi driver from the airport ... the most stressed-out job in the universe and he was really nice. And the tuk tuk driver was only taking us for a few pence.'

'But everyone's lazy and slow with no idea about time-keeping and stuff. It's just the impression I get. You know, the girl in the guesthouse asleep at the desk ... no towels, no soap.' She picked nervously at the damp label on her beer bottle.

'But Emm, isn't that the charm of the place?' said Maca. 'It's a modern city but so laid back. Even when the going gets tough, it's always *sanuk*'.

'What's *sanuk*?'

'*Sanuk* means fun. It's the Thai way of life.'

'I hadn't noticed,' said Emma moodily.

'And we *farang* have it so easy in Thailand,' Maca persisted. 'For us, it's all so cheap.'

'Cheap labour and poor service.'

'You think the Thais are lazy then, Emm? Don't kid yourself. Most of them work nonstop for piss-poor pay. Like our waitress ... after cleaning up late at night, she'll be serving breakfast first thing in the morning.'

'Suppose I'm lucky to be a student,' admitted Emma.

'She probably left school at fourteen to work in Bangkok,' said Maca. 'And now she has to watch us living off the fat of the land and telling her what to do.'

'Hey guys, this is getting a bit serious. What about some food?' interrupted Ben as he thumbed through the menu. 'There's some weird things in here ... how about the duck's blood cake with oyster sauce or the fried pig's entrails? What d'you think Emm? Food now or later?'

But Chuck had other ideas. Food was not on his agenda.

'Think it'd be cool to see some *muay Thai* tonight ... that place off Sukhumvit Road?'

'We went to Sukhumvit Road last night,' said Emma. 'But what's *muay Thai*?'

'Kick boxing ... it's like a national sport. They use the feet, knees and elbows and belt each other just about anywhere. You'd love it.'

'No, I wouldn't,' said Emma. 'You don't want to go, do you, Ben?'

'Dunno ... but if these two guys are going, well, why not. Come on

Emm, join in.'

She sat silently as the lads planned the trip around her. Chuck was keen, Maca was ready to go along with anything and Ben was warming to the idea. Emma was the only problem.

'Why not Emm? Since we're here, we've got to see it,' urged Ben.

'You can't use that argument on me this time,' she said curtly. 'I'm going to get an early night. You can watch two men beating each other to a pulp if that's what appeals to you.' Her bitter glance at Ben was not lost on Maca and Chuck.

Alone that second uncomfortable night in their cheap guesthouse, Emma thought of the two men she had just met; Maca, with his easy Australian manner, so well-informed but free of pretension, and Chuck, strangely diffident and shy, with his attractive American accent, striking good looks and serious glasses. If she were marooned with them alone on a desert island, which one would she go for? Choosing between them proved impossible so it would have to be a hybrid ... Maca re-bodied with Chuck's physique.

But there were many more important things to think about. Sleep was impossible as she lay and agonised about Ben, wondering what he was up to with his two eccentric friends out on the dark streets of Bangkok. It seemed an eternity as she waited for the sounds of his return.

4

That evening Ben met up with Maca and Chuck at the end of Khao San Road by the tourist police post. Maca called a tuk tuk and agreed a fare without bothering to haggle, and they all squeezed themselves into the seat behind the driver. As the bar with the Thai boxing was at least forty minutes away in the heavy evening traffic, they had decided to catch a ferry boat down the river where they could pick up the Skytrain to Sukhumvit Road.

'I'm sorry Emm's not going to see the boxing,' said Ben, 'but she's a bit squeamish about things she hasn't seen before ... like in Spain she refused to come to the bullfight.'

'Gotta keep an open mind,' said Maca cheerfully.

The tuk tuk quickly arrived at the ferry pier near Thammasat University where radical campaigners for democracy had been violently suppressed in the early seventies. Now the area was peaceful, a centre for trading in traditional medicines and Buddhist amulets, tiny Buddha images worn on a pendant round the neck. A row of small shops, their open fronts spilling goods onto the pavement, ran down to a square of well-restored shop-houses. People were shopping and eating and sitting in the cool of the evening under the frangipani trees whose richly-scented flowers were scattered on the ground.

'I like this place,' said Maca. 'It's just how old Bangkok should be preserved.'

They walked into the ferry terminus building, through stalls selling tourist trinkets and a profusion of fruit and cooked foods. The sun was falling and casting a soft glow from the west, the heat of the day beginning to moderate as they reached the pontoon to wait for the ferry.

Wider than the Thames in London, the Chao Phraya river was muddy and brown and, unlike the Thames, it was a busy thoroughfare. The slowest boats were trains of barges moving at a snail's pace behind a tug, the fastest the brightly coloured long-tailed boats, slim passenger craft carrying up to forty people. Their bows were dramatically flared upwards and hung with plastic flowers as offerings to the aquatic spirits, the engines high up behind the driver powering a long prop-shaft at the back.

From the pontoon Ben watched the long-tails screaming along the river like demented insects, kicking up sheets of spray. His ears were assailed by the noise of their engines, by the roar of traffic from the road, the scream of metal on metal as the pontoon lifted on the waves and the shriek of the boat-boys' whistles. The river was vibrant and alive. Nothing was quiet and inscrutable here.

'Okay mate, this is ours, the Chao Phraya River Express,' said Maca, pointing to a long shark-like ferry coming down the river. It reversed into the jetty in a surge of foaming water as a deck-hand flicked a rope over a bollard, giving a brief moment for passengers to jump ashore. Ben and the others then joined the rush to get aboard and within seconds the powerful engine was again spewing fumes, pushing the boat fast through the murky water.

The three pleasure-seekers stood on the open deck at the stern, enjoying the scenery and the hot wind in their faces. Maca pointed out the sights to Ben; first the glittering spires of the Grand Palace and its temples, and then to the right the tall Khmer-style stupa of Wat Arun, the Temple of Dawn, backlit by the setting sun. On the left was Chinatown and on both sides, wharves and markets that would have been familiar in the days of Joseph Conrad more than a century earlier. Old wooden houses built on stilts over the water clung to the banks, their verandas crowded with pot plants and washing.

The river then took a sweep to the right, giving a clear view of the many tower blocks built when Thailand was booming in the late eighties and early nineties. There were offices, apartments and hotels, the most famous of which, the Oriental Hotel was set in leafy gardens on the edge of the water.

'You wouldn't believe the luxury in those places,' said Maca. 'Some of the top hotels are half empty, so some old bugger from the backside of Melbourne gets a luxury room thrown in with his package tour. He and his sheila are king and queen for the week and within spitting distance there's people living in slum conditions.'

'But not all the Thais are that poor,' said Ben. 'There seems to be money around.'

'Yes, but it's the contrast that gets to me … it's so in-yer-face.'

They got off the boat beneath Saphan Taksin, a massive road bridge over the river, and walked up the ramp from the pontoon.

'Look at that,' said Ben. 'They're still completing the top floors of that block. Looks like flats … forty or fifty storeys at least.'

'It's not a new development,' said Maca. 'I guess work stopped when the economy collapsed in 1997 and now it's been abandoned. That's boom and bust for you.'

In contrast, their next form of transport, the Skytrain, looked a gleaming success story. They climbed a flight of steps to the ticket concourse and up to the elevated track where a train was waiting and sat down on the yellow plastic seats. The carriage was powerfully air-conditioned and Ben was able to breathe easily again, his sweaty skin and tee shirt rapidly drying out. All was spotlessly clean and starkly modern with straps and metal poles for standing passengers to hold onto.

'Why's there no Thai girls dancing round those poles?' quipped Maca.

The view from the overhead railway was panoramic, the urban landscape of extravagant modern buildings relieved first by the greenery of Lumpini Park and then the manicured golf course and race track of the Royal Bangkok Sports Club. After changing trains at Siam Station, Ben sat high above the street as the marble facades of department stores, McDonald's outlets, green trees, Thai temples, expressways and traffic jams slipped smoothly past his window.

They got off at Nana Station and followed the stairway down to Sukhumvit Road where Ben was unable to ignore a woman on the steps begging with two tiny children, one of them crying lustily.

'You'll see plenty more of those before we're home tonight,' said Maca as Ben dropped a coin into her bowl. 'The Thais give to the poor to make merit for the next life, but you hear horror stories ... like heavily drugged children being hired out to the beggar to boost their takings, and beggars being delivered in taxis to their pitch and handing over their earnings to their protectors. Same as with the bar girls, it's always the big guys who control the cash flow.'

They walked up Sukhumvit Road, past glittering office buildings and banks, world class hotels and shopping malls, all dedicated to the *farang* and the upper end of the tourist industry. This was the place to shop for curios, carvings and handicrafts, for silks and designer labels, fake watches and flick knives, for leather and live skin. It was just an anonymous tourist trap and Ben did not much like it.

He and Maca followed Chuck to an open-air bar down one of the *sois* where the Thai boxing had already started. The clientele were mainly older *farang* males of all shapes and sizes, in singlet or tee shirt, shapeless shorts and trainers. As always there were bar girls sitting waiting at empty tables or draped over the men whose wallets they hoped to infiltrate. Next to the bar through screens set up to deter freeloaders, Ben could just see a floodlit boxing ring.

'Come inside sir ... only 300 baht,' droned the tout. In the enclosure there were twenty or thirty tables with a mixture of Thai and foreign spectators watching the boxing. They paid to go in, took a table and ordered beers and food from a waitress in a very short skirt.

The fighting was brutal, the boxers wiry and thin, their sinewy bodies glistening in the heat and glare of the tropical night. They were barefooted, their ankles strapped up with white bindings and wore loose shiny shorts and boxing gloves. Heads down in combat, their gumshields gave them a ghastly grimace. They moved fast, showering blows on each other with their fists and more damagingly with their feet, knees and elbows. The feet were brought up in a scything action, belting the opponent in the kidneys. Often the fighters came together in a clinch, hammering each other with their knees before the referee broke them apart again. As a round ended, steel trays were brought into each corner to catch the water that was poured over their sweating bodies, the coaches screaming advice as they massaged bruised legs and arms. Soon another round began. It was rough stuff.

Ben wondered how the fighters could take such a pasting. They already looked exhausted and had a haunted look in their piggy little eyes. One of them was grotesquely ugly, battered beyond belief from a long career in the ring. His shorts were too big for him and in the middle of the fight he was making pathetic attempts to pull them up with his gloved hands. When at last both men went the distance, the referee held up the arm of the victor. There was little applause from the floor and nobody took much notice as the boxers came round the tables begging for tips.

'I hate this bit,' said Ben. 'These blokes do it for our benefit but they're hardly getting given anything. Do they fight only for tips?'

Chuck claimed to know how the sport operated in Thailand.

'No man, they're usually paid for each bout,' he said. 'The guys who fight on telly or at Lumpini and Ratchadamnoen have real money and status. But down the bottom end it's shit, and this is the bottom end ... fighting outside a bar. At least if they know who's gonna win, they can fix it and not belt each other too hard.'

Ben could see two fit young boxers ready for the next bout.

'These guys always do the ceremonial bit before the fight,' said Chuck. 'See their headbands. They'll dance around in the ring to honour the spirits of *muay Thai* before getting stuck in.'

Studiously ignoring each other, the men began a slow ritual dance to the wailing oboe music and strident drumming, strutting like fighting cocks and kneeling and bowing down to the canvas. After a few minutes, they removed their headbands and made final adjustments to their kit. Then the bout started and the three friends watched several furious rounds before they were distracted by their food arriving. As they were arranging the dishes on the table, Ben realised that something had happened in the ring.

'Damn, I missed it! One of them's down,' he said. The boxer was writhing on the canvas and being counted out. 'What's going on, Chuck?'

'Probably been kicked in the calf. You can take almost anything on the shin, but a good kick to the calf poleaxes you. That's it, he's finished.' For the man on the ground, his agony had only just begun. His seconds were with him and he was hauled to his corner, while Ben and the others concentrated on their curries and beers.

The next fight was between two small boys. Ben paid them little attention, though they were full of bile and energy, hitting each other for all they were worth. He noticed that while one was only in shorts, the other had a tee shirt on and hair pinned back with a grip. Then it suddenly dawned on him.

'Blimey,' he said to Chuck in astonishment, 'that one's a girl.'

'No sweat,' said Chuck lazily. 'She can take care of herself okay.'

'But it's pretty vicious, isn't it? Fine maybe for adults if there's medics handy. But not with kids ... and certainly not a girl.'

'Yeah, but Ben, safety standards here aren't the same as in the States, and you gotta let'em make some bread. Anyway it's great sport.'

'This isn't sport, Chuck! It's just to sell more beers,' insisted Ben.

'Yeah, but the girl's the aggressive one,' said Chuck. 'I'm more worried about the little guy.'

Ben was about to press his point when Maca broke in.

'Kids isn't so bad, but it's boxing between bar girls that makes me puke,' he said. 'Like at Lamai on Koh Samui there's lady-boxing every week and the bars all put up a girl to have their faces pushed in.'

'Get real, man! Amateurs can't hurt each other,' said Chuck.

'They sure can. It's like a street fight and they're often badly matched. One lovely girl I saw was the tiniest thing. The other one was bigger and hurt her bad.'

'But they're all in it together,' said Chuck.

'No mate, they're competitors every day of their lives. The big girl was mean, like she enjoyed smashing that beautiful face. The little'un was in a real distress after ... showed me her split lip and the egg on her shin. Made me feel crook,' said Maca staring into his beer.

'So the *farang* like to watch bar girls brawling then?' asked Ben incredulously.

'Yes, they buy beers and bay like animals. The women are the worst.'

'But the bar girls get a few baht for fighting,' said Chuck, 'and it's gotta be voluntary.'

'What's ever voluntary when you're a bar girl!' said Maca sharply. 'At least when they're lying on their backs they're making some bloke happy and not hurting each other. No, mate, choice doesn't come into it.' There was passion in his voice.

They sat in silence as the next bout began. One of the contestants was a *farang* from Eastern Europe, an ox of a man, tall and muscle-bound. He was followed into the ring by his opponent, a tubby little Thai with the doleful face of an oriental dog.

'This one's a foregone conclusion,' said Ben as the fight started. 'That Thai bloke couldn't punch the *farang* in the face even if he stood on a box. He just can't reach.'

'Yes, but the face isn't the only target,' said Chuck. 'The Thai guy looks tough and the *farang*'s slow ... got no boxing skills at all.'

Chuck was right. In the third round, the foreigner ended up sitting on the floor with a look of utter surprise on his face. The referee counted him out and the Thai fighter was loudly cheered by the audience. But Ben did not applaud; he was not sure what to think of the backstreet *muay Thai* scene. He was certain Emma would have been appalled and he was glad she had stayed behind at the guesthouse that night.

'Right then guys,' said Maca theatrically. 'We've done booze, food and aggro, so now for the go-go bars.'

Ben again thought of Emma and wondered how he was going to explain away being out so late drinking with Maca and Chuck in the *sois* and bars of Sukhumvit. She was not going to like it.

5

O kay, that's enough kick boxing,' agreed Chuck. 'So, where to next?'

'Has to be Nana Plaza,' said Maca.

'I went there with Emm,' said Ben. 'She hated it.' He knew he was on dangerous ground if Emma found out he had been there again, but as Nana Plaza was only a few hundred yards away from the boxing ring, it was unavoidable. He would feel pretty stupid in front of the lads if he went home early just because the little woman disapproved.

They all stood on the kerb waiting for a gap in the steady flow of taxis and tuk tuks.

'Better use the pedestrian crossing,' suggested Ben.

'Whatever for? Drivers never stop!' said Chuck knowingly. But as he crossed the road, it was streetwise Chuck who stepped on one of life's banana skins. Dashing across the *soi,* his big mistake was to ignore a primary rule for avoiding collisions between pedestrians ... he was foolish enough to look an oncoming Thai girl in the eye.

Later in the bar, Maca explained the rule's fatal effect.

'You see it's like this, Chuck. When there's someone coming towards ya', you just gotta avoid eye contact. Look'em in the eye and you're dead ... specially if it's a sheila and she's a smasher.'

'Bullshit, man!'

'Dinkie die mate ... even a smart-arsed American in Bangkok.'

It was as the three men plunged off the kerb into the traffic, cheating death, that Chuck spotted her crossing the road towards him. She was perhaps the loveliest Thai girl he had ever seen, a siren, his nemesis. Petite with an elfin face and in a tight crop top, she had the flowing black hair and belly button of a Greek goddess. Their eyes met and as they closed at speed in the middle of the road, irresistibly drawn together like heat-seeking missiles, they could not help running headlong into each other.

As with most banana skins it all happened in a nanosecond, but for Chuck it seemed agonisingly drawn out in time. Momentarily stunned, he was appalled to observe his glasses leave their allotted place on his nose and fly beyond his reach, slowly falling in a downward parabola. He saw the road come up to meet them and the lenses shatter across the tarmac like slow motion water droplets in a shampoo ad on TV.

Then, as he recovered his equilibrium, he became horribly aware of a battered green and yellow taxi driven in all probability by the Grim Reaper bearing down on him at speed. Having the presence of mind not to hang around in the middle of the road to be scythed down, he made it to the pavement just in time to see the remains of his glasses being pulverised under the nearside wheels of the taxi. Still feeling shocked, Chuck looked around myopically for a silver lining to his banana skin but sadly the bird had flown, the tasty Thai girl had disappeared.

'Fuck her!' he swore angrily under his breath.

'You'd be so lucky,' said Maca, ducking away as Chuck swung at him in *muay Thai* fashion. 'Got any spare specs, mate?'

'Yeah, but right now I can't see a damned thing. Tonight I'm screwed!'

'Well Chuck, it's Nana Plaza, so you can be if that's what you want. Thai tits are too small to see at the best of times so you might as well touch base.' Maca had grasped that he could tease without mercy as Chuck was too blind to catch him. 'So Ben, me old mate, where shall we take the dim-sighted Yank then?' he laughed.

'Me and Emm went to the G-String … got more girls than the other bars,' said Ben. 'Why don't we go there first?'

'Okay, we can have a few beers and then move on to Caligulas.'

The G-String was exactly as it had been the night before, the girls at the door calling 'Hallor dalling, come inside,' followed by the plunge into the surreal glitter of lights, plastic and chrome and the sudden shock of bare skin. Ben recognised several of the dancers, though he was disappointed the girl in cargo pants was nowhere to be seen.

They filed into the long padded seats and sat and goggled, or at least Ben did. Chuck could not see anything unless it was within a few inches of his nose, while Maca was unfazed, as if this level of female display was nothing out of the ordinary.

The evening featured Puss in Boots, or to be more precise, puss only in boots. Some of the girls wore cats' ears and whiskers, while others had fluorescent designs on their bodies which glowed iridescent in the purple light. Down one end of the bar, a Thai man was casually painting a girl's skin, his ordinary every day canvas. He worked fast without talking, while the girls chattered together comparing their designs. Ben could see vivid tropical flowers, stylised birds and suggestive slogans; 'I go with you', and 'Love me short-time'. As he watched, a garish scorpion flowed from the brush of the artist, its claws angled down towards the girl's crotch.

Soon it was changeover time and the painted ladies filed up onto the platform and each found a pole. It was a bizarre sight, the slim forms writhing around their poles, the paint glowing brightly in the darkness.

'Blimey mate, see the handprints on her buttocks ... nearly shoved his thumbs up her arse.' Maca was almost animated.

'Where? I can't see a damned thing,' said Chuck in frustration.

'Sorry mate, you must've been too hands-on before you got yourself a sheila. Don't say they didn't warn you though!'

Chuck looked pained but ignored him.

One beer was enough before they left the G-String and went on to Caligulas, Maca's favourite place. It was probably the largest of the clubs, full of *farang* standing around tall tables, perched on bar stools and mingling with the girls. Maca ordered beers, while Chuck peered blindly about him looking thoroughly miserable.

'Hey, what's going on over there?' asked Ben. 'Something's about to start.'

In the corner some curtains had been drawn back, revealing two girls at first awkwardly ignoring the honeyed sounds of Westlife's 'My Love'.

'What are they doing?' demanded Chuck.

'Well it's these ladies … they're having a shower … and they're rubbing soap on each other,' said Maca. 'And Auntie Gladys, look where that one's putting her hand.'

'Where?'

'Never you mind, it's not for the infirm. Cripes, see her move!' he hooted loudly.

'What's she doin', Maca?'

'Wouldn't miss this for anything, Chuck. And, ooh look, two more girlies … first proper tits I've seen in Thailand. Yeah, and they like beer too … got a bottle each. No, they don't like beer, they're pouring it down their nipples. Oh yes, they love it … they're licking it off each other.'

'Holy shit!'

'And now one of them's on her back, and you know where she's sticking the bottle?'

'I think it's utterly disgusting,' said Chuck. 'It's a waste of good beer.'

'Tell you what gets me,' said Ben. 'They sell us the most expensive beer in Bangkok and then put us off drinking out of a beer bottle for life.'

'But I can't see anything,' moaned Chuck again.

'So get in close and sniff 'em instead, mate.'

'Think I'm a pervert? I'd look a jerk!' Chuck wailed bitterly.

Ben could now see that the next display was about to start on a small circular stage in the middle of the room.

'Chuck, it's a sex show! Won't that be nice,' said Maca.

'Get lost you stoopid dude!'

'If you can't be polite I shan't tell you about it,' said Maca as a naked woman, definitely no longer a girl, lay on her back on the floor and lit a cigarette.

'Well, Chuck,' he rambled on, 'there's this lovely young girl and she's having a smoke. It's really quite Clintonesque! No, not a cigar this time … but just see where she's putting it. And she ain't inhaling either!'

'You wait 'til I get my glasses, you asshole,' threatened Chuck.

'And look, the lady's got some balloons … so now what's going up the Khyber? Yes, I know what it is … it's a blowpipe!'

Chuck heard the bang as the first balloon was shot down by a well-aimed dart.

'Wouldn't be allowed in the States,' he said. 'What if one of the darts goes into the crowd?'

'But this lady never misses. They call her Dead Eyed Dick ... or should it be Fanny,' said Maca grinning broadly.

Now the woman was standing up, showing her rapt audience the contents of a bucket. In the bottom was something dark and squirming.

'Shall I tell you what the lady's got, Chuckie boy? It's froggies ... a bucketful of froggies. And you know what she's gonna do with them?'

'Eat'em maybe?'

'Yes, eat them ... but what with? Think about it, baby! Then they're going to be reborn, resurrected. We're gonna see a miracle!'

'Don't mind missing this one,' said Chuck frowning.

Even Maca, the unshockable commentator, fell silent. How could he begin to describe such a thing.

'It's a freak show,' said Ben. 'But we all come to see it. Why ever?'

'Because every white-knuckle ride's gotta be tried maybe?' said Maca.

The show continued at Caligulas until late, though it puzzled Ben why the bar owners thought the *farang* would want to witness frog-abuse. It was, of course all done to pull in the punters and sell more beer.

With this in mind the girls on stage that night kept themselves busy writhing around, rubbing oil on themselves, spreading their legs and inserting various implements into each other. But as Ben sat and watched, he kept asking himself why the tourists flock to see Thai girls using their most intimate parts to shoot bananas and ping pong balls into a glass, to blow trumpets, draw pictures with felt tip pens, extinguish the candles on a cake, crush beer cans and even take the tops off bottles of cola. Only the live fish were missing from the menu.

'The frogs was a bit of a turn-off,' he said as they got up to go.

'Wouldn't have missed it,' said Maca, back in frivolous mode.

'I did miss it,' said Chuck, mortified.

They exchanged the pounding of the music and the smoky atmosphere of Caligulas for the noise and exhaust fumes of the traffic. It was late, very late as they raced through the sodium-lit streets, the tuk tuk driver flirting casually with disaster.

Back at the guesthouse on Khao San Road, Ben tried to slip into the room and get into bed without waking Emma.

'So where did you go? Sukhumvit?' she suddenly asked him out of the darkness.

'Yes. We watched the *muay Thai* and had some food and a few beers.'

'But it's far too late … we've got to be up in a few hours to get the bus.'

'Oh shit, I'd almost forgotten.'

'Was it only *muay Thai* then?'

'Yes, well … that's what we went for. Course we had a drink after.'

'What sort of bar?'

'An ordinary bar.'

'Ordinary for Bangkok you mean?'

'Yeah, Emm, ordinary.'

'Like Elvis Presley singing psalms on a Sunday! Ben, I can see right through you like there's nothing there.' She lay curled up in her sarong on the far side of the bed giving him her back. She did not move when he lay down beside her and he did not dare to touch her.

Ben was exhausted and quickly fell asleep, but he slept fitfully. All too soon he would have to face up to a hangover, an early morning bus ride to the island and the constant chill of Emma's silent censure.

6

The next morning after a restless few hours on the hard double bed, Ben and Emma slept through the alarm. Or, as Ben was forced to confess, he sat up and switched it off as soon as it rang and then dozed off again.

'Ben, why the hell did you do that? It's eight o'clock and we've got to be at the bus in half an hour.'

'Oh sod it! And you haven't packed our stuff yet.'

'Me pack? While you're out all night looking at tits?'

Ben was horribly aware of his hangover, his mouth like a monkey's armpit, his eyes swollen and bleary. The last place in the world he wanted to be was in this grotty room at war with Emma.

Barefoot and in sarong, he padded down the narrow corridor to the showers, but he had forgotten his shower gel. By the time he had found it, the shower cubicles were all fully occupied and his bowels were now responding tumultuously to the night's rich food. He was going to have to do business with a squatter loo, just a nasty little hole in the floor. Hunker down, take aim, then, 'Shit! No paper!'

'Look, Ben,' protested Emma back in the room, 'there's no time for breakfast. If we order something, they'll probably take ages getting it and we'll miss the bus. You were crazy staying out so late last night.'

They both made it down to the street by eight thirty but there was no minibus, no Chuck and Maca and the travel agents had not yet opened up.

'Christ, I could do with a cup of tea,' grumbled Ben.

'That's your problem. I'm not having you dumping me here with all the bags and the bus going without you.'

Emma was encouraged when a minibus drove up and stopped by the kerb, but the driver got out and disappeared, leaving the engine running in a growing fog of diesel fumes. After a few minutes he came back and switched it off.

'You ask him Ben,' insisted Emma, so Ben went and asked.

'Is this the minibus for Koh Samet?'

'Bus go Ban Phe. You have boat ticket?'

'Nobody said anything about boat tickets.'

The man shrugged silently and walked away. After ten minutes he reappeared.

'Tickets,' he demanded abruptly.

'Who's got them?' Ben asked Emma.

'You have,' said Emma.

'No I haven't. Surely you paid and put'em in your wallet.'

'I didn't,' she snapped.

'Dammit, you must have, Emm.' Emma was not enjoying this.

Other passengers were now arriving. They were all told to leave their packs on the pavement and board the minibus. The inside was hot and claustrophobic, the sticky plastic seats packed tightly together with little leg room. Soon after nine, Maca and Chuck showed up, Maca looking pale and crumpled.

'Where've you two been?' asked Emma.

'Last night? Sleeping,' said Maca innocently.

'Running it a bit tight aren't you?'

'Stay cool, Emm baby,' said Chuck.

After twenty minutes' sweaty confinement inside the parked minibus, a new driver got in and they at last moved off into the traffic.

'Ben,' Emma suddenly shrieked in alarm. 'Are our packs on the bus?'

'I left them outside, but I didn't see them go up on the roof. I wasn't watching.'

'Ask the driver then. We'll have to go back if they're still on the pavement.'

Maca and Chuck were in the front seat just behind the driver and at

Emma's insistence, Ben poked Maca in the neck.

'Can you ask if they put our bags on the roof?'

Maca leaned forward and spoke to the driver against the loud Thai pop music filling the bus, then turned and shouted back to Ben.

'Him say, "Ugh, many bag on top. You wait." So you'll just have to wait, mate.'

'We're shafted if they've been stolen,' moaned Emma.

The minibus was now in heavy traffic, often gridlocked and then surging forward for brief sprints, the air conditioning unable to cope with the heat and humidity. Ben and Emma sat jammed in together, hungry and thirsty and overwhelmingly anxious. Emma had a feeling that the bus was going round in circles and not making any progress out of Bangkok to the east. It seemed to be negotiating complex one-way systems and taking elaborate rat-runs to avoid the worst blockages. When at last it pulled into the forecourt of a hotel, Ben jumped out to check the roof. Peering in through the door, he told Maca and Chuck the good news that the packs were there, safely stowed on top.

'Chill out man … cool it, cool it,' said Chuck.

'No worries, mate,' said Maca. 'This is Thailand. Things look a bit hairy but it all works eventually. There's not much theft despite us being the rich guys.'

'Yeah, that's what I said to Emm,' said Ben.

Emma glared and cursed him silently.

The driver soon reappeared from the hotel lobby with two more passengers, a white-skinned woman of the Anglo-hockey stick type in a pale cotton frock, followed by a large Scandinavian neanderthal in jeans. They both climbed in and Emma found herself pressed hard against the man's thigh. Smelling strongly of booze and radiating heat, he began to talk in broken English interspersed with guttural grunts.

'I feel so sick … please I sit by the door. Last night I meet this German guy and we go drinking … now hangover very bad. Driver, wait me please.' He got out of the minibus, walked slowly across the hotel forecourt and stood bending over a porcelain pot filled with lotus and lily plants. Emma looked on appalled.

'He's going to puke in the dragon pot!' she gasped.

'Gross!' said Chuck.

But he did not spew up; instead, putting a finger to one nostril, he blew hard through his nose and directed a well-aimed gob of snot into the lilies.

'Holy shit,' said Chuck.

'Nice one, mate!' said Maca admiringly.

The beast climbed back in beside Emma and continued talking in a relentless monologue. Emma would have done anything to get away as far as possible from his massive belly, stubbly receding chin and piggy eyes. It was as much as she and Ben could do to bring themselves to be civil and only their enforced proximity for the next few hours prevented Ben from being thoroughly rude. But contrary to all expectation he turned out to be one of the more engaging characters they had met so far, proving that travelling confounds first impressions and broadens the mind.

His name was Stig Ruud and he was from Norway, a long-distance truck driver and proud owner of a pink nineteen fifties convertible Chevrolet which, he proudly told them, comes out in the summer for a week or so when the retreating snows permit. Taking his winter holidays in Thailand, he freely admitted spending much of his time in bars, chatting to the girls but emphatically denied ever shagging them.

'What, never?' asked Emma.

'No never,' said Stig showing his teeth.

Even taking his denial with a pinch of salt, she found him to be a harmless sort of guy whose naive assumption that anyone would enjoy talking to him proved to be broadly correct.

The passengers in the minibus had little in common except travelling, but they all talked freely, learning about each other and sharing their Asian experiences. The woman who had got in at the same time as Stig was Clarissa. She was very English, in her mid-thirties and had recently given up a lucrative job in the City of London as a corporate lawyer. She was excitable and talkative, enjoying being off her employer's short leash and discovering who she might actually be.

'I gave it all up because the solicitor I worked with was a rotten bastard,' she told them. 'Couldn't stand a woman being better than him. But he got a partnership and I didn't, so I left. Now I can do more eventing and dressage … and of course go travelling.' She laughed a brittle, irritating laugh.

'So you like horses, eh, Clarissa? Beaut' animals,' said Maca. 'Go try the outback … take yer swag and some tucker and ride a few thousand miles. Then you'll know if you've got the arse for it.'

'Gosh, yes, kangaroos and koalas,' said Clarissa with relish.

Emma watched out of the window as the high-rise buildings of Bangkok were slowly left behind. But the eight lane expressway and the urban sprawl surrounding it seemed to go on for ever. There were endless factories and industrial sites, some belonging to multinational companies. The land was flat and featureless, the open spaces dried up and colourless, giving her the impression that this was an ecological disaster area, the awful consequence of global capitalism. She was deeply disappointed, expecting that the real Thailand should have revealed itself now that they were out of Bangkok. Maybe there was no amazing Thailand; perhaps it was all an elaborate con-trick.

But when they reached the smaller roads, rural Thailand gradually materialised. She could see houses that looked like real family homes set in groves of fruit trees among jungle-clad hills, substantial farms with fields of pineapple and what Maca told her was tapioca. Rubber trees stood in long straight lines, each with the V-shaped slash where the rubber tapper every morning cuts back a slither of bark and inserts the cup to catch the latex. Then behind one of the big plantations was a row of horseshoe-shaped Chinese graves set into a hollow in the hill from which generations of owners could enjoy an eternal view of their earthly estate.

The road was now narrow and twisty and there were many slower trucks ahead of them. If the minibus driver was lucky, overtaking was just possible. Emma's defence mechanism was to look sideways at the wheels of the vehicle they were passing and not to look ahead; better not to know if you are about to be wiped out in a head-on collision.

After three hours they arrived in Ban Phe where the boats leave for Koh Samet. Like every other small Thai town, it looked as if it had been planned by someone with a pencil and a ruler but very little imagination.

It had straight, well-paved roads and featureless buildings of two or three storeys, all linked by a spaghetti of electric cables.

They stopped in a street outside one of the rough concrete buildings, apparently a tour operator's office. As they got out of the minibus, they discovered that its air conditioning had not been totally ineffective; the outside world was even hotter. The bags unloaded from the roof, they were left standing around aimlessly in the entrance to the office.

'So what now? More waiting?' complained Emma impatiently. 'When do we get tickets for the boat?' she asked the driver.

'You wait here ... I coming,' he said as he stalked off into the back room. Ten minutes later she found herself trudging down to the jetty with the others, her heavy pack on her back, already soaked in sweat.

The town was a fishing port with several jetties, this one used mainly for tourist boats going to the island. There were booths selling boat tickets and accommodation, stalls with brightly coloured clothes, inflatable beach toys, sun lotions and all the necessities for a lazy beach holiday. Emma cautiously picked her way over the jetty's broken wooden sleepers which rattled loudly under the wheels of the pick-ups and motorbikes taking supplies to the boats. Alongside lay the brightly-painted wooden ferries used for carrying passengers, food and water out to the beaches. Beyond them was a rusty ice crusher flanked by trawlers, the crew lolling around in their underpants, washing and eating after a night's fishing.

They were shown to one of the ferries, a two-decker run by a resort on the island. Ben, Emma, Maca and Chuck sat and lounged on the upper deck, relieved after the long drive to be able to sit back and relax. Savouring the distinctive marine smells of tropical timber, oil and paint, Emma felt that the holiday was now at last about to start for real.

The engine throbbed into life and the ferry began backing away from the jetty. There was a hot following wind as they moved off down the harbour, but turning to port round the end of the harbour wall, amazing Thailand at last came in sight. Heading out into a translucent blue sea dotted with distant islands, a cooling breeze flowed over them, soothing their pent-up frustrations. Left behind was the heat and hassle of the mainland, ahead the long-promised tropical idyll. Maca and Chuck remained unimpressed while Emma and Ben sat entranced.

The crossing was about forty minutes, the island already clearly visible, a low wooded spine of hills lying a few miles out to sea. Its main village was at the closest point to the mainland but the boat did not stop there, instead following the long east coast of the island. Running close under the shore as it rounded a headland, they saw the first of the many beaches of dazzling white sand. Perhaps a mile long, it was fringed with chalets and scattered with bright umbrellas, a jet ski buzzing round like an angry wasp.

They sat watching the beaches go by one by one, the bays becoming smaller and more intimate. Finally they reached a rocky point and slowed as they came into a deep crescent-shaped bay, Ao Sapporot, their destination. The beach was a perfect stretch of sand, sullied only by clusters of low buildings along the shore and a red and white communications mast on the hills which rose gently behind.

'Cool thing is,' said Chuck, 'Koh Samet's got no roads, only a rough track. Proper roads ruin a place ... more buildings, more trippers, more trash and stuff. Samet's getting busier but it's a National Park and it's just about hanging on.'

The ferry picked up its mooring out in the bay and they all climbed down into a flat-bottomed landing craft with an outboard motor which was standing by to shuttle them to the beach. It took them ashore through the breakers and they jumped off into knee-deep water, carrying their packs high to avoid the spray.

'So this is Thailand at last. The beach!' said Ben in raptures.

'No man, not *the* beach. This one's handy for Bangkok but it's a bit crowded. Almost but not quite paradise,' said Maca.

'Looks like paradise to me,' said Emma, taking in the sweep of the bay, the crystal clear water and the unbroken green of the jungle.

Now they had to find accommodation. Emma felt a twinge of apprehension but Maca and Chuck were much more casual.

'Let's stop for a beer, guys,' said Chuck.

'Shouldn't we find a place first? With all these people coming off the boat, it'll be filling up, especially as it's weekend,' said Emma.

'Keep cool, Emm. It's never the wrong time for a beer.'

Maca and Chuck headed for a nearby bar, while Ben and Emma

made for the left hand end of the beach where there was a secluded group of chalets almost hidden in the trees. Sinking into the soft sand under the weight of their packs, they struggled sweating up the beach. Inside the palm-thatched reception area, Ben could see a sleepy-looking woman, heavily pregnant, behind the desk. She seemed too hot and tired even to look up.

'Do you have any rooms?' he asked her.

'Have.'

'How much are they?'

'Four hundred baht up to eight hundred baht, family room with aircon.'

'Can we see one of the cheap ones?'

The woman called over her shoulder in Thai but there was no response. She slowly got up and selected a key from a rack.

'No problem, you wait,' she said.

Eventually a dumpy girl with a radiant smile appeared from the kitchen and led them round the back to a wooden hut raised a few feet off the ground on concrete piers. Four steps led up to a small veranda with a rattan sofa. The girl unlocked the door and they peered inside a damp-smelling room almost filled by a double bed. A doorway led through to a wash room with a concrete floor, a squatter loo, a bin of water under a tap and a plastic scoop for showering. Emma looked dubious.

'You like?' asked the girl. Emma and Ben exchanged glances.

'Yes, fine, we'll take it,' said Ben.

'Okay, you check in, pay one night.'

They went back to the reception hut and, with sweaty hands, filled out a form for the pregnant lady and paid for their first night. They were both mad with heat, thirst, fatigue and frustration. After many months of expectation and days of travelling, they were now being held back by a few minutiae from their final release into this perfect cliché of a tropical paradise. At last they shouldered their rucksacks and walked painfully up to their hut.

'I've got to have a shower,' said Ben. 'I'm going crazy with this heat.' He dumped his pack on the floor, stripped off and began pouring delicious scoops of icy water over his head. 'Emm, it's brilliant. I thought I was going to die,' Emma heard him say, but the sounds of splashing were followed by an oath. 'Shit, no soap! Emm, can you pass me a towel?'

'What towel? There aren't any in the hut.'

'Damn. Can you go and get me one?'

'Why didn't you look before showering. I'm hot too you know.'

There was silence as Emma went off to ask for towels and soap, Ben waiting wet and uncomfortable.

'You have to pay for soap and a deposit for the towels,' she said when she got back. 'I didn't take any money with me, but they said I could pay later.' She passed the towel to Ben who dried himself and quickly dressed.

'I'm going to join Maca and Chuck,' he said. 'I'm desperate for a beer.'

'You sodding dare, Ben … I'll kill you. You wait while I shower too.'

When Emma had showered, they both went down to where Maca and Chuck were sitting under a beach umbrella, well into their third Singha beer.

'Aren't you worried about getting a room?' Emma asked Maca.

'Too easy, Emm, we've got one. The girl brought us the check-in forms and we did it all from here. Beer's priority.'

'You smooth bugger,' said Ben. 'We had a shower but there were no towels or soap. Can't think why they didn't tell us at reception.'

'Why should they? Everyone knows you don't get towels and soap.'

Ben then announced that he was starving hungry and asked for a menu.

'Best standby's a good old cowpat,' said Maca in mock pommie accent.

'Whatever's cowpat?' asked Ben.

'It's Thai for fried rice. Yeah really! Call the girl over and say "kor cowpat moo" and she'll get you a pork fried rice.'

The girl came to the table and Ben said, 'kor cowpat moo'. The others ordered too, and within minutes, there on the beach in the middle of the afternoon, a sumptuous meal was spread before them.

'A tropical beach, a cold beer and cowpat moo for a couple of quid. Can you beat that?' said Ben, looking pleased with himself.

Hunger, thirst and tiredness relieved, Emma now had a chance to sit back and look around. The beach was breathtaking, the view out to sea what dreams are made of. The holiday huts were a little ramshackle with more concrete and corrugation than she would have liked, but the natural beauty of the island at last justified all the travelling.

Nearby at one of the bamboo tables a little further along the sand, Stig, the truck driver and Clarissa, the corporate lawyer were sitting together, lost in conversation.

'Bet they're talking about his old car!' quipped Maca. 'Like, "I'll buy you a Chevrolet, if you'll just give me some of your love, Clarissa babe."'

'Or maybe they're talking about dressage,' said Ben.

The afternoon slipped by as lazy tropical afternoons do, Maca and Chuck exerting the minimum possible physical effort. That was why, Emma decided, they were such accomplished travellers; for not rushing on to the next beach but instead staying peacefully put.

'So when shall we eat tonight?' asked Ben to nobody in particular.

'Meet here at seven?' said Maca. 'I'll tell Stig and Clarissa in case they want to join us … should be good for a piss-take. But now's my siesta time, so see ya later.'

Emma was not sure whether she was included in the party, nor if she wanted to be. After his night out with these two crazy travellers in Bangkok, Ben was cosying up to them and had bonded with them so strongly that she hardly felt a part of his life any more.

7

Well before seven that evening, Maca and Chuck were out on the beach, comfortably installed on bamboo chairs, beer bottles in hand. It was already inkily dark. Maca had bagged a brace of English girls who he hoped might be game and was liberally applying his easy Aussie charm, while Chuck was being mysterious and American, his soft brown eyes smiling from behind his spare pair of glasses.

Two tables had been put together on the sand and were laden with beer bottles, each one in a red striped polystyrene jacket to keep it chilled. Around the table sat Ben and Emma, Chuck and Maca, Clarissa and Stig, and the two English girls, Samantha and Nadia. Nobody had bothered to dress up for the evening except the English girls who had made an obvious effort with long skirts and makeup, Nadia, her short hair scraped back and shiny with oil. To Ben they looked like tourists and not travellers at all.

Behind the tables was a magnificent display of seafood. Tiger prawns, sea bass and red snapper, tuna, squid, mussels, crab and lobster were all waiting to go on the barbecue which was fired up and glowing. Further along the beach other eating places had set up their tables on the sand, each lit with an oil lamp. These and the electric lighting sparkled and reflected off wet patches on the sand, picking out the spume of the waves swirling in the darkness a few yards away.

'Hi, I'm Ben and this is Emma,' said Ben to the English girls as he sat down.

'I'm Sam and this is Nadia … we're travelling together.'

Ben thought them a bit odd.

'Sam? Why Sam?' he asked.

''Cos Mum called me Samantha,' she said tartly in strong estuary English.

'Oh, right.'

There was an awkward silence, quickly rescued by Maca.

'How ya goin' Sam? I'm Maca, and this is Clarissa from Blighty and Stig from the North Pole. And my friend, Charles ... the only shy American.'

'Call me Chuck,' he said, looking shyly around the group.

'Howlongyoubin in Thailand, Stig?' said Maca, asking the universal opener.

'Pattaya one month. Always good, Pattaya.'

'Pattaya good for the ladies, yah?'

'Yah, I like,' said Stig. 'It's the best.'

'But I just adore Koh Samet,' enthused Clarissa. 'These are the good old days!'

'Golly yes, by Jove!' said Maca mercilessly. 'And Sam, howlongyoubin here?'

'Three weeks and I detest it,' said Samantha. It was quite a conversation stopper.

'Why?' asked Maca in surprise. 'Whatever's wrong with Thailand?'

'Well, there's nothing'd make me want to come back. Land of Smiles, my arse.'

Ben eyed Samantha across the table. She was in her early twenties with a golden tan, dark, close-cropped hair, large vulnerable eyes and a full body, tightly packaged in a skimpy top. Not bad at all, he thought, though Nadia's a bit butch.

'Had some nasty experiences then?' he asked Samantha.

'Not really, but the Thais cart us around like animals without telling us what's going on. They're inefficient, can't read a clock and never give a straight answer to a simple question. Smiley when they want to be, but at other times totally offhand.'

'Well, I like them as they are,' said Maca. 'We're their livelihood but they keep their dignity.'

'They don't have to be so rude!' said Samantha.

'Maybe we get the response we deserve,' he said provocatively. 'And we don't want'em ending up like these Americans with their plastic McDonalds politeness.'

Ben could see the fire in Samantha's eyes as she responded.

'Well, I'm talking about the basics. They just don't react normally!'

'But it depends what's normal ... your normal behaviour isn't the same as theirs. Maybe it's a language problem ... they're embarrassed because they can't understand, so they just giggle. They'll clam up if there's any tension or if they sense you don't like their country. Probing questions make them uncomfortable too ... they'll just tell you what they think you want to hear.'

'But you've got to be able to ask for things!' said Samantha angrily.

'Yes, but you gotta keep'em smiling. Harmony's number one.'

'Even when I'm paying them!' Samantha gripped the arms of her chair and glared at Maca.

'Maybe that's it ... you standing on your rights. You mustn't demand or complain ... and don't ever expect an apology from a Thai. They may seem humble, but make'em lose face and you'll just get passive resistance. It can be frustrating but it's better than confrontation, American-style.'

'Sure man ... shut up about Americans and pass on this spliff,' said Chuck. A soggy hand-rolled cigarette went on around the table, only Clarissa passing it on unpuffed.

'Anyway, I like lazing around and being harmonious,' said Maca. 'That's why I'm here ... for the Thais and their gentleness.'

Intense and unsmiling and armed with a fresh bottle of beer, Samantha now tried another justification for not liking Thailand.

'And what about sex for sale,' she said. 'In Bangkok it's totally open. Nadia and me went to the nightmarket in Patpong Road. The touts outside the bars were disgusting, trying to drag us into them sex shows. Showed us these cards ... "pussy eat banana, boy fuck girl". Stuff like that.'

'Sam, it's the same the whole world over,' said Stig lolling back in his chair, his five o'clock shadow creased into a permanent smile.

'Yeah, but Bangkok's swarming with'em. And they're all on the make

'... not like the working girls in London who really are on the skids.'

'How do you tell the difference?' asked Ben.

'I pass through Kings Cross on my way back to Hackney and you see real despair ... drug dependency and that. The girls here just want to make a fast buck. They even look like they're enjoying it.'

'Yeah, the English hookers are as miserable as hell, aren't they,' said Ben, shooting himself in the foot. 'Who wouldn't want the Thai girls!' Emma glowered at him.

'Trust you to lower the tone,' she said, angrily pulling out a packet of cigarettes and lighting up. Ben looked away and grinned at Chuck.

There was a brief pause, but Maca had not yet finished sparring with Samantha.

'Generalisations are dangerous, Sam. Most of the sex workers you see in the *farang* bars are from Isaan ... that's the rice farming region in the North East which is dry and very poor. Thousands of men and women from there leave home and come to the cities to make a bit of cash.'

'But they don't have to be prostitutes do they,' broke in Samantha sharply.

'No, though they may have little choice. Some are sold into prostitution when they're very young. Or the job agency gives the parents a cash advance which the girl can only pay off by selling herself. And there's kids to feed.'

'But I bet it's not always like that,' said Samantha, cradling her bottle in her hands.

'No, maybe some of them just want to get on in life. But don't forget, they're not all Thais. The illegal immigrants from Burma, Lao and Cambodia are the most at risk. If they're run across the border and tricked into prostitution here, it seems hard to condemn them as sluts.'

'Exactly,' said Emma. 'Don't stigmatise the women, blame the men who buy them. Why's it a disgrace to be a prostitute but macho for a man to shag'em?'

'Yes, Sam, don't be so judgmental. It's all because of poverty,' said Nadia, nervously speaking up for the first time.

The surprised silence that followed was broken by Clarissa.

'Nadia's right. Can you imagine poverty and what you'd do to escape it. I've just given up my job because I've done okay, but think what it'd be like for a Thai peasant to have steady money. Some of them are so poor. You should've seen the hotel porter's smile when I gave him a twenty baht note.'

'Dinkie die,' said Maca. 'When I think about sitting here on my Aussie arse drinking all day, I nearly die of guilt.'

'Have another beer to deaden the pain then,' said Ben.

'Well I'm as dry as a dead dingo's donger, so I don't mind if I do. But seriously, Ben... Thailand's rich compared to Laos or Cambodia. And in rural Thailand the family's still everything, even if people do have to leave home to find work.'

'So you're saying rural poverty here's not so bad then?'

'Not really ... in Thailand there's still a poverty of opportunity. Back home you can get up and go, but here there's so much under-employment and wasted talent. Even if you've got enough to eat, what sort of a life is it selling noodles from a roadside stall when in the West you could be a teacher or doctor.'

'Like we're all going to be when we go back home,' interjected Ben flippantly.

'And take America where our Chuck comes from. Anyone can start an internet company aged twenty five and bugger off and tan their ass in Thailand for a year or two before getting back on the merry-go-round.' Chuck ignored him and said nothing.

'All this breast-beating's making me hungry,' said Clarissa. 'I could eat a horse.'

She called for menus and they all ordered red and green curries, noodles and fried rice and more beer.

'I suppose I'm a case in point,' she said. 'I can plan my life. I've had real choices. Of course it doesn't always go to plan ... worst of all when my horse died. But I've put my career on hold, let my house in Islington and returned my company car. I was working sixteen hours a day, half of it over the Atlantic going to meetings in New York. It was grim but now I'm flying for free with my Air Miles.'

'Alright for some,' said Samantha sourly.

'Yes, but there's always a price. Corporate law was exciting and I'm glad I did it, but I'm glad I'm not doing it any more. No more grovelling to my clients and worrying about professional negligence claims. Escaping my mobile's amazing.'

'So we're all running away from something then. Is that what we're doing?' asked Emma, drawing on her cigarette. 'Me and Ben couldn't make any decisions after uni, so we went travelling to avoid growing up.'

'Speak for yourself,' said Ben indignantly. 'I went travelling to learn about other parts of the world.'

'Crap, you didn't. You just weren't mature enough to face up to work ... so why not sponge off your parents and bugger off abroad. What parts did you learn about in the go-go bars then? Tell me that!'

Ben was saved from having to answer Emma's broadside by the food arriving at the table, but when everyone was dipping in, she pressed her point.

'So maybe we're all in transition or putting off difficult decisions ... like me and Ben not getting jobs, Clarissa leaving hers, and Chuck and Maca forever drifting around the place. But what about you?' she asked the two girls.

'Well, I don't see it as running away,' said Samantha. Me and Nadia gave up our jobs to come out here ... Thailand first, then Malaysia and Singapore. But it's all a bit different for us ... life I mean.'

'Why is it? In what way?'

'Well, there's no horses in Hackney ... silver spoon up me arse more like. None of this university stuff ... just got a few GCSEs and I'm lucky to be a secretary. I've struggled up from the bottom and now I'm a supervisor ... well, I was until I gave in my notice. It was partly because I broke up with my boyfriend. Then me and Nadia came out here together.'

'And now you hate Thailand?'

'Well, not hate it exactly, but it's not what I expected. We've worked for our holiday and now we want to relax and not be fighting with the Thais.'

'But why do you see everyone as hostile?' asked Emma.

'Maybe because where I come from, life's always a struggle and you have to battle for every little thing. And there's so many decisions to make, so many choices. I don't just mean work, I mean life in general … what you want to be, who you settle down with and stuff. It's like I'm always at a turning point and about to get it wrong.' Samantha clung to her empty beer bottle.

'How nice,' said Clarissa. 'Getting older means I don't have so many options left.'

'Sounds great,' said Samantha. 'Fewer nooses to stick your neck into. I envy the Thai workers here on the beach with no prospects, just blue sea and sky.'

'You can't really believe that,' said Ben. 'Everyone wants opportunities and not to be stuck in a hole.'

Samantha was sitting stiffly upright, but the alcohol had loosened her tongue.

'I'm sure getting older can be tough,' she said, 'but I always think of my Auntie Ada. She's lived in Hackney all her life … it's the whole world to her. She was a cleaner, married to my Uncle Ken. He snuffed it a few years back and now she's got the ideal life, safe and settled. She's got her pension, has tea with her friends and watches her favourite telly programmes. My cousins take the grandchildren round at weekends and she makes 'em fat with piles of cakes. There's no decisions to make and she doesn't want anything different. I really envy her.'

'Sounds awful,' said Emma. 'Moving on's not easy but it's exciting too.'

Some serious eating from the collection of dishes in the middle of the table was not going to stop Clarissa challenging Samantha.

'No Sam, your auntie just made the best of a bad job. It's you who's got everything … your health, good looks and boyfriends if you want them, sexual freedom without being seen as a slapper. Career, money, travel, control of your life. Your auntie had none of these. She was messed up by the war I suppose, and by womens' low status … no expectations and no chance of anything better. You were born at the best possible time … you can have whatever you want.'

'No I can't. Anyway I'd rather have fewer options and more security.'

I'd like an easy life, like the Thai workers here on the beach.'

Maca guessed Sam's bluntness was because she'd drunk too much and perhaps to tell these middle class plonkers how easy they'd had it in life.

'Look Sam,' he said. 'Try telling that to the girl who served our food tonight. Imagine what she'd give for the money you earn, for regular hours and holidays … all dreams beyond belief. People get trapped, the Thais too, desperate to move on in life. That's why some of them even sell their bodies.'

'But I could never ever do that,' said Samantha. 'Never!'

'It's easy for you to say that, but you've never been so hopeless. Lots of the bar girls have children, and women'll do almost anything for their kids.'

'Well, maybe, but work on the island still looks an easy option to me.'

'Okay then, imagine being a worker on this beach,' said Maca. 'The island was almost uninhabited before it was hit by tourism and now all the guesthouses need cooks, cleaners, waiters. So there are hundreds, maybe thousands of migrant workers here, most of them from Isaan, the North East. It's hard to make a living farming rice, so families send their young away to find work. The waitress is from there … her broad face and dark skin are typical Isaan. I'll bet she sends money back to her Mum and just scrapes by herself … you wouldn't believe the long hours and low wages. She may go home in the rainy season to help on the farm, but that's her world … never been anywhere else and never will.' He stared out at the bright lights of the distant fishing boats and paused for breath.

'Sounds all right to me. Not a bad life,' said Samantha defensively, but even Maca was now beginning to get irritated with her.

'No way! The beach workers have the same problems you talk about … new aspirations and no security. Thailand's changing fast with crazy materialism. It's all there in the shops even in Ban Phe … televisions, videos, motorbikes, clothes, cosmetics. And the Thai soaps on the telly are showing a new urban life-style, raising expectations sky high. And of course she sees us, the *farang* always on holiday. Like you, Sam.'

'Why me?'

'Because you're a princess ... well dressed and made up, the world at your feet. And we *farang* never apparently do any work. All we do is sit around drinking and eating the best food, reading trashy novels, and having sex. Unreal! Seeing us, it's getting much more difficult for a Thai beach worker to accept her limited horizons.'

'So what's the future for a girl like the waitress, Maca?' asked Emma.

'I guess she'll fall for one of the men working here, get pregnant and go home to have the baby. Then she'll come back to work leaving the child at home with Mum. If he's a good guy, they'll register the marriage, he'll contribute to the child's upkeep and she'll be faithful to him. But he may go and work somewhere else and find another girlfriend. So she just keeps on serving food and wiping tables ... if the tourist trade doesn't collapse. There are worse places than Koh Samet, but it's not much of a life. What do you think, Sam?'

'No ... maybe not,' she said shifting in her seat.

'Of course, many of the girls dream of marrying a *farang* ... which means big money. And they think Europeans make good husbands! How about that, ladies?' said Maca with a silly grin.

'Sod the men,' said Samantha, 'I'm sticking with Nadia.'

Nobody laughed and Maca and Ben exchanged glances.

Such evenings go on indefinitely, the warm night, the unlimited alcohol, good food and company giving little reason to leave. More bottles of beer were emptied while the serving girls waited late into the night, their early breakfast shift coming ever closer.

It was Emma who made the first move to go to bed, followed by the other women.

'Ben, you didn't let me sleep last night, staying out late with the lowlife, so I'm turning in. Are you coming?'

Ben looked a little apprehensive.

'Yeah, well soon anyway. Just one more beer.'

Maca, Chuck, Stig and Ben stayed up into the small hours, gazing dopily into the flame of the oil lamp as they discussed whether Samantha and Nadia were gay. A few hundred yards away in the hut, Emma lay on the hard bed unable to sleep. Thailand was still not the escape from reality she had hoped for and she knew she would soon have to face up to making some serious decisions of her own. She pretended to be asleep when Ben at last blundered clumsily into the hut.

An hour or two later they were both roughly woken by the storm. An unseasonable squall of rain swept across the island, the wind howling through the trees, causing the tin roof of the hut to crash and strain as if it was about to be ripped away. It was almost morning when the storm subsided and they finally fell asleep.

8

In the early hours, the rain pounded on the tin roof of the hut with tropical ferocity. For what little remained of the night, Ben was dimly aware of the hum of the distant generator that supplied power to the resort and of the pounding of the waves, still agitated from the night's storm. He could hear the drips falling from the trees and running off the eaves onto the ground and could smell the rich scent of wet earth.

At his home in Haywards Heath the dawn is always silent except for the hum of traffic and the clink of milk bottles. The birds are either too chilled to sing or have been decimated by domestic cats. But Ben was learning that here in Thailand the world wakes up noisily. First are the cockerels, very early and very vocal. The dogs often join in, barking and howling at each other. Then comes a chorus of bird song, including sometimes the distant pulsing cry of a nightjar. Ching-choks, the tiny near-transparent lizards that inhabit every building and climb like Spiderman across walls and ceilings, make a distinctive sound like clicking tongues. An invisible gecko lizard is more intrusive, loudly repeating 'tukkae, tukkae' from somewhere under the floor. Happy with the flow of rain water into the hollows, the bullfrogs are in full throat calling their ladies with their bizarre 'oink-oink, oink-oink'. And as the morning begins to heat up, insects hidden in the trees one by one begin a continuous chorus of high-pitched shrieking.

Around the huts can be heard the sounds of talking and laughter as the daily routine begins at first light. The workers' flip-flops slop down the path as their home-made brooms swish away the night's fall of leaves. After the storm there is much for them to do. Rubbish has blown into the restaurant, chairs are overturned and rotten branches lie scattered over the pathways. Long before the *farang* surface, they are up and about, having crawled out of their rough wooden huts or from behind the bar where they slept under a table with a mosquito net thrown over it.

The sleeping *farang* make no sound, except perhaps an occasional groan. They are on holiday, indulging in a serial hangover. Silently cursing the sounds of the morning that wake them too early, they stay late in bed and so miss the best part of the day. But in a flimsy beach hut, it is hard to stay asleep once the island has begun to stir.

After his late and alcoholic night, Ben was finally disturbed by the morning noises and by the light pouring in through thin cotton curtains. It was damp and sweaty in the hut and he was feeling seriously dehydrated. He went cautiously out onto the veranda in his sarong and surveyed what he could see of the world. Everything was wet and leafy, the ground dark and sodden, though he was surprised the storm had not done more damage. He was most intrigued by the chickens; red, original chickens, very skinny with long necks and legs, running everywhere like mini-dinosaurs. A bamboo ladder stood against a palm tree where a nesting box kept their eggs safe from the many rangy dogs on the island.

As he went back into the hut, Emma was just surfacing.

'Christ, you look bleary,' he said. 'You okay Emm?'

'Yes, but no thanks to you. Think I need more sleep in this climate, and I'm not sure I'm over the jetlag yet.'

They threw on their shorts and wandered down to the restaurant, an open-sided building by the reception hut. Breakfast was black coffee, scrambled egg and bacon, toast with butter and jam and a plate of fresh fruit.

It was a big surprise when Chuck and Maca appeared a few minutes later and joined them at their table.

'Bit early for you guys!' teased Emma.

'G'day Emma. I like an early brekkie ... sets me up for a busy day.'

'So what are you going to do today then?'

'I'm easy Emm, but one thing's for sure ... I'll be flat out like a lizard drinking.'

'Well, I'm not sitting around doing nothing!' said Ben scornfully.

'Chill out man,' droned Chuck.

'Slow down, Ben. Time's on your side ... you've got lots of it for once,' said Maca.'

'Walk the middle path, seek Nirvana.'

'Yes, but how exactly?' Ben asked, slightly puzzled.

'Well, you get your bathers,' said Maca, 'you pick up a book, a bottle of water and sun glasses and you find a deckchair. You sit on it and read the book. Get too hot, you walk to the sea and throw yourself in. Get too hungry, you eat food. Even roll a spliff.' He filled his mouth with scrambled egg.

'Very droll,' said Emma finishing the last slice of papaya.

'Anyway, I'm going for a walk,' said Ben. 'Want to come, Emm?'

'No thanks, I'm doing it Maca's way today. Didn't get much sleep you know.'

Incapable of doing nothing, Ben had his usual urge to explore his new surroundings. He left the others and walked to the rocks at the end of the bay and across the headland until he could see the next beach through the trees. Along the way he passed several Thais selling sweets, cooked food and fruit, carrying their loads in baskets balanced at each end of a bamboo pole and slung across one shoulder. Most were middle-aged women and walked with a rolling gait to handle the weight, the pole flexing with the rhythm of each step.

Ben stopped one of the fruit sellers and looked in her baskets. There was papaya, pineapple, watermelon, pomelo, mangoes, bananas and coconuts, the soft fruit carefully packaged in white styrofoam trays and covered in cling-film. He chose a coconut and the fruit lady cut its top off and gave him a straw and a plastic spoon to scoop out the soft, unripe flesh. The milk was fresh and cold with a pleasant sweetness; he wondered how anyone could drink cola when this god-given nectar was falling from the trees.

Returning to Ao Sapporot, he then headed inland and walked up the dusty track towards the dry monsoon forest. Beyond the chalets were the huts of the workers, half hidden in the trees. He was surprised how ramshackle they were and was even more disgusted by the rubbish littered everywhere; polythene wrappers, broken furniture, scraps of timber and plastic, old shoes and tin cans. It looked as if nobody cared that the garbage generated by the tourists was left scattered to the four winds.

Nearing the workers' huts, he came across some Thai men squatting on the ground cooking something over a fire. They welcomed him with warm smiles as he approached. Out of curiosity he went closer but could hardly believe what he saw; they were roasting rats. Bamboo sticks had been pushed through the rats' bodies from nose to tail and the men were slowly charring them in the flames. He tried not to look appalled, though he could not help thinking of the feast he had eaten with the others the night before. One of the men saw him staring at their breakfast.

'Eat mouse. You like?' he said with a broad smile.

'No thanks, maybe next time,' said Ben, feeling he had been caught intruding.

When he got back to the beach, he passed by two European girls in brief bikinis who were having a massage under the trees with some old Thai women. They looked pale and exposed next to the dark-skinned masseuses who were covered up in trousers, long-sleeved shirts and wide-brimmed hats. Further on along the sand, rows of *farang* were lounging in deckchairs and reading novels, some of the girls lying topless under the pitiless heat of the sun.

Taking a deckchair from the stack against a tree, he rejoined the others who were sitting more sensibly in a shady place at the top of the beach.

'Hey Emm, you're looking chilled out,' he said.

'I'm hot, sweaty and bitten by ants, but yes, chilled out I suppose. Stupid expression.'

'American lingo,' said Maca.

Chuck remained unprovoked and looked vacant. Having lit up that morning, he had already found the meaning of life.

'So what did the Pommie explorer find on his travels?' asked Maca.

'Lots,' said Ben. 'Dunno how you can all just sit here.' He was determined to tell them what he had seen, even if nobody was in the least bit interested. 'There were these men cooking rats and two gorgeous girls being massaged, and I saw more rubbish than in the whole of Bangkok.'

'Eating rats! How disgusting,' said Emma. 'Glad I didn't see them.'

'Why not?' said Chuck. 'Meat's from dead animals, not supermarkets.'

'But I mean rat! Are they so poor they have to eat rat?'

'Maybe rat's a delicacy,' said Maca. 'Anyway, it's a bush rat not a sewer rat and country people here eat everything … frogs, snakes, lizards and rats from the paddy fields. The kids go out and collect'em. And there's crickets, termites and scorpions … and grubs that live in bamboo. You look for the boreholes in the bamboo, cut it with your parang and the inside's squirming with grubs. You saw them on the stalls outside Nana Plaza … the working girls from Isaan love'em.'

'But I'd never eat stuff like that,' said Emma.

'Why not?' Maca demanded. 'You eat some shonky things out of the sea like oysters and prawns … just as disgusting. Course it's the aborigines that really know about bush tucker. Witchetty grubs are the best.'

'Then I had a brilliant coconut from one of the fruit sellers,' persisted Ben. 'So much milk and the meat's delicious.'

'Better than buying drinks in cans, making more trash,' said Chuck. 'Coconuts are local too.'

'I can see why they like the plastic packaging though … it's so light. The woman must've been half dead carrying the coconuts.'

'Yeah, and have you thought how far she's walked with all that weight?' said Maca. 'They buy the fruit and stuff and put it in those wretched plastic trays, catch the first boat at dawn with two full baskets and walk the length of the island. It's one hell of a walk, three or four miles. Rocky headlands, roots to trip you up, steep climbs and bloody hot. Then they walk back again.'

'But my coconut lady was all smiles,' said Ben. 'They're tough, these people.'

'It's the blind fruit seller blows my mind,' said Chuck. 'I saw him carrying those baskets last time I was here … he has to walk very slowly, step at a time.'

'Have to hand it to people like that,' said Maca, 'not that he's got any choice.'

'I was surprised to see masseurs on the beach though,' said Ben. 'After Bangkok, I thought massage was part of the sex industry.'

'Not always,' said Maca. 'Prostitution's supposed to be illegal so massage is an obvious cover. But Thai massage is straight ... Wat Po's the top training school.'

'Yes, we were surprised to see massage in a temple,' said Ben.

'The Thais take it very seriously ... the masseurs over there'll be proud of their skills.'

'Well, I won't be asking those old crones for any extras,' he said. 'Wouldn't mind a bit of the Euro-tottie they're working on though.'

'Go on then,' said Emma indignantly, glaring at him. 'Try your luck if you dare.'

'Spoiled for choice,' he said with a smirk. 'Don't mind if I do!'

Emma frostily changed the subject.

'You know, it's odd,' she said, 'the foreigners wearing so little compared to the Thais. Even the older tourists are in thongs and go topless with their tits bobbing about, but the masseurs on the beach are all covered up. Same as those Thai kids over there.'

They all turned to look. A group of young Thais were fooling around in the waves, the males in swimming shorts, the girls in shorts and tee-shirts.

'Thai girls are so modest they swim in their clothes,' said Maca. 'If you see one here in a brief bikini, she's probably a hooker hired by the day from Pattaya.'

'Pattaya? That's the big sex resort, isn't it,' said Ben.

'Sodom-on-Sea,' said Maca. 'Just your place, eh Ben?' Ben grinned. 'And Thai women cover up because they don't want to go black,' Maca went on. 'Beauty means white skin. Dark means peasant working in the fields, Isaan farmers, *baan nawk*, the back of beyond. Pale's the colour of urban lifestyle, Chinese money. That's why they're so keen to keep out of the sun.'

'Who's stupid then, the Thais or the *farang* roasting on the beach? We all complain about the heat but then lie in the sun and risk skin cancer,' said Emma.

'But Emma, it's cool getting a tan,' said Chuck.

'Is it? In the pharmacy in Bangkok next to the tanning lotions, I saw rows of skin whitening creams for the Thais. Guess people want whatever they haven't got.'

'Yeah, the Thais think we're mad wanting to sunbathe,' said Maca. 'And Thai men seeing foreign chicks half-dressed like bar girls think that means they're available. Surprises me our women don't get molested more often.'

'In another culture, you mustn't give the wrong signals,' said Emma.

'Good on yuh, Emm. It's plain offensive going topless and wearing skimpy clothes in town. Don't know why *farang* women are so insensitive.'

'Maybe because the Thais are too tolerant,' said Chuck. 'They just smile and take us as we come.'

There was a pause as they watched the Thais noisily playing in the sea.

'Well, folks, it's time for a plate of cowpat moo. Anyone peckish?' asked Maca.

As they wandered off to eat, they passed the masseuses who were now sitting waiting for customers. 'Massage, massage,' they called out, smiling broadly.

'Don't fancy being mauled by those old biddies,' said Ben.

'Prefer a topless chick in cargo pants, I suppose,' hissed Emma under her breath.

'Say na'more!' said Ben, unabashed.

Maca heard the exchange.

'Once a bloke, always a bloke,' he guffawed. 'Sorry Emma, it's true … though I'm a feminist kinda guy myself, honest!' There were loud hoots from Chuck.

Lunchtime was clouded by the obvious tensions between Ben and Emma, by lack of sleep and by the increasing heat. Eating only made them all hotter and more uncomfortable. Emma was the first to say she was going back to the hut to crash out for a bit.

'I'll be with you in a moment, Emm,' said Ben.

'Don't rush,' she replied icily.

He followed her a few minutes later and found her lying on the bed facing the wall, a sarong knotted round her waist. She ignored him and said nothing as he sat down beside her. Looking down at the curve of her back and the scarp of her hips and thighs, he ran the tips of his fingers slowly up her spine and into her hair. To his alarm, she turned on him angrily.

'How dare you do that after all the foul things you keep saying in front of me. Don't you dare touch me!'

'Emm, it's a siesta. You know what siestas are for,' he said resentfully.

Abruptly Emma sat up and faced him, cradling her bare breasts protectively in her folded arms. Briefly distracted by the pink line along her bikini top where she had caught the sun, Ben was totally unprepared for the outburst that followed.

'I don't care what you think siestas are for. Why don't you push off and find someone else to fuck.'

He could hardly believe what he was hearing.

'Emm, it's you I want,' he protested, 'but since we got to Thailand we haven't once …'

'Haven't what?' she broke in, her eyes ablaze.

'Yes okay, I know it's hot and you're tired, but come on Emm, not another headache.'

She rounded on him indignantly.

'You just don't understand anything, do you … don't even begin to!' Ben looked shocked and began to sweat.

'Don't understand what?' he said weakly.

'See! If you understood, you wouldn't have to ask.'

'I only want to know what you're ranting on about.'

'So I have to tell you then I suppose … that you don't understand my feelings … you don't know how to treat me properly and never have.'

'But Emm, why all this shit? Why now?'

'Why now? Because I should've had it out ages ago … or just split up. I've left it far too long and now it's too late.'

'Left what too long?' said Ben, propping himself defensively against the door.

'All the things I should've said to you before.'

'Like …?'

'Oh, what's the point!' she cut in sharply.

'There's lots of point.'

'Okay then, you've asked for it ... I'll tell you like it is. Ben, you're just a little boy when it comes to serious relationships. You're so insensitive ... you hurt me whenever you feel like it. And you don't know how to love me ... because the only person you love's yourself.'

Ben looked stunned.

'Come on Emm, what did I ever do to hurt you?'

Emma rolled her eyes in exasperation.

'The big problem's your mother, treating you like the sun shines out of your arse. You don't know how to behave because mummy lets you get away with everything. Well, I'm not making the same mistake. I can't hack it any more.'

'Come off it Emm, I do love you ... you know that,' he said as gently as possible.

'That's what you always say as if it answers everything. You just like playing the lover-boy, don't you.'

He cautiously moved towards the bed, his hand held out to her.

'No really, I still think you're gorgeous. And Emm ... did I ever tell you how stunning you look when you're cross?'

Gasping for breath, Emma paused in astonishment before slapping his hand away in fury.

'Well, that just about beats it. Why the hell did I let you drag me here?' she shouted, almost beside herself. 'I could like Thailand but not with you I can't.'

'Sod it, Emm, it's you who's ruining things, you and your moods. We can sort it out if only you'd stop sulking. We always have before.'

'No, we only ever shelve the problems. We never face up to them ... maybe because we know we can't.'

Emma was now sitting on the edge of the bed, feeling naked and vulnerable. She untucked her sarong from her waist and tied the ends behind her neck to cover herself. The fan swished loudly above them as she gathered strength to close the confrontation.

'Well, I'm not going to talk about it any more, not now. It's too bloody hot. So lie down and shut up, Ben ... or just bugger off.'

Ben saw she was deadly serious and was not going to listen to him, so he decided it was best to bugger off. Feeling numb, he walked out into a world full of bright sunshine and palm trees and pulled the door closed behind him with a resounding crash.

9

Unceremoniously ejected from the hut, Ben now had to face the day alone. Maca and Chuck were having a siesta and Clarissa, Samantha and Nadia were nowhere to be seen. All he could do was to walk. From the rocks at the far end of the bay, he found the path over the headland and, with the shriek of the insects in his ears and the heat now almost unbearable, he followed it to a tiny beach of white sand on the other side.

Slipping off his sandals, he walked into the waves up to his knees. The water was refreshing and the sea breeze offered a little relief from the heat, but he suddenly felt overcome with tiredness. He lay down on the sand under the shade of the nearest tree, a bizarre species half growing over the rocks. It had smooth, green bark punctuated every few inches with spiky thorns, and though it was bare of leaves it was in full flower, a riot of outrageous red blossoms. Lying listening to the sea and studying the bare, angular branches above his head, he watched a tiny yellow bird with a long beak tapping nectar from the flowers.

After a time he sat up and looked at the view, a seascape of tiny islets lost in an infinity of blue, and high above him a sea eagle soaring and wheeling in the thermals. But the beach itself was not without blemishes. Caught in the crannies among the rocks was a tangle of bamboo poles with broken lines, the wreckage of floats that had marked fish traps in the shallow waters. The sea had brought in scraps of expanded polystyrene, a shoe, a disposable nappy. The island was near perfection, but it was, he thought, unnecessarily spoiled; just like his friendship with Emma.

Sitting on the sand, he asked himself how a long relationship could so suddenly self-destruct when everything should be at its best. University had not been all fun; they had been short of money, it was always cold and there were the pressures of exams. But now, with money in their pockets and in the exotic place they wanted to be, for no apparent reason everything was falling apart.

Feeling restless, he got up and went back the way he had come, this time walking out to the end of the headland and scrambling across the rocks where the waves were crashing ashore. A few hundred yards out to sea just off the point, a wooden fishing boat with a tall flying-bridge was at work. He watched as it held its ground against the current, dipping and plunging in the swell. The crew had laid out a long circular net and were now slowly hauling it in hand over hand. The boat, back-lit by the sun, was almost in silhouette, the light dancing in the net like shoals of silver fish. But as the net was finally brought aboard, he could not see any fish at all; it looked a meagre catch.

When he got back to Ao Sapporot, he still had more time to kill before he dared disturb Emma. With nothing to read and his swimming things in the hut, he sat on the beach and watched as a load of ice was brought ashore from the ferry. The landing craft was beached in the shallows piled high with sacks which the men were unloading into a rusty trailer behind a tiny two-wheeled tractor. They had backed it down into the shallows as close as possible to the boat, but the trailer was too full and the tractor could not haul it out. When they decided to unhitch the trailer, disaster struck. Much to his amusement, the tow bar of the trailer reared up in the air, tipping most of the ice backwards into the sea. There was much laughter and shouting from the men.

With this impromptu entertainment over, Ben was left sitting in his deckchair, feeling bored and a little resentful, staring out to sea. He was wondering what to do with himself for the afternoon when from behind him came a siren call.

'Massage, you want massage?'

He looked around and there, standing smiling at him, was a petite and pretty Thai girl.

'No thanks. Well, I don't know really,' he said, unsure what to do.

The idea of being massaged in public on the beach did not appeal very much, but the girl's manner was totally disarming. He found himself warming to the idea.

'Yes, okay then,' he said. 'How much is it?'

'One hour, two hundred baht.'

'Right, so where shall we go then?'

They walked a few yards to a shady spot behind some rocks, the girl carrying a plastic picnic box in which she kept her massage kit. She pulled out a blue cotton sheet covered in Disney characters and laid it out on the sand, weighted with a stone at each corner.

'Lie down ... take off shirt,' she said, and so Ben's massage began.

Although at first he was lying face down and could not see her, he was comprehensively charmed. Despite her limited English, she was chatty and easy to talk to.

'This your first time in Thailand?' she began.

'Yes, and my first ever massage as well.'

'How long in Thailand?'

'Just a few days.'

'You like Thailand?'

'Yes, it's great, though Bangkok was heavy going. Couldn't get out fast enough.'

'Bangkok no good ... I work there five years. Much better here,' she said as she manipulated his calf muscles. 'You married already?'

'No, I'm with my girlfriend. How about you?'

'Have boyfriend.'

'And where does he work?'

'Boyfriend work Ban Phe ... say island too boring.'

'So what do you think of Koh Samet?'

'Like very much ... make good money, but today wait long time for customer. Be very rich if working all the time.' She paused for a moment as they both contemplated what it means to be rich.

'You come from where?' she asked.

'England.'

'England good ... Arsenan, Liverpoon! And what work you do?'

'I don't work. I'm a student ... just graduated.' The girl looked puzzled.

'But how you get money if you not work? Holiday expensive.'

'Dunno … borrowing mainly.'

There was a silence; he had lost her completely. How can you eat if you did not work today? How can you have holidays when you never work? Her English was not good enough for her to span the gulf between them and for a few moments she quietly concentrated on her work.

The style of the massage was not particularly sensuous which came as a surprise to Ben. She started by digging her fingers and knuckles into the soles of his feet. Then she moved up his calves, kneading them hard with her thumbs; he was amazed how sore they were after carrying a rucksack around. Next came a pummelling of the buttocks, concentrating on the muscle around the hip joints. After that she worked on his spine, firmly easing each vertebra, pushing and poking and shifting. At the top of his back she applied some strong-smelling ointment and firmly rubbed it in around the neck and shoulder muscles; that was the best bit.

Then after about twenty minutes she told him to turn over; now he could lie back and look at her as she worked. She returned his smile and led in with her next question.

'Thailand poor and very hot, so why *farang* pay so much to come Thailand?'

'Because it's a beautiful place with such beautiful people,' he said with feeling.

'*Jing jing*? We beautiful?' she said flirtatiously. 'But I want travel too! You take me aeroplane, go England?' She laughed her infectious laugh and gave him the full force of her smile.

'Yes, of course. I'll take you in an aeroplane any time. For that smile, anything.'

'Tomorrow go?' she said to more cascades of laughter.

'Why not,' said Ben. There were many reasons why not but it seemed a great idea.

'So how did you get into massage?' he asked her. She was a stunning girl and there was an obvious way she could be making lots more money.

'Work hotel before … cleaning, cashier, four year, but money no good.'

'But surely you don't earn more as a masseur?'

'Money good, high season, so now work strong every day. Rainy season no many tourist.'

'And how long've you been doing massage?'

'Two years. Get number massage two years ago.'

'Number? What's that?'

She showed him a yellow laminated card attached to her purse with her photo, name and licence number.

'So how do you get a licence?'

'Pay money. *Paeng jing jing* ... expensive. But first learn massage.'

'Who taught you then?'

'Old lady massage, here on the beach. Pay too much!'

'So you say you've been doing massage for two years, four years in a hotel here and five working in Bangkok. That's eleven years' more work than me. That can't be right ... you're not *that* old.'

'I'm twenty four,' she replied.

Ben was puzzled, trying to do the sums in his head.

'But that means you started work aged thirteen. That's impossible.'

'Possible,' she said.

'But why? What about school?'

'Father die. School cannot.'

'Your father died when you were fourteen?'

'Thirteen,' she replied.

Ben was silent for a moment, trying to take it all in, unsure how much more he should ask. Her face was impassive, though her father's death must have been the defining event of her life.

'So what happened when your father died?'

'I'm the oldest ... have to work. Mama have four ... no, five children, so she sell farm. Six thousand baht!' Her laugh had a hint of bitterness. 'Then I go Bangkok ... work for four hundred baht a month, send money home.' Ben was aghast. After earning only four hundred baht a month, massage on Koh Samet now looked pretty good.

'So your family were farmers? Where abouts?'

'Buriram.'

'Buriram? Where's Buriram?'

'Isaan … before Surin.'

'Oh yes, the North East. Rice farmers?'

'Yes, rice.'

This was the pattern that Maca had talked about, of farming people having to leave home as migrant workers to find paid work. They had casually talked about it together the night before but now Ben felt moved by the girl's story. Gently kneading his right hand, she seemed to sense his thoughtfulness and gave him another of her radiant smiles.

'Now I like my work,' she said cheerfully. 'Work, work, work every day, meet *farang* like you, learn English. Have many friends, stay beautiful place. Send money to Mama … she happy she have good daughter.'

'So where is your mother?'

'She home, Buriram. Mama not work, she sick sometime.'

'So you pay everything for her?'

'Yes, work for Mama, for sisters.'

'As you're the oldest, you have to earn money for the others?'

'Yes, always work for family.'

'But it seems awful you being sent to Bangkok … you were just a child. Whatever work did you do?'

'Work in big house, washing, cleaning, cooking.'

'And were you with the same family the whole time?' he asked her.

But his question was never answered. A few yards away, a girl in a sarong and pink bikini top suddenly appeared over the rocks that screened them from view. She saw Ben stretched out on his back, the pretty young masseuse leaning over him, and abruptly turned and walked briskly back the way she had come. He caught a glimpse of Emma out of the corner of his eye, but it was too late to call to her as already she was gone.

The masseuse silently went on with her work, then spoke in a quiet voice.

'She your wife?'

'No, she's not,' he said without elaborating, the easy flow of conversation now at an end.

'Sid aap,' said the girl after a few moments, so Ben sat up. She made him clasp his fingers round the back of his neck, and, putting her knees into the small of his back, she hauled him over backwards, stretching his spine. Finally, holding him firmly from behind, she twisted him first to the left and then to the right, giving his back a thorough flexing.

'Fin–ish,' she said in a sing-song voice and sat back down on the blue cotton sheet.

'Thanks, that was great,' he said, fishing for his money. The girl took the two hundred baht without looking at it and stuffed it into her pouch.

'*Korp khun ka*,' she said. 'Tomorrow, same time?'

'Well yes, maybe. Don't really know,' he said.

She breezily folded the sheet, picked up her plastic box, slipped her feet into her flip flops and walked off along the beach to look for more customers, leaving Ben feeling strangely unsettled.

Wandering back to the beach bar to give himself some thinking time before facing Emma, he found Samantha, the stroppy Cockney sitting at one of the tables with Clarissa, the classy thirty-something. He joined them and ordered a fresh lime juice.

'I've just had my first Thai massage,' he announced.

'How was it?'

'Great … well, quite a battering really. The girl was fantastic.'

'Was she now? The pretty one was it?' teased Samantha.

'It's more of a passive work-out than a sensuous thing … yoga without effort. But after all the booze and late nights I feel good on it.'

'So you're paying a sexy girl to rub your body!' joked Clarissa.

'Yes okay, the girl was great. And she's very open about herself … father died young and she had to work in Bangkok as a servant. Awful losing her childhood, but she doesn't seem bitter.'

'Maybe expectations are different in Thailand,' said Clarissa. 'You work your life through, fulfil your family obligations and die. Then you're reborn according to the merit you accumulate in your lifetime. I picked up a book on Buddhism when I was in Bangkok.'

Facing out to sea, Ben did not see Emma coming up behind him until she quietly pulled out a chair and sat down next to Clarissa, carefully avoiding his glance.

'Ben's just been telling us about his massage,' said Samantha, and then a little maliciously, 'He's been telling us about the masseur too …

very pretty apparently.'

'I know all about it,' said Emma, hatchet faced, leaving Ben struggling for something neutral to say.

'Fancy a drink, Emm? I've just had a lime juice and it was sensational.'

'Why not. Make yourself useful, even if it's only ordering a lime juice.'

He turned and beckoned to a sleepy waitress.

'Busy day?' he asked Clarissa to fill the awkward silence.

'Reading my book on Buddhism. Hardly moved all day ... so me and Sam are planning to go and see the sunset. You two want to come? It's not far.'

'What do you think Emm? I wouldn't mind.'

'Do what you like. I'm going to have my drink and hang about here.'

'So when are you going?' asked Ben. Clarissa looked at her watch.

'Any time now if we don't want to miss the sundown.'

Clarissa, Samantha and Ben got up and left Emma alone with her lime juice and went off up the dusty path into the interior. Where they turned left onto the main track which ran down the centre of the island they passed an exceptionally tall tree, underneath it a brightly painted model of a traditional Thai house. On the steps of the house were several tiny figures and some bowls of oranges.

'Whatever's that for?' asked Samantha.

'It's a spirit house,' said Clarissa, 'for making offerings to the spirits of the tree.'

'Is that a Buddhist thing?'

'Sort of ... it's an older animist practice that's been absorbed into Buddhism.'

'Seems funny to mix religion and superstition,' said Ben.

'Well, is it? People everywhere have the same reaction to natural things like big trees. In France a cliff or a spring often has a shrine to the Virgin or to Our Lady of Lourdes. I'm not sure it's so different,' said Clarissa.

After a few hundred yards they found a sign board with a crudely painted arrow saying, 'Sunset'. A steep path took them down through wind-sculpted bushes and when they came out into the open, the sea lay a few hundred feet below them. Several *farang* were scattered in small groups on the gently sloping cliff, sitting on their haunches like troops of monkeys, waiting for the sun to go down. Samantha wandered off and sat on her own while Ben and Clarissa chose a vantage point a little higher up.

'I always enjoy guessing where the trippers are from,' said Clarissa. 'If they're pale and puffy and badly dressed like me, they're probably British. The big ones are the Dutch, Belgians and Germans and the Scandinavians are like blonde Vikings. And I hate the Mediterranean girls ... golden-skinned and gorgeous.'

Ben bit his tongue and said nothing.

As they sat and looked around them, they could see two men and a girl on the rocks below, the girl slim with blonde hair and wearing only a pair of dark blue pantaloons. She had small breasts, tanned all over, and was showing off to the men, rolling down her waistband and inspecting her bikini line. Then the pantaloons were off and she was in the water, splashing and shouting.

'What do you think they are? Swedish?' asked Clarissa.

'Don't know, but she's a babe,' said Ben.

Loud voices reached them from the water.

'California of course. They're so vulgar!' she hissed.

'Wish they all could be California girls,' said Ben. 'Guess I can handle the vulgarity.'

'Typical male!' said Clarissa tartly.

The brief distraction over, they sat back and enjoyed the spectacular view. To the right they could see the coast of Thailand, a line of mountains sleeping like dragons in the warm evening light, the buildings of Ban Phe clearly visible at their feet. Further down the coast the outlines of an oil refinery were suffused in the glow of the sunset, an oil tanker at anchor a mile or two out, a tiny detail in a vast canvas. The sea, a deepening blue, was dotted with fishing boats; Clarissa counted over forty of them. The sky became a blaze of colour as the sun settled lower, ever growing in size, though disappointingly it disappeared into the haze on the horizon before it finally set.

'Well, there you go ... can't win'em all,' said Ben.

They watched the changing hues for some time until Clarissa broke the silence.

'Ben, what's up with you and Emma? Are you two okay?'

'I don't know ... not really sure.'

'What's going on then?'

'Seems Emma's changed since we got to Thailand ... always easy-going before and nothing ever bothered her, but now she overreacts to everything.'

'You seem to be bugging her.'

'Yes, I can't say anything right.'

'Maybe the travelling's unsettled her ... no routine or commitments, expecting to be on a high all the time,' suggested Clarissa.

'Yeah, maybe that's all it is. Hope so.'

'I'm still on honeymoon after throwing up my job, but it's scary when I think about it. Having regular money coming in's a bit like sex ... when you're getting it, it's no big deal, but when you're not it's the end of the world.'

Ben gave her a sideways glance.

'Same with you and Emma,' she went on. 'You're both in the melting pot just like me.'

'I take life a day at a time but I'm not sure Emma can switch off in the same way,' he said.

'Maybe she's facing up to decision-time and you're not,' said Clarissa pointedly.

Rejoining Samantha, they walked back to the beach in the gathering darkness and found Emma still at the same table with Chuck and Maca, already enjoying a dinner of *pad Thai, tom yam goong, tom ka ghai* and Singha beer. Pulling up another table, they joined the party. It was perfection, sitting there on the beach, the surf just visible in the moonlight. But Ben was not looking forward to the end of the evening when he would go back to the hut with Emma. After the argument he had no idea what to expect, though he knew it was not going to be easy.

The group broke up soon after they had finished eating and by the time they reached their hut, the tension had subsided a little, Emma now more subdued than angry.

'You're wanting to talk things out then,' said Ben as they went inside.

'Not tonight … I feel drained,' she said. 'But anyway, it's too late. I've already decided.'

'Decided what?' asked Ben anxiously.

'About us of course.'

'Us?' he said, nervously shifting his feet.

'I've checked the boat times to Ban Phe and I'm taking the twelve thirty tomorrow. I'm going back to Bangkok.'

His eyes widened in shock.

'What d'you mean, Emm? Going back to Bangkok? You mean alone?'

'Yes, I do mean Bangkok, and I do mean alone,' she said sharply.

Picking up a towel, she disappeared into the shower room leaving Ben sitting on the bed, a look of total bewilderment on his face.

10

The morning after Emma dropped the bombshell that she was going back to Bangkok, she and Ben slept in late. She was exhausted by the travel and culture shock, by the heat, the alcohol and late nights, and not least by the emotional turmoil of the previous few days. When they woke, Ben lay lazily dozing in bed, but before he could pull himself together, Emma was out of the shower and dressed.

'I'm going to breakfast,' she said, and walked out onto the veranda and disappeared.

Breakfast was a dismal affair. Both felt bleary after their long night's sleep and were reluctant to talk or catch each other's eye. Small-talk seemed insincere when there was so much that needed to be said.

Breakfast over and back at the hut, Ben sensed this was to be the moment of truth. As he sat down on the edge of the bed wondering what was coming next, Emma stood at the window, nervously twisting her hair.

'This has been on the cards for a long time, Ben. You know I wasn't mad keen about coming to Thailand,' she said. 'Though I suppose it isn't all your fault … if I hadn't come, this wouldn't have happened.'

'But I'm glad you did come.'

'Okay, that's nice but it doesn't change anything, does it. It hasn't worked out and I want to get away for a bit.'

'So you're saying I'm dumped?'

'Ben, sometimes you're just like a fourteen year old,' she said scornfully.

'Well, what then?'

'Suppose you could call it a trial separation.'

Ben looked stunned.

'How long for?' he said in a weak voice, putting his head in his hands.

'No idea.'

'But what are you going to do? Go back to England?'

'No, I can't ... I'd have to buy a new air ticket. Maybe Chiang Mai where I wanted to go in the first place,' she said pointedly.

'Yes, but I still don't understand why.'

'Course you do if you think about it. But then you don't think, do you.'

'That's rubbish, Emm!'

'No Ben, when it comes to relationships you don't seem to understand anything ... I told you all that yesterday. You just want to play games, play at being passionate, but it never goes any deeper. That's how you are, I guess ... suppose someone may like you for it but I'm not sure I can any more.' She turned away and stared out at the trees.

'But we've come a long way together ... doesn't that mean anything?' he said, determined not to let his voice shake.

'So you haven't got it yet? Do I have to rub it in?'

'But why split up now, just when we've got to Thailand?'

'Because Bangkok made me realise what sort of person you really are. I'm not sure I can trust you any more.'

'Shit, Emm, have I ever been unfaithful?' he said angrily.

'I've no idea, but by God I know you've wanted to.'

'What the hell do you expect? A bloody saint?' Ben retorted, raising his voice. 'Of course I've wanted to, just like every other normal bloke, but I haven't, have I. And I've seen you eyeing Chuck!' He wiped the beads of sweat from his brow.

'Give us a break,' said Emma angrily. 'It's *you* keeps going back to the brothels. How do I know you won't get it next time?'

'Come on Emm! What's so bad about strippers?'

'Oh, get lost,' she snapped, turning on him in fury. 'Problem is you're obsessed ... if there's any tottie going by you just gawp. You're so obvious sometimes.'

'That's ridiculous ...' he said lamely.

Emma ignored him and opened up a new line of attack.

'And you keep on making macho comments in front of me, like you want to impress the lads ... to insult me, humiliate me.'

'Emm, that's utter crap. I only want one girlfriend ... but I can't pretend I'm blind when there's something worth looking at.'

'Don't I know it! At the most difficult time for me, just after an argument, the minute my back's turned, what happens? You've picked the prettiest masseur on the beach and you're off with her hidden in the rocks.'

'No, Emm, it wasn't like that at all!' Ben shouted indignantly, jumping to his feet.

'But how do you think *I* feel? I might've changed my mind about going if you'd showed me any sensitivity but not after that I won't.'

'For Christ's sake Emm, that's crazy. She's a really nice girl ... not available, got a boyfriend.'

'So you really, really like her, do you? Found out if she's available, did you? I bet you did!' They were now shouting in each others' faces.

'No! It's just Thai massage ... like acupuncture, going to a doctor or something.'

'A doctor! So you're lovesick, I suppose. Well, you can stay here with your nice little masseur and make sexist comments all day with Chuck and Maca. I don't care a damn. I'll be on the twelve thirty boat.'

'Oh, fuck off then if that's what you want,' Ben said, slamming his fist down hard onto the window sill.

'Well I *am* fucking off ... and you can piss off while I pack,' Emma yelled back.

Saving his breath, Ben grabbed his mask and snorkel and stormed out of the hut.

At the next beach, floating weightlessly over heads of coral, watching the coloured fish cruising effortlessly through the rocky canyons, he felt strangely detached. It was like being on another planet.

As he walked back up the beach at midday, he determined to heal the rift, but climbing the steps to the hut his confidence evaporated.

'Emm, can I do anything to help?' he asked. It was obvious Emma had all but finished packing.

'No, nothing,' she said, pausing. 'But as you'll be staying on, do you want to keep the torch and mosquito coils? And what about splitting the malaria pills?'

'I don't give a damn, I just want to know when I'll see you again.'

'I told you, I'm not sure … not sure about anything.'

'But we can keep in touch. I must know where you are.'

'Yes, thanks, I'll email. Will you be going anywhere in a hurry?'

'No, suppose I'll stick around here with Maca and Chuck for a bit.'

'Right,' she said, closing the top of her rucksack.

'Hope you'll be okay, Emm.'

'I'll be fine on my own,' she said with more confidence than she felt.

And then their emotions came spilling over; first love, first parting.

Emma put one arm around his neck, her head down. Ben put his arms round her waist and gave her a squeeze. Her tears flowed briefly and he tried hard to contain his, staring hard at her bulging rucksack.

'I'd better get the boat,' she said.

'Yes, it's time.'

But it was not yet time; it was still early and the ferry was late leaving. Emma carried her pack down to the beach and they sat and waited silently on the sand. When the moment came, she got up and walked through the shallows to the shuttle boat without looking back. There were few people around in the heat of the day and nobody except Ben saw her go. Once on the upper deck of the ferry, she waved briefly to him. He waved back at the distant figure, then turned away towards the resort to avoid having to watch her boat leaving the bay.

The experience of being left behind was far more gut-wrenching than he had ever expected. It was totally incomprehensible and had all happened so fast. Suddenly he was alone for the first time in years, alone and desolate.

At that moment Chuck and Maca came down to the beach bar, so he went and joined them, grateful for any distraction. He guessed they would soon wonder where Emma was.

'Well, guys, looks like I'm a bachelor now,' he said. 'Emm's gone back to Bangkok. Got some things to do ... money and stuff.'

'That's a surprise ... she didn't say anything last night. There's cash machines in Ban Phe if that's all she wants.'

'No, it's a bit more than that.'

Ben was relieved that neither of them was into talking about personal things.

'When's she coming back?' was all that Maca asked.

'Expect I'll go and meet her in Bangkok.'

'We'll miss her ... I liked the pink bikini,' said Chuck. 'Been together long?'

'Yes, for ever ... three years.'

'Wow!' Chuck was impressed.

As they ate in the midday heat, the conversation was low key. Maca talked of moving on to Koh Chang, the big island to the east, Chuck about setting up websites. Trying hard not to brood about Emma, Ben was thinking how easy it is to make close friends with other *farang* but how difficult it is to get to know the Thais. He put this to Maca and Chuck.

'It's so frustrating. I'm interested in Thailand and what makes people tick, but we don't really talk to them. We order food and beers, complain when things go wrong, and they're nice and friendly. But it doesn't go any deeper.'

'I'm with you on that,' said Maca. 'They're warm on the outside but also very private. Language can be a big problem too ... so few of them speak much English.'

'I've learned almost nothing about their lives,' said Ben. 'I did a course on Third World Development for my geography degree and I thought being here would teach me something, but it just doesn't seem to happen.'

'It's a very different culture, difficult to penetrate ... maybe that's what makes it so interesting.'

'My first real contact was with the masseur I met yesterday,' said

Ben. 'She's really nice ... very open about herself and she's not had an easy life.'

'Is that the pretty one?' said Chuck.

'Hands off mate,' said Ben, more forcefully than he intended.

'But Ben, you've got to watch'em,' said Maca. 'They're smooth talkers and they'll give you a sob story about sickness and death, moneylenders moving in and that sort of stuff. But then they'll ask you for money to save the family from ruin, so you end up wondering how much of it to believe.'

'Her story's a sad one but I don't think she's softening me up for money. She seems honest enough, working hard to make ends meet.'

'Of course the sob stories are usually true.'

'Yes, it's a tough place,' said Ben.

Having eaten, Chuck and Maca went off to their hut, and Ben, not wanting to face an empty room, found a deckchair on the beach. He sat and read a novel about Thailand, 'The Beach' by Alex Garland, hoping to learn something about the country from it. But it told him nothing.

Unable to concentrate, the hot afternoon dragged by, giving him too much time to be miserable. He kept glancing up, distracted by every fruit-seller and *farang* who went by on the sand. When he saw a familiar figure coming along the beach carrying her plastic box, his heart beat faster, a blend of pleasure and confusion. She was much smaller than he remembered but just as pretty, and he had not forgotten the smile.

'*Sawasdee ka,*' she said.

'*Sawasdee krap,*' he replied, collecting himself.

'You want massage?' Without waiting for an answer, she chose a different place in the shade at the top of the beach next to the gnarled trunk of a fallen tree, spread out the sheet on the sand and weighted the corners just as she had done the day before, chatting easily to him.

'What you do today? Where you go? Where your girlfriend?'

This time he was able to look at her more freely as he relaxed with her. She was neatly dressed in close-fitting blue cotton trousers and a long-sleeved tie-die shirt and wore a baseball cap with a curved peak, making her look younger than her twenty four years. Her face was strong-boned and perfectly oval, framed by her long, glossy hair, which was held back from her forehead with a headband to allow her to work. He liked her button nose, the strong white teeth and her golden skin which was clear and unmarked. But most of all he liked her smiling eyes which were large and round but still very Asian.

'My girlfriend's gone to Bangkok. I don't think she'll be back here, but we'll keep in touch by email,' he said as he lay down on his front.

'She not like Koh Samet?'

'Not much. Not that keen on Thailand.'

'*Mai pen rai*. Never mind.'

'Well I'm not going to be lonely am I.'

'Up to you,' she said enigmatically.

'It's great meeting you,' said Ben, 'but I don't even know your name yet.'

'Called Fon,' she said.

'Fon? What does that mean?'

'Rain,' she said simply.

'Rainstorms … rainfall? That's cool … and I'm Ben.'

'Hi Ben. You welcome Koh Samet.'

As Fon dug her knuckles into the soles of his feet, Ben wanted to go on asking her about her hard life. Without eye contact it was difficult, but he was determined to try.

'Fon, you were telling me all about yourself yesterday. It seems awful a child having to leave home to work in Bangkok.'

'No problem. Many people leave Mama Papa to find work. My village very poor … and now I like it here.'

Ben pressed his point.

'But your family was split up … and you were sent away when you were so young.'

'Yes, I cry, cry, cry,' she said with a laugh.

'You left home at fourteen to earn almost nothing?'

'Yes, but I was given food so Mama not have to feed me.'

'And what were the people like you worked for? Were they kind to you?'

'Kind to me? Only small girl … sleep in kitchen, work every day.'

'What do you mean? No days off?'

'No days off. Once a year have holiday at *songkhran,* Happy New Year Thailand. Take bus night time to Buriram, very far. Get there early morning, stay Mama one day, sleep, then get bus back to Bangkok.'

'Only once a year! A kid aged fourteen … and no days off.'

'Work seven days a week.'

'For four hundred baht?'

'Four hundred baht.'

Ben was moved to silence. For the injustice done to this girl, the theft of her childhood, he felt a welling up of compassion. Though he knew it was ridiculous, he wanted somehow to make it up to her, to compensate her for what she had been deprived of.

'But Fon, you don't seem bitter … you smile all the time.'

'Yes, I look happy, but I cry inside. Family not together and Papa die.' Ben saw his chance to ask the big question.

'So tell me, how did your father die?'

'Papa die on the road,' she said.

'You mean an accident? A crash?'

'He strong man, very handsome. Crossing road to farm … big car come too fast.' She paused for a moment. 'But I have his photo … I never forget. I take it out and talk to him and he take care me when things are bad. I love my Papa.'

'Fon, it's so sad,' said Ben, lying face down, eye to eye with Mickey Mouse on the blue cotton sheet. 'How did you all cope?'

'When Papa die, Mama have babies already. She very busy, have no time for me. I carry water, feed pigs, take care little sisters. Too hard being the oldest, but it make me strong.'

'How many sisters?'

'Three sisters but one die already. Have one brother.'

'They're at home in Buriram?'

'No, all working. Young sister Jinda's here … she work resort, cooking.'

Then it was turnover time when Ben could lie on his back and gaze at Fon as she massaged his hands and arms.

'So childhood in the North East must be hard,' he said.

'Everywhere life hard. We live, we grow old and die. Live a good life, maybe not suffer so much next time. Long life, short life, no problem.'

'Yes, but Fon, life's for living. You only live once.'

'You think so?' she said with a surprised look, before brightening a little. 'Fon nearly die when small baby … dirty little girl, black face, wet nose.' She wiped her sleeve across her nose and shrieked with laughter. 'Get sick, very hot … Mama no have money for medicine, think I die. Then soldier Cambodia come.'

'Who?'

'Cambodia not far … can hear guns every night, pow pow, pow. Khmer Rouge fighting, maybe come inside Thailand, steal everything, kill us all. But this soldier like my Mama too much, give me shot every day.' She indicated her bum with a wiggle of the hips and giggled. 'So Fon get better, not die.' Her face lit up again and she burst into laughter, irrepressible mirth salvaged from near tragedy.

Ben was again moved by a sense of empathy for this modest life, for someone who had survived a tough childhood with grace and dignity and had made so much from her poor beginnings. He reflected on his own privilege, his secure family background, cushioned by so many material advantages. And as Fon manipulated his calf muscles, chatting happily to him, he could not keep his eyes off her.

'So I not dead, I massage good … meet many people like you,' she said cheerfully. 'And I have Joy to look after.'

'Who?'

'Joy. You not see her? Little girl, Joy, who live with me.'

'But whose child is Joy? Why's she with you?'

'My sister have baby called Joy … sister die already, so Joy stay with Mama. But when Mama get sick, I go Buriram, bring Joy back here with me. Sister Jinda take care daytime while I massage.'

'Okay, got it! So you and Jinda look after Joy, your niece, as she's an orphan.'

'Yes, I'm the oldest, have money, so look after Joy. She's four and love me too much. I fight for her so she not suffer like me.'

Ben wondered what the future held for the child.

'And what does your boyfriend think of all this, you bringing up your sister's child?'

Fon hesitated before answering.

'What him think? She my problem, my family.'

'But you may have your own children one day.'

'Yes, I dream. Many girls want rich man but Fon not want. Want good man ... to be together with family,' she said, wrapping her arms round herself in symbolic embrace. 'Rich man him butterfly.'

'Butterfly?'

'Yes, butterfly ... have too many ladies.'

'Right! So rich men are all butterflies?'

'All men butterfly ... unless too old!' She shrieked with laughter. 'And young men dangerous!'

'No, we're not!' said Ben.

'Yes, even my Papa. I love my Papa, but he have ladies too. When he die, they bring children, ask for money. So I have brother, sister in Buriram, and I don't know who they are.' She looked solemn.

'But your brother and your other sister? You're in touch with them?'

'They both stay Bangkok. Sister only nineteen, work hotel cleaner, Sukhumvit. Brother, I worry he no have work ... maybe get trouble *yaa bah,* trouble with drugs.' She mimed sticking a needle into her arm and grimaced.

'You don't know where he is then?'

'No, Bangkok somewhere. Mama not know.'

'And you feel responsible for all of them?'

'Papa dead, Mama sick litty bit. I'm the oldest, so have to take care.'

Ben wanted to ask her about the sister who had died, leaving Joy an orphan. What did she die of? Who was the father and did he contribute to the child's upkeep? But it seemed too intrusive to ask.

At that moment they were joined by another young masseuse who came and sat on the sheet beside them. She chatted briefly to Fon in Thai and the two of them broke into smiles, glancing across at Ben.

'Are you two talking about me?' he asked.

'Telling Gaeo you my new boyfriend, and she say very handsome.' Fon burst into peals of laughter. 'Gaeo my friend, number one, hundred

percent. We massage together two years … always *sanuk*, always funny.'
Ben learned that Gaeo was a mother of three small children who were
at home with their grandparents in the North East. A few years older
than Fon, she looked tired but she had gentle eyes and Ben took to her
immediately.

Then Fon sat him up, did the final stretching and twisting and the
massage was over.

'Okay, Ben, fin-ish. Today many people … tired already. Now find
Joy, cook rice.'

'Well, my hour was great, Fon … the massage too,' said Ben.

'Tomorrow massage?'

'I never say no.'

'What time tomorrow?'

'Start nine o'clock, then all day long …'

'Okay, up to you! *Sawasdee ka Khun* Ben.'

And with that the two masseuses picked up their plastic boxes and
walked off along the beach.

Relaxing in the bar that evening, Ben broke the news to Clarissa that
Emma had gone back to Bangkok to give herself some time and space.

'It came as a total shock,' he said mournfully. 'We looked forward to
this trip for ages and now we get here and she pushes off.'

'Life's little ironies,' said Clarissa. 'It's like karaoke. In the bath
you're Pavarotti, but you've forgotten the words … then, when you've
got them on the karaoke screen, you can't remember the flipping tune.'

Clarissa was curious to hear more about Emma but Ben was
reluctant; he was much keener to talk about Fon. He told her the story of
Fon's childhood, how he admired her struggle to survive, and how good
it was to meet a Thai who was willing to open up to a stranger. And he
had to admit how taken with her he was.

'Yes, I knew it,' said Clarissa, 'typical man … out of control as soon
as there's a pretty girl about.'

'No way, Clarissa, you've got it totally wrong. Emm's just gone off for a bit and I only met Fon yesterday. Anyway, I don't believe in love at first sight,' he said. 'Liking, yes, but not love.'

'What about lust?' said Clarissa, looking at him very directly.

'Come on, this is just a girl off the beach with a child and a boyfriend … hardly speaks English. It can't come to anything, so I'm not going to get involved.'

'Don't be too sure … looks dangerous to me,' was Clarissa's reply.

11

Ben woke slowly the next morning and reached out his hand to find Emma, but she was not there. He felt strangely disorientated, the inside of the hut, its damp smell, the unfilled double bed all unfamiliar. It took him a few moments to pull himself together and to remember what had happened the previous day. The airless night had left him bleary and unrefreshed despite a long sleep, so he dragged himself to the shower where he shuddered under the impact of the cold water on his skin.

He did not fancy a full breakfast but decided on coffee and a plate of fruit. Sitting alone, he was relieved he did not have to face Maca and Chuck or any of the other travellers. After breakfast, he surveyed the mess in the hut. His things were strewn everywhere, a jumble of used clothes and books, his medicines smeared with sun lotion which had leaked, and on the floor and in the bed, the inescapable grittiness of sand. He began to tidy up listlessly, the morning heat building up as the sun rose higher in the sky. He dumped his underpants in the water scoop and washed them in shampoo, he sniffed yesterday's tee shirt and pronounced it wearable. He flicked through the floor of the hut with the hand-made broom from the veranda, but his activity did nothing to distract him.

Even after only two days in the hut with Emma, her absence was almost palpable and he felt a sense of loss and longing which he could not quite understand. Though he still greatly regretted the bust-up, he was now almost over the initial shock.

It was not too painful thinking back to the good times at university; the first snog at the end of an alcoholic evening, followed by more serious fumblings at her flat, paralytic in party clothes after the Union ball. And he remembered the times they stayed with her parents at their suburban home in Swindon; there often seemed to be arguments when they were there, though she always quickly got over them. This latest spat was her most serious sulk so far but, he guessed, it would not last too long. If he emailed her in a day or two, she would soon soften up and they could get back together again as if nothing had happened.

So what was lowering his mood if it wasn't Emma? Had he gone cold on Thailand and travelling? Or was it Fon that was unsettling him? The very thought was disturbing, so he decided he would have to do something positive to try and calm himself. He grabbed his novel, his sunglasses and sun cream, fumbled around for the keys in the still untidy room and went outside and locked the door.

Once on the beach, the novel again failed to engage his interest; he could not even begin to focus his mind on it. Sitting on his towel on the sand, he watched the passers by on the beach; foreign couples, fruit vendors swinging their heavy baskets, a boy selling brightly coloured sarongs. Lying on his front to tan his back, he could put sun block on his shoulders and lower back but there was a bit in between he could not reach. With nobody to do it for him, he would just have to burn.

Totally alone, he spoke to no one until a woman came up to him, looking agitated.

'I came here for a beach holiday,' she said in a very British accent. 'I've been here two days and it's driving me crazy. How do I get off this island?' A day or so earlier Ben would not have known what she was talking about. Now he understood.

Unable to sit still, he went to buy a drink and was pleased to find Maca, Chuck and Clarissa sitting round a table on the sand, each playing their part as Aussie, Yank and plummy Pom. Clarissa was sounding off about the glories of dressage, Chuck was droning on about Thanksgiving, while Maca was extolling the 'beaut ute' he'd bought dirt cheap for driving into the outback at weekends.

Ben sat down, wondering what he could bore them with, and ordered his favourite lime juice.

'So what ails you, Ben, alone and palely loitering?' asked Clarissa.

'Sorry?' said Ben, perplexed.

'La Belle Dame Sans Merci,' said Clarissa. 'Coleridge.'

Ben was little the wiser.

'Yeah mate, no worries … it always turns out wrong in the end,' said Maca cheerfully.

'Thanks, pal. I'm okay really, just a bit shattered.'

Chuck was busy checking through the contents of a small rucksack.

'Water bottle, mask and snorkel, towel,' he said aloud.

'Where are you going?' asked Ben.

'Maca and me are heading down the island. It's a long, sweaty walk but there's a beach down south with some decent coral. Wanna come, Ben?'

'How long are you going for?'

'Well, most of the day I guess.'

Ben hardly hesitated.

'No, I don't think so. I'll hang out here,' he said.

'Okay mate, you can keep Clarissa company then,' said Maca.

Chuck and Maca set off, leaving Clarissa with a glum-looking Ben.

'Why didn't you go too?' she asked him. 'I thought that was your sort of thing.'

'Just didn't feel like it.'

'A bit down because of Emma?' she persisted. 'Isn't it better to do something?'

'No, it isn't that … well, I don't think it is.'

'What is it then?'

'Nothing really.'

'So it's going to be a massage today maybe?'

'Wouldn't you like to know?'

Clarissa saw that Ben was not going to be drawn.

'Right then, I'm going back to my Buddhism,' she said and went off to her hut.

With a sinking feeling Ben realised he was now alone for the day. He chose a deckchair under the tree by the usual massage place, hoping for some relief from the heat and stared out at the deep blue of sky and water, squinting into the dazzling light. On this, the east side of the island, the sun tracked along the beach all day, penetrating under the trees at the top of the beach. Since nine that morning the heat had been ferocious and it was impossible for him to escape it. Even a swim only gave him a brief respite and by the time he had walked back up the super-heated sand, he was already hot and sticky again.

Sitting in the deck chair under the trees he felt tired and lethargic. Why after only a few days on the island did he feel so low? The row with Emma and the overwhelming heat did not explain his unease and he now began to accept that the hollow in the pit of his stomach was because of Fon.

He had a strong urge to go and find her but he had no idea where to look. He could see some masseuses working at the far end of the beach but as he did not have the nerve to go and ask them, there was nothing he could do but wait. At home he knew the rules of the game but here he felt totally lost.

At midday he did not feel like eating as it was far too hot, so he stayed on the beach carefully scrutinising every female figure that passed by. Several times he thought he saw her, but in the distance one young Thai woman looked to him much like another. Then he saw two of the older masseuses coming in his direction. They were solid, stocky women from the rice fields, well dressed for the sun, their broad-brimmed hats shading their smiling faces.

'Hello, massage! Want massage?'

Ben was unsure what to say.

'Thanks, maybe later …' he said, but they quickly understood.

'You want Fon?' one of them asked him.

'Yes, but Fon's not here.'

'She work that beach,' said the other, pointing in the direction he had walked his first day on the island. 'She braiding Thai lady.'

'Braiding?'

'Yes, plaiting hair with beads.'

When they had gone, Ben got up and walked across the rocks to the next beach, relieved to be doing something at last, his toes sinking into the wet sand as he followed the water's edge, looking for Fon. Coming back along the beach above the high tide mark, he reached a group of tourists sitting on the sand, and suddenly he saw her. She was kneeling behind a deckchair, plaiting the hair of a young Thai girl in a bright red bikini. In the next chair sat a big barrel of an old man, a European of some sort, grotesque and hairy, his right hand wandering casually across the girl's navel and bikini pants. With Ben's attention divided between this bizarre couple and Fon, she gave him her finest smile.

'You want massage,' she asked sweetly.

'Yes, of course I do.'

'Okay Ben, see you later. You wait me please, usual place.' Her hands continued plaiting at great speed.

Ben was surprised and confused. He could not intrude, he could not stop and talk to Fon across the girl and the grizzled old *farang,* so he just had to keep walking.

As he retreated, he tried to analyse what he had seen. The girl in the deckchair was one of the prettiest of Thai girls, young and fresh. At least in his sixties, the man was powerfully built with greying hair across his chest and back and was wearing tight lycra swimming shorts. It was beauty and the beast. And as he glanced back he saw that Fon was now sharing a joke with him, totally at ease, almost flirtatious, her bewitching smile and infectious laughter squandered on this disgusting old gargoyle.

He walked back to Ao Sapporot, mulling it all over. But finding Fon had brought his appetite back so he went to the beach bar and ordered a plate of noodles which he ate greedily. He paid his bill and was overjoyed to spot Fon again soon after, this time sitting nearby under the trees at the top of the beach. She greeted him warmly and called him over.

She and some of the other masseuses were gathered round a little old lady who was selling food from two big baskets. Ben felt suddenly self-conscious; he did not know these people, he could not speak their language, nor begin to fathom what they were thinking. They were all eyeing him in a girlie, giggly sort of way that embarrassed him.

'No problem,' said Fon seeing his diffidence. 'Come Ben, sit.'

Ben sat where he was told, but he found it impossible to squat as they were doing, their hands thrown forward as counterweights. Nor could he comfortably sit cross-legged as a lifetime of sitting on chairs meant he was not as flexible as they were. So he half sat and half squatted and felt thoroughly awkward.

'We eat *som tam*,' said Fon.

'What?' he asked.

'*Som tam Lao*. Hot, hot, hot.'

'What's *som tam Lao*?'

'This *som tam*.' She pointed to a bowl of sliced green vegetable in a grey sauce, flecked with red chillis that one of the older women was already eating. 'Made with green papaya, crab legs, chilli ... and *plaa raa*.'

'What's *plaa raa*?'

'Fish sauce. Not plain fish sauce but rotten fish sauce.'

'Sounds terrible!'

'But all *farang* have to try *som tam Lao*.'

The little old lady was preparing each bowl of *som tam* individually to order; with or without palm sugar and peanuts, hot or very hot. She was swathed in clothes and under her broad-brimmed hat her face was a pattern of deep wrinkles, her teeth broken and red from the betel nut she was chewing. Out of this wreck of a face the liveliest eyes smiled and twinkled. As Ben watched the bony hands and wrists rhythmically pounding the ingredients in a heavy mortar, it crossed his mind that this frail old bird had walked all the way along the island from the ferry carrying her heavy load, while he had been too lazy even to go and swim with Maca and Chuck.

She had now finished preparing a dish of *som tam* for Fon who thrust it in front of Ben.

'Eat,' said Fon. '*Nit noy*.'

'What?' he said as the smell hit him.

'*Nit noy* ... little bit,' she said, grinning from ear to ear as she passed him a spoonful.

Everyone was watching. Ben had never before been defeated by exotic foods and did not want to look feeble, so he took the spoon and tentatively put a little *som tam* into his mouth. First came the taste, the taste of fermented fish, and then the pain. It did not hit him immediately, but in seconds his mouth was a searing, exquisite agony of burning chilli. The fire brigade turned on the tear ducts, his nose streamed, he gasped for breath. Fon then began to demolish the rest of the bowl, placing each spoonful very deliberately into the pale pinkness of her dainty little mouth.

'You not like?' she enquired mischievously. '*Som tam* too hot?'

Ben was hardly able to speak, blowing his nose and gulping air.

'God, that was disgusting. I thought Thai food was supposed to be brilliant.'

'Not Thai food,' said Fon. 'This special *som tam ... som tam Lao.*'

'Lao? But surely you're Thai?' said Ben.

'Yes Thai ... but Mama Lao, Papa Khmer from Cambodia. Family speak Lao and Khmer,' said Fon.

Gaeo, whose English was better than Fon's tried to explain.

'Some of Lao and Cambodia were part of Thailand before. Long time ago, France make trouble for Thailand ... King Thailand give Lao and Cambodia to France. So Isaan people, Laos and Khmers are the same ... same same but different.'

Ben thought he understood; that the modern political borders so recently imposed by the European powers do not always reflect cultural and linguistic boundaries. As a result both Lao and Khmer culture are intermingled in northeastern Thailand and that was why they were now eating *som tam Lao.*

'How you know all that, Gaeo?' asked Fon.

'Because I stay school longer than you,' Gaeo replied.

Fon fell silent for a moment, but not for long. There were other less serious things to talk and laugh about.

Ben watched as she amused the little group of masseuses with an outrageous anecdote. She seemed unaware that Ben was watching her intently, enjoying every moment though not understanding a word. He listened to her rapid-fire talk as she rocked back and forth with the drama of her tale. Salacious perhaps, scurrilous certainly, she kept her audience rapt and entertained. Intoned in the musical flight of the Thai language, her voice resembled birdsong. It seemed inconceivable to him that such a torrent of sound could mean something, but much meaning it clearly had. Seeing him left out, she tried to explain. Yes, it was salacious; she had been retelling Gaeo's confidences about her own married life.

'Gaeo, she married long time, have children,' she said. 'Husband go Isaan, see family, but Gaeo think him have lady Cambodia. When him come back, have sex with her, no problem. Next morning wake up, she very sleepy but husband want sex again. She say, have sex last night. But husband have sex with her again, get up, dress, not speak, say nothing! Then go work!'

Gaeo did not seem the least bit embarrassed and laughed along with all the others.

While they were talking, a couple Ben had not seen before came along the beach and joined the party. Fon jumped up and greeted them, just as she had earlier greeted Ben. He did not take to the tarty-looking Thai woman and he thought her *farang* boyfriend with his silly moustache, his tight Speedo swimming trunks and sagging stomach, looked a complete prat. The man turned to Ben and gave him a limp handshake.

'Hi, I'm Gunther,' he said, sounding very Germanic.

'I'm Ben. So you know Fon already, do you?'

'Yes, every day I come massage with Fon. I like very much.'

Ben fervently hoped he would drop dead or at least go away.

The German's Thai girlfriend had a weathered face with acne scars, her hair had once been permed and she wore a faded bikini top and sarong. They both seemed to know the masseuses well and Gunther was making it no secret that he fancied Fon like crazy.

The two of them pulled up deckchairs and settled down on the edge of the group. The girlfriend pulled out a piece of embroidery and became engrossed while Gunther seemed determined to chat to Ben.

'You like Koh Samet? First time in Thailand?' Ben hardly bothered to reply, but Gunther was not easily put off. 'Where do you stay? How much you pay for room?'

To Ben's relief Gunther then got up to buy drinks after first, disarmingly, offering him one, which Ben, being English, politely refused.

'You sit here,' Gunther said to his girlfriend. 'I'll get the drinks … you're just paid to look pretty.'

When he returned, she did not thank him for her Jack Daniels and coke, but held her towel to her nose and pulled a disgusted face.

'*Nagliat maak!* Towel smell pussy!' she shrieked.

Delighted at his girlfriend's wit, Gunther then held forth to Ben, while she quietly went back to her embroidery.

'Yes, I first come Thailand thirteen years ago. Work VW factory, Wolfsburg … good money. Go holiday three times a year … holiday more important than money.'

'So you're a car worker? You like it?'

'Ya, good, but I like holiday more. Every day same same, sit on beach with girlfriend, have massage with Fon.' He stroked the hairy caterpillar on his upper lip which looked as if it was about to crawl into his mouth.

By now the masseuses had eaten and talked enough and they and the little old lady wandered away down the beach, leaving Fon behind with Ben, Gunther and the girlfriend. Ben hoped his waiting might at last be over as Fon began to lay out her blue sheet on the sand, but he was to be disappointed.

'Massage now, okay?' she said to Gunther.

'Yah, good,' Gunther replied, leaving Ben sitting dejectedly with the girlfriend.

'You like Jack Daniels?' she asked him. 'Gunther buy me Jack Daniels and cola … six, maybe ten glass every day. He very good to me, pay everything.'

'He's your boyfriend?'

'Yes, special boyfriend. Have American before but him *kee niew* … stop sending money.'

'So Gunther lives in Germany … and how about you?'

'Stay Pattaya. You know Pattaya?'

'I've heard about it,' said Ben. 'What do you do there?'

'Work bar, cashier.' She gave Ben a nervous smile.

'And do you like it?'

'Okay, fifty-fifty. Good money and better than ricefield Isaan. But I not tell my Papa.'

'Not tell him what?'

'Not tell him I work Pattaya. If him know, him angry. Mama know already but not tell Papa, not tell family.' Her giggles flowed freely, released by the afternoon alcohol.

Ben wondered at the generosity of Gunther to this very ordinary girl. Why would he choose her and why was she so keen on spending his money? One Jack Daniels must be almost a day's wage in Isaan. And why waste a good quality bourbon by swamping it in cola. A tot of Mekhong, the local whisky would taste exactly the same with cola at a fraction of the price.

He watched Gunther enjoying his massage and flirting openly, while Fon responded with smiles and laughter. He felt a biting jealousy which he could not suppress or justify; he wanted his massage and he wanted to be alone with Fon, but he knew he would just have to wait.

He waited for what seemed an age until at last Gunther's massage was over. As Gunther went off to buy another Jack Daniels for his girl, he sidled over to where Fon was packing up her things.

'Can I have my massage, Fon?' he asked.

'Yes, can, but later. Have booking four o'clock … maybe one hour, maybe two, not sure.'

Ben looked at his watch; it was just before four. After a long day of waiting, he had no choice but to wait yet more. Fon gave him a warm smile, gathered up her plastic picnic box, and walked briskly away to her next appointment, leaving him feeling bereft and abandoned.

12

As Ben sat on his deckchair and waited for his massage, he could clearly see a small figure in blue top and baseball cap some way along the sand, crouched over one of the tourists who had booked a four o'clock massage.

For something to do, he got up and walked the length of the beach, paddling knee deep in the water. When he got near to where Fon was working, he could see her chatting happily with her customer, a fit young western guy, but as he passed by she did not wave or acknowledge him.

Time dragged heavily. He could not risk going back to his hut in case she finished work and disappeared while he was away, so all he could do was sit and wait. The sun was falling and the mosquitoes were active when at last he saw her coming back along the beach. She had been working all day and it crossed his mind that the only food she had eaten was that gut-wrenching *som tam*. Though she must be very tired and hungry by now, she looked cheerful enough as she came up to him.

'Okay Ben, massage. You wait me longtime ... same dog!'

At the sound of her laughter his spirits revived.

'You're not too tired?' he asked.

'No problem. High season, have to work strong.'

'We can leave it for today if you like.'

'You wait longtime already, so lie down English dog.'

Fon laid out her blue sheet under the trees in their usual place by the fallen tree trunk. Ben lay down on his front and she started to massage his feet and legs.

'So what you do today? Swim, sleep in the sun, read book?' she

112

asked.

'No, nothing ... waiting for you all day, just wanting to see you again.' He had to tell her exactly how it was, though lying face down he could not see her reaction.

'*Pak waan* ... sweet mouth,' she said. 'All men say like this to me.'

'No Fon, I really mean it. I'm different.' He twisted his head round for a glimpse of her smile, the smile she used to such effect on all her male customers.

'No, you not different,' she said. 'All men same same.'

'So you don't trust me then?'

'Better have woman friend, like Gaeo ... can tell her everything.'

'Yes, but it's very special, the feelings between a man and a woman,' said Ben.

'Sometimes too strong ... handsome man dangerous. Wrong man big trouble, but Gaeo always friend hundred percent.'

'That's great, though it's not the same, is it? It's not the same as being in love.'

Fon was quiet for a moment, then asked the obvious question.

'Your girlfriend yak-yak you? You and she boxing?'

'Boxing?'

'She boxing you?'

'Oh, fighting ... right. Well, suppose so, a bit.'

'When she come back Koh Samet?'

'She's not coming back.'

Ben had told Fon this before and did not want to elaborate, so he asked her a similar question.

'How about your boyfriend? Where's he now?'

'I think he go Isaan ... then come back Ban Phe. Always working.'

'What's the point of a boyfriend who's never with you?' he asked.

'Boyfriend, girlfriend often apart. Husband, wife work different place, leave children with grandmama. But it's okay, no problem.'

'No, it's terrible,' Ben insisted. 'Families shouldn't be split up.'

'Sometimes no possible to be together when you poor.'

'But why be married if you can't be with the person you love?'

'Always you *farang* talk of love, marry for love. You make crazy for girl, same drug, same movie. No Ben, fall in love bring tears, break hearts. Thai woman want good man, marry for children, have money, feed family.'

Ben felt Fon's slender hands working deep into the muscles around his neck. He gave in to the sensation and was silent for a moment, thinking about what she had said. Then he remembered the peculiar couples he had seen earlier in the day, the ugly old man and the German with their Thai girls.

'Who the hell was that old guy with the girl whose hair you were doing today? Where was he from?' he asked her.

'Don't know, maybe Russia.'

'And where did he meet the girl? You were chatting to her a lot.'

'She from Pattaya, work bar.'

'But how did she end up here with him?'

Fon seemed surprised by the question.

'Pay money of course,' she said.

'You mean she's a sex worker?'

'Yes, she bar girl. Sell sex.'

Ben's fears were confirmed.

'But he's hideous. How could she?'

'Old man okay … have money. Young man make her work too hard!' She shook with laughter.

'So he picks her up in a bar in Pattaya and brings her here?'

'Yes, bar lady like very much … get away from bar, have holiday. Paid every day, good money.'

'How much?'

'One day, one thousand baht.'

'But how can a pretty young kid go with a revolting old man?'

'Don't know. Fon not sell sex … sell sex I die!' She clasped her hands around her throat and let out a fake shriek of anguish. 'Better work strong, make small money.'

'So why does she do it?' asked Ben.

'Girl not like school, want easy money, easy life. From Ubon, Isaan, she eighteen go Pattaya. She virgin … first night man pay 15,000 baht.'

'That's a bit over two hundred pounds. Blow me!' said Ben.

'So now she work bar … boom-boom with *farang*.'

'And she ends up in bed with an old man. How old is he anyway?'

'She say he sixty two and very kind, pay everything.'

'But how can she ever enjoy sex again.'

'She like Thai boys … sleep with boyfriend. But him not work, always take her money.'

'Christ, so you mean she's doubly screwed … by the old Russian and by a slob of a Thai who gets into her pocket as well as her pants. But she looked so nice.'

'You like her?' asked Fon pointedly.

'Yes, she's a stunner,' said Ben.

Fon went quiet and concentrated on her work.

'Too many mosquitoes,' she said, brushing one off Ben's back. 'Better we go down the beach.'

They picked up the sheet and moved away from the trees into the relative cool of an evening breeze that was springing up nearer the sea.

As the massage went on, Ben now wanted to ask about Gunther and his extravagant girlfriend.

'So who's the German with the Thai woman? You seem to know them.'

'Yes, always come for massage. He want sex with me … massage in room. Girlfriend she say okay no problem.'

'The bastard tells his girlfriend he wants sex with you?' asked Ben aghast. 'But he's supposed to be her boyfriend, isn't he?'

'He come holiday with her many times. He good to her, give money.'

'So she's a hooker too?'

'Yes, have many boyfriends send her money. She want marry *farang* … but until then she bar lady Pattaya.'

'My god, how can people live like that,' said Ben.

'Easy you talking … some people not have money, so work bar.'

'They could work hard just like you do. You'd never sell yourself.'

'Massage better … can make good money.'

'But you worked for nothing in Bangkok and were a cleaner here on the island … you could have escaped all that and be rich by now.'

'No problem, I happy my life,' said Fon. 'I look after Mama, Joy, make merit. Not rich, not too poor, then I die. Next life maybe better.'

Ben thought for a moment. Despite the smiles, her outlook seemed so bleak.

'But Fon, you're young and attractive. You've got to enjoy this life right now.'

'Cannot think of myself, family more important ... so work every day. Evening tired, look story on TV ... pretty girl fall in love, have big house, big Benz. But life not like that for me.'

'Does life have to be all work though, *every* day? Have you ever been anywhere for fun and not just for work?' he asked her.

Fon answered him almost angrily.

'How I go holiday? Expensive! *Farang* come holiday, bring girl from Pattaya ... go in sea no clothes on, drink too much, get another girl, have more sex. But me not *farang,* not same me!' she said accusingly.

'Come on Fon, that's a bit hard. I'm not like that either.'

'No, you good *farang.* I like!' She dispelled the tension with peals of laughter, but her smile quickly disappeared. 'And *farang* women as bad as men ... smoke, drink, go street like bar girl, show their body on beach ... Thai men look at them, think they sell sex. Why they do like this?'

'What's so wrong with having a good time? Men do, so why not women too?' said Ben, lying flat on his face on Fon's blue sheet. 'Just because a woman's not all covered up doesn't mean she's up for it.'

'So *farang* woman only have sex with husband?'

'Well, no, they sleep with their boyfriends if they want to.'

'Can sleep with anyone? Not same Thai woman. Thai woman only sleep with husband.'

'Go on! Tell me another. Did I dream Bangkok?'

'Ben, Thai girl virgin, not sleep with men, not go crazy like *farang* woman.'

'*Farang* women don't go crazy,' said Ben.

'Yes, but *farang* woman like sex too much. For woman, sex not important except make baby. If she want too much sex, better she go Pattaya.'

Ben was quite taken aback by her negative view of the *farang* on holiday.

'Come on, Fon, sex isn't that wicked. It's a pleasure for women too, isn't it? You can still respect a woman who likes it, can't you?'

'Thai woman keep herself for husband, not like bar girl,' she said quietly.

'And Fon, the crazy *farang* on holiday ... that's all it is, people letting off steam. We spend our lives doing exams or locked up in an office saving up, freezing cold, desperate to escape. So what do we do? Rip off our clothes, get pissed and jump in the sea. And there's nobody watching, so you can score if you want to.'

He immediately regretted this last comment, but either Fon did not understand or it troubled her more that holidays were a terrible waste of money.

'But Ben, you go holiday, and when money finish you have nothing,' she said.

'That's no problem if you enjoyed it.'

'Okay for *farang*, but Thai people cannot. Must pay room, buy rice ... Mama Papa sick, pay doctor. Okay buy TV, VCD, video, then you have something, but pay holiday, same burn money ... you only get smoke.'

'Sure Fon, but going travelling you learn so much about the place and stuff.'

'Learn what? About drinking, about sex?' she said emphatically.

'Not fair, Fon. What I mean's this ... you're only young once. Life's beautiful, so you've got to live it ... you don't have to feel guilty about that. The *farang* are here for the time of their lives, for one special holiday.'

'One holiday? But same *farang* keep coming back,' she said triumphantly.

Ben decided to try a different tack.

'And Fon, what's so special about virginity? I don't go for sex with bar girls, but two people who respect each other can decide what they want to do together.'

'So you *farang* get drunk, have sex, do what you like. But my life's my work ... what I do for my family.'

'Sounds awfully hard.'

'Yes, and for Thai woman getting harder. Before, Papa always go work ... Mama stay home for family. But now woman working too, and when man not work, woman still do cooking, cleaning, take care children.'

'So you don't think much of Thai men then?'

'Better have woman friend. Men sweet talk me, but I not sixteen anymore.'

Ben sensed this was aimed at him.

'But Fon, I had to tell you what I feel. I like you too much to shut up.'

'No problem, I know men talk sweet. *Farang* always try their luck with me, ask me go room for massage. But no, no, never! I can look after myself now, not like before.'

Ben did not dare to ask exactly what she meant by this so tried a safer question.

'Your little sister, Jinda. What's she like?'

'Jinda, she same me, same face. But she virgin. When man come sweet talk, she run, run. She scared of man.' Fon's face lit up. 'No have boyfriend, no have problems!'

'I must meet Joy and Jinda,' said Ben.

'Can,' said Fon. 'Joy over there.' She pointed into the trees behind them.

As Ben sat up and turned around he caught a glimpse of a little girl ducking behind a tree. When she did not reappear, Fon called to her and the child came dancing down the beach towards them. She wore a well-washed yellow dress that was too big for her skinny frame and looked like a hand-me-down. The buttons behind the neck were not done up and she kept hitching the dress back onto her tiny shoulders. Her hair was wild and her oval face and cheeky smile strongly resembled Fon's. She bounced right up to them, grinning from ear to ear.

'This *Khun* Ben,' said Fon.

'*Sawasdee ka, Khun* Ben,' said Joy, briefly bowing her head and holding her hands together under her chin in a traditional *wai* greeting. She looked directly at him, not in the least afraid of the big *farang*.

'Fon, she's lovely. Joy's the right name for her.'

Fon glowed with pleasure and pride.

Joy had disappeared and Ben was sitting up facing out to sea as Fon manipulated his shoulders, when he heard her speaking in Thai to someone behind him. He looked round again and saw Joy dragging a young Thai woman down the beach. She had been sent to find Jinda. But Jinda hardly spoke any English and, on meeting him, could only giggle in embarrassment. The two sisters seemed so very different.

As Fon finished the massage and started to pack up, it suddenly dawned on Ben that after all the waiting and their brief time together, the day was now over. Fon would soon disappear with Joy and Jinda, leaving him totally alone.

'*Hiu khao*. Very hungry,' said Fon. 'Shall we go eat?'

'Eat? You mean with me?' He could hardly believe what he was hearing.

'Yes, why not? You not like?' She hooted with laughter.

'I like very much.'

'Okay, go shower. See you here, half hour. We eat good place.' She pointed along the beach to where in the gathering darkness the restaurants were setting out their bamboo tables on the beach for the night's entertainment. So Ben's day was not yet over after all. He went back to his hut, had a quick shower and put on a clean tee-shirt and cotton trousers and was back on the beach well within the half hour. But Fon, Joy and Jinda were not yet there. He waited and still they did not come. Once again he was waiting for Fon. He had no idea where she stayed and would not dare to go looking for her even if he did, so he sat on the fallen tree by the massage place, anxiously looking at his watch. Had he misunderstood where they were to meet? Perhaps they were already down at the restaurant. It was now a full hour since Fon had gone to shower and he could bear to wait no longer. He got up and started off along the beach but had only gone a hundred yards when he heard a voice.

'Ben, where you go?' It was Fon coming out of the trees with Jinda and Joy.

'Just going to look for you,' he said, too relieved to be annoyed. 'No problem ... we go eat.'

Ben was entranced by how Fon looked. She had changed into a blue dress with a high waist, an embroidered bib over the bust and short gathered sleeves. Her hair was loose and she had taken some trouble with her makeup, accentuating her eyebrows and smiling eyes. Perhaps this was why she had taken so long. Joy was in her best dress and had been powdered around the neck and face making her look like a little ghost. Jinda, in jeans and tee shirt, seemed more relaxed than before and was laughing and joking with Fon, while Joy was rushing in circles, grabbing Fon by the hand, and wanting her all to herself.

Ben thought the walk along the beach in the thickness of the night was magical. On their left were the restaurants with their glowing barbecues, already packed with people, to their right the crashing of the waves. Walking to the far end of the beach, they came to the last of the eating places beyond the main group of restaurants. He wondered whether she had chosen this quieter one because she was with a *farang*; local eyebrows might be raised if she were seen out at night with a foreigner.

'Come, sit,' said Fon. 'What you like Ben?'

He inspected the seafood on display and chose tiger prawns.

'We eat pork, fried chicken and noodle,' she said.

'What'll Joy have?' he asked.

'She look when food come ... not eat much.'

Sure enough Joy was too excited to sit still, dancing on the moonlit sand, lost in childish fantasy. First she mimed as a karaoke singer with an invisible microphone, then picked up some leaves for a mobile phone with which she dialled the world. But the best game of all was jumping on the heads of the long shadows cast by Jinda and Fon. Ben saw her looking down at the shapes and crept up behind her. As his shadow came towards hers with arms raised, she let out a shriek of delight and escaped away across the sand.

As they ate, it was not easy for Ben to talk with Jinda, and Fon seemed a little tense, lacking her usual sparkle, her serious face very different to the daytime one. He tried asking her about her work.

'Good day today? Many people?'

'Yes, good day. One braiding, four massage ... one thousand baht.

Now very tired.'

'And tell me a bit about Jinda's work.'

'She look after Joy, and when I finish massage, she cooking, Montego Resort. But she not work tonight.'

'Sounds a good arrangement.'

'Joy now four. When five, she go school. Jinda cooking daytime and I pay her less.'

'So you pay her for looking after Joy?'

'Yes, I have money so I give to Jinda. She my sister.'

'That's good ... better than English families.'

'And tomorrow I go Ban Phe, send money to Mama. Gaeo come too.'

'So you and your mother have bank accounts?'

'I have ... Mama not have. I send money to Mama friend, telephone to say money in bank already.'

As she was speaking, a brilliant idea was forming in Ben's mind.

'Fon, I've got to go and check my email. When are you going?'

'Have booking nine o'clock ... go eleven thirty. We go together?'

'That'd be great,' said Ben. 'Let's do it.'

Fon then exchanged a few words in Thai with Jinda.

'Jinda and Joy come too,' she said. 'Can eat Ban Phe ... go market, buy food. Half day no work, *sanuk dee*. Have holiday, like *farang*!'

Then the food was served, the many plates squeezed onto the table around the flickering oil lamp. Joy sat and toyed with her food, constantly wriggling and putting her feet up on the chair, displaying her skinny knees and whinging a little. Fon fed her bits of rice, Joy wanting her undivided attention. When the food was finished, Fon called for the bill and Ben paid it. It was time for Joy to go to bed, so they walked slowly back along the beach peering at the fish on display and discussing the bars and eating places. On reaching the spot where Fon would go up to her hut, Ben again felt the pain of parting. The question slipped out; he just had to ask.

'Can I walk back to your room with you, Fon?'

'No, cannot. You go bar, find friend.'

'Right,' he said, looking disappointed.

'So you come Ban Phe tomorrow?'

'Yes, I'd really like to.'

'Okay, eleven thirty boat.'

The parting was brief, Joy holding Fon's hand and now looking tired and subdued. Ben felt suddenly excluded as he watched them disappear into the darkness. He headed for the beach bar, sat down at a table and ordered a beer, but seeing Clarissa sitting alone a few tables away, he got up and joined her.

'So you've been left on your own too,' he said to her as he sat down.

'Yes, Samantha and her sidekick left yesterday and Stig, the mad Norwegian, got the boat this morning.'

'Are you pining for him?' teased Ben.

'Not exactly, but he was good company. Quite a revelation really.'

'And no Maca or Chuck?'

'Probably doped up in their hut.'

There was a silence before Ben broached what he really wanted to talk about.

'Well, I've had a fascinating day ... or an hour or two of it at least.'

'Let me guess. Massage was it?'

'Yes, but it's not so much the massage as the chance to talk. You never get to talk to Thai people and I've learned so much from Fon.'

'So what's she told you then?'

'We talked about tourists and about Thai families and sex mainly.'

'Bet you did.'

'No seriously, there were some real surprises. She doesn't condemn the sex workers, but she's got strict views on chastity, and being respectable seems crucial for her.'

'So you mean a girl's a virgin or married ... or else she's a whore?'

'Yes, I suppose that's about it.'

'An attractive young masseur must have to be careful with her reputation in a small place like this,' said Clarissa.

'It's a bit nineteenth century though, the fallen woman and stuff ... weird given Thailand's reputation for sex tourism. And Fon's really suspicious of love relationships ... talks of marriage as an economic partnership. And definitely no sex outside marriage. It's so different here.'

'Rural societies are always traditional, I guess, putting the family first and so on. But it looks like Thailand's changing fast, and I bet there's horrific double standards ... abstinence for the ladies while the men screw around.' She rolled her eyes and broke into a smile.

'No joke though Clarissa, I really admire Fon's principles. Most of her money goes looking after Joy and her mother, and she says her sister Jinda's a virgin. They're both pretty wary of men.'

'Maybe Fon has reason to be ... you said there's a boyfriend in the background somewhere. And the child you told me about ... Joy is it? You don't really know who the mother is, do you. And does Fon claim to be one of the virgins?'

Ben did not have the chance to reply to all these questions as they were interrupted by Chuck and Maca noisily joining them at the table after their day's snorkelling. Already well-oiled, they ordered more beers.

'Great beach, mate,' said Maca. 'Wasn't Aussie coral but it was good. You should've come with us.'

'Yeah, you dunno how to live, man,' said Chuck dreamily.

For the rest of the evening Ben was quiet and lost in thought and after a couple of beers with the lads, he went back to his hut to sleep. It had been a frustrating day with a good ending, though the next day's trip into Ban Phe with Fon was looking much more promising.

13

As the eleven thirty ferry out of Ao Sapporot came clear of the headland, its brightly-painted hull began to lift in the gentle swell. The on-shore breeze moderated the heat of the day and the sea sparkled and danced to the rhythm of a perfect cloudless morning. Ben watched from the stern as the island fell behind in all its beauty. At this distance, apart from the mast for cellphone reception, Koh Samet looked undeveloped and unspoiled. Beautiful though it was, he felt relieved to be getting away from where the tensions with Emma had come to a head, even if only for a few hours.

On board with him were Fon, her friend Gaeo, sister Jinda and little Joy. Fon had already squeezed in two hours of massage that morning and only just managed to get aboard the last boat shuttling passengers to the ferry anchored in the bay. Ben had taken the first boat with the others and was terrified she would not make it in time. From the ferry he watched as she splashed through the shallows, desperately trying to roll up her tight jeans, laughing and joking with the boat boys. Now they were all comfortably installed in deckchairs on the upper deck, Fon trying to dry out her jeans. The three women were absorbed in excited chatter which had them in fits of laughter, while Joy was rushing around under Fon's anxious eye. It was a party all the way, every ounce of enjoyment being extracted from a mundane trip to the bank to send money home.

Forty minutes were spent watching the island pass by the port side before the ferry nosed around the end of the massive stone breakwater that created a safe haven and made Ban Phe a major fishing port. The long jetty was crowded with boats, the wooden planking of the walkway and the bustle of pick-ups and motorbikes already familiar to Ben. It was only a few days earlier that he had come here for the first time en route to the island with Emma but it seemed an age. So much had happened in so short a time.

Joy led the way along the jetty, pulling Fon by the hand and talking incessantly. They passed through the stalls and wooden shacks selling beach clothes and fruit and reached the road. It was a busy urban street, lined with featureless three-storey concrete buildings, their facades covered with signs and hoardings advertising every modern temptation from Pepsi to mobile phones.

'First we go eat,' said Fon, leading them to a food shop a few hundred yards up the street. Furnished only with concrete tables and chairs, it consisted of a long, narrow space under a commercial building open to the winds with no front or rear walls. As it was still early, there were no other customers. She walked through as far from the road as possible and chose a table on the edge of what should have been a garden at the back. Ben sat down on an uncomfortable chair and took in the surroundings. The inside had not seen any paint for many years and the concrete floor was scattered with empty beer cartons and junk. On the wall by their table was a dog-eared poster of the fishes and flora of Thailand stuck on with yellowing tape. He was a little alarmed. How safe was it to eat in a place like this?

Fon ordered the food and in no time the table was laden with pork ribs, tiny fish fried to a crisp, a rice soup and *laab*, a northeastern dish of minced beef, cooked with all sorts of green bits and pieces. The meal was to be eaten with sticky rice, the staple food of Lao and Isaan. Ben had not tried sticky rice before and was not too sure about it. The opposite of the western fixation for fluffy rice grains that do not stick together, it was congealed into one glutinous blob. He watched the others as they ate the sticky rice with their fingers, rolling it into a ball, dipping it in the sauce and popping it into their mouths. But what struck him most of all was the containers; the rice was served to each person in a finely-woven basket with a lid and a wooden base. He picked his up and admired it.

'Beautiful,' he said. 'Where can you buy them?'

'You like sticky rice?' asked Fon slightly bemused.

'No, the basket … great handicraft. I'd like to take one for Mum.'

'She eat sticky rice?'

'No, I mean for display, to look at.'

'*Farang* want to look at basket! Too much sun, go soft in the head,' said Fon with a mocking grin before adding something in Thai. When the others erupted in laughter, Ben sensed it was indecent and at his expense, though he adored her every little attention.

The food was quickly eaten and Fon called loudly for the bill. She paid the girl and they abruptly departed; there was serious business to be done. They all walked together along the edge of the road, close to the roar of the traffic. There was no pavement and it was dusty and hot, the heat radiating from the tarmac. They walked for about ten minutes, leaving behind the concrete shop houses and crossed an open area between the fishing port and the old centre of the town. Ben felt the sweat trickling down his back, his tee shirt clinging to his wet skin.

Ahead of them was a large white building, the branch of the Bangkok Bank where Fon had her account. Fon and her posse went inside, while Ben tried his luck with the cashpoint on the outside wall. He inserted his card and his baht came popping out, much to the wonder of an old man nearby, marvelling at the miraculous fountain of money.

Inside the bank he found Fon wrestling with the intricacies of paying-in slips, taking two thousand baht from her own account to put into the account of her mother's friend. This was the monthly payment that enabled her mum to survive in relative comfort. Enjoying the air-conditioned calm of the bank, he was relieved it all took some time.

Back outside again, it seemed that Fon had something on her mind. She told Jinda and Gaeo to wait with Joy in the shade for a few moments and asked Ben to follow her.

'Ben, I want to show you something,' she said, looking serious.

'What is it?'

'Come with me.' She walked away at some speed despite the heat, talking as she went. 'Ben, you ask me about my dreams. Joy soon five, go school …'

'Yes, but where are we going?'

'Look school, school for Joy.'

She took Ben a few hundred yards to a small private school, tucked away in modern buildings beyond an orchard of fruit trees. The school was in session and children in neat, practical uniforms could be seen at work in spacious classrooms and playing in the playground. Fon clearly knew the place well and walked around freely, without embarrassment. Apart from a few glances at Ben, the children politely ignored them.

'So that my dream, my dream for Joy,' she said as they walked back to the road.

'I hope the dream comes true ... but it must be expensive, Fon.'

'Maybe can ... if many tourists come Koh Samet.'

Ben was impressed, though he wondered how she could possibly afford the fees just from working as a masseuse.

They walked back to the others who were still patiently waiting where they had left them. Fon then braved a superheated phone box to call her mother's friend and tell her the money was in her account, while in the cool of Thai Farmers Bank, Gaeo was making a money transfer to her family in the North East. Crossing the road again to the post office, Gaeo then helped Fon to fill out a form for registered mail; they kept making mistakes, ripping the form up and starting again. Fon explained to Ben that she was sending some cash to an elderly and wayward relative.

'Sister my grandbrother she not work ... drink too much, buy lottery. I send her little bit money, so she can eat.'

'Why's it you who has to give it her?' asked Ben.

'They know I have money, they speak Mama, so Mama ask me to give. Big family, big problem.' With a resigned look, she handed the envelope with the money over the counter.

This last payment finally done, they all went on down the road through the old town, a narrow street of tightly-packed wooden shop-houses, each with its ground floor shop and living-space upstairs. They walked past crowded clothes shops, hardware stores, beauty salons and dealers in farm and fishing equipment, Ben happily tagging along, no longer bothering to ask where they were going. Soon they reached a market.

'Buy food for this evening,' said Fon.

The market was an open-sided iron shed full of stalls selling fish, meat and vegetables, clothes, plastic goods, buckets and bins. It was quiet as it was still early afternoon, but the stalls were all manned by weathered women patiently waiting for a sale. Ben noticed one exception, a pretty young girl. When she turned to smile at him, he saw she had only one eye, the other an empty socket.

Fon was buying food in brisk and businesslike fashion, choosing and bargaining and passing the packets back to Jinda and Gaeo, buying enough meat and fish for a small army. They then went back into the street where Fon called three motorbike taxis. She jumped onto one of them and with Joy squeezed between her and the rider, they shot off down the road. Gaeo and Jinda got on another and noisily departed in a cloud of smoke. Ben had no idea where they were going but the third bike set off with him clinging on behind, in hot pursuit of Jinda's yellow tee shirt which he could just see disappearing into the distance.

His motorbike was now going much too fast. It weaved through the traffic and braked hard at an intersection, avoiding a collision by seconds. As it took the next corner the world tipped sideways and then righted itself, his brain filled with images of bodies bouncing and sliding down the road and of bare limbs lacerating on loose tarmac.

After a few more spine-tingling moments, he realised he had returned to the fishing port through the one-way system and that the others were already walking away towards the ferry. He paid forty baht to the driver for not quite killing him and set off after Fon, his legs feeling strangely unfamiliar. When he caught up with her, she smiled at him with a mischievous glint.

'You like motorbike taxi?' she asked. 'Sorry Ben, no need to hurry … wait next boat one hour.'

But Ben was not complaining. He was still alive and though waiting for Fon was painful, waiting with her was no problem at all.

'Ben, you wanted to look email,' she reminded him bluntly. 'Why you not do it?'

'Yeah, of course, I'd forgotten,' he said, feeling a bit stupid.

'We wait you over there, clothes shop.'

Ben was surprised that emailing Emma had totally slipped his mind. Keeping in touch with her was important, but he had become so absorbed in chasing after Fon that it had totally gone out of his head. He crossed the road and found the internet cafe where several travellers were intently huddled over their computer monitors in silent communion. He sat down and nervously opened his Hotmail account. As he scanned his inbox, he saw with a jump that there was a message from her sent the previous night. So Emma had made the first move.

> To: ben-the-bill80@hotmail.com
> Subject: Chiang Mai
> *Dearest Ben, I'm shocked you haven't emailed me, gobsmacked, gutted even. I was half expecting an apology but maybe you're too busy with sun, sand and massage. I'm busy too as I've met some people and we're getting the train tonight to Chiang Mai to do some hilltribe trekking. I was going to wait for a message from you, but as I'll be in the jungle for a bit, thought I'd email first.*
>
> *Just to say I don't want to part on bad terms without talking things through a bit, so can we get together in Bangkok? When I'm back from CM, I'll meet you at the Regal Hotel off Ratanakosin Avenue near the Grand Palace. It's a bit pricey but no need to book. You check us into a room for the night of 25th and I'll be there in the evening. Email me if you're not coming, but if you don't come, then stuff you. Gotta get packed and meet the others before the train.*
> *M.*

The message was typical Emma. Ben could just hear her saying this sort of thing and felt almost reassured by her bluntness. He suddenly missed her and felt funny that she was heading off to Chiang Mai without him. As he wanted to keep his options open, it was important how he now played his cards.

> To: melldoyma66@hotmail.com
> Subject: Stuff and Things
> *Emm, How could I email you from Koh Samet, there's no*

cyber palm trees! So I've made a special trip into Ban Phe, but I'll have to be quick as the boat goes back soon.

I'd love to be going to Chiang Mai. Who are the blokes then? Bring me back some opium or a stick of rock and see you on the 25th. And Emm, I do miss you, honest. It came as a real shock you walking out on me like that. I had no idea you were so screwed up and I didn't mean to get up your nose. Got a bit over-excited in Bangkok I guess, but for me you're still a cool dude. So enjoy, and see you at the Regal. Suppose I'm paying! Love, Ben.

He clicked on 'Send', quickly read a message from his little sister, paid and rushed out of the shop. He found Fon in the back of the clothes shop where she was waiting for him, fooling around with the others and trying on clothes. The shop was little more than a wooden shack built over the beach by the pier. It was intolerably hot inside, the generator which rumbled loudly in the background only adding to the heat. Gaeo and Jinda were sitting on the floor eating fried chicken and sticky rice out of plastic bags and offered some to Ben, but he did not fancy it.

Jinda then took a skimpy little tank top with a Union Jack design from the rail of clothes, hid behind a crate to try it on and quickly emerged to shrieks and cat-calls.

'You look like bar lady, Jinda,' squealed Fon. 'Give it to me … I want to be bar lady too.' The sisters went behind the crate together before Fon reappeared in the Union Jack top looking a million dollars as she played the fashion model pounding the catwalk. With an insolent pout and hand on hip she sailed down the seedy inside of the shop, leaving Ben utterly transfixed by the swing of her body and the exaggerated wiggle of blue denim. Flashing him a grin, she disappeared behind the crate. When the laughter had died down, she popped her head out again to see his reaction.

'I your England flag, Ben. I wave for you.'

'Fon, you look amazing … but then you always do.'

It struck Ben that this was the first time Fon had behaved provocatively in front of him; the sparks flying between the two of them must have been obvious to the others. Perhaps she was no longer the defender of Thai female modesty now she was not in public on the beach, or was it, he dared hope, because she was growing to like him.

When she had changed back into her tee shirt, they all wandered out onto the jetty. Instead of going straight to the ferry which was soon due to leave, she stopped and chatted casually with some women at one of the kiosks. Ben had no idea what was going on and was bothered about missing the boat. Fon tried to explain.

'Go speedboat ... better more and not expensive,' she said. As she talked, Ben began to grasp that a speedboat from one of the beach resorts was running back to Ao Sapporot and could take them as passengers.

They all walked slowly along the jetty, climbed aboard the speedboat which was lying alongside and sat down amidst vegetables and beer bottles. The long-haired boat-boy in baggy shorts and singlet started up the forty horse outboard and soon they were out beyond the breakwater, bumping and thumping over the waves. Ben stood up in the slipstream and howled with joy while Fon crouched uncomfortably in the bottom of the boat, holding a supermarket catalogue over her face to keep off the sun.

In no time at all they were back at Ao Sapporot, wallowing through the surf and splashing onto the beach. It was early afternoon and Fon would now have to get back to work for the rest of the day. She quickly answered Ben's silent enquiry.

'Have plenty food, cook tonight. You come eat?'

'You bet,' he said.

'Okay, see you here, seven o'clock. Maybe we go disco later.' She took Joy by the hand and with the bags of food in the other, sailed off up the beach. Ben watched her go. He could now enjoy a pleasant afternoon looking forward to an evening together with good eating and perhaps even a disco. The vibes were now very positive indeed.

14

Time slipped easily by for the rest of the day as Ben swam and lazed on the beach. He could relax because that evening he would be with Fon and because he knew exactly where she now was. As he swam he could see her at work with Gaeo over by the rocks, and later when she walked along the beach looking for customers, his eyes followed her every move. He could not help watching her and he could not concentrate on anything else. Once she disappeared from view but her plastic box with her massage kit was still sitting under the trees so she would not be very far away.

He now had time to think about his growing obsession; why had he fallen so totally for Fon? There was of course the powerful appeal of the exotic. Fon was every man's Asian dream, and though he had seen many gorgeous girls in Bangkok, her charm and personality were no less than dazzling. But the strangest feeling was his sympathy and admiration for her; he was moved by the sad story of her childhood and he greatly respected her solitary struggle to provide for her Mama and Joy. These were all reasons for his fixation, though by now it had gone beyond the rational. He realised he was besotted.

It worried him that there were still many things about her that were puzzling. Though there seemed to be a growing chemistry between them, he could not really be sure what if anything she felt for him. She was always flirtatious with her customers and could turn on the charm at will, so perhaps he was just another dupe for her to play games with. Her claims to modesty also seemed at odds with her recent provocative behaviour. He was confused by her insistence on propriety and reputation while at the same time being an outrageous tease and an accomplished mistress of innuendo. Then there was the shadowy boyfriend she had mentioned a couple of times and her reluctance to talk about the death of her sister, the mother of Joy. It was all made more difficult because he could not read the signals in so different a culture.

Now sitting alone waiting for the evening, he found himself talking freely with her, practising the verbal foreplay of seduction which streamed through his head in a pleasurable glow. He could say to her whatever he liked and he daydreamed erotic dreams. More than once, a little carried away, he was embarrassed by a stirring in the swimming trunk department that kept him briefly confined to his deckchair.

Ben's afternoon went slowly by in a heated reverie. Come dusk and mosquito time, he went to his hut and showered. He arrived early at the meeting place, the fallen tree at the top of the beach and sat and waited. Then he saw a small female figure coming towards him. The light was behind her and he thought he recognised the distinctive gait.

'Hi, Fon,' he called, running towards her. He wanted to hold her and kiss her but suddenly he realised it was not Fon but her sister. Jinda laughed out loud, guessing his mistake. He followed her into the trees until they reached a group of workers' huts where he saw Fon, dressed as she had been all day, in the middle of cooking.

Beside the huts was an open-air kitchen, a simple wooden structure with a corrugated roof, gas cylinders, plastic basins for washing dishes, and pots and pans strewn around in disorder. Under the trees were a couple of rusty tin tables with plastic tops and some chairs. Fon was holding a pan over a gas ring and stirring hard.

'Hi, Ben ... cooking for you,' she called to him. 'Very hot and too many red ants.' She bent down and brushed them off her ankle. 'You hungry?'

'You bet,' said Ben. 'So is this where you live?' he asked her.

'No, this house Gaeo,' she said, pointing with her wooden spatula. 'Her husband away, so we cook here.'

At that moment Joy came shooting out of Gaeo's hut, saw Ben and with a shriek hurled herself at him, shouting his name. He caught her and lifted her into the air, twirling her round until he was dizzy.

'Food ready now,' said Fon. 'Pork ribs, fish, *tom yam* and sticky rice.'

'No *som tam*?' asked Ben.

'No *som tam*,' said Fon. 'But sticky rice always have.'

The plates of food were put on the tables and Fon, Jinda, Joy, Gaeo and Ben sat down on the tin chairs, the feet sinking into the sandy soil. Ben felt honoured. He guessed this had all been done for his benefit, that it was not usual for Fon to entertain a *farang* and that it could only be done with other friends around.

'Food good?' asked Fon.

'Yes, the best ... the best ever,' said Ben with conviction, good because it had been done specially for him and by Fon.

They ate hungrily from the wobbly tables and soon the dishes were all empty. There was no standing on ceremony and they immediately started clearing up.

'Ben, you go Gaeo's room, take Joy,' said Fon.

Gaeo showed Ben into her hut where he was left with Joy, sitting on a double mattress on the floor and flicking through a magazine for Thai TV. In the room was a television, a fridge, the mattress, a mosquito net and clean clothes hung up behind a curtain.

Joy was wriggling around, wanting to play with Ben. Frustrated that she could not make him understand, she switched on the television and trawled through the channels with the remote control. Then Fon's head came round the door.

'You okay, Ben? Me and Jinda go shower,' she said, before disappearing again.

Ben was a little surprised when a few minutes later, she and Jinda came back after showering, wrapped only in towels. Defying the towel to fall off, Fon then threw her arms above her head and pirouetted around twice on tiptoes.

'Fon sexy? You like?' she sang out with a laugh. Ben liked very much and said so. At that moment Gaeo came back into the hut and, with much merriment, they began to go through the clothes stored behind the curtain.

'Jinda have clean clothes but I not have, so borrow from Gaeo,'

Fon explained.

There was little choice, most of it working clothes, and Fon ended up with a clean tee shirt and a pair of shapeless brown shorts to wear.

'We put on shirt now,' she said to Ben, 'so you watch TV ... not look.' Still only in her towel she came up to where Ben was sitting on the mattress, knelt down behind him, wrapped her arms round him and clasped her hands over his eyes. 'You eyes closed, okay!'

It was very tactile, her body pressed hard against his back, the first contact between them that was not professional massage.

'What if I look?' he demanded, stirred if not shaken.

'I kill you,' she said.

With Joy dancing around in front of the television and Ben's eyes glued uncomprehendingly to a Thai soap opera, Jinda and Fon noisily got dressed.

'Ben, you can look now,' said Fon as Jinda shrieked in protest, zipping up her jeans just in time.

'You look great, Fon,' said Ben, 'in whatever you wear.'

'Sweet mouth... men always the same!' Fon did another little dance, this time with Joy, the two of them falling about the place like puppies.

With Ben sitting on the mattress in front of the television, Jinda and Fon chatted with Gaeo in Thai. Gaeo produced a bag of cosmetics which they sorted through, while Fon picked up a mirror and gazed lovingly into it. In fits of giggles, Fon and Jinda started to put on make-up, concentrating hard; a little eye-liner, some talcum, an eyebrow pencil, but no lipstick. Fon caught sight of Ben looking at her in the mirror and smiled.

'What's the war paint for?' he asked.

'What you say?'

'The make-up. Where are you going?'

'Dancing,' she said breezily. Ben felt a surge of anxiety.

'Where?'

'Diamond Bar. Maybe go Meridian later.'

He was none the wiser, nor did he care so long as he could go dancing too. With the make-up ritual over, he now realised the sisters were about to make a move.

'Who's going dancing?' he asked.

'Me and Jinda,' said Fon. 'Gaeo cannot … married woman, wait husband. Joy sleep here with Gaeo.'

'But what about me? Am I coming?' he asked, on tenterhooks.

'No. *Farang* men not dance with us … only ladies. You want to go?'

'Course I want to. More than anything.'

'Okay then, we take you … this time.'

Grasping her glossy black hair in both hands, she twisted it tightly into a rope and coiled it at the back of her head, securing it through with a pin. Now for the first time Ben saw her with her hair up in formal Asian style, displaying the elegance of her neck, her finely-sculpted head and profile. Her simple act of sinuously throwing her arms back and arranging her hair, he found distinctly erotic. It was made sweeter when he noticed that the pin she had pushed through it was an ordinary blue biro. So little adornment achieved such effect on this lovely girl.

When at last she was ready, Fon slipped into some green plastic flip flops, swept out of the room and headed off towards the beach in the darkness with Jinda and Ben following close behind. Reaching the path along the shore she stopped, told Ben to wait and disappeared with Jinda into the darkness under the trees. Ben was now getting used to this sort of thing, so he stood and waited for them. After about ten minutes they came back with another girl of about the same age.

'This Goong,' said Fon. '*Goong* means shrimp … she big so they call her Shrimp!'

'Hi, Goong. *Sawasdee krap,*' said Ben, careful not to shake hands. Thais do not shake hands Maca had told him.

'Goong come from our place, Isaan. We not know her before but now she friend Jinda. She massage here six months,' said Fon.

Goong had an open and fresh innocence about her. Her nicest feature was her smile which went from ear to ear, her eyes crinkling up and almost disappearing from view.

The four of them got under way again and soon reached the last night spot at the end of the beach. The Diamond Bar consisted of a wooden building thatched with palm fronds on a terrace among the rocks. It was stylishly done in the manner of a South Sea island beach hut and was decorated with fish nets, dried puffer fish and other trappings. Even the coloured lights hanging in the trees added to the atmosphere and did not look too tacky. The bar itself was well-stocked with bottles, a fridge, sound system and all the modern amenities. Somewhere a generator was beating steadily for their sole benefit. A sign boldly declared, "Kitchen open 10.00am to 11.00pm", though the place seemed totally dead; there was nobody about.

Fon directed everyone to a table and called loudly in Thai. A bleary youth emerged from behind the bar where he had been asleep in a hammock and brought them drinks. Beer in hand, Ben then looked around him and took stock. It was hard to believe he was sitting under the stars at the end of a tropical beach of white sand, looking at the brightly coloured lights of the bars and restaurants around the bay. Only months after getting his Geography degree, here he was on Koh Samet enjoying a whole new world of experience, out for an evening's dancing with three Thai girls, all of them accepting him warmly into their inner circle and one of them perhaps the most bewitching woman in the world. Though he was still sober, he could not quite believe that this was not just some fevered fantasy. Feeling well-pleased with himself, he began to wonder what was going to happen next. Where was the disco and the dancing?

Jinda and Goong disappeared behind the bar and chatted to the boy over a pile of CDs, and as the powerful sound erupted from loudspeakers in the trees, they started dancing on a small concrete space next to the bar. The Lao songs from Isaan were their favourites and had them both leaping wildly. When Jinda came and dragged Fon onto the floor, they danced together, leaving Ben watching from the table. For a moment he felt an irrelevance; the music was unfamiliar and he was worried about looking ridiculous on the dancefloor. But he was given little chance to be a wallflower as Fon came back to the table and grabbed him firmly by the hand. Willingly he followed, and, like a maniac, he danced as he had never danced before. He had never enjoyed dancing so much, but best of all was watching Fon. She was an elegant and graceful dancer, but so very sexy at the same time. He could not take his eyes off her as she danced in borrowed brown shorts and flip flops, her hair pinned up with an old biro, taking a brief and joyful respite from the weight of her family responsibilities.

As they danced, the bar was theirs alone. The three girls chose a variety of CDs; Thai pop, sixties and seventies, rock, the whole range of western music. Ben in his tidy shirt and cotton trousers was soon soaked through with sweat. It was totally intoxicating, with Fon dancing like a angel. They danced on into the night and it seemed to him that their orgy of energy and sound never need stop. But then without warning they were plunged into total darkness as the sound of music gave way to the sound of silence; the bar's generator had given out. The girls all shrieked with surprise as they bumped into things in the darkness, loudly laughing and joking. There was to be no more dancing at the Diamond Bar that night.

'Can you ride motorbike?' Fon asked Ben.

'Not very well. Why?'

'Then we walk.'

'Walk where?'

'Meridian,' she said without explaining.

The three girls picked their way out of the Diamond Bar in the darkness and went back in the direction of the coast path, Ben following on behind. They soon came to a steep headland which formed the end of a bay. With Fon in the lead, they picked their way through the huts and started to climb almost vertically upwards into the forest. Under the canopy of trees it was impossibly dark. The path, if there was one at all, was rough and rocky, criss-crossed with eroded tree roots as hazardous as tripwires.

They reached level ground at the top of the cliff, the path coming out of the trees into low scrub. Walking was now easier as the clouds had cleared and the moon was sailing white and enormous over the sea. Ben could see the dark spine of the island, the sea shining in the moonlight and a distant view of surf breaking on sand. Stumbling along at the back of the line, trying to see where to put his feet and to keep up with the others, wanting to look at the view and listening to the sounds of the surf and the insects of the night, he thought he must be dreaming. But the best bit of the dream was there in front of him, confidently leading the three of them over the rocky ground in her flip flops and brown shorts.

At the end of the headland the path dropped down again to the water's edge and from there they walked on squeaky sand from beach to beach. Up ahead were the tables and chairs of a bar set up on the sand, the table lamps winking in the dark. One beach followed another, one lotus eaters' paradise improved upon by the next.

Finally they climbed a flight of stairs almost lost in the trees and reached a bar full of people and palm trees and pulsating with music. This was the Meridian, the prime place to dance and be seen on Koh Samet. Much larger than the Diamond, it was alive with travellers and backpackers, a great scene, a cool place to hang out. Ben was entranced.

Fon chose a table where they could look out over the sea and they all sat down. Ben went to the bar and bought colas for the girls and beer for himself. It was still drinking time and nobody was yet dancing.

'You like? *Sanuk dee mai?*' asked Fon.

'Yes, it's wonderful. I think I've gone to heaven,' said Ben.

'Heaven? Okay, I come too … see you next life,' she said joyfully.

The music was too loud to talk easily so Ben sat and exchanged smiles across the table with her and watched her eyes sparkling with laughter and lightness. He could not begin to fathom what she felt about their relationship, if indeed there even was one.

'Come, Jinda,' said Fon, 'Dancing!' Fon got up and made for the dance floor, followed by Goong and Jinda. This time Ben did not hesitate and went with them. He watched the girls dancing, ignoring him totally, but then they casually took him into their circle and they all danced together.

Ben enjoyed himself more at the Meridian than he ever had at university or in some dingy Brighton club. This was the place to be, by the sea and in the open air, with people from all over the world mixing easily, enjoying freedom and warmth. He was with the ones he liked the best, these children of Isaan with their innocent sense of fun, joyfully embracing the global culture of music and dance. And he was with Fon, without whom he felt edgy, agitated, incomplete and in whose company he now felt total euphoria.

The music pounded and provoked, each new track providing fresh vigour. The evening seemed to go on forever, a night of great music, a natural high free of artificial stimulants. Ben was now on iced water as he was sweating profusely, and even the three Thais who usually seemed so cool, were now more than glowing.

He did not want it ever to stop, but it was getting late and as the bar would soon close, he wanted a final dance with Fon. She let him dance with her for a few moments, smiling up at him, then turned away and mixed with the others on the crowded dance floor. Perhaps it was too public for them to be seen as a couple, Ben guessed, though he did not really understand what was going on.

When a slow track came on that none of them liked, they all returned to the table to recover. Fon looked at her watch and pronounced it time to go.

'Bar close in ten minutes. Can walk back okay, Ben?'

'Yeah, suppose so. What's the alternative?'

'*Sorngthaew*.'

'You mean a pick-up? How much is it?'

'Maybe 400 baht.'

'Okay, no problem, I'll pay. Let's get a *sorngthaew*,' he said without hesitation.

Leaving behind the noise of the Meridian, they wandered out into the quiet of the night and walked for a few moments. Just up the track was a battered pick-up truck with no bumpers and missing one of its front wings. Fon went over and Ben could see her talking to the driver, who had been asleep in the cab. They all climbed into the open back of the pick-up and sat down on the hard, narrow seats on each side, Fon getting in first, followed by Ben who sat immediately behind her. The track was dusty and rough with steep rocky patches. The moon illuminated the way ahead, the vehicle pitching and bucking on its hard suspension as it plunged into the potholes, still muddy at the bottom even though it was well into the dry season.

Ben found it hard work clinging on as they were bounced around against the sides of the truck, so he held onto a steel hoop just in front of Fon to steady himself. Without a word, she then leaned back and nestled herself into the crook of his arm. Holding on firmly, he cushioned her from the battering, cradling her body against his, their contact natural and easy. She remained silent, no longer chatting or joking, the high mood of the evening now over, though for Ben it was a rare moment of closeness and intimacy.

When the pick-up pulled into the track behind the beach at Ao Sapporot, they all got down and Ben paid the driver. Goong disappeared into the darkness with no pause for goodbyes and he, Jinda and Fon walked back along the beach together. At the usual place by the fallen tree, he knew that Fon and Jinda would turn inland and go back to their hut without him. Now should be the time for a warm parting from Fon, perhaps a kiss, but he knew that was not how it was going to be.

'Really great evening, Fon. Thanks,' he said. Fon looked at him and smiled and without a word turned and walked away into the trees with Jinda.

Ben felt as if his heart had been cut out and cast into the sea. The exhaustion was beginning to come over him as he went back to his grubby little hut. It had been a great day with Fon; taking the boat into Ban Phe that morning, eating with her in the evening and finally and best, the dancing; a day in which all his expectations had been aroused. But now it was over. Even after showering, he was hot and uncomfortable and had difficulty falling asleep.

15

When Ben awoke during the night with a pounding head and raging thirst, thoughts of Fon immediately filled his hazy brain. As he tried to escape into oblivion, he could see her smiling face, he could hear her voice teasing and arousing him. It was pleasurable, tantalising, sweet and sad.

Disturbed by the cockerels at first light, Fon again came to him, but as he lay sprawled on the bed in the sticky dampness of the morning, he realised he was missing Emma. Their relationship had been so comfortable and familiar that it was hard to be apart from her. In just a few days on the twenty fifth, they would share a luxury room at the Regal in Bangkok and he was looking forward to it, though confusingly, he also wanted Fon.

When he dragged himself out of bed, he felt lethargic and low. Standing on the bare concrete floor of the wash room, he contemplated the cracked ceramic of the squat loo as he poured scoops of cold water over his head. Squatting down he could feel the tightness in his legs from the walking and dancing the previous evening, which now already seemed an age ago.

At breakfast he realised that from where he was sitting, he would see Fon as she came down to the beach to start work; she always arrived at about eight thirty to walk up and down offering massage and manicure to the first of the tourists to claim their deckchairs and loungers. So when he had finished eating, he decided to stay at his table in the hope of seeing her. To pass the time, he went over to the shelf of paperbacks and picked up a copy of "Trainspotting" which he recognised from the movie still on the cover. He stared at the title page but the book was not "Trainspotting" but "Togtitting". 'Norwegian or something,' he muttered to himself.

Then everything began to happen at once. Maca and Chuck came into the bar to order breakfast and joined him just at the very moment he saw Fon walk by on the sand only fifty yards from him. Though he was sitting exactly where she might expect him to be at this time of the morning, she did not even turn her head to see if he was there.

'How y'doin' Ben, me old mate?' said Maca. 'Hardly ever see you around these days.'

Ben could see that Fon was now talking to a middle-aged man and pointing out a place for a massage. 'Having a great time,' he said. 'Ban Phe yesterday and boogying last night.'

'Go on your own?'

'No, went with Fon.'

'Goodoh! I should've guessed,' said Maca.

Ben watched Fon as she spread out her sheet and started the massage.

'You two been busy then?' he asked, now glad of someone to talk to.

'Snorkelling, chilling out and stuff,' said Maca. 'So when are you thinking of moving on, Ben?'

'Go to Bangkok on the twenty fifth, then maybe back here. Not sure yet.'

'Watch this space!' said Maca with a wider than usual grin.

As Ben now knew where Fon would be for the next hour, he went up to his room to wash a few clothes. When he returned to the beach she had just finished the massage and had been joined by the two middle-aged masseuses and the little old lady who sold *som tam*. Looking amazingly fresh and well-slept despite the late night, she saw him coming and called him over.

'Come, Ben, sit. You want *som tam*?' teased Fon.

'Like a hole in the head.'

'Too much *bia Chang* last night?'

Ben was now feeling much more at ease with Fon's friends as

they chatted noisily around him. Fon explained to Ben what they were laughing about.

'Gop and Pornpun want to throw their husband, marry old *farang* ... as old as possible.'

'Why old?' asked Ben.

'Old *farang* soon die ... get his money quick! Everyone want to marry *farang*. Everyone except me!'

As they were talking, a middle-aged Thai lady, neatly dressed in a blouse and long skirt as if for town, came up to them in an unhurried way, greeted them and sat down on the edge of Fon's blue sheet. There was a long conversation in Thai, none of which Ben understood. She then took out a set of Tarot cards and put them down in a pile while they gathered round her in a circle. After they had all contributed twenty baht, she began her Tarot routine. Ben had not seen this done before and could not follow what was going on.

Placing the cards one by one face up on the sheet, she scribbled elaborate mathematical calculations on a notepad and slowly and deliberately read each of their palms. When it came to Fon's turn, Fon solemnly sat and waited. There was a definite stir in the group when the Tarot lady made her pronouncements, Ben sensing sidelong glances in his direction. After the last palm had been read, she gathered her cards together and slowly departed.

'What did she say about you, Fon?' asked Ben expectantly.

'She say there's a man from far away who loves me. Soon I go long journey ... go Europe.' This time there was no laughter and Ben was not quite sure how to respond.

'How did she know?' he asked.

'She not blind, Ben ... you follow me like dog!' she said. 'Would you like to come to England then?'

'Yes, I like. Everyone go aeroplane, have holiday. But England cold and no *som tam* ... so Thailand better.'

Ben too knew that taking her to England was an improbable dream so he would have to seize the day right here on Koh Samet.

'Okay, can I have a massage then?' he asked.

'Yes, can, but later ... evening, when *farang* go inside, okay?'

Not okay, thought Ben, but at least the certainty of an hour with Fon later in the day was something to look forward to. So once again he sat lethargically waiting while Fon trawled the beach for work in her quest to make ends meet and feed her family.

The one ripple to hit the beach that day was the arrival of a group of Russian tourists. The men were powerfully built mafia types and from their arrogant behaviour they seemed to be wealthy and used to having their own way. Their women were young and good-looking, sunning themselves in skimpy bikinis. The boys were tearing up and down the beach on noisy 250cc trail bikes and screaming around on jet skis, coming dangerously close to the swimmers.

Ben was sitting on the beach near the Russians and could hear their high-pitched voices as they argued loudly with their Thai tour guide who was in floods of tears. Standing by was a Thai policeman who quietly listened and tried to mediate. The Thai restaurant workers watched the confrontation, disgusted at how these foreigners could so disturb the proper harmony of personal relations.

Soon afterwards Ben saw a softly spoken Thai man offering a bamboo flute for sale to one of the mafiosi. After trying the flute, the Russian bluntly offered less than half the asking price. There then began a tough bargaining session, the Russian showing off to his friends who had all gathered round. They were laughing and joking noisily as the Russian aggressively beat the price down until the seller reluctantly accepted. Ben was incensed. Here was this bastard foreigner who probably had illegal millions stashed away, screwing a decent man into the ground just to impress his friends. For the Russian the money was nothing, the display of bullying everything. He felt angry that any *farang* with a little money in his pocket could buy Thailand on the cheap and vowed he would never again bargain too hard.

That afternoon Fon was finding plenty of customers on the beach. As Ben's massage was pushed back later into the evening he began to wonder if he was going to miss out altogether, until at last he saw her coming towards him.

'Okay Ben, you next,' she called, and so belatedly his massage began, the sun now falling into the sea on the other side of the island. Again they talked and talked, revisiting many of the same themes, of life and love, of money, marriage and commercial sex. Fon told Ben that *farang* men often brought girls with them from Pattaya because there were very few women selling sex on the island, though there were some.

'You saw that girl yesterday selling coconuts on the beach?' she said. 'She sell more than coconuts.' Ben hooted with laughter.

'Does she sell bananas too?' Fon did not seem to see the joke.

'Once I go Meridian dancing with girlfriends,' she said. 'I sit at table with Thai lady and she say, "You not have *farang* yet tonight?" She sell sex ... think I sell sex too.'

'Why the hell ...? The last thing you look like's a tart.'

'Because Thai girl in bar sell sex, that's why.'

'Is that really what people think?'

'Same same when they see Thai girl with *farang*,' she said gravely.

'So they see us together and think you're in it for the money?'

'Yes. You know that, Ben.'

'No Fon, I'm sorry, I didn't realise.' He shrank from this awful truth.

Perhaps a Thai woman shouldn't go into a bar alone, but a presumption that any Thai girl seen with a foreigner must be a whore appalled him. It demeaned her and every other Thai woman, making genuine relationships between the races so much more difficult.

By the time the massage was finished it was almost dark and Ben was wondering what would happen next. The mood was good and he did not want the day to end so soon, but as he slipped Fon her two hundred baht, she resolved things very simply.

'Ben, Joy waiting me. I eat with her tonight.' She packed up her box and they walked slowly to the place where she always went off to her hut. 'See you,' she said, and Ben's day was over. As always she did not look back.

The next few days went by in much the same way, Ben keeping his eye out for Fon, always in orbit around her. He sat and chatted with her in her quiet moments and with Gop and Pornpun who were often there. The two older masseuses were pleasant company, accepting him as the young *farang* in ardent pursuit of Fon.

He was now uncomfortably aware that the twenty fifth of the month was getting closer when he was to go to Bangkok to meet Emma. He wanted to see how Fon would take it when he told her he was leaving, so he chose a time during a massage when he was lying on his back and could watch her reaction.

'Fon, I have to go to Bangkok … in two days,' he said to her without warning.

'You go? Okay you go,' Fon replied impassively. She said nothing for a few moments, then asked the inevitable question.

'When you come Koh Samet again, Ben?'

'Maybe come back … don't really know when.'

'Up to you, up to you,' she said calmly, keeping up a steady rhythm with her hands.

Ben was devastated. Was she totally cold? Did she not care a damn? Now it was he who was in turmoil.

Fon serenely concentrated on her work, until a second question slipped out.

'You go Bangkok, see girlfriend?'

'Don't know,' lied Ben shamelessly. 'But I do know I'm really going to miss you.'

'Sweet mouth,' she said, this time conceding a smile.

'Fon, the night before I go, let's eat together,' he said. 'We can walk to another beach, just you and me.'

'Maybe, if I got time.'

He desperately hoped this was her way of saying yes.

On the evening of the twenty fourth, Ben was waiting in the darkness at the end of the beach where Fon had told him to meet her. It was to be their first time alone, their last evening together. Fon was late so he sat scrutinising the figures that came towards him along the beach, backlit by the lights from the bars. At last in the distance he saw an almost child-like figure in a close-fitting skirt or shorts. He flushed with pleasure when he heard her voice.

'English dog still waiting? Okay, let's go.'

They climbed the low headland he had crossed the day Emma told him to bugger off and get out of her life, and came to the first small beach where there was a pretty waterside restaurant.

'How's this Fon? I really like this place,' he said.

'Yes, nice ... but no, we go next one.'

She steered him along the path where a few days earlier Ben, lying on the sand, had watched the tiny bird in the flowering tree. They went on past several more bars and restaurants before she finally chose one to her liking. It was just a thatched roof with a sandy floor, the bar area decorated with snake skins, a stuffed anteater and a buffalo skull.

Ben sat down opposite Fon at a heavy wooden table, leaning forward on his elbows, eye to eye with her. For the first time he could take in how she looked that night. She was at her best, glowing like a fresh-faced teenager with no make up or jewellery and in a tight top which flattered her arms and tiny bust. And she was wearing a very short skirt, her bare thighs spread provocatively apart on the bench.

Ben was now much in need of a beer. Fon asked for a bottle of Spy, a sticky red alcopop and chose some pricey seafood, ordering in Thai from the boy. They both ate hungrily, the rich food adding to the warmth of the alcohol. When Ben slipped off his sandals and found his feet meeting hers under the table, she did not move them away. He wanted to hold her hand across the table but so early in the evening he did not dare.

'I little bit drunk already,' said Fon with a giggle, gazing at Ben across the table.

'Good ... me too. And alone with you at last.' He paused, carefully timing his first move. 'Fon, I really love being with you,' he said.

She shyly averted her eyes.

'Same me, Ben,' she said quietly, looking up again with a smile he would kill for.

'But it's much more than that ... I'm falling for you in a big way.'

'Ben?'

'Fon, I think I'm in love with you,' he said solemnly.

'No Ben, please. Cannot … not possible,' said Fon, shifting backwards on the bench, the smile fading from her face.

'Why? What's impossible?' he said in alarm.

'Have too many problems, Ben. Cannot be with you … cannot marry you.'

Ben was disconcerted; whoever had said anything about marriage?

'Well, can't we just spend some time together and get to know each other better?'

'You not understand yet? *Farang*, rich … better find rich girl. You go university already, I not go school … no good for you.'

'Fon, that doesn't make any difference … I like you for what you are. I'm crazy about you … think about you all the time.'

'But you have English girlfriend … can still think about me!'

'That's not fair, Fon,' he complained.

'Why you choose me, Ben? I not understand.'

'I didn't choose you … it just happened. You talked to me and I liked you and I admire everything you do. You see, I'm always happy when I'm with you, so I want to be happy all the time.'

'Impossible, Ben,' she said, her eyes now flashing angrily.

'But tell me, Fon, do you love me at all? Even a bit? You just haven't said.'

'What you want me say? If girl love boy, he know … she not have to say.'

'But I've said lots to you …' Ben gripped his beer bottle tightly in both hands.

'You say too much … try catch me with sweet words, like fly in honey.'

'No, Fon, it's not that at all.'

Seeing his hang-dog look she relented a little.

'Okay Ben, I like you … you have good heart.' She showed him the top joint of her tiniest finger. 'And I like you little bit more each time.'

'Or is it that you just can't say it out loud?' he persisted.

'Ben, love is same beautiful bird … put it in cage, it die,' she said.
'Yes, but if you don't catch it, the beautiful bird flies away.'

They sat and smiled at each other until Fon's face clouded again.

'Anyway Ben, what you mean … love? Like in movie?' She paused. 'In movie boy always get girl, no problem. But Fon cannot follow heart … have too many problems.'

'Problems? Like what?'

'Ben, I poor, no time play being in love. Have to work like buffalo, make money for Joy.' Her face was tragic. 'Papa die young. In Bangkok I suffer many bad things … not forget. Now I have Joy, but family not together, far from home. I want people to love me but I not always trust … only person can trust is me.'

Ben was taking it all in, but there was something important still troubling him.

'Fon, I don't understand about your boyfriend.'

'Boyfriend? Why you ask about boyfriend? Thai men want one thing, then go. Only come back if girl get money.'

'But Fon, I'm not like that. I think of you every moment. Even when I wake up at night, I can't get you out of my head.'

'Why you say this, Ben?' she demanded. 'Why you look at me all the time like mad dog? What you want me say?' She held up her hands in mock despair.

'I just want to know how you feel,' he said quietly.

'Okay, Ben, I tell you little bit more.' She spoke very deliberately. 'I want you here, Samet. When I see you on beach and go work, I feel strong. When you not there I think, where Ben? Then I miss you.'

'Thanks, that's nice.' It was a touching little tribute.

'But keep cool heart, Ben. You say too much, too quick. How you so sure? You not know me yet.' Her eyes were anxious.

'It's the way I am,' said Ben. 'I just get carried away and can't shut up.'

'But for me, fall in love take long time. Give my heart dangerous.'

'It's wonderful too, falling in love,' he said eagerly.

'Yes Ben, but Fon only say when my heart same rock.'

'You mean when your love's as steady as a rock? Then you can bring yourself to say it?'

'Yes, I 'fraid my heart … have to be sure. Can only tell you when my heart same rock.'

Ben was elated but exhausted; it had been an amazing evening. He felt he now understood Fon a little more and that they had drawn closer together. Then Fon said it was time for them to go back. As they followed the path in the darkness, she turned to him and said, 'Come Ben ... big big moon tonight.' She took him by the hand over the sand to the rocks where they could look out along the restless, silvery lane of sea that led up to the moon.

Ben was not quite sure who made the first move. As he pulled her up onto the rocks, her body brushed against his, the brief contact like an electric discharge. Somehow their arms became entwined around each other, her slim body fitting tightly against his.

'Ben, you big, you so big,' she laughed.

'And Fon, you're so very very small.'

There was no kissing, just a savour of scented skin, a nuzzling of cheeks, the sensation of soft abundant hair. Ben's arm was firmly around her waist, holding her hard to him, while the other hand wandered far enough to discover that she was not wearing a skirt; it was in fact a pair of shorts with a panel across the front, only pretending to be a skirt. Then, as suddenly, she was pulling away from him again, tossing her head and escaping his hold.

'Enough Ben ... too dangerous. We go home.'

They were comfortable with silence as they walked along the shore and over the headland back to Ao Sapporot, until Fon asked Ben which boat he would be taking the next day for his return to Bangkok.

'The nine thirty boat, so I can catch the ten thirty bus,' he said.

'Okay, I come early morning, say goodbye. See you eight o'clock, maybe seven.' Then she turned to him with a look of excitement. 'Ben, what your room number?'

'Hut 107, up the back there. Why?' There was a wicked twinkle in her eye.

'Please Ben, please you not lock door. Maybe I come to you in the night.' With a shriek of laughter, she broke away and ran up the beach and into the trees, leaving Ben in a state of high agitation.

16

Ben went to bed in a ferment of excitement, leaving the door of his hut unlocked. After an alcoholic evening it was perfectly possible that Fon would come to him in the night. Even a nice girl's 'no' is not always what it seems and in every relationship there has to be a first time. He lay and imagined the sound of the door swinging open, of her bare feet on the wooden floor cautiously approaching the bed, her hand held out towards him in the darkness. But as he tossed and turned for hours on end, the fantasy became more and more improbable and he knew he was going to be disappointed.

He had only a few hours sleep before his alarm clock woke him at seven. After taking a shower, he attempted to pack his rucksack, but for some reason his things were obstinately refusing to go back into it. His clothes were sandy, damp and smelly and he longed for the Regal in Bangkok, for hot water and a little luxury.

He made it to the beach bar well before eight, sat down at a table, ordered a coffee and fruit and waited. Thinking back over the events of the previous night, he decided he was going to have to overlook Fon's tease about the unlocked door; if he dared challenge her she would only accuse him of being a sex-crazed foreigner. Despite his irritation, the glow of the evening was still with him, but it began to fade as he waited and waited and still she did not come.

By half past eight, he was in turmoil. Where the hell was she and what was she up to this time? Why promise so sweetly to see him off and then not turn up. By nine o'clock he was beside himself.

Ben was becoming resigned to the wrecking of his send-off when suddenly Fon was standing there next to him. She looked a little concerned but still managed a disarming smile. His anger quickly ebbed away and he felt more like putting his arms around her and bursting into tears than tearing a strip off her.

'Fon, where did you get to? The boat goes in a few minutes.'

'Not see you ... looking for people on beach,' she said.

Ben guessed she had come down to the beach by another path and when she did not find him, had gone touting for customers.

Seeing his disgusted look, Fon deftly offered another reason for being late.

'And Joy have fever ... not sleep all night.'

'Oh, how awful. I hope she's okay.'

'It happen before. She get very sick.'

He was immediately concerned for Joy and also for Fon who must have had a bad night caring for the child. Then came the intoxicating thought that this could be why she had not come to his hut in the night. Unsure what to make of it all, he paid for his breakfast, shouldered his pack and the two of them went and sat together on the log under the trees. 'Joy have problem with stomach, she cry, cry. Before, in rainy season she sick, go hospital Rayong. Pay, pay, pay ... always worry she sick again.'

'Poor little kid,' said Ben. 'Do you know what's been wrong with her?'

'Doctor say her stomach stuck ... and medicine very expensive.'

The mood between the two was subdued and distant, light years from the euphoria of the previous night, Fon wearing the weight of her responsibilities on her face. Ben was wanting a better goodbye than this, but when Gop and Pornpun came and sat with them, his last chance of saying anything personal was lost.

As Fon chatted happily to them in Thai, he suddenly realised he did not have an address or phone number for her. In the excitement of the previous night he had forgotten to ask her for them.

'Fon, is there a mobile I can get you on and can you give me an address?' he said anxiously.

'Why you write me? Say what?'

'Come on Fon, just so we can keep in touch.'

'Okay, have card hotel … can write me there. Give you number Gaeo's mobile.' She got up and walked away in no apparent hurry, leaving him awkwardly sitting with Gop and Pornpun, unable to talk to them as their English was minimal.

The time ticked by and Fon did not come back. At twenty past nine, Ben realised that the shuttle boat for the ferry was already loading up. His heart began to pound and his mouth went dry. How could this all go so horribly wrong? But just as the boat boy was starting up the outboard motor, Fon reappeared, calm and cool and not unduly rushed.

'No problem, Ben,' she said, 'small boat go ferry two times. You go second boat … not get so wet.'

He watched as the overloaded boat went out through the waves, giving the passengers and their luggage a thorough soaking. He put the hotel's card and the tiny scrap of paper with Gaeo's mobile number faintly written in pencil into the safest place in his wallet and tried to say goodbye properly, but everything became a blur.

He could not later remember what passed between them before he picked up his rucksack, splashed through the shallows and got aboard the boat for its final run to the ferry. There was little that could be said; the real goodbye had been on the rocks in the moonlight the previous night.

Ben thought he would come back to Koh Samet to see Fon again, but he could not be entirely certain. He was utterly miserable and wondered how she was feeling. He had been looking for the signs but she was giving nothing away. Perhaps, he wondered, it was all much worse for her; while he could come and go at will, she could only wonder and wait.

By the time he was aboard the shuttle boat and could look back to the beach, Fon had already disappeared. Once on the ferry he climbed to the top deck, and stared towards the distant shore. He was sure he could see her standing by the water with a small child, both of them waving energetically. Had she gone to get Joy to wave him off? Was Joy suddenly better? Then the two tiny figures stopped waving and wandered off along the beach hand in hand.

He tried to control his emotions as the ferry pulled out of the bay and the beach began to disappear behind the headland. At first he was not successful, but the further he got from the little world of Ao Sapporot, the more his depression began to lift. He now had other things in his life to face up to.

On landing in Ban Phe, he turned right and walked the five hundred yards to the bus station. Already soaked with sweat, he was relieved to see a blue inter-city bus waiting with a Bangkok board in the front window.

He bought a ticket and the attendant showed him to a numbered window seat. The bus was clean and modern and to his relief was air-conditioned.

He sat and stared out of the window at the handful of people straggling slowly through the heat towards the bus. One of them caught his eye, a gaunt-looking western man hovering in the shade for a final smoke before boarding. Aged about sixty with thinning grey hair and a sallow, hawklike face, he was wearing a yellow long-sleeved shirt, pale blue trousers and white plimsolls. Ben watched as he climbed aboard the almost empty bus and was shown to the seat next to him. The man turned out to be an American who had worked in the Philippines as an engineer for many years and was now based in Texas. He told Ben that he had been coming to Thailand since the early eighties and had recently returned from visiting friends in the North East. Ben's interest immediately revived.

'What's it like in Isaan? I'd love to go,' he said.

'Well, it sure is poor ... poor as shit.'

'What do you do when you're there?'

'Teach English in school, just voluntary. At first the kids are real scared of an old *farang*, but I know how to make'em relax. Sometimes they come to my place for lessons. Yeah, I love it there,' said the man.

As the bus moved off, he politely said he wanted more space and moved to a pair of empty seats.

Ben was curious about him and now had plenty of time to speculate. Whatever made an old guy like that keep coming back to Thailand? He guessed that although the regular sex industry in Thailand was totally open and up-front, the unripe fruit must always be kept under the counter. Perhaps the vulture-man was unfortunate in his appearance and it was unfair to make this connection, but he did seem very odd. Both the Philippines and Thailand were known for the trafficking of children, often orphans like Joy. Watching out of the window as rural Thailand rolled by, he found the thought of it totally repulsive.

On the long road back to Bangkok, everything looked the same as before except that the towns were now the battleground for an important general election. In a day or two polling was due and the streets were festooned with campaign posters. Everywhere the same candidate's face beamed down benignly on his electors. Ben did not know who he was, but if campaign spending could bring in votes, this guy seemed to have it all sewn up.

The traffic jam into Bangkok began in Sukhumvit Road far from the centre of town. As he stared out at the passers-by, Ben was becoming anxious about seeing Emma that evening; he had no idea what would happen between them. Familiarity, alcohol and crisp white sheets at the Regal might prove decisive, but he still did not know how he was going to reconcile his feelings for Fon.

At the Eastern Bus Terminus he got down into the heat of the city, to be hit by touts offering taxis. The fare to the Regal seemed excessive so he walked out into Sukhumvit Road and picked up a metered taxi. The battered green and yellow Nissan looked almost as old as its driver; Ben could not take his eyes off the old man's cadaverous skull, the jaw and cheekbone devoid of flesh like a death's head, though he was still full of life.

'I drive taxi forty three year … start driving age eighteen,' he said.

'Amazing. You've got to be tough to last that long in this traffic.'

'Now sixty five. Not enjoy taxi any more.'

'So when do you retire? When'll you stop work?'

'Finish sick o'crock,' said the taxi driver.

After a long crawl through the traffic the taxi dropped Ben off at the Regal Hotel on Ratanakosin Avenue. At the top of the wide marble stairs a uniformed doorman opened the door to him. Feeling distinctly out of place in his baggy shorts and *bia Chang* tee shirt, he checked in at the reception desk, surrounded by package tourists in a sea of expensive luggage. Following a porter, he then padded noiselessly in smelly sandals along deep-carpetted corridors to his room, where the porter made an ostentatious display of opening the curtains and adjusting the air conditioning, holding out for a tip. Ben hated this, unsure how much to give and feeling tired and impatient to be alone.

When at last the porter departed clutching a twenty baht note, he was able to look around the room and finally relax. It was a standard international hotel room with a double bed, television and mini-bar, anonymous and characterless but overwhelmingly comfortable. The bathroom was stacked with soft white towels, the end of the toilet roll was neatly folded in a V-shape and there was a paper sash across the sitdown toilet; so very different from the steaming shit-holes of Koh Samet. Now all he had to do was wait for Emma.

When he opened his rucksack, the dank smell of the beach hut came wafting out. He had a hot bath, drawing out the dirt from the pores of his skin, put on the nearest thing he had to clean clothes and read what his Lonely Planet guidebook had to say about Chiang Mai where Emma had just been. After buying a Bangkok Post in the lobby, he sat on the bed and learned more about the general election. A top Thai businessman, Thaksin Shinawatra, the face on the election posters, seemed to be ahead of the game and was tipped to be the next prime minister. Then he lay and relaxed, happily cocooned in his room and listened to the distant hum of the city, enjoying a welcome respite from Thailand on ten pounds a day, courtesy of his interest free student overdraft.

Outside the hotel, Bangkok was as always red in tooth and claw, its countless millions, many of them rural migrants, locked in a relentless struggle for survival. By the big intersection on Ratanakosin Avenue, twenty four hours a day, the traffic pauses when the lights go red. As they turn to green, the race is on, the motorbikes in the lead leaping forward noisily over the canal bridge. The girls riding pillion sit side-saddle, rather than compromise their modesty by sitting astride the machine. They are closely followed by speeding pick-ups, buses, taxis, tuk tuks and trucks, engines roaring, spewing fumes into the humid evening air. Under the arch of the road bridge, people are sleeping by the edge of the canal. On the pavement a family assembles sweet-scented white jasmine

157

blossoms on strings for sale as offerings to Buddha and the spirits. Every bit of luck must be carefully nurtured; life on the streets is precarious and unforgiving.

That evening, anyone sitting inside the hotel lobby at six would hardly have noticed a young European woman as she came in from the street and stood waiting at the reception desk. When she reached the receptionist, she made her enquiry, looked puzzled for a moment, then left the hotel. She came back some hours later and again went to the desk. The receptionist was attentive and repeatedly checked the computer screen, but this time the girl became agitated; she had evidently not been told what she wanted to hear. Slowly and indecisively she went back to the lobby doors and hesitated at the top of the marble steps. She stood framed in the doorway for a moment or two as if unsure what to do.

She was an attractive girl with dark brown hair and a healthy tan, wearing ethnic jewellery, a fresh white tee shirt and blue cotton harem pants. Hovering briefly by the door, the breeze ruffling her loose-fitting clothes, she looked out at a world which was ignoring her. There were signs of distress on her face as she went down the steps and turned right towards Khao San Road.

Up in his room Ben was getting distinctly pissed off and increasingly anxious. He was frustrated that if Emma did not show up that night, there was absolutely nothing he could do about it. He had no idea where she was and had no immediate way of contacting her; their overdrafts did not stretch to mobile phones. The only thing he could do was wait. By eight o'clock he was getting hungry so he decided to slip out for some food.

As Khao San Road was only ten minutes walk away, he headed in that direction, taking a perilous short cut across the four lane highway. He then realised he should have left a message at reception in case Emma arrived while he was out, so he stopped at the first place he came to, had a quick bowl of noodles and headed back to the hotel. Shortly before nine he sat around in the lobby for a few minutes but hating the package tourists, went up to his room.

As he waited in the room he became more and more agitated. He had a strong sense of déja vu, that it was his role to be kept dangling by women who had too much hold over him. Emma was his lover, sister and best mate all rolled into one and he still needed her; they had come for a holiday in Thailand together and now he felt very alone. Perhaps by not turning up she was giving him a final message.

In desperation he decided to raid the mini-bar. As he downed the bottles of chilled beer, he became maudlin and morose, thinking back to the good times with her. But when Fon began to dominate his thoughts again, he felt thoroughly confused and distressed. Sick with longing, he began to realise that if Emma had finally walked out on him, his way was now clear with Fon.

It was past midnight when he fell unconscious across the bed, fully clothed and with the light on. Sometime in the night he woke up, his bladder bursting and staggered to the bathroom, then undressed and got into bed. In his dreams, Emma and Fon ran rings around him, disturbing what little remained of his night's sleep.

17

The following morning Ben slept through to nine o'clock. When he woke, the luxury of his room at the Regal came as a surprise, but cold reality and the trauma of Emma's no-show quickly came back to him. His penalty for drinking the contents of the mini-bar was a thumping headache and a serious case of Sahara tongue. Throwing on his clothes, he went downstairs and asked at reception if there were any messages for room 127 before finding the hotel coffee shop; he would spoil himself for once with a full hotel breakfast as a consolation for the disasters of the previous day.

Waiting for a menu, he spotted a sign on the table: 'General election today. It is illegal to serve alcoholic beverages on election days.' The very thought of beer was stomach-turning.

Realising that the lavish buffet breakfast cost only marginally more than ordering from the menu, he helped himself to a coffee and orange juice and sat down and admired his surroundings. The place was an extravaganza of polished marble and teak, more a palace than a coffee shop. The ceiling was at least two storeys high, there were potted palms everywhere and a fountain was spouting water in front of a photo montage of a tropical seascape. At the entrance to this earthly paradise stood an angel in a pink jacket whose job it was to open the door to each guest and to smile sweetly. If she got pregnant, fat or reached twenty five she would, he guessed, be instantly redeployed to the kitchens.

To the sounds of piped music and falling water, he then started on a marathon relay of muesli and yoghurt, bacon and eggs and a cornucopia of fruit. As he ate he looked around at the princes and the paupers in the restaurant. The Thai staff were as handsome as princes and princesses, the waiters in black trousers, waistcoat and a bow tie, the waitresses in neat white blouse and long black skirt. Yet these were the paupers, beholden to the every need of their wealthy paymasters, the package tourists.

He watched the holiday-makers drifting into the coffee shop for their buffet breakfast blow-out. Unlike the smart uniformity of the Thai hotel staff, they came in all shapes and sizes. Many seemed middle-aged with rotund middles, some were grey and balding, the women with hair tortured into tight curls. Styleless in baggy shorts, garish shirt or singlet, they were loud and gauche, their legs fat or spindly, and wearing brand new trainers that were far too big for them. Ben decided he did not much like them.

They struck him as being the uncultured masses of the package tour tribe, Mondeo men, promoted beyond their own mediocrity to be royally treated in the top hotels of Thailand. In front of the fountain, she in long tee shirt with pudgy white legs and no apparent shorts was being photographed with a smiling Thai waiter. He at the next table could be heard complaining that the butter was too hard and the toast had gone soggy. 'Do better than this in Brenda's Butty Bar on the bypass,' Ben heard him say.

Ben was nauseated, a mixture of disgust at what he saw around him, at his own capitulation to the deadly sin of gluttony and by his anxiety about the day ahead.

As he began to think about Emma again, his anger alternated with concern and he felt lonely and lost. Emma was unpredictable at times but it was not like her to fail to show up; she was not totally thoughtless. The murder of a Welsh girl in Chiang Mai had been in the news and they had not yet caught the killer. Could something awful have happened to her there?

It then crossed his mind that he had not read his email since agreeing to meet up with her at the Royal; the previous night he had been far too drunk to think of anything as sensible. So when he had finished breakfast, he headed out towards Khao San Road and stopped at the first internet café he found. Hot and bothered, he opened his in-box. There was a message from Emma sent the previous night.

To: ben-the-bill80@hotmail.com
Subject: Expletives Not Deleted

    Bloody Ben flipping Farnsworth. I came to the Regal several times and asked for you, but were you there? Oh no! And did you bother to email? Chiang Mai was brilliant, great crowd of people and I could be myself for once without you getting on top of me. They've all come back to Bangkok and are going to Angkor Wat in Cambodia at the end of the week. I couldn't go because of meeting you here, but now I'm damn well going too. I'd rather be with them anyway and after all your insults I just can't take any more.
Yours never again,
Emma

Ben gazed at the computer screen in shock. He was overwhelmed by a succession of responses; disbelief, jealousy, frustration, fury. He had to restrain himself from smashing his fist into the screen.

'She demands an expensive hotel room and doesn't show up, then heaps shit on me!' he raged silently in the calm of the cyber café. 'Maybe she's still in Chiang Mai getting screwed senseless and not in Bangkok at all.'

Then he began to get a grip on himself and to think more rationally. Perhaps she had got the wrong day or time, or even the wrong hotel, though none of these things rang true. Then an idea suddenly struck him. He closed his email and ran back to the Regal. Streaming with sweat, he went to the reception desk. On being given the answers he expected, he counted to ten, stayed calm and went up to his room. He took off his tee shirt and dried himself with a towel, the air conditioning a glorious relief. Picking up his Lonely Planet guide, he opened it at the section headed, 'Bangkok - Places to Stay - Budget - Sukhumvit'. After making a note of the first hotel listed, he ran downstairs, plunged out into the heat again and legged it back to the cyber café on Khao San Road. He felt thoroughly vindicated as he hit the 'Compose' button, but hot and very far from composed.

To: melldoyma66@hotmail.com
Subject: Told You So

Emma you prat, it's your fault. I was at the Regal all the time. I've just asked them if they had a Mr Farnsworth staying in the hotel and they said no. Is that who you asked for? Then I asked if they had a Mr Ben. 'Yes, Mr Ben come yesterday, stay room 127.' Bloody brilliant. Couldn't you have sussed that one out? Was the torrent of abuse really necessary?

So first of all, tell me where you are. It's nearly time for me to check out of the Regal and I'm not footing the bill for another night on the off chance you'll turn up. But I'd still like to see you, so I'm moving to the Georgia off Sukhumvit Road on Soi Seven. Phone 02-373-8763. Budget place, old-style, and handy for the Eastern Bus Terminus. I've chosen it because you hate Khao San and I'm hoping you'll come and see me there. I'll wait for you at the Georgia for at least two nights.

Please contact me asap. Go to Cambodia if you have to, but just get this. Waiting for you not to show up last night was horrible. And I wouldn't be running around in the heat and sitting in this cyber café in a pool of sweat asking to see you if I didn't think a lot of you.

Love, Ben.

PS Anyway Angkor's only a heap of old rocks.

He re-read the message and sent it off and walked slowly back to the Regal. Checkout was at twelve so he decided to make the most of his last hour of luxury. He changed out of his clothes, stuffing the sodden tee shirt into the air conditioning vent to dry. After showering, he slowly began to pack, using the nasal test to decide which clothes were dirty and which very dirty. This time his tube of toothpaste had burst open and half the contents were smeared around the inside of his spongebag, mingling with the medicines and plasters. He longed to stay in the comfort of the Regal and to get himself properly cleaned up, but no, he was committed to a cheaper place where he would wait for Emma.

Closing the door and with his rucksack feeling exceptionally heavy, he took the lift down to the reception desk.

'Bill for room 127, please.'

The girl printed off the bill.

'Here we are, Mr Ben,' she said.

He glanced at the total and again regretted raiding the mini-bar. Somewhat poorer he shouldered his pack, descended the marble steps of the Regal and was back on the road again.

Maca had told him that a cool way to cross town was by boat on a *klong*, one of the old canals that were the main thoroughfares before most of them were filled in and Bangkok became overwhelmed by the motor vehicle. And so, city map in hand, he headed for the canal near Wat Saket. He had seen photos of this golden temple and recognised it sitting high on its artificial hill as he approached from the Democracy Monument. Following the walls of an old fort, he found his way down to the *klong*. The water in the canal was dark and murky. A boat about the dimensions of a large bus was moored alongside and was filling up with passengers. He climbed aboard, scrambling through the narrow gap between the awning and the gunwale and sat down on one of the highly-polished wooden seats.

Soon the boat was packed with people, ordinary workers on their daily treadmill. The big diesel roared into life and the boat moved off at speed along the canal. Despite the blue and white striped side-screens, flecks of spray found their way through the gaps and onto his face and lips. Peering out, he could see the wooden houses on either side, tightly packed together, a reminder of old Bangkok. Many of them were rickety and roofed in corrugated iron, their verandas packed with pot plants and washing and all the clutter of a crowded life. Several times they passed shiny brown children swimming in the filthy water.

The boat came to a landing stage and the boatboy flicked a rope over a bollard before passengers leaped out and the boat pulled away again. Climbing precariously along the gunwale, he collected the fare from Ben; it was all of seven baht. Avoiding the roads, the boat trip had taken less than half the time by taxi and traffic jam.

Out in the street he hailed a motorcycle taxi and asked for the Georgia Hotel on Soi Seven. Riding pillion with a heavy rucksack was not going to be easy and he began to think he had made a fatal mistake. The bike took off at speed, weaving in and out of the traffic, then cut through the central road divider, apparently to do a U-turn. But to his horror it accelerated the wrong way down the opposite side of the dual carriageway; they were now closing at speed head-on with a large beige Mercedes bus. Like a gunsight aimed at his heart, the Mercedes star became indelibly etched into the part of his brain that stores recurrent nightmares. Then, at the last possible moment, when he could see the whites of the bus driver's eyes, the bike swerved sharp right, shooting across the path of the bus into the safety of a side street.

Ben let out a shriek of terror and exhilaration. Almost, but not quite, dying is life-enhancing, the ultimate adrenaline rush. Sky diving, bungee jumping, the wildest of extreme sports surely have nothing on this, 'The Bangkok Motorbike Taxi Experience'.

They had just succeeded in turning right without doing a U-turn, cheating almost certain death and saving at least five minutes in a traffic jam. The motorbike maniac would live to ride again and earn another forty baht, while Ben had been delivered alive but trembling to the door of the Georgia Hotel.

The facade of the Georgia was unprepossessing, but on stepping down into the foyer, it had a pleasant old-world atmosphere of faded elegance. The hotel had once been top-notch and modern but was now slipping into genteel middle age. Ben checked into a budget room with fan on the fourth floor and was hugely relieved; he really liked the place. The balcony in his room looked down onto a leafy garden with coconut trees and to the swimming pool beyond. The low roar of the nearby expressway was constant, but so was the sound of birdsong. It would be no hardship to wait here for Emma for a couple of days.

Now the middle of the afternoon, he was starving hungry as he had not eaten since his gargantuan breakfast. He went down to the restaurant and found it open, but seeing email terminals for the use of guests, decided first to check whether there was anything from Emma and found a brief message from her sent only a few hours earlier.

'Sorry Ben,' it read. 'I'm not going to answer you by email but owe you a phone call. I'll try the number at the Georgia later this afternoon when you've had a chance to settle in.' The message ended, 'Love, Emma.' This was all very enigmatic.

He made for the restaurant; waiting for a woman yet again was not going to spoil his appetite. Ordering a Thai green curry, he felt calmer as he sat and read the Bangkok Post, which was neatly clipped to a mahogany rod in the style of a London club. The green curry was a revelation, a myriad of flavours that exploded in his mouth and of obscure and exotic vegetables, herbs and spices. The menu told him that it contained galangal, kaffir lime peel, coriander seed and root, roast cumin seed, fresh lemongrass, pea eggplant and sweet basil leaves. Surely this was culinary heaven and for less than the British price of a McDonald's globalburger.

As he went up to his room, Ben began to think about Emma again. He had come back to Bangkok solely to sort things out with her, but their night at the Regal had fallen foul of Murphy's law. The following few hours could be crucial, but as he waited for her call, the combined effects of his alcoholic blow-out, of running to and from the cyber café in the heat that morning, plus a belly-full of green curry were beginning to tell. He lay heavily on the bed and dozed off.

The next thing he knew was the jarring ring of the telephone in his ear and the sweaty sensation of his tee shirt adhering to his armpits. He grabbed the phone and said hello in a sleepy voice.

'Christ, Ben, you're not pissed again are you? Mid-afternoon!'

'Where are you, Emm?' said Ben not bothering to answer her question.

'Khao San Road.'

'But you hate Khao San. Why there for God's sake?'

'Because I'm with my mates. They wanted to stay here.'

'They?'

'Yes, they.'

It was not a good start and Ben knew it.

'Look Ben, I'm going to have to be quick. It's a thousand degrees in this phone box and I can hardly hear because of the traffic.'

'So when am I going to see you?'

'Don't know … not immediately. I've got things to do before going to Cambodia.'

'You're going?'

'I told you in my email.'

There was a jingle as she put more coins into the box.

'For definite?'

'Look Ben, I really want to see Angkor and I've had so much fun with these guys. Sorry I dragged you back to Bangkok ... thought it'd be different after being apart for a bit. Just don't hold your breath, that's all.'

'Emm, I don't get you.' He tried to keep the panic out of his voice.

'Ben, you're being a bit slow.'

'But this hotel's really great ...' he said uselessly as Emma abruptly cut in.

'Damn, I'm running out of money. It's just eating the stuff.'

'Emm, for pity's sake tell me your guesthouse.'

'Whatever for?'

'Well, the phone number at least ...' he begged, but Emma did not reply. The line had gone dead.

Ben put the handset down and lay back, looking out of the balcony door at the Bangkok skyline. He felt physically sick and very alone.

18

Lying on his bed in the middle of the afternoon at the Georgia Hotel, the ceiling fan slowly stirring the humid air, Ben tried to take in what had just happened. In their brief and bitter exchange on the phone, Emma had not even begun to admit that failing to find him at the Regal had been her mistake, let alone apologise. She had flatly refused to meet up with him, she had conceded nothing and given nothing away. He felt desperately let down, comprehensively dumped thousands of miles from home in a hellish city, alone in a cheap hotel room with nothing but an expanding overdraft to worry about and too much time on his hands. The precious trip to Thailand that he had so much looked forward to had turned into the ultimate nightmare.

Black thoughts succeeded each other at random. Emma had told him she was staying in Khao San Road, but this could have been a lie. Perhaps her money in the phone box ran out so quickly because really she was still in Chiang Mai. Then again if she was in Bangkok with a new boyfriend, how could she possibly get to see him, even if she wanted to.

He lay and seethed, staring out at the phallic towers of the Sukhumvit skyline. But as his anger turned to depression, his thoughts drifted back to Fon. Then the doubts really began to gnaw at his guts. Koh Samet seemed ages ago and somehow he could not even remember clearly what Fon looked like; he longed for a decent photo to rekindle the dream.

As he turned it all over in his mind, he had to admit he hardly knew Fon at all; they could not be more different in their backgrounds and experience. Her English was basic and it would take him years to learn Thai. Nor could he afford to bring her to England. What would she do there anyway, an exotic flower uprooted from her own culture, wilting in the freezing cold. And there was her unshakeable devotion to Joy and her family; she would never leave them behind and she could certainly not bring them with her. It all seemed hopeless and even irresponsible to chase after her. But then he thought of their romantic meal together and the clinch in the moonlight afterwards, and his feelings for her revived in all their fury. He wanted her dreadfully.

It struck him that it was now futile to stay on at the Georgia waiting for Emma; the only thing to do was to pack up and go straight back to Koh Samet; he could phone Fon on Gaeo's number and tell her he was getting the bus the next morning. But then he began to have second thoughts. Fon would probably not be around to take the call and he might get Gaeo's husband who did not speak English. So he quickly abandoned the idea.

Resolving to stick with his original plan of giving Emma two days to change her mind and get in touch, he went downstairs to the computer terminals and sent her a short email. He told her he regretted the brevity of her phone call but that he still hoped she'd contact him at the Georgia.

For want of anything better to do, he sat in the lobby watching the comings and goings of the hotel guests for a while, then decided to see what Sukhumvit Road had to offer at that time of the afternoon. He wondered whether he would see anything of the general election which was now in full swing. The coverage in the Bangkok Post had told him it was a major event in Thailand's political history and that there were great hopes for the future.

He walked slowly up the *soi* past elegant residences standing in large gardens and came to Sukhumvit Road with its crowded pavements, the traffic nose to tail, filling the canyon of tall buildings with fumes. Wandering aimlessly, he spent some time in the cool oasis of Asia Books in The Landmark Hotel and bought himself a novel and a Thai language tape. To build bridges with Fon, he could at least attempt to learn some of her language.

As he walked, a sign on the pavement advertising a massage parlour caught his eye. 'Thai massage can relief sickness,' it said, 'stimulate evacuation system, cause lively emotion and help to release seriousness.'

This was exactly what Ben needed; to have his seriousness released. He could at least check it out.

A little nervously, he opened the glass door of the massage parlour. Inside were some nondescript Thai women lounging on sofas reading magazines and beyond them the massage beds screened off behind curtains. It was all very clinical.

'What massage you want?' asked the unsmiling receptionist from behind her desk.

'Not sure. Maybe come back later.'

'You have massage before?'

'Yes.'

'What kind you have?'

Ben was beginning to regret this.

'Thai massage.'

'Thai massage can. Oil massage and "special" also can.'

He suddenly felt disloyal to Fon; to be massaged by someone else was a bit like being unfaithful.

'So what's oil massage?' he asked disingenuously.

'Lady have Johnson baby oil. Rub it on man … same baby.' She laughed a hysterical laugh.

'What about the "special"?' he asked.

'Lady take off everything, rub oil on body, then rub body on man. Not same baby!' There was more hysteria.

'Okay, I'll have a massage, but how much are they?'

More than an hour later he gave the masseuse a tip, got dressed and went out into Sukhumvit Road.

By the time he was back at the Georgia, it was evening and the sun was falling. There had been a phone call for him from Emma, though she had not left a number. Trying not to think too much about her, he went into the restaurant and ordered an iced tea. With nothing else to distract him, he found himself looking at a middle-aged man reading a newspaper at the next table. When the man suddenly put the paper down and glanced up, he caught Ben's eye.

'I've finished with the Post if you want it,' he said.

'No thanks, I've read it,' Ben replied.

'It'll be interesting to see how the election goes, don't you think,' said the man chattily. 'Looks like Leekpai's on the way out. Thaksin's the one ... done wonders in telecoms, so now they'll want him to work his magic on Thailand too.'

'Don't know anything about Thai politics,' said Ben.

'Been following it since I first came out here ten years ago. Fascinating place.'

'So what are you doing in Thailand?' asked Ben.

'I'm on holiday. You too?'

'Yes ... well, travelling.'

'Travelling alone?'

Ben hesitated a moment before replying.

'Well, no. Well, I wasn't ... alone I mean, not until a few days ago. Came to Thailand with my girlfriend.' He had not meant to say so much; it just slipped out.

'Sounds like there's a story there somewhere,' said the man, though to Ben's relief he began talking at some length about himself. He was a company director, was divorced and always took a long holiday in Thailand every winter. 'Sex tourist,' thought Ben. He introduced himself as John Russell, Jack to his friends, and was in his mid-forties and from Huddersfield in the north of England. Short, dumpy and almost bald, he was not very prepossessing to look at, but Ben immediately liked his pleasant, open personality. Within minutes the two of them were firm friends and had decided to meet up in the restaurant at eight and then, perhaps, to hit the town together that night and cruise the *sois* and byways of Sukhumvit Road.

So it was, that later that evening they sat down for dinner at a quiet table in the restaurant of the Georgia. Jack ordered the green curry on Ben's recommendation while Ben, who had already eaten well that day, chose something lighter.

'So you're a company director. Your own company?' Ben asked him.

'Yes, it is. I'm in residential care homes.'

'You run a home for old people?'

'Two in fact, for my sins.'

'What's it like?'

'Used to be good, lots of DSS money. But now there's problems with the local authority contracts and hellish regulation ... mindless care standards and so on.'

'Must be cool being a company director.'

'No, it's hands-on stuff ... working all hours to keep afloat. Got a big overdraft and if there's cash flow problems, we'd go down in a big way. I'm on a treadmill ... impossible to sell up at the moment.'

'Do you actually like the work though?' Ben thought it sounded awful.

'Sometimes ... it's what I do. And do you like your work?'

'Don't know yet ... I've only just graduated.'

'Lucky guy ... it's all ahead of you then. But choosing a career isn't easy, is it?'

'Haven't really tried,' said Ben cagily, quite glad Jack seemed to like the sound of his own voice.

'When I started out in business with my "ex", we made a conscious choice ... it was going to be something in tourism or residential care. We decided old people are more important. And the demand's always guaranteed!'

'Great if that's what you like doing.'

'It was fine for a time but it's not that easy keeping up the ideal. When margins get tight, you can't do a first rate job. Keeping staff's a problem too, though I've got a good manager. That's what lets me get away every year and keeps me sane ... well anyroad, somewhere between daft as a brush and barking mad.' Jack thoughtfully fingered the generous folds of his double chin.

'So why do you come out here so often then?' asked Ben.

'It's the best antidote to death and decay. Working with old people all the time gets you down. And it's always grey outside with the rain running down the windows, so I can forgive myself escaping for a bit.'

'Sure, but why Thailand?'

'You know why, Ben! Beautiful country and all that … but it's for the women of course.'

Ben was amazed at his frankness.

'Got a Thai girlfriend, then?'

'Yes of course … always have.'

'You mean not the same one?'

'Never the same one.'

Ben was not quite sure what to say.

'So what's it you like so much about them?' was all he could think of.

'Well, their only demands are on my pocket … any emotional hang-ups and I move on. They're like healers and therapists and make me feel good about myself. The warmth and friendship's the best bit.'

'Hope you don't mind me saying, Jack … but surely they're only with you for the money.'

'No offence, lad. But please they're not just prostitutes, they're courtesans with real finesse … never use their mobiles or the remote while I roger'em. Not like the short-time girls.'

Ben was getting even more sceptical.

'Yes, but I'm still not sure you can buy their friendship.'

'No, you can't, so I try to deserve it. But then again as the Buddhists say, everything in life's illusory, so maybe friendship's an illusion anyway. Though I tell you, Ben … a Thai girl in my bed feels real enough to me.'

'It all sounds too good to be true,' said Ben with unintended irony.

'I don't have to justify myself to you, Ben, lad,' said Jack. 'You can easily find a girl at your age, but I couldn't cope without my annual break. These women bring my stress levels down and set me up for another year's work.'

'I get your meaning, but can you really value their friendship?'

'Look at it this way, Ben … I saw my parents through their last illnesses, so I really know what old age and dying's all about. Back home the families are grateful for what I do for their old folks and think I'm wonderful … it never occurs to them I only do it for the money. And I value what the girls do for me too even though I pay them … it's exactly the same.'

'Never looked at it like that,' said Ben, playing with his spoon and fork.

'I'm paid to care for the old folk and it burns me out, so I take a break and give a Thai girl a bit of cash to sort me out. Same same as the Thais say ... sex and death are both pretty intimate.' Jack savoured his green curry sauce with the last of the rice.

'But Jack, you can pay for sex anywhere, can't you?'

'Well, as I say, it's not just about sex. I need a good cuddle, to have my back scratched ... these girls are so good at the pampering side. They're farmers' daughters, young and optimistic, not hard-bitten bitches, and they seem to enjoy the whole thing. It's like having a real girlfriend without any of the hassle.'

'But what about them? How do they recharge?' asked Ben.

'Maybe by not doing it for too long ... their shelf-life's quite short.'

'Some of them look worn out to me.'

'Funny thing,' said Jack, ignoring Ben's comment. 'There's plenty of male prostitutes in Bangkok and the female sex workers use'em a lot. As I said, if you're in the caring professions, you need to be cared for too.'

'Prostitution! One of the caring professions!' said Ben, much amused.

'That's just what it is,' said Jack. 'And Ben, the green curry ... it's sensational.'

There was a lull before Ben dared ask a more personal question.

'So you don't ever get involved with the girls, emotionally I mean?'

'No, can't afford to ... it'd be a disaster for both of us. It's not that I don't care about them. I'm courteous and kind ... never ask them to do anything I wouldn't've asked the wife, and I keep it safe. And I give'em a good time ... go to the beach, have a real little honeymoon. But then I make it clear we'll probably never see each other again and that's that. Am I shocking you, Ben?'

'Well it's certainly a new angle on it.'

'Look Ben, this isn't a perfect world, but if they're sex workers by choice and aren't getting shafted by the big bosses, it's not so bad a job. We both enjoy it.'

'And after you've said goodbye to your sex goddess, you go back to the old biddies!'

'Yes, the opposite ends of the life cycle … young women in their prime and physical wrecks seeing out their last days. Life in the raw!'

'Bizarre, isn't it,' said Ben. 'At home we spend shed loads keeping the senile alive, while here the girls risk their health for the price of a few drinks.'

Jack seemed lost in thought for a moment as Ben finished eating.

'Since I've chuntered on about Thai women so much,' he said, 'maybe I can show you some of the local bars and girlie places.'

'But it's going to be dry tonight. Alcohol's banned on election day.'

'Don't believe that one, you ninny. We'll be served alright.'

'Yes okay, I'd like to,' said Ben without hesitation.

'Let's go to Freddie's Massage Parlour. It's got a goldfish bowl … where you choose your woman through a glass window.'

'Guess I'm up for anything.'

'You're on then. We'll finish off your education with a doctorate. How'd you like to be a Doctor of Philandery … from the University of Life?'

'I'm looking forward to the practicals,' said Ben as they got up and left the restaurant.

19

They walked up the *soi* together, Ben the fresh Geography graduate and Jack Russell, the round-bellied little terrier, company director and care home proprietor, both looking forward to a night out rutting for bar girls. They came to a doorway at the foot of a tall building where a simple sign said one word, "Freddies". As they went inside and climbed a blind stairway Ben heard a buzzer going off. Passing through a glass door into fierce air conditioning, he found himself in a bar empty of people other than a Thai barman. A tank in which a large silver fish was languidly swimming caught his eye.

'That's an arowana,' said Jack. 'Very expensive, and they're supposed to be lucky.'

'It looks so sad and ugly,' said Ben.

'But I bet they take more care of it than the women in the goldfish bowl.'

As Ben glanced around, an older Thai women in a short red dress appeared from a door behind the bar, her painted face creased into a synthetic smile.

'Welkaam, *Pompui*. Been long time,' she said, taking Jack's hand. 'Who you friend?'

'This is Ben. I've brought him to see you.'

She pointed her hand at Ben like a pistol and gave him a damp handshake.

'You drink first, then come see girls,' she said and walked away.

As they went over to the bar Ben saw the goldfish bowl for the first time. At the far end of the room was a large plate glass window behind which about twenty women were sitting in rows. They were in bright red dresses, quite formal and old-fashioned, none of them revealing. Most were young, though he guessed some of the older ones were the wrong side of forty. Sitting on red-carpeted steps like a mini-amphitheatre, they were not talking or smiling, just staring into space. Ben's eyes were standing out on stalks. This was a shop window; these women were for sale.

They sat down at the bar and ordered beers and to Ben's amusement the barman served them without question, election or no election.

'Looks as if you've been here before,' he said to Jack.

'Aye lad, suppose I have, once or twice.'

'What was it she called you? Pompey or something.'

'*Pompui*. It's like "fatso" … means you look prosperous, so I'm quite chuffed.'

'But I can't get over the goldfish bowl. What's on offer?'

'Want to find out?' teased Jack.

'I'm still stone cold sober!' protested Ben.

'Well, this is what they call a massage parlour! Get my meaning?'

'It's not like the place I had a massage this morning.'

'No, they're different. Thai massage is straight and serious, but here you pay your thousand baht and choose a girl, she takes you to a private room with showers and soap and away you go. If she gets you to heaven, you give her something for the extras. It's as simple as that. If you want to take her out, you'll have to pay the bar.'

At that moment the barman who had been hovering nearby gave them a leery smile.

'Ladies very horny … you like?' he asked.

'Got a headache,' said Jack with a smile. 'Want to doff yer britches, Ben?'

Ben squirmed and said nothing.

'No, sorry squire, Ben-lad's having a layday too if that's the right expression.'

The barman looked totally confused. 'He want lady, ugh?'

'Not tonight Napoleon, but thanks all the same,' said Jack.

Perched on his bar stool, Ben watched as the barman pressed the buzzer and the women, still sitting in their tidy rows, broke ranks and relaxed. No longer on display for the two men, they slipped off their shoes and picked up magazines, one girl wrapping an old blanket around herself to keep warm.

As he sat and stared through the window, Ben noticed that the walls inside were all mirrors to make it look as if there were more girls than there really were. It was difficult to tell what was real woman and what was only a reflection; all was illusion in the world of the goldfish bowl.

When, after a few moments, the barman again pressed the buzzer, Ben watched intently as the scarlet women moved smartly back to their places. A western man with greying hair came into the bar and was intercepted by the same mamasan who steered him towards the goldfish bowl. While they stood in front of the window discussing the merchandise, the women avoided eye contact with him, sitting as motionless as meat in a supermarket freezer. Eventually he made his choice and one of the women took him away to the private rooms. Ben was aghast; he would have died of embarrassment standing there sizing them all up.

He watched the women relax again after the punter had gone, but then his jaw almost dropped open. There was a little girl in the goldfish bowl, playing happily with a Barbie doll dressed in a red ballgown.

'Who's the little girl with the doll?' he asked the barman.

'School holiday ... come with big sister,' said the barman before smartly retreating into the back room.

'Ben, if you say things like that, he'll think you're wanting the kid. He's probably gone to check the tariff.'

'Oh, come on Jack!' said Ben, looking uncomfortable.

'You bet it's not a sister though ... daughter more like,' said Jack. 'Most of these women have children and that's why they're here.'

'But it's awful a child being exposed to all this ... Mummy being taken into the shower with the dirty old men. How the hell do they explain it to her?' asked Ben.

'It's just normal ... it's how they live,' said Jack passively.

'Well, there's lots more I want to know about them,' said Ben. 'Are they on drugs? And what's it like to be taken away and molested?'

'Dunno, but they make a damn good pretence of enjoying it,' said

Jack with a grimace.

'And how much do they get paid? The place seems dead tonight.'

'Well, you don't know, do you. The rooms at the back could be full by now.' Jack looked at his watch. 'So, Ben, what shall we do then? Have another beer or move on?'

'Let's go. I feel a bit of a voyeur sitting here.'

He took a last glance through the window before they went down the stairs and out into the heat of the night.

'So now you know where Freddies is,' said Jack. 'Where d'you want to go next?'

'No idea really, but what about the Eleganza Hotel? My guidebook calls it "infamous" and says it's mostly used by sex tourists.'

'Yes, the Eleganza … had its heyday in the Vietnam war with American troops on R and R, but now it's mainly used by Middle Eastern men and paunchy ex-GIs coming back to relive their experiences.'

'Sounds awful,' said Ben. 'I'll have to see it.'

'Right then. We can walk that way before going on to Big Bazzas.

And we could stop off at the fortune-teller in the next *soi* if the queue's not too long. It's a ladyboy and she's a gem.'

They turned the corner into the busy *soi* and found the fortune-teller squeezed behind a portable table, his back to the door of a jewellers' shop, half blocking the narrow pavement. Three bar girls were huddled round the table, giggling loudly as he predicted their certain doom.

Dressed in a dark blouse and skirt, the fortune-teller's long wavy hair was held back by little-girl hairgrips, revealing extravagant earrings. His eyes were lively, reflecting the oil lamps on the table, his face angular and gaunt with the pallor of someone who comes out only at night. The bony wrists, heavy with bangles, deftly flicked the cards onto the table.

Pausing for a moment, he looked up at Jack and Ben.

'Okay, only fie minute. You wait me please.'

'Shall we?' said Jack.

'Well, you can if you want to,' said Ben. 'How much is it anyway?'

'Hundred baht … almost a day's wage for the locals, but worth every satang.'

When the fortune-teller had finished with the girls, he motioned to

Jack to sit down on the stool opposite him and started his routine.

'Up to you ... anything you think for future inside card. You do like this, fifty times.'

Jack shuffled the pack and put it down in front of him. With a flourish, the fortune-teller then took the cards one by one from the top of the pack, placing them in a pattern face up on the table. In a high-pitched, nasal monotone he began his performance.

'You lucky more, lucky so much. Later no problem, for car, for plane ... not have accident. Good. Future, later, up to you. Maybe before sometime you hungry, you not eat something, you drink, you eat every day.' He glanced up at Jack. 'You have in family lady? My wife, girlfriend, boyfriend ... you have, not have?'

'No,' said Jack.

'Uh huh ... sorry! Be careful for lady people somewhere straight. Up to you, you can try, for future. She good seventy per cent, she bad thirty, coming soon to see you. She *pompui* little bit, she wife, she lucky more to you, you take care her a lot. Have father? Have? Not have? You tell me, I tell you.'

'No, he's dead,' said Jack smiling broadly.

'Sorry, no problem ... him never die in your heart. Mother have?'

'No. Dead.'

'Sorry, no problem ... in family, miss you so much!'

'But they're all dead, Romeo,' said Jack cheerfully.

'Be careful for body, maybe here and here, fifty-fifty now,' persisted the fortune-teller, pointing to his stomach and knees. 'You welly, welly good heart also ... you want people look soft in your heart.'

'You're right there, matey.'

'Big job, not lucky quickly. Later money come see you so much, for job, for business, for work hard.'

'I can't wait,' grinned Jack.

'Later you lucky number one the world! Thank you sir, what you want to know? You ask me no problem.'

'How's Huddersfield going to do in the League? You know, second division.'

'Sorry sir, I not know that one sir. Thank you sir, *korp khun ka*,' said the fortune-teller accepting Jack's hundred-baht note with both hands and pouting sweetly.

'That was weird,' said Ben as Jack got up to go. 'So Jack, money come see you so much. You lucky number one the world.'

'Yes, I'm chuffed, but I still don't know if Huddersfield's going to be relegated.'

The neon-lit streets were throbbing with activity, with foodstalls, taxis and tuk tuks, and everywhere skinny Thai girls in tight jeans, not all of them beautiful, tottering dangerously on platform heels. As he walked with Jack towards the Eleganza Hotel, Ben found himself following a most unsavoury-looking lady of the night. Despite being very overweight, she was wearing a tight yellow Chinese-style cheongsam dress which only just covered her rump. Beside the driveway to the hotel entrance there was a small Buddhist shrine. As she approached the shrine, she put her hands together and bowed deeply, almost showing her knickers. Ben was scared something would split.

'That's even weirder,' he said to Jack.

'Why so? These women are tolerated. If they fail to follow the Eightfold Path they need to make merit like everyone else. There's no hypocrisy round here ... though she ought to suffer in hell for that skirt.'

'Yes, I don't think much of the bar girls' dress sense.'

'That's why I like the go-go dancers,' said Jack wryly. 'They never dress badly ... they don't dress at all!'

After what he had seen that evening, Ben thought there could be no more surprises, but just as they got to the Eleganza they passed a young Muslim man smartly dressed in stylish jeans, polo shirt and trainers holding hands with a blue pillar box. She was swathed from head to toe in Islamic dress, even the slot for her eyes covered with an opaque gauze. Ben felt he had now seen everything; this crazy place was where all worlds collide.

The Eleganza Hotel turned out to be a huge nondescript tower block. In the lobby a few men, some Middle Eastern, were sitting around on plush sofas. Ben looked unimpressed.

'The coffee shop's where it all happens,' said Jack. 'It's one of the oldest pick up joints around.'

They went down the stairs into the basement and came to a doorway with a desk set up like a checkpoint. There was a notice over the door which read, 'Weapon Free Area. Liquor and Beverage are not Allowed to Bring Inside.'

They went through into a large and gloomy room like a canteen. It was very run-down, the drab decor unmaintained, the tiled floor worn and dirty. Two juke boxes, one playing western music, the other songs from Isaan, loudly competed for dominance. At the tables sat Thai women of all ages, the most ghastly looking slags and slappers that Ben in his limited experience had ever seen. One of them sitting nearby was fixing him with her beady eye. He felt distinctly uncomfortable and wanted to bolt back up the stairs.

'Well, this is the coffee shop of the infamous Eleganza. Like it?' said Jack.

'No, it's just about the most awful place I've ever been in.'

'Well, you ain't seen nuttin' yet. Wait 'til you see the Bier Kellar later on tonight. But now we're here, do you want to see another goldfish bowl?'

Ben was not sure he did.

Walking back down the lobby, Jack steered him towards a small flight of stairs leading into the bowels of the building. They went down the stairs and along a corridor and there it was. A bored-looking girl sitting at the desk opposite the window ignored the new arrivals but there was an excited flutter in the goldfish bowl. The women put on their best pouts.

'Christ,' said Ben, 'it's the Widow Twankie.'

The goldfish bowl was filled with pantomime dames of the most voluptuous sort. They were in lace-up boots with high heels, a short frothy underskirt displaying ample legs, their tight bodices and low-cut blouse bursting with cleavage. Large tumbled curls, plump rouged cheeks and mascara laid on with a trowel completed the picture. Ben hardly had the nerve to look at them but Jack was coolly surveying the field.

'Nowt to my taste, but obviously the clientele here love 'em like this,' he said, smiling at the women who sweetly responded. When Ben turned and retreated down the corridor, the women's disappointed eyes followed him. As he took a quick backward glance, one of them blew him a parting kiss.

'Maybe we should go on to Big Bazzas next,' said Jack as they left the Eleganza. It's mainly Australian expatriates there and good for a quiet drink. I hope Bazza's in tonight.'

'Who's Bazza?'

'He's the Australian who owns the place ... great raconteur and good company unless he takes against you.'

'He does, does he?'

'Yes, sometimes. It's like an initiation first time you go in ... every spade's a bloody shovel. Oh, and Bazza weighs half a ton, and he does *The Times* crossword faster than you can read the clues.'

By this time they had crossed Sukhumvit Road and were heading down one of the *sois* on the other side.

'In case Bazza's there tonight, I ought to tell you one of his best stories,' said Jack. 'Wouldn't fancy my chances if I told it in front of him.'

Ben tried to keep up with Jack in the crowded street and to listen at the same time.

'Bazza's got this new girlfriend who takes him to her home in the North East ... just a wooden house on stilts and all the animals living underneath. Now Bazza snores big-time, a gurgly, wet whoopee cushion of a snore. That night he goes to bed with his girlfriend and he starts snoring. The girlfriend can't sleep, the family can't sleep and the animals under the house can't sleep. The animals wonder what beast their mistress has bedded. They've no idea what this wild, warbling sound can be. The dogs begin to howl and whimper, the pigs start snorting, the buffaloes bellow and the geese honk. This wakes up the dogs next door who join in the barking ... then the next house and the next. In the morning everyone looks ashen. The local headman wants to know what set the animals off. But it was nothing ... just big Bazza the Aussie windbag in full cry.'

'Nice one, Jack,' said Ben, not exactly splitting his sides.

'Yes, and knowing Bazz, there might even be a grain of truth in it.' Jack mopped his brow as he turned the corner. 'Well, we're here. This is it, the world famous, the one and only ... Big Bazza's bar!'

20

When they came off the street into the welcome chill of the air conditioning, Ben was surprised that Big Bazza's bar was so small. The bar was a narrow room almost filled with a U-shaped counter enclosing a working space from which the girls served the customers, a motley collection of older *farang* men perched on bar stools nursing glasses of beer. The walls were hung with posters and with framed photos of past hijinx in the bar. There were several shots of girls in short skirts going upstairs, of pallid *farang* backsides with trousers at half-mast and one of Bazza himself stranded like a whale on an anonymous tropical beach.

'The drinkers in here are usually expats working as engineers and so on,' explained Jack.

Ben thought they looked a rough lot.

'But where's Bazza?' he asked.

'I've a horrible feeling he's not here. Maybe he's gone upcountry on snoring safari.'

They found vacant bar stools and ordered drinks. A strikingly pretty bar girl in blue skirt and white blouse poured two large Chang beers into chilled glasses. With Ben's interest very definitely engaged, Jack broached the unavoidable topic.

'So, Ben lad, what do you think of Thai women then?'

'Wow!' he said dreamily, 'they're mind-blowing, but I'm not sure I even begin to understand them.'

'Well I've tried pretty hard,' said Jack, pleased to talk on his favourite subject. 'Though it isn't their looks that blows my mind. *Farang* women are just men with tits, but here they're real women.'

'Better not let the feminists hear you, Jack,' teased Ben.

'They're half the problem, matey. Nowadays a Yorkshire lass can't be a mother and home-maker anymore without feeling guilty. But the Thais can still be proper women.'

'Maybe with a lower status?'

'Maybe, Ben. But my point's that they're feminine right through and that's what I find so attractive. And going with a Thai girl for a few weeks can still be a game ... as a guy you've got all the cards but she keeps you guessing. Go clubbing in Huddersfield and you get jumped on by some inebriated tottie with fat legs wanting a one-night stand ... but here there's still a bit of subtlety.'

Ben was definitely not convinced.

'Tell us another Jack!' he challenged. 'Even when you're paying?'

'Yes, even then it's a game. That's what makes it fun.'

Ben paused in thought for a moment, staring into his beer.

'But Jack, I still feel uncomfortable with the idea of paying for sex.'

'Me too, if you mean straight prostitution ... girls servicing several men a night. But as I say, my girls are courtesans and I give'em money to help their families. It's never a quick shag for a fixed fee.'

'But it's not that great for the girls, is it,' insisted Ben.

'Not if they get pushed into it ... by poverty, drugs, children to feed and so on.'

'Exactly! That's most of 'em, isn't it? Which is why commercial sex bothers me.'

'The girls that go with the *farang* can usually look after themselves, but it's the ones getting screwed by Thai men for a few baht that I worry about.'

'And what about the girls working with Asian tourists?' Ben asked.

'They've got their own clubs and places in Bangkok. The punters from Japan, Hong Kong, Taiwan and so on insist on pale skin ... that's what beauty means to them, while we like these dark skinned Isaan girls.'

Mention of Isaan made Ben think again of Fon. Sent to work in Bangkok, she had somehow avoided being a bar girl, but her life seemed so hard and unrewarding.

'What do you think it's like for a girl from a poor farming family who stays behind in the village?' he asked Jack.

'She'll end up with a Thai boy who'll get her pregnant and then be unfaithful,' said Jack. 'She's last in the pecking-order in the home. Mother-in-law kicks her round the place and she does all the house work … maybe the farming too. It can be tough.'

'And what does she get out of the deal?'

'She gets food and protection … but she shouldn't be too interested in sex herself or she won't be respectable.'

'Is it always that bad, Jack?' asked Ben dubiously.

'No, probably not. If she raises sons and runs the household, she'll be powerful … even more so if the men are always drunk or away working. I'm sure lots of Thai families function better than ours do, but a girl from a poor farming family probably fears the worst, so it doesn't seem much to give up when she has a chance to work in a bar and be independent.'

'But being a sex worker isn't that great either, is it.'

'Well, it depends. If she saves and gets out early, she can buy a farm or small business for her family and maybe get married.'

'But she has to sit in bars all night waiting to be screwed by some old pervert.'

Ben suddenly realised this was more than tactless but Jack passed it by.

'Yes, that's what they have to do,' he said. 'And then they can look a million dollars, send money back to their families and walk tall … exactly what every girl wants. And the alternative? Grubbing around in a rice paddy for life, carrying babies and waiting for her husband to come home and infect her with something nasty.'

Ben was still not persuaded.

'But isn't a bar girl a social outcast compared to a farmer's wife?' he asked Jack.

'Yes, she's outside the mainstream, though a successful sex-worker has plenty of support from the other girls and she won't want to be rescued. When she does go home, she'll keep quiet about her past and they'll love her for her money.'

'There must be lots who can't save, or get sick though, aren't there?'

But Jack did not answer him as they were distracted by a noisy party of men coming in from the street, led by a shaven-headed Australian with a massive beer belly, the girls greeting them with excited shrieks. They watched as the Australian ordered beers, talking loudly in monosyllables, every second word an expletive.

'That's a real rough diamond ... must be a Queenslander,' said Jack under his breath.

'Pity any girl who fall into his hands,' said Ben.

'Yes, but if he's got money and treats her properly, being grotesque's no problem.'

'Bet they don't often get a nice guy like you, Jack!'

'Yes, but I'm not a soft touch anymore. Two women sent me identical begging letters last month ... got'em from a letter-writer or off the internet. You know the sort of thing ... father dying, buffalo sick, mortgage lender about to seize the farm ... unless of course I come up with the money. Lets face it though, their problems are all basically the same and the sob stories usually true.' Staring with distaste at the Australian, Jack rocked back on his stool and took a swig of his beer.

'So you've never had longer term friendships with Thai girls?' Ben asked him. 'You talk about enjoying the courtship thing.'

'As I said, I try to remain dispassionate ... love affairs with Thai women aren't easy at the best of times. You see, there's this fundamental problem ... for the Thais, a man's willingness to provide is a much bigger part of the love equation than it is with us. So the *farang* fears his Thai girl doesn't really love him because she's too keen on his money ... and she thinks he doesn't love her because he's so reluctant to hand it over. The Thais detest a man who's a meany, while we want a woman who's not interested in our money. It's the very definition of incompatibility.'

'Sounds dodgy,' said Ben, 'and even worse with bar girls who are only in it for the money anyway.'

'Yes, it's amazing how many men fall for a bar girl and want to marry her. They go back home and keep sending her money, but she's promised to marry several blokes and she's milking the lot of them.'

'Surely it catches up with her?'

'Maybe, but she can stop'em visiting her at the same time and if there's a problem she just dumps whoever's the meanest.'

'Serve the buggers right if you ask me,' said Ben.

'Well, everyone's in it for what they can get, aren't they,' replied Jack.

'I like the story of the *farang* who shacked up with a girl in the North East. He'd come out to Thailand to stay at her home for the winter months and was keeping the whole family going. But he didn't realise one of the men who was always around the place was in fact her husband. Whenever the *farang* turned up, the husband moved over and kept his mouth shut.'

'That's outrageous,' said Ben.

'But who's worse? The foreigner who buys the woman or the family who hand over their daughter and take him for everything they can get?'

Their attention was again drawn to the big Australian who this time was noisily challenging one of the bar girls to drink a bottle of Bacardi Breezer against the clock. Ben thought her a classy looking girl, far superior to the foreign roughneck, but to his surprise she threw back the bottle and downed the sickly contents in four seconds. Wiping the excess from her mouth and gasping for breath, she looked distinctly green.

'Well, I've been doing all the talking again,' said Jack. 'How about another beer?'

'Thanks. I'll have a Chang.'

'So Ben, tell me about yourself. You hinted at a bust-up of some sort.'

'Yes, it's pretty simple. Came out here with my girlfriend and we split up … and now I've got involved with a Thai girl.'

'Emotionally involved?'

'Yes. She's called Fon and she's a masseur on Koh Samet.'

'Does she tap you for money?'

'No. Other than paying for a daily massage, there's no mention of money. And she says unmarried women should keep themselves for their future husbands, which makes her a bit different.'

'Sounds frustrating.'

'And there's a little girl she looks after called Joy, her dead sister's child.'

'Any idea what happened to the sister and why Fon took on the child?' asked Jack.

'No, nothing. Though I understand why she doesn't like talking about her sister.'

'Maybe Ben ... maybe. So Fon's had a tough life, has she then?'

'Yes, her father died when she was thirteen and she was sent to Bangkok to work as a domestic ... been working like a donkey ever since. Her mother's sick too.'

'Sounds familiar,' said Jack. 'But watch yourself, lad. In Asia, the literal truth isn't always that important ... life's an illusion, so why worry about a few little white lies.'

'What do you mean?'

'Well, take chastity. Being a virgin isn't a matter of real substance, is it ... so you just tell people what you want'em to hear. Thailand may look westernised but the old ways are only just beneath the surface. Same same but different as they always say.'

'Suppose that's what makes a relationship with Fon so difficult. With an English girlfriend I know the rules and when things go wrong, I have some idea why. But chasing Fon's another ballgame.' He stared glumly into his beer.

'And what are you hoping for?'

'Everything I guess. Though I can't see much future for us here ... nor at home for that matter.'

Ben looked across the bar to where the girl who had sunk the Bacardi Breezer was all over the ugly Australian. Her arms were wrapped around his neck and she was laughing and joking with him.

'See that,' said Ben. 'How can she go for such a disgusting old bloke.'

'It's amazing what these girls tolerate. Looks like she really wants him ... but then he's got money.'

'Imagine bringing home a slob like that.'

'They'd welcome him with open arms, Ben. He thinks he's jumping into bed with the girl but in fact he's marrying the whole family. If he's generous with'em they won't thank him because that's exactly what's expected of a rich *farang*. And the more he shells out, the more they'll think his money's unlimited. They won't believe him when they've bled him dry.'

'I think you're trying to warn me off,' said Ben.

'No lad, I'm just telling it the way it is. At first the *farang*'s a star, but one day when she wants more money he'll say no and there'll be a god almighty bust up. She'll tell everyone he's tight as sticky shit and then it's downhill all the way. And if he's bought'em a house, it has to be in her name. Trouble at mill ... know what I mean!'

'Well, that's not my problem,' said Ben. 'I don't have any money and I just want a relationship with Fon right now, that's all.'

'But, Ben, if she's the traditional girl she says she is, she won't go for anything temporary,' said Jack. 'A sexual relationship means permanence. You know, the old-fashioned thing that if you've been seen kissing the girl, you've got to marry her.'

'Maybe, but I really don't understand the game she's playing.'

'These girls keep their cards close to their chest.' Jack paused for a moment. 'Though if there's no money in it for her, then I guess she really likes you.'

'So why does she hold back all the time, Jack. I don't get it.'

'Maybe you're a big risk for her, Ben. If she goes with you, it could break her heart and ruin her reputation ... they'll think you're paying her for sex. And how does she know you won't fly away and not come back? Her whole life's at stake, but for you it's only a holiday romance.'

Ben drained his beer glass and put it down on the bar feeling mildly irritated. How could Jack, with his casual attitude to Thai women ever understand how serious he was about Fon?

'Well, Jack, I've learned a lot tonight,' he said. 'Some seminar.'

'What's more educational than talking about Thai women. Shall we move on?'

'Whatever you suggest,' said Ben.

The last stop that night was the Bier Kellar, the bar in a basement on Sukhumvit Road that Jack had talked about. They went down a

190

short flight of stairs and through some double doors into a dark interior heaving with gloomy-looking women waiting for their next contact. It smelled of dampness and mould, intermingled with stale beer. As they sat down, Ben was beginning to feel he had had enough for one night.

'Do you want another beer or shall we head back?' asked Jack.

'I think I've seen it all now, but before we go, what about this place? There's at least ten women to every man in here.'

'This is the bottom end, free-lance girls who haven't managed a pick up yet, the last chance saloon. Makes the go-go bars look polite and charming, doesn't it.'

'Amazes me some of the older ones ever get a hit,' said Ben trying to look around without attracting attention.

'Bernard Trink who writes about the bar scene in the *Bangkok Post* says that when they're past their screw-by date, the oldies make their money selling methamphetamines to the younger girls. "Speed's" a massive problem country-wide.'

'I'm not surprised if they take it,' said Ben. 'You'd need to be on something to tolerate sitting in here every night.'

In the taxi back home, the driver was the talkative type, hoping to earn a commission by taking them to another night spot.

'Want massage? Ladies?' he called over his shoulder.

'No thanks.'

There was a brief silence before he broke in again.

'You like Thai girls?'

'No,' said Jack.

'Why you not like?' the driver asked in shock.

'Because I only go for Japanese girls.'

Jack leaned across and whispered to Ben that Thai men are mad about Japanese girls for their pale skin and legendary performance.

'Why you like Japanese girls?' demanded the driver.

'Because they're always begging for it.'

'Beg for what?'

'Whatever you want! Those mini-knickers and tight little arses …
they just love it from behind!'

The driver lost concentration and narrowly avoided colliding with a
tuk tuk before again interrupting.

'How you know Japanese good?'

'Because I can't resist'em … it's the angel faces and silky white skin.'
Jack made a low moaning sound as the driver started weaving erratically
across the traffic lanes, pulling frantically at his collar.

'Okay,' said Ben, 'don't wind him up any more. I want to get
back alive!'

On reaching the Georgia, they got out of the taxi holding their
sides.

'Right Jack, when did you have a Japanese girlfriend then?'

'Never, you ninny. Give me a Thai girl anytime,' he replied with a
laugh.

'Guess they're my fantasy too,' said Ben.

'So get your skates on lad and forget about your girl on the island. It's
all waiting for you out there on the streets and the night's still young.'

After Jack had gone up to his room, Ben sat in the garden by the
pool looking up at the bright lights of the surrounding buildings framed
against the night sky, thinking about what he had seen in the past few
hours and wrestling with his conscience.

21

After his late night out on the town it suited Ben that the restaurant at the Georgia served breakfast at any time between seven in the morning and eleven at night. As he lay dozing on his bed in the middle of the morning, tracing the pattern of cracks in the ceiling, he half expected Emma to phone. He felt hungover in the heat, images of Thai girls and of Emma and Fon tumbling through his mind.

He wanted to catch a bus and go straight back to Koh Samet but instead he faced the day alone in Bangkok. Though he still hoped Emma might call, he was now regretting his futile gesture of waiting for her at the Georgia.

After breakfast he checked his email and found a brief message from her.

To: ben-the-bill80@hotmail.com
Subject: Over and Out
   Thanks for hanging on at the Georgia for me, but don't put yourself out. I called you there but remembering your ratty mood last time, I'm emailing to say I'm still going to Cambodia.
   I can tell you all about it later. As we can't change our flights home, we'll be on the same plane back to London, so see you at Bangkok airport! Enjoy!!!
Emm.

The message made Ben swallow hard; he was finally on his own. This was the feisty Emma he still liked and the thought of meeting up with her for the flight, though still weeks away, was oddly reassuring. But now he had too much time on his hands to sit around thinking how thoroughly he had messed things up. The tears pricked at the back of his eyes as he tried to adjust to the new reality.

It was already too late to travel back to Koh Samet that day, so in spite of the doubts Jack Russell had sowed in his mind, he decided to call Fon on Gaeo's mobile to say he would be coming back to the island the next day. He went down the hotel stairs and to the call box across the *soi* but it was being used by one of the staff. When it came free, it was like plunging into a super-heated oven. He assembled a pile of coins, found the scrap of paper on which Gaeo's number was written and tried to decipher the dialling instructions. When at last he managed to dial the number, there was no answer. Not understanding the noises the phone was making, he dialled again and sweated. When still nothing happened, he dialled yet again and sweated some more, then gave up in disgust. Either there was no reception on the island or Gaeo's phone was switched off. He felt almost relieved. At least he could tell Fon he had tried.

The rest of the day was now an empty canvas with nothing sketched in. He had a swim in the hotel pool and sat in the sun and tried to read. He saw no sign of Jack Russell and spoke to no-one, so in the afternoon he went out and took a bus to a fruit and vegetable market mentioned in the guidebook. It was in a huge modern building but was still a traditional Asian market. The traders were typical Thais from the countryside and the porters wheeling barrows laden with cabbages in baskets were coolies in baggy shorts and dirty white singlets. It struck him that Bangkok, with its millions of rural migrants still had something of the village about it. This was very much a city of contradictions and contrasts.

As he walked through the crowded market, he noticed an old lady dressed in faded black pyjamas propped up against her fruit stall. She looked as if she had had a hard life in the rice fields, her dark face lined by the years. Frail and bent, she seemed to be muttering to herself, though as he came nearer he realised she was having a spirited argument on her mobile phone.

That evening, alone in Bangkok and finally free for the first time, Ben felt restless. After the sights he had seen with Jack Russell the night before, he could not just sit in his room and contemplate his navel. He decided to head off to Sukhumvit Road to have a few beers and see how the dice would fall.

The next day, despite another very late night, Ben was up early. He collected his laundry, paid his hotel bill and took the Skytrain to the Eastern Bus Terminus where he caught a bus for Koh Samet. This time the journey seemed long and tedious. Apprehensive about how things would go with Fon, he could not concentrate on reading and just wanted to get there.

When the bus arrived at Ban Phe, though Fon was now only a few miles away, still his low spirits did not lift. Once the boat was outside the breakwater, heading into the open sea and as their reunion came closer, he began to feel more positive. By the time the boat picked up its mooring in Ao Sapporot he was in a state of high excitement.

He stood in the bow of the landing craft, straining to see if she was on the beach and as it bumped onto the firm sand, he was the first off, splashing through the waves to the shore. At this time in the afternoon she was usually working or looking for custom, but she did not seem to be there. He left his things at the reception desk of the huts he had stayed in before and went to their usual massage place beside the fallen tree. He walked to one end of the beach and then to the other but there was no Fon. When he bumped into Fon's friend, Gop, she immediately saw his anxious face.

'You looking Fon?' she asked.

'Can't find her anywhere. Has she gone away ... to Isaan?'

'Maybe she go Mama house.'

'Could you see if she's in her room for me?' he asked.

He thought of going with Gop but knew Fon would not like him being seen hanging around her hut. Then as he waited anxiously, he remembered talk of Fon's boyfriend. Yes, perhaps that was it; Fon was in the hut with her boyfriend. His guts were grinding as he waited.

Still smiling, Gop came back a few minutes later.

'Fon not there. Go other beach,' she said, pointing the way.

Ben hurried across the headland to the beach where he had found Fon plaiting the girl's hair a few days earlier, but she was nowhere to be seen. Then, just as he turned to go back he saw three sleeping forms spread out on the soft sand under the trees at the top of the beach. As he went up to them he recognised Gaeo and Pornpun, but the third, in shapeless brown trousers, her face covered by her arms, did not look like Fon.

Gaeo had now sensed his approach and was stirring. He put his fingers to his lips to silence her but too late, she had warned the sleeping figure that he was there. Fon rolled over and sat up, rubbing her eyes and peered obliquely at Ben. She looked different, darker than he remembered, her hair loose and crumpled. It was not at all his memory of the girl who had taken him to eat at the far beach and had surrendered to a brief clinch in the moonlight.

'You come already,' said Fon. 'Why you not phone?'

'I called you on Gaeo's number but the phone was switched off.'

'I surprise you come already,' she said.

'Fon say she dream you come back,' said Gaeo with a grin.

Fon put her face in her hands and peeped out at Ben.

'Have nightmare,' she said with a laugh.

Ben began to relax a little.

'Well, I'm here now,' he said, half apologetically.

'Ben, I not sleep. I sick … yesterday go doctor, buy medicine.' She seemed to be sniffly and to have a slight cold.

'What sort of medicine?'

'Have many colour.'

'And did they make you better?'

'Yes, little bit, but today very tired.'

Pornpun and Gaeo, now fully awake and ready for work, picked up their plastic boxes and walked away towards Ao Sapporot, leaving Ben alone with Fon.

'Why you come back Koh Samet?' she asked him unsmilingly.

'Because I said I'd come back … because you're all I ever think about.'

'*Pak waan*. What you want from me, Ben?'

'Just to be with you,' he said in a strangled voice.

'But you can't be with me, not here. I have my work, have Joy … look like bar lady when you follow me like dog.'

'Let's go somewhere else then … to your village. That's what I'd like most of all.'

'High season cannot … lose money. House dirty … you not like.'

'I'd love it … to meet your mum and see where you were brought up.'

'Okay Ben, later maybe … but now go back. Today look after Joy.'

Ben realised his happy return was now almost over for the day. As they walked back to Ao Sapporot together, Fon asked him what he had done in Bangkok and he gave her some evasive answers. When they came to the place where she always disappeared, she gave him a strained smile and walked away into the trees without a word.

This had hardly been the reunion he had longed for and as he checked into a hut, he went over everything that had been said. The idea of going to Fon's village had come to him on the spur of the moment but she had not dismissed it out of hand. He could think of nothing better.

He now dreaded an evening alone, though it was possible Maca and Chuck were still around. He thought of asking for them at reception; Maca's name was Mackintosh, though he knew from bitter experience he would not need the surname.

In his tiny hut he unpacked his rucksack, then went down to the beach bar and ordered a beer. Even before it had arrived, he heard a familiar voice. It was Maca rolling in, with Chuck only a pace or two behind.

'How's it with you guys?' asked Ben.

'Cool,' said Chuck.

'Good,' said Maca.

'Have a cool time in Bangkok?' asked Chuck.

'You bet. How about a beer?'

They sat down together as if Ben had never been away.

'So you were on your own in Bangkok, were you Ben?' asked Maca.

'Guess I was.'

'Must've been wild,' said Chuck.

Ben played the innocent.

'Well, I did the tourist thing … went to this amazing fruit and veg market.'

'Fruit and veg? Far out, man!'

'In the market they were selling turtles. Not sure if they were for food.'

'Course they're for food. What else?' hooted Chuck.

'And there were frogs and eels and catfish, all black and squirmy.'

'Sounds good tucker.'

'Oh, and bamboo cages with birds in them … far too small to eat. Saw a woman buy a cage full.'

'Was there a temple nearby?' asked Maca. 'They release'em at temples to make merit. Maybe the turtles too. It's a Buddhist thing, to get you a better reincarnation next time round.'

'Pull the other one! They release birds as a good deed?'

'Yeah mate, dinkie die.'

'But some poor kid has to catch them in the first place. So he gets a black mark then, just so the rich can let'em go again?'

'Seems a crazy way of merit-making,' said Maca.

'Don't really understand Buddhism,' admitted Ben, 'life being illusory and impermanent and stuff, but I do love the feel of a Buddhist country.'

'Me too,' said Maca grinning. 'Most of the CDs, designer labels and stuff are cheap, impermanent fakes. And even the girls are an illusion … half the prettiest ones are ladyboys.'

'Yeah, and man … reincarnation's far out,' said Chuck in rare flippant mood. 'If I kill myself smoking dope, maybe I'll come back as a buffalo. But how do I get to be a human again? By being a good buffalo?'

'Don't knock it,' said Ben. 'Buddhism's tolerant and adaptable, not like most religions.'

'Sure is. It's right up to the minute,' said Maca. 'Thai monks get free transport and internet access, and even the mummified monk in the glass case at Wat Khunaram on Samui wears dark glasses.'

'Well, I'm into making merit too,' said Ben with a wry smile, 'though in Bangkok I did go for an oil massage.'

Chuck and Maca looked suddenly attentive.

'Tell us about it then!' hooted Maca.

'Okay guys,' said Ben, warming to the subject. 'You see I missed Fun so much I just had to have a massage ... tried an oil massage to see what it's like. You know ... research sort of thing!'

There was a chorus of guffaws before he went on.

'The massage girl was fully dressed, sorry to say, so there I am starkers on this trolley like a slab of dead meat, and she's rubbing baby oil into my buttocks. Not much of a turn-on really ... but we had a nice chat.'

'That's your story and you're sticking to it, huh?' interrupted Maca.

'Well, there were these awkward silences,' Ben persisted, 'so I asked her a bit about herself. Says she used to be a hotel cleaner, but massage is a nice little earner ... know what I mean. And of course she wouldn't be doing massage at all if she was a good girl, would she, nudge nudge ... and did I want a "special"? Of course I said no thanks, though by this time I'm getting into the mood and trying to think of England. Then Buddhism comes up and we chat about that ... which means we've done sex and religion. So now for politics. It was election day and I say to her, "I see you've got an election today?" She looks kind of surprised, and you know what she says?'

'No we don't,' roared Maca, demanding the punch line. 'What did she say?'

'Solly,' she says. "Me? Election today? No ... *you* have election!" I almost fell off the frigging bed.'

When Maca and Chuck at last stopped laughing, Maca pressed Ben for more details.

'But it didn't just fizzle out there, did it? What about the climax to the story?'

'Climax?' replied Ben with an innocent look.

'Don't tell me you went into that whorehouse and got all oiled up for nothing.'

'It was only ten thirty in the morning,' he protested.

'So you Poms can't make it before tea time, eh?' said Maca. 'She must at least've offered.'

'Offered what?'

'Drop it, mate! Did she offer you a hand job?'

Ben paused in near embarrassment.

'Well, yes she did … but it was going to cost me.'

'What did she say then?'

'Say? She didn't say anything … it's not the most difficult thing to get across in sign language!'

They all fell about laughing.

'But did you accept?' Maca insisted.

'Let's put it this way. When I go for a haircut, I don't waste money having my hair washed … I wash it myself.'

Chuck and Maca cracked up again.

'Man, you can have whatever you want in them massage places,' said Chuck, when he could draw breath. 'But that's for the crazies. Like I said to my ex-girlfriend … blow-jobs suck!'

There was so much raucous laughter that the couple at the next table turned and stared before relative peace was restored.

The rest of the evening continued in similar vein, and somehow the discussion came round to choosing the most congenial ways of killing oneself. Ben's favourite means of suicide was to be run off the top of a cliff by a rampaging mob of topless women with big tits.

'Where d'you get that one from, you perverted Pom?' taunted Maca.

'Somewhere in my adolescent subconscious I guess,' said Ben.

Chuck came over all patriotic and, to save the nation, decided to be a suicide bomber at a summit meeting of George Bush, Bill Gates and Michael Jackson.

Typically Maca chose a softer option. To renewed laughter he told them the Thais believe a surfeit of sex and gorging on durian can both be fatal, so he was going for a simultaneous orgy of durian and sex. Chuck expressed doubt that Maca's choice satisfied the strict criteria for suicide, and that anyway Maca would never be motivated enough to do himself in, let alone get round to buying the durian. The late night suicide debate became long and heated.

Ben was relieved that Maca and Chuck did not ask him about Emma and he told them little more of what had happened to him in Bangkok. It was all good traveller talk about ganja, go-go bars and moving on to the next beach. But even in an alcoholic haze and despite good company, Ben could not forget his close proximity to Fon. He wanted the morning to come as soon as possible. The stalemate with her could not go on forever; it was just too painful.

22

The next morning Ben was at the beach early, having breakfast and waiting for Fon. At nine thirty she appeared, carrying her usual box of tricks and came over to his table looking fresh and happy. She seemed to have forgotten her cold.

'So you still here? Not go Bangkok?' she said with a cheeky grin.

'Course not. I've come back to talk to you.'

'Okay, I listen … but not like sweet talk.'

Ben summoned up as much sincerity as he could muster.

'Fon, I missed you like hell when I was in Bangkok.'

'*Gohok!* You lie me already,' she retorted.

'No, Fon, I really mean it,' he pleaded, quite taken aback.

'You not look other girls? Not go with lady?' she demanded.

'Course not.'

'Never?'

'How could I, Fon? I was thinking of you most of the time.'

'No good! I want you think me *all* the time,' she said, and then without warning burst into peals of laughter. Ben had the feeling he had been subtly sent up. It was always so hard to tell the difference between Fon being deadly serious and a deadly tease.

But Fon had work to do and this was not the time for idle talk. She quickly changed the subject.

'Today I phone Mama, Buriram,' she said. Ben did not understand and Fon did not stop to explain. 'Now many people … go find work.'

And with that she was off, swinging away down the beach, offering massage, manicure and hair braiding to the horizontal tourists. Today was work as usual, seven days a week, Ben or no Ben.

But Ben did not feel put out. Already he was able to relax with her again and after Bangkok the beach was blissful. Most importantly, she was as sensational as he remembered and his heart was thumping wildly for her.

Half way through the morning he noticed her sitting with Jinda on the fallen tree at the top of the beach taking a break. As he wandered across to join them, he sensed they were in holiday mood.

'I bored,' said Fon. 'Go aeroplane, have holiday! Me buffalo, always work … want to take off, go sea in bikini.' She mimed tearing off her clothes, flinging her arms around in wild abandon.

'Well why not?' said Ben. 'I'll take you.'

'We go England? Tomorrow?'

'It's my dream to travel with you in Thailand, Fon … Buriram maybe.'

'Buriram not fun. *Mai sanuk.*'

'But it's your home and I want to see it. I've been reading about Phnom Rung, the Khmer temple and I want to go there too.'

There was a brief pause in the banter as Fon stood up and gazed out to sea. Then she spoke intently with Jinda for a few moments before the two of them broke into smiles and looked across at Ben.

'Okay,' said Fon. 'We go together.'

'What?'

'We go … you and me. Jinda come too.'

'Where to?'

'Buriram. See Mama.'

'You really mean it? When?' said Ben in shock.

'Tomorrow, maybe. Gaeo take care Joy … can, no problem.'

Ben could not believe his ears. After last night's fiasco when Fon had seemed so unwelcoming, everything was now turning around. But that was not all.

'Tonight have party my room. We cook food, have music, dancing.'

'Can I come too?' Ben dared to ask.

'Cannot … party for lady. But yes, okay … you want?'

'More than anything ... except going to your village. I want that the most.'

Ben spent the rest of the day walking on air. Fon was busy with her work and left the beach earlier than usual to prepare the food, so he missed out on a massage. But it did not matter; he had an evening with her to look forward to. He was to be allowed to see where she lived and she was going to take him to her home in the North East. Even with Jinda as chaperone, it would be like going to heaven.

Chuck noticed his serene expression and asked him what drug he was on. He wanted to say he was in love, high on nature's greatest narcotic, to shout to the world that love, love, love is a dangerous drug and that he adored Fon and was addicted to her. But he knew he had to tone it down a bit.

'Hey you guys, I think I'm in with a chance with Fon. She's taking me home to see her mum,' he said, looking pleased with himself.

Chuck hooted derisively.

'You watch yourself, man ... sounds dangerous. I wanna wedding invite.'

'Get lost, it's just a platonic relationship ... so far anyway.'

'How long you going for?'

'A few days I suppose.'

'Well, me and Maca are moving on to Koh Chang soon, so when you're finished with Fon, come and join us there.'

That evening Ben waited on the beach and Jinda fetched him and took him to where she and Fon lived with Joy. He had not seen these huts before. They were built on a slope, hidden in the trees near where the generator throbbed steadily twenty four hours a day.

Fon's room was in a longhouse of four rooms, each separately occupied.

The hut was roughly built of softwood covered with thin fibreboard and had a low-pitched corrugated roof. It was high at the front where the ground fell away, the rear squatting close to the dry yellow earth. Ben knew it was the custom to remove shoes before entering a home so he slipped off his sandals as he climbed the steps, closely followed by Jinda. Fon was inside cooking, surrounded by Gaeo, Gop and Pornpun, who were already there for the party.

Ben looked round the room. Its framework, the rafters and the underside of the corrugated roof were all visible as it had no lining or ceiling. Crawling over the timbers was a tangle of electric wires and here and there the earthy trails of ants. At one end were two fabric-covered boxes with zippers down the front used as hanging cupboards for clothes. There was a pile of dry washing waiting to be sorted and more piles of clothes neatly folded and stacked on cane shelves. Two windows with rough wooden shutters opened onto the jungle at the back of the hut. Between them was a dressing table with cosmetics and a mirror, a table fan, a television and video and a sound system with speakers.

Then to his dismay, Ben saw at the other end of the room, covered in colourful bedding and cushions, a large double mattress. He was assailed by black thoughts. Why ever would Fon need a double bed?

Joy was lying quietly on the mattress looking sorry for herself and did not jump up in her usual excited way when Ben came into the hut. Fon explained why.

'Joy sick. *Bpen khai.* She very hot.'

'Oh no,' said Ben. 'Have you taken her temperature?'

'Cannot. Not have.'

'You ought to get a thermometer so you can check how ill she is.'

'If she sick tomorrow, cannot go Buriram.'

With this new setback added to the shock of the double bed, Ben's face fell even further.

Looking hot and tired after a day's work, Fon now immersed herself in juggling the demands of a grizzly child at the same time as cooking for seven people. She put on a video for Joy, a Taiwanese version of King Kong dubbed into Thai, but it did little to cheer her up. Joy was lost in misery, gazing at the television with big offended eyes, hugging a shapeless soft toy to her chest.

Fon was squatting on the floor, cooking with an electric wok and an electric rice cooker. Somehow she managed to produce fried pork, chicken, fish, vegetables and rice which they all ate with their fingers, sitting round in a circle on the floor. Everyone was used to sitting with their legs crossed except Ben who found it distinctly uncomfortable.

Joy was still being cranky and was extracting the maximum attention from Fon's attempts to make her eat something. Fon, with infinite patience coaxed her down from the bed and fed her rice and chicken, a spoonful at a time. When Ben put his hand to her brow, she cringed away with a 'don't touch me' look of fury, but she did not seem to be too feverish.

After they had finished eating, the plates were stacked outside and then the party started for real. Gaeo and Gop had been drinking steadily and were plying Ben with generous tots of Mekhong whisky and Three Fingers Chinese brandy. Gaeo in particular had been knocking back the alcohol which was making her talk too much. She fixed Ben with sad eyes and began a sorrowful lament about her husband's philanderings. Her ramblings were difficult to follow but Ben thought he had the gist of it. She confided to him that her husband had another lady and was probably with her now. As she still loved him, she was hurt and unhappy, but there was nothing she could do; she and the children depended on him and she could not rock the boat. The others seemed to take no notice of her, covering their embarrassment with laughter.

Then Fon turned the music up and Gaeo was drowned out. Gaeo, the married woman who could not go dancing with them at the Meridian, now picked herself up and became the most energetic dancer of all. Even Joy decided she was feeling better and began prancing about. The music was Thai pop which had some good dance rhythms and the small room was soon bursting with sound, the floor drumming up and down. Their sense of fun was contagious and Ben got up and danced with them in the tiny space, afraid his big *farang* feet would tread on someone's toes or trip over the flex of the fan.

As he danced he tried to put the double bed to the back of his mind. It looked new and must have been bought since Joy came to live with Fon; he told himself Fon slept there with Joy and perhaps with Jinda. It was a magnificent bed, fresh and bright, and he could not bear the thought of any male sharing it with her other than himself.

After a time, Gop and Gaeo were beginning to look the worse for wear and Gop sat down and lay back full length, her head resting on the hard floor. Gaeo was rapidly turning green and rushed over to one of the open windows at the back of the hut. She leaned out for a few moments, her hands on the sill, retched briefly and then slowly turned back into the room, looking shamefaced, but not for long. A moment or two, some water and a tissue later and she was dancing again.

When everyone began to flag, Gaeo and Pornpun joined Gop lying on the floor. Jinda started to get Joy ready for bed while Fon was tidying up after the meal. When the music was finally turned off, the dull thump of the generator filled the silence.

'Fon, that was fun. Thanks for including me,' said Ben.

There didn't seem to be much Thai smalltalk in response to this except a smile, while the others just picked up their things and disappeared into the darkness.

'So what about tomorrow?' he asked Fon.

'Tomorrow? Go Buriram. Joy okay, no problem.'

'What time? Which boat?'

'When we ready, afternoon maybe.'

Stupid *farang* questions. Ben got the message and left. It had been a fantastic evening but now it was over.

Fon, Jinda and Ben did not catch the ferry to the mainland until three o'clock the following day as Fon had decided it would be better to travel on the bus overnight and to arrive in Buriram first thing the next morning. It was going to be a long journey.

On the ferry the mood was upbeat, Fon talking and laughing with her sister as if they had not seen each other for years, Ben happy to watch and wait and occasionally be the butt of their jokes. When they landed in Ban Phe, she did not behave as if there were a bus to catch, but wandered into the clothes shop where she had played the fashion model on their trip to the bank a week before. She dumped her bag on the floor and pointed to a tiny plastic stool.

'Ben, you sit. I go with Jinda, *raan tat pom*.'

'Where?'

'Hair cutter. To have my hair cut.'

'How long'll you be? When are we getting the bus?'

'Five o'clock,' she said decisively.

The shop girl brought Ben a mug of water and he sat on the stool and waited. When five o'clock was getting close, he began to feel agitated as the bus station was a good few minutes walk away, but when Fon breezed in again after more than half an hour, she still seemed relaxed and unhurried. The untidy ends of her hair had been trimmed and she was looking pleased with herself. There was no sign of Jinda.

'So what now?' Ben had decided not to ask about bus times again.

'We get *sorngthaew*,' she said.

'Why? Where to?'

'Bus go from Rayong, not Ban Phe.'

Out on the street Jinda appeared from nowhere and Fon stopped a cruising *sorngthaew* and chartered it into Rayong. Jinda was put in the back while Fon got in the cab with Ben next to the driver. It was a pick-up designed for midgets and the driver insisted on winding up the windows and switching on the feeble air conditioning which made it airless and oppressive. Ben sat sweltering while Fon chatted with the driver as if they had known each other all their lives.

Arriving in town, they spilled out onto the pavement near the bus depot.

'You eat now?' asked Fon.

Ben was a little surprised.

'Now?' It seemed a funny time to eat, not even late afternoon.

'Why not? You not hungry?'

After eating at a noodle stall on the pavement, they wandered off to the bus station, bought tickets and boarded a bus which was about to leave for Buriram. It was more than half empty so they ignored their allocated seats and chose the ones they wanted. Jinda decided to sit at the front and Ben and Fon sat together towards the back, just far enough forward to avoid the smell of the lavatory cubicle. As the bus pulled out for its long overnight journey, Ben realised that this would be only his second time alone with Fon at night and his very first time to sleep with her.

Fon took a keen interest in the passing countryside, enthusing at the first tall limestone pinnacles they passed and appreciating everything

208

along the way. She chatted non-stop, though he could not afterwards remember much of what she said. The denim of her jeans was pressed hard against the thin cotton of his trousers, she was leaning up against his shoulder, she was turning and talking to him excitedly, she was resting her hand on his knee and he was loving every moment of it.

Then she said she was cold in the fierce air conditioning so she got a blanket and put it over both of them. As they snuggled beneath it, she took his hand in hers and played sensuous games. They clasped and unclasped hands, twining them together, playing, caressing, teasing. She explored every sensuality to be found in the fingers, stroking his palms and the back of his hands with hers. Ben felt strangely excited by so limited a seduction, sweetly innocent but full of sensation and promise. He felt impossibly happy to be on the bus with her, rushing through the darkening countryside towards Buriram.

As time went on Fon began to look sleepy, wriggling around like a cat to make herself comfortable. Curled up on her side, her bare feet tucked against the seat, she gently rested her head and shoulders on his lap. With a volition of its own his hand strayed across her thighs to her bare feet, up to her shoulders and into the nape of her neck, his fingers exploring the mass of black hair. She stayed motionless and silent, at ease with the modest intimacy of the moment.

The bus journey became timeless and Ben did not want it ever to end. He did not want to sleep because that would have been a waste, but sleep he did. There were stops at large towns on the way when shadowy figures got on and off the bus, sudden and stark in the glare of the white strip lighting. Finally came a stop when Jinda appeared from the front to wake them; they had arrived in Buriram. As he got down from the bus, it seemed as if they had driven in a huge circle; the bus station and the surrounding streets looked exactly the same as the featureless water-stained buildings of the town they had left some eight hours earlier. It was three thirty in the morning and a moonless night.

'So what now?' he asked Fon.

'Wait bus to Nang Rong, then go bus to village. Or we take *sorngthaew* all the way.'

'How much for the *sorngthaew*?'

'Maybe five hundred baht.'

'*Sorngthaew*,' said Ben, though with no passing traffic, he wondered how on earth they would find one at this unearthly hour of the morning.

Fon went in search of one and within five minutes reappeared in a small pick-up with two tight rows of seats in the cab. Their bags thrown into the back, Jinda climbed in next to the driver while Ben and Fon took the rear seats. The decrepit vehicle crawled off into the darkness, the oncoming traffic flashing angrily at its badly aligned headlights. A mile or two further on they stopped at a filling station where the driver asked Ben for an advance on his fare to pay for fuel. Then the pick-up's engine would not start and they had to get out and push-start it across the forecourt. Dawn was not even in prospect but it was already a laugh a minute.

There had been some unseasonal rain and the lights of the traffic shone on the wet road, the damp earth giving off a warm smell of dust and dung and deep countryside. Though the roads were straight and well-paved, this was the real, rural Thailand that Ben had longed to see. He had left behind the artificial worlds of Bangkok and backpacking and ahead of him lay new and authentic experiences of Thailand.

After some time they reached the outskirts of a town. It was still dark and there was nobody about. When Fon leaned forward and spoke to the driver, he drew into the side of the road and stopped.

'Okay Ben, get out,' she said.

'What are we doing? Where are we?'

'Nang Rong. Go shopping.'

'Shopping? Now? In the middle of the night?'

'Yes, now. Not ask questions!'

Ben obediently got out without a word and stared around at the bleak concrete streets of Nang Rong.

23

Fon and Jinda climbed out of the pick-up and walked briskly down a side alley towards the Nang Rong market with Ben following on behind. There was just a hint of the dawn as they reached the open-air market, a tightly-packed clutter of wooden stalls covered with grubby awnings. After the rain the air was heavy with humidity, the ground a dark soup of liquid mud. Despite the early hour, the market was alive with activity, the faces of the buyers lit by the harsh light of the bulbs swinging from the stalls. Ben picked his way through the puddles, trying not to submerge his sandals in the filthy water.

The market stalls were weighed down with vegetables and fruit, few of which Ben could identify, and with fish which were still gasping and squirming. Fon chose a live fish to be collected later and bought meat, vegetables and herbs which she passed back to Jinda to carry. She attracted many sidelong glances, a self-confident young woman with her six foot foreign boyfriend in tow. As she went among the stalls, she freely sampled the fried insects and wriggly bamboo grubs.

'Here Ben, you eat,' she said as she popped a grub into his mouth with a wicked twinkle. Ben bit on it and it filled his mouth with a tasteless doughy mush.

Jinda and Ben were soon laden with plastic bags full of food. They went back for the fish, now cleaned and de-scaled, and waded through the sludge back to the road. The pick-up was waiting and they drove on through the town and out into the dark countryside. After some time, a glow of light appeared on the horizon and for the first time Ben could glimpse the endless rice fields, scattered houses of wood and concrete and the occasional school or police post as they sped along the dead straight road.

'Soon come to village. Not far now,' said Fon.

A few minutes later the driver slowed down and pulled over onto the verge in front of a cluster of houses set back from the road. So this is it at last, thought Ben as he climbed down from the cab and looked around at a world that was dripping and dismal.

He followed Fon and Jinda as they crossed a slippery wooden plank over a drainage ditch and walked towards a small house from which an elderly woman was emerging. It was Fon's Mama, a tiny woman in a sarong, with a weathered face the same broad shape as those of her daughters. The greetings were low-key and the moment casual and easy as if this sort of thing happened every day. All Ben could do was to smile awkwardly and look around while everyone loudly talked about him in Thai.

The tiny single-storey house was dwarfed by a tamarind tree and by the larger house next door. It was built of concrete blocks skimmed in cement, with wooden doors and window frames all unpainted. A bamboo pole fixed to the roof was topped with a television aerial and ceramic pots stood under the eaves to catch rainwater for drinking.

He was glad when at last Fon took him inside, adding their shoes to the collection outside the door. A narrow room with white strip-lighting ran the length of the house to a cooking area and washroom at the back. On the right were doors to two small bedrooms, each almost filled by a double mattress laid on the floor and draped with mosquito nets. As he looked in, he wondered where they would all sleep that night.

The floor of the main room was covered with thin blue lino but there was hardly any furniture. The sole focus of the room was some rattan shelving with a television taking pride of place. On the top shelf was a ceramic Buddha still in its cellophane wrapping, a vase of artificial lotus flowers and a picture of King Chulalongkorn in a frame decorated with shells. A split-bamboo bed, a sack of rice in the corner and a spittoon half full of red betel spit were the only other things in the room.

Fon showed Ben through to the kitchen which was bare except for an electric rice-cooker and wok, a twin-tub washing machine and a glassfronted food cabinet, its feet standing in bowls of water to repel the ants. As they went out of the kitchen door at the back of the house, it was now almost light. Ben could see that this was the place for washing the dishes; just a muddy space with a duckboard, a clay pot for water and a blue plastic basin.

The small piece of ground at the back of the house was overgrown and neglected. Fon led him through the tangled vegetation and showed him banana and papaya trees, ginger, galangal and taro plants and a vine of pepper leaves used for chewing with betel nut. Beyond the wilderness, the vegetable gardens and rice fields began. Neighbours were already going to work in the fields, some of them casting curious glances at the house where the visitors had just arrived. One, an elderly man with a battered face and a wicked grin came across with a couple of bottles of beer and offered them to Ben who politely refused. He could think of nothing worse at that time of the morning.

'So the house is almost new?' he asked Fon.

'Yes, I build it for Mama,' she said proudly. 'Old one no good ... roof leak, wood broken. New house expensive ... one window twelve hundred baht, door eight hundred. Mama think she have good daughter. I die if she work like people on Koh Samet.'

Ben thought of the little old lady who flogged up and down the beach every day selling som tam. He could not imagine Fon's mother carrying those heavy loads.

'Come, Ben, see buffalo. Baby born yesterday,' said Fon, her face lighting up. She took him round the side of the house through the mud to the buffalo wallow where a tiny pink calf was suckling a black buffalo cow which gazed at them head down, her massive horns swept back behind flapping ears.

'Wow, a real live buffalo. I must get my camera,' said Ben, rushing back into the house. As he photographed Fon standing in front of the animals, she made great play of the *farang* getting excited about something so ordinary.

'Why you like buffalo? Not have, England?'

'No, we only have cows.'

'Smile buffalo. *Farang* take your photo!'

'And what are the buffaloes for? For milk?' asked Ben.

'No! You joking me!' Fon laughed at his stupidity. 'Buffalo pull cart, plough rice field, make manure … and for meat. But now, have small tractor. Before many buffalo, but soon all gone, soon no more buffalo.'

'So you had a buffalo cart?'

'Yes, I ride behind Papa, take vegetables to market, carry rice. No have cars before. Never go very far … this our village so we stay here, happy family.'

'The buffalo looks dangerous.'

'No, not dangerous! When small, Fon ride buffalo, have race. Beat buffalo hard with stick … always want to win. Sometimes fall off, come home black face. Papa angry little bit, but no problem … he love me.'

'And what's that wooden building over there, the small one with its floor above the ground,' asked Ben.

'That one, rice barn where we keep the rice before. Now sell the rice and take it away. Very different today,' said Fon.

'Yes, everything changes.'

'But still we have Buddha … temple not change so much. Today, Ben, we go wat with Mama, take food for monks. You come too.'

They went back into the house where Fon's mother was filling some jars with food for the monks. She, Fon and Ben then set off together, crossing the road and walking through the dewy grass. The temple was a modern concrete building with a red corrugated roof in Thai style, surrounded by mango trees and betel palms. Next to it was an open-sided pavilion of rough-hewn wood with a flight of steps leading up to a high wooden floor. Ben, still feeling bleary from the overnight bus ride and suffering mild culture shock, followed the others up the steps, kicking off his shoes.

They joined four or five middle-aged ladies who were watching a group of saffron-robed monks with shaven heads sitting cross-legged in a circle on a raised platform, silently eating from enamel bowls. Fon motioned Ben to sit down on the floor with the women. While the monks were eating, the women waited quietly, only occasionally exchanging words, and sometimes holding their hands together in prayer.

When the monks had finished eating, the women removed their

dishes and, sitting round on the floor, shared the fish, meat and sticky rice that remained. There was lots of low-key banter and joking, most of it directed towards Ben. The women gave him shy looks, asking questions through Fon and teasing him about his capacity for chilli. When they had eaten enough, the women sat back and chewed betel nut wrapped in a wad of pepper leaves, the red pulp visible on their lips. Ben noticed them occasionally rocking forward on their haunches, their heads down, as if bowing to a deity. But no, they were spitting the bright red residue through the gaps in the floor boards down onto the earth below.

Fon supervised the cleaning up, collecting the dirty dishes, taking water from a waist-high clay pot and washing them in a bowl and tipping the scraps through the floor for the chickens, the last in the pecking order. As she worked, two of the monks sauntered across and chatted to her. Ben guessed they were asking questions about her *farang* friend and wondered how she explained him away. Then the women collected up their bowls and slowly began to return to their homes. Ben followed Fon and her mother back across the road to the house, already beginning to feel a little more comfortable with rural Thailand.

When they got back from the temple, Fon led Ben out of the house past the buffaloes and the rice barn, through the mango and jackfruit trees to where a group of women were sitting on mats near some low wooden huts. This gathering, Fon explained, was to celebrate the birth two weeks earlier of a little girl. The teenage mother was cradling a tiny baby with a pale oval face and a head of thick black hair. Fon and Ben's arrival caused quite a stir and she invited them to come and join her. Dressed in sarong and tee shirt, her hair tied back with a red ribbon, she smiled happily at the honour being done to her baby as the visitors sat down.

Ben found a corner of the mat to sit on and slowly took in the surroundings; the low wooden houses, the banana trees, piles of sticks and firewood, washing out on lines, an old motorbike, the dry season dustiness and all the clutter and mess of rural Asia.

With much joking and laughter, one of the older women then tied a twenty baht note to his wrist with pieces of string. Fon explained as best she could that the money was for the child and that he must now keep the string tied to his wrist for good luck.

As they sat and talked, Ben noticed that the local males sat apart from the women, the boys playing and tumbling, the teens and older men drinking beer together on the steps of one of the huts. A skinny youth who was the baby's father came across to greet them and then returned to his friends. One old man was rolling around making incoherent noises and Ben asked Fon if he was a mental defective. But no, he was just blind drunk, halfway through the morning of a long hot day.

Ben was curious about some of the characters around them and asked her about a wizened old woman cradling a tiny girl on her lap.

'She grandmama,' said Fon. 'Her daughter have baby, but papa have new lady. She not see daughter long time, not know where she is. And daughter not send money … big, big problem.'

When Ben slipped the child a fifty baht note, she disarmingly brought her pudgy little hands together under her chin in a traditional *wai* of thanks.

Fon was now making a fuss of another old crone who looked different to the others, a touch more exotic, her dark skin pulled tight over prominent cheek bones. Her lips were bright red from chewing betel nut and a torrent of curly black hair flowed from beneath a woolly blue hat. She was full of life and fun.

'She come from Cambodia long time ago,' Fon explained. 'Have too much fighting, too many people die. Before, she have husbands, but they die too, all die.'

'How many husbands?'

'Three … and she have children, but not know where they are. War finish, Pol Pot dead already, but Cambodia still dangerous. Step on bomb, you die. If you lucky, you lose leg.'

There was much boisterous talking and laughter with Fon the centre of attention, and there were many glances at Ben. He imagined the inevitable questions to Fon about life on the island, about the significance of the tall *farang* and the dream of marrying out of rural poverty.

After one loud outburst, Fon told Ben what the old woman from Cambodia had just said.

'She say most *farang* are fat with big bellies and always smell bad.

But this one doesn't smell at all!'

'Thanks a million, Fon.'

'Yes, but maybe she not come close enough!'

Early that afternoon, Fon and Ben joined a tractor load of labourers going out to harvest the rice. They climbed onto the wooden trailer and sat down on the floor with the other workers. The tractor was just a small engine mounted on a single axle with large knobbly tyres, handle bars for steering and a hitch attached to the trailer. They puttered off across the road and down a track through the houses and orchards, the trailer crashing heavily into the potholes, and soon reached the rice fields.

Stretching to the horizon, the landscape of small fields, each separated by low earth banks, was relieved only by patches of woodland, bamboo and fruit trees. Here and there stood a substantial tree, a survivor from the jungle which had covered the area not so long ago. The tracks were well built, sometimes following ditches and concrete-lined irrigation channels flowing with crystal-clear water. Ben was impressed that this infrastructure for the control of water to the paddy fields, essential for the production of rice in a region of low rainfall, was so elaborate. Now at the beginning of the dry season the fields had been drained and the rice was brown and ripe and ready for harvesting.

After several spine-jarring minutes the tractor stopped and they got down and joined some farm workers resting in the shade a few hundred yards away. On a rise in the ground under the mango and cashew trees stood a wooden shelter with a corrugated iron roof. A dozen or so farmers, both men and women, had stopped work in the midday heat and were now about to eat. Rice straw had been spread out under the trees to sit on and as Fon and Ben arrived the food was just ready; sticky rice, meat that was sizzling on a barbecue and raw beef dipped in seasonings. Ben decided to risk the raw meat which was succulent and tender, eaten with newly sprouted leaves from a nearby cashew tree.

The workers ranged from women in their late sixties down to a handful of little boys. Ben noticed one young girl who was obviously pregnant, her bare feet dry and callused from a short lifetime of work in the fields. He asked Fon about her.

'She seventeen. Boyfriend go work Bangkok.'

'Tough to have a baby and then be apart,' he said. 'When'll he come back?'

'Don't know. Maybe he like Bangkok … maybe he not come back.'

When they had finished eating, the workers began putting on short rubber boots, straw hats with wide brims and a face cloth wrapped around the head and neck to keep out the dust. Ben was determined to join in the work and asked Fon for a sickle. The Thai rice farmers swathed in clothes and the tall *farang* in floppy shorts and tee shirt then spread themselves across the end of a tiny field and advanced shoulder to shoulder into the standing rice, leaning forward and cutting the waist-high rice stalks. Ben's neighbour showed him how to grasp a bunch of stalks with the left hand and then cut through it by pulling the sickle back towards the body. He felt incompetent at first but after half an hour was beginning to get the hang of it.

He wondered how much the owner of the field paid the workers for their labour and jokingly asked Fon what he would be paid for his hour's work. She told him that when she was a child, everyone used to work together to bring in the rice and that cash did not usually change hands. But the old ways were breaking down and they now paid a hundred and twenty baht for a full day's work. Because of this there were times, she said, when the price of rice was so low that farmers could not afford the cost of bringing it in and so had to leave it unharvested.

It crossed Ben's mind that a day's wage for a rice farmer would hardly buy a pint of beer in his local pub back home. He knew that rice farming in Asia was still labour-intensive but he had not realised it was in such crisis. As he cut at the rice a handful at a time, he began to understand the human cost of a lifetime of back-breaking labour in the heat of the rice fields. It seemed to him a tragedy for these people that as the price of rice was falling, their unremitting physical work offered them so little reward; they were trapped in an old way of life that was in decline. On the other hand it struck him that if basic living standards could be maintained and changing aspirations did not seduce them away to the cities, a village like this could offer many compensations. A life on the land free of urban pressures and surrounded by family and friends strongly appealed to his romantic side.

But he could see many signs of instability and change. The story of how Fon had been sent away to work in Bangkok was just one example. Yet she had done well and the money she now sent back to her mother was helping to sustain a rural community no longer able to survive on its own. But this was hardly a satisfactory solution and he could not begin to guess what the future held for villages like this one.

His back was beginning to ache when his reverie in the rice fields was broken by Fon calling loudly to him. The tractor was about to run back to the road and they would have to go if they did not want to face a long walk home in the heat of the day. Bumping along the track, he longed for a shower and a cold drink and dreamed of the air-conditioned luxury of the Regal in Bangkok.

As they arrived home, an elderly neighbour from the next house was just beginning the long task of threshing his rice crop by hand. Ben watched as the old man pounded the bunches of rice stalks against a board, the grains falling off and collecting in what looked like blue mosquito netting. Gripping the bunch of rice stalks with two sticks joined together by a short length of rope, he beat them again and again to dislodge all the grains. His wife then winnowed the rice by pouring it into a basket from above her head while their daughter fanned hard with hand-held fans. From where he was now sitting in the house, Ben could see the dust and straw mixed in with the rice being blown away on the breeze. Finally the women spread a small quantity of rice on round bamboo trays and repeatedly tossed it in the air, teasing out the remaining stones and bits of stalk.

After some time the old farmer seemed to tire of his labour and wandered into the house where Ben and Fon were in front of the television lazily watching the heavyweight fight between Lennox Lewis and Hashim Rahman in Las Vegas. The old man sat down on the floor, leaned against the wall, his head in his hands and gazed impassively at the screen. He was just in time to see Lewis get his revenge, knocking out Rahman with a single blow to the jaw. As the camera lovingly replayed the final punch in slow-motion and Rahman again crashed to the canvas, he clicked his tongue, slowly got up and went back to his work without a word.

'God, if only he could see Las Vegas,' said Ben.

'Las Vegas good?' asked Fon. 'He like?'

'Well, it's kind of different! People are better paid for a start ... and for getting knocked out, that boxer's just netted more than a rice farmer earns in a lifetime.'

'Good life better than money,' said Fon quietly.

'True, but today's taught me a bit about being poor, Fon. Rice farming's so tough.'

'Yes Ben, but today not so bad ... cutting rice easy.'

'So what's the hard part then?' asked Ben.

'First we have to plough ... big big job, too hard. Then planting ... standing in the water bending down, pushing every plant into the mud by hand, one, one, one, in rows. Your back break, blood come out fingers ... pain everywhere. We mend the walls to keep water in the fields, and kill the weeds and bugs. Then cut the rice, carry home, beat and clean it in machine or do like old man today. Dry the rice, go rice mill, then take rice to sell.'

'It's so labour intensive ... just so much work.'

'Yes, rice farming too hard ... so farmer eat *yaa bah*, amphetamine. This work terrible, Ben, it kill you. Now have machines like rice mill, but have to pay, pay, pay ... make small money.'

'What's a rice mill like then?' he casually asked her.

'Rice mill? You want look?'

Fon jumped up, grabbed him by the hand and dragged him out of the door. On the other side of the road was a tin-roofed building emitting a steady throbbing sound and a cloud of black smoke from a tall exhaust pipe. She took him inside and showed him a bizarre wooden structure with ladders and walkways connected by a series of drive-belts to a watercooled engine which was thumping away loudly in the background. Brown rice in a vat at the top of the machine was flowing slowly downwards in an elaborate process of shaking and polishing that Ben could not begin to fathom out. The contraption was producing a shower of husks at the back of the shed and a precious trickle of white grains which slowly filled a sack at its base.

'Old time, the women do rice by hand in a wooden bowl,' said Fon. 'One hour, three kilos maybe. Now rice mill very quick but expensive.'

'And do they still thresh the rice by hand like your neighbour was doing just now?'

'No, old man like to do it that way. Now have big blue machine come on tractor ... but have to pay.'

Ben was beginning to wonder whether with all these new costs, rice production could still be profitable.

'So after all this work, how much do they get for the rice?' he asked.

'Ordinary rice, about four baht a kilo.'

'Four baht only pays for a piss in the bus station! But after what they've spent, do they make any money? Is any of it profit?' he asked as they wandered back to the house.

'Today, grow more rice but make small money. New seeds expensive and need insecticide and fertiliser ... no buffalo, no have buffalo shit! Borrow money buy tractor ... so pay bank, pay petrol. Pay men to cut rice, pay to bring rice home, pay machine for beating rice, pay rice mill, pay to go market. Work all year but pay too much, so maybe sell rice but make no money. Sometimes no rain or rain come wrong time ... then rice spoil, farmer lose.'

'Sounds like hell. And I suppose that as the farmers only sell at the end of the season, they're desperate for credit to pay for everything first?'

'Yes, borrow, borrow ... then bad year, cannot turn back the money. Borrow money from mill owner ... send him brown rice for milling and he keep most of it for himself. Borrow from bank ... big big problem.'

'So what if a farmer can't pay off his bank loan?'

'Bank take farm,' she said solemnly.

'Then the family loses everything? Home, income, the lot?'

'Yes, lose everything ... even their daughters. Two year ago, my uncle borrow to buy tractor for ploughing. But rain no good, small rice ... so cannot pay bank every month. Now he work all year, only pay percent.'

'You mean he can only pay the interest? There's not enough to pay off the loan?'

'Yes, he work for the bank ... to stop them take the farm.'

'What a hole to be in. Is there any way out for him?'

'Uncle have pretty daughter, only eighteen. So she go work Pattaya, sell sex ... boom-boom with *farang* every night. Maybe she save farm, save family.'

'God, what a price to pay.'

'And she very shy. To talk with *farang* in bar, go room with *farang*, she drink too much. She *mao lao* ... drunk every night. Now cannot stop drinking, have big problem with drink.'

'Poor kid,' said Ben with feeling.

'Yes, and maybe she get HIV ... then she finished.'

24

As soon as they got home from the rice mill, Fon took a shower in the washroom at the back of the house, leaving Ben sitting outside pondering the pressures that drive farmers' daughters to become bar girls. How would it feel, he wondered, to be a father who through ill-fortune had so failed his family that his favourite daughter was now a feast for any foreign sex tourist.

His thoughts were interrupted when, after an eternity of splashing sounds, Fon reappeared glowing and wet, her sarong tucked in above the bust, her hair dripping and shiny black. As always, he could not take his eyes off her; the figure-hugging sarong, the bare arms and shoulders and her bewitching smile.

'Okay Ben, you not smell but you go shower,' she commanded him.

The washroom was a dark space under a lean-to behind the house, the only facilities a squat toilet and a plastic scoop floating in a murky concrete water tank. Ben could not close the door as there was no proper catch and there was nowhere dry to hang his clothes. But the shower was a relief, the cold water from the scoop exploding onto his hot skin in an exquisite agony. It was only a pity that he had to climb back into his sweaty shorts and tee shirt as he had not had a chance to settle in and pull fresh ones out of his rucksack. Hopping around on one foot, trying to juggle towel and clothes in the sodden space, it was impossible to get dry. In the heat and humidity of the afternoon, the benefit of showering was undone almost as soon as he emerged.

Coming back into the kitchen, he watched the kittens playing among the pots and pans just as a puppy launched an attack, chasing them into the front room and out onto the veranda. He followed them through and found Fon sitting on a bench in front of the house, irresistible in her green sarong.

'Come sit with me, Ben,' she said. Ben willingly obeyed.

'Fon, it's great to see where you were brought up,' he said. 'This is a wonderful place to be a child.'

'Is it? Maybe. We were happy here, all of us.'

'How many were you? You did tell me.'

'Me number one, then brother Somchai, Jinda and little sister, Nok. Mama always busy with babies so I have to work too.'

'Sounds a hard life.'

'Good life before Papa die.'

'How old was he?'

'He thirty ... die on the road over there.' She pointed to the place a few hundred yards away where a moment's chance had changed her life.

'Before, in old house, we all sleep in one room. As I go bed Papa tell me about Cinderella, pretty girl who work, work, not go to party ... then fall asleep in his arms. Not forget his smell, good smell. Morning wake up, he not there ... already go farm before too hot.'

'Cinderella. That's you, isn't it?'

Fon did not answer but gave free rein to her thoughts.

'Then I get up, go school,' she went on. 'Not have money ... but every day we eat rice, not thinking strong, always happy. Now want family again ... to be together.'

'But I'm sure it wasn't always fun. You said you were very ill once.'

'Ill many times, very thin. But when I go school, get strong.'

'I'll bet you were naughty too.'

'Yes, ride buffalo, boxing with Somchai, climb mango tree. One day go swimming, muddy pond. Take boat and fall in ... boat sink. Man come, say, "Where my boat?" He angry, we run, run.'

'Sounds a perfect childhood.'

'Finish too soon when Papa die.'

There was a brief silence while Ben turned everything over in his mind; the near destitution of a family, Fon being sent away from home, a village child working in a distant adult world. He wanted to know more about it.

'You were only a child when you were in Bangkok. Did they really make you work?'

'Yes, all the time. Big, big Chinese family, big, big house. Grandmother, grandbrother, uncles, aunts, children. Many, many servants to clean house, cook, go market, take care baby, wash clothes,' she said with a wan smile.

'But lots of servants means less work?'

'No, too much work ... they angry if they see me not working. Wake five o'clock, work all day ... last to bed, eleven at night. Always last to eat.'

'Unbelievable. And no day off?'

'No holiday, no problem ... but have to look down, be nobody, be nothing. Small boy throw food in my face ... cannot angry, have to smile.'

'That's disgusting. Why didn't you leave?'

'Work always like that ... cannot leave. I lucky, have food, help Mama.'

'But that's no life for a kid, living with people who don't value you.'

'Not so bad. I work good and big boss give me more money. And did it kill me? No, it make me strong.'

As they sat talking in front of the house, a little girl of three or four came and squatted on the ground in front of them. She had a tiny face with clear, steady eyes that focused not on Ben but on Fon. She gazed and gazed, listening to the strange language, adoring the stylish lady returned home from afar.

'I think she like me,' said Fon, smiling back.

'She certainly does. I'm sure you were exactly the same only a few years ago and just as pretty. She must wonder about the world outside the village.'

'Yes, same me long ago. But many things happen to me since I leave home ... go Bangkok, work massage, meet *farang*. Before, not see *farang* ... never. We scared! And when we naughty Mama say *farang* eat us.'

'But they didn't, did they ... though this *farang* wouldn't mind a nibble.'

'Okay, Ben, you like?'

Hitching up her sarong, Fon flashed him a radiant smile and an extra inch or three of bare thigh.

Fon's recollection of an idyllic Asian childhood reminded Ben of the destructive wars that had swept through the region at the time. Ever since university, he had wanted to visit Thailand because his final year dissertation had been about the intractable problem of Cambodian refugees held in camps at the Thai border. After all that book learning, it was now tantalising to be so near to Cambodia, Laos and Vietnam where the Indochinese wars had raged for so many decades.

He guessed that the road in front of the house where he was now sitting had been built with American money as a strategic route for getting troops to the Cambodian border. Or it had perhaps been a small part of the lavish foreign aid given to prevent Thailand falling to communism. A car speeding along that road had killed Fon's father.

Then his thoughts turned to the more recent events that had devastated Cambodia so close by, a tragic history that he had immersed himself in when writing the dissertation. In the seventies the Khmer Rouge had seized power and in an obscene social experiment caused the deaths of a third of the population, spreading instability and displacing floods of refugees into neighbouring Thailand. Even after the Vietnamese invaded Cambodia, there had been fighting and civil disorder until so very recently. He asked Fon what she remembered of the conflict.

'Hear bombs in Cambodia, old house shaking. Sometimes people come Thailand to be safe ... Khmer Rouge follow with guns. We hear police car go by, wee-wa, wee-wa, wee-wa ... hide under table, afraid we die. Many bad dreams ... never know who kill us. Then one day Papa cross road to farm. Big car come too fast … all finish.'

That evening Fon's mother quietly produced a big meal from the things they had bought in the market early that morning. They all sat round on the floor, taking the sticky rice in their fingers and dipping it in the sauces. There was pork rib in a salty sauce, tiny fish caught in nearby ponds fried to a crisp and eaten whole and a green soup with a fungus which had a distinctive earthy flavour. When Ben dipped his rice into a bowl of soup which was thick and dark, almost black, he noticed Fon looking at him intently.

'You like?' she asked, smiling broadly.

Ben tasted it.

'Why? What is it?'

'*Rok kwai.*'

'Whatever's that?'

'*Kwai* means buffalo … *rok* I not know in English. When buffalo born, *rok* come out, understand?'

Ben was afraid he understood all too well and the dictionary confirmed his fears. This was buffalo placenta soup.

'Fon, how could you?!'

'Buffalo eat it, so must be good,' she said with a wicked grin.

Fon's mother said very little as they ate but clearly enjoyed seeing her daughters and their exotic friend enjoying her cooking. During the meal a couple of women came into the house and casually sampled the dishes before drifting off again. Six half-grown ducklings wandered in and as Jinda shooed them out, like cartoon characters they ran on the spot on the slippery floor without moving, before shooting out of the door. Then when everyone was full to bursting, Fon and Jinda cleared up, rinsing the dishes outside the back of the house.

Jinda went off to see a friend and Ben was left alone in the house with Fon who at last raised the subject he had been waiting for, the sleeping plans for the night.

'Cannot sleep here tonight,' she said. 'Too many people, too many cats. Mama not let me clean house, boxing little bit, so better we go Nang Rong, stay hotel.'

'We?' he asked in surprise.

'Yes, you and me.'

Ben's pulse raced, he could hardly believe it. Him, her, a hotel room … tonight? In his dreams! He wanted to ask more but he did not dare; he would just have to contain himself and wait.

They collected their things together, Fon her bag and Ben his rucksack and went out to the road to wait for a bus back to the town. They could see down the road for at least a mile and so had several minutes warning that it was coming.

Then without explanation Fon took Ben's hand and led him fifty yards along the road where she stopped and pointed to a spot near the verge.

'This is where Papa die,' she said.

Ben stared at a mark on the tarmac, a dark stain almost like a pool of blood, blood spilled a decade ago. He shuddered at the thought of a violent death right here, so very close to home. Surely that could not be her father's blood.

They went silently back to where they had been waiting. Fon squatted down on her haunches while Ben stood and stared down the road for the bus. After some time he thought he saw one coming.

'Is that it?' he asked.

Fon got up and looked.

'Bus come,' she said, giving Ben her bag and running back to the house.

'Where are you going?' he called after her.

'To get Jinda,' she shouted as she ran.

Ben's heart sank.

'So Jinda's coming to the hotel too?' he asked when she rejoined him at the roadside.

'Of course Jinda's coming. Go hotel together.' She paused for a moment and eyed him with a quizzical look.

'Ben? Ben? What you thinking?' Seeing Ben's embarrassment, she shrieked with laughter. 'What you think I am? Bar lady, Pattaya?'

The hotel in Nang Rong had a smart air-conditioned lobby but the fan rooms they checked into were very basic. Fon and Jinda shared a room, with Ben in the next one along. After the overnight journey they were all ready to sleep early. Ben's double bed felt very empty but he slept well until he was woken all too soon by a loud knocking. He stuck a bleary face round the door; it was Fon looking infuriatingly fresh and breezy.

'Morning, lazy *farang*, we go breakfast.' It was almost light.

'Christ, what time is it?'

'You not hungry?'

'No, it's sleep I need.'

'*Kee-kyet!* Ben, you so lazy.'

Ben dressed quickly and joined Fon and Jinda in their room where, with lip gloss and eyebrow pencil and much jollification, they were putting the finishing touches before facing the early morning world of Nang Rong. Even this, so early in the morning, was *sanuk*, irrepressible fun.

The three of them wandered out into the drab streets of the town and found a market with food stalls on its fringes. They sat down on tin stools by one of the stalls, an old motorcycle and sidecar loaded with food and cooking utensils.

'What you eat for breakfast, Ben?' asked Fon.

'Muesli and tea.'

'What's moosly?

'It's a sort of rabbit food.'

'Not have rabbit food, Ben. You like egg? *Farang* eat egg for breakfast.'

Bowls of noodles were quickly produced for Jinda and Fon, followed by Ben's tea in a glass with a spoon sticking out, tea of a dark earthy colour with a pale yellow pool of something nasty at the bottom. It turned out to be condensed milk and was disgustingly sweet. His eggs came in a mug, two eggs broken in together and hardly cooked, the whites still runny and transparent.

'*Nagliat!* How you eat that?' said Fon.

'Not exactly the Hilton, is it,' he grimaced.

After barely surviving his breakfast, Ben went back with them to the hotel. He had kept quiet but now he just had to ask what they were going to do that day.

'We go village, then Phnom Rung. You like temple?'

'Yes, that most of all. I've never seen a Khmer temple before.'

They walked through the town to the bus station where they sat down opposite their bus, a large open pick-up with a steel canopy over the back, and waited. After about half an hour Fon decided it was time to board. The bus started up and went about two hundred yards but stopped again while more people got on with their goods and animals. Ten hot minutes later it finally moved off, Ben sitting next to Fon, sweltering in the confined space. Opposite him was a fat boy in a padded jacket zipped up to the neck, a farmer with a chicken on his lap and a gaggle of old women.

Only in the West, Ben thought, do you sit on a bus sullenly avoiding eye contact. If you are Thai village folk who have just been into town to market and are packed into a bus together, of course you talk. And if there is a pretty girl in stylish jeans and colourful top next to her foreign boyfriend, you want to find out everything about them. He was aware that all eyes were on the two of them.

Tongues soon loosened and Fon found herself engaged in good-natured chit-chat. One old woman was talking nineteen to the dozen, causing much amusement.

'What's she saying?' asked Ben.

'She ask we come from where and if we married already. Then she ask we going to get married … so I say no, not want *farang*. And old woman, she say, "If you not want the *farang*, can I have him?" What you think Ben? You like?' chuckled Fon.

'Yes, very funny,' Ben replied. 'But Fon, if they know we're not married, what do they think? It's obvious we're together.'

'Thai girl with *farang* sell sex. That's what they think.'

On getting back to the house, Jinda and Fon went into a huddle with their mother in the kitchen. Things sounded tense but after a time Fon came over to where Ben was sitting.

'Talk with Mama. Brother Somchai not send money. Say he send thousand baht ... it not come. But no problem, today holiday so we go Phnom Rung. Mama come too.'

'What time are we going?'

'When we ready,' said Fon.

It was not exactly a village outing, but a pick-up had been taken for the trip and the neighbours were invited to pile in. Ben's hopes of getting to the temple in the cool of the morning were frustrated as they began an indefinite wait for anyone who wanted to join them. At last, late in the morning they climbed aboard and the pick-up pulled out onto the road and slowly gathered speed, bouncing on its hard springs. Ben found himself sitting at the back next to Fon and opposite some middle-aged ladies who had come for the day out.

The hot air rushed through the open body of the pick-up, bringing with it all the smells and sensation of rural Asia. For mile after mile the rice fields passed by on either side, the green of the trees contrasting with the muted browns of the ripening rice. In some of the fields that had not yet been harvested, Ben could see the workers swathed in clothes moving slowly forward cutting at the ocean of rice a handful at a time.

Several times he saw rice being threshed manually, the workers beating the rice stalks to dislodge the grains, raising clouds of dust. Once there was a mechanical thresher powered by a shiny blue Ford tractor doing the work of many hands. Its arrival was clearly an event, watched by crowds of onlookers, relieved of an unpleasant job but perhaps aware that mechanisation brings change.

As they neared the temple there was a downpour of rain and the rich smell of hot earth flooded the pick-up. Everyone moved forward into the lee of the cab to avoid the spray that was coming through the front and open sides. Sitting at the back, Ben enjoyed the closeness of the wet road rushing past beneath him, the water flying up from the wheels and leaving a foamy wake on the dark tarmac. Then it was dry and hot again and the vehicle began to climb, its engine labouring. He looked back at the road, a black ribbon falling away across the plains behind them, through limitless rice fields to the furthest horizon.

Ben had been reading that the temple of Phnom Rung was once part of the Khmer empire which for many centuries had controlled much of northeastern Thailand from its centre, the great city and temple complex at Angkor Wat in Cambodia. Started in the tenth century, Phnom Rung was built in the crater of an extinct volcano, still dominating the landscape for miles around. Now its restored ruins made a good day out for both foreigners and Thais. Phnom Rung had become a major tourist attraction and its huge vehicle park was surrounded with stalls selling all that the sightseer could need, from souvenirs and trinkets to broad-brimmed hats.

Everybody got down from the pick-up and made for the shops. Ben found one selling the dried heads of tiny deer with bright red horns and what were claimed to be tiger teeth and the tusks of baby elephants. He had plenty of time to browse as the rest of the party seemed more engrossed in shopping than in going to the temple itself. Getting impatient, he urged Fon to make a move and leaving the others behind, they paid their entrance fee and climbed the rough laterite steps up to the temple.

The heat was pitiless as they walked the stone-paved avenue towards the sanctuary, but the beauty of the temple distracted from the discomfort as Ben came under the spell of its ancient red sandstone buildings. They were quite unlike anything he had seen in the West, free of the classical influence of the Mediterranean civilisations. Though cruder than Greek and Roman buildings, their effect was robust and dramatic, the last imprint of a vast civilisation and empire that had retreated south and decayed many centuries earlier.

They climbed a series of stairways and crossed the 'naga bridges', paved causeways decorated with the heads of stylised serpents. They were now traversing the symbolic abyss between earth and heaven and were approaching Mount Meru, the heavenly palace of the gods. The way led to the main sanctuary, a tower of immense stone blocks, the upper part covered in elaborate carvings and surrounded on each side by entrance halls and antechambers, their roofs and gable-ends a mass of mythical figures and symbolic motifs.

On the lintel over the main entrance were intricate carvings of Hindu deities to whom the temple was first dedicated before Buddhism pervaded the region. According to Ben's leaflet which he stopped to read in a shady spot, the lintel depicted Vishnu, a lotus growing from his navel, reclining asleep on the milky sea of eternity. It was an enchanting place and for Ben a small miracle that he was here with Fon, briefly able to share with her the ancient culture that was her heritage.

From the highest point of the temple grounds they could just make out the blue backbone of the Dongrek mountains across the border in Cambodia. Puffy thunder clouds towered in the deepest of blue skies and far to the east a rainstorm blotted out a stretch of forest in a veil of white. It was a rich landscape of jungle and cultivation merging from green into blue and overlaid with irregular dark patches, the shadows of passing clouds. Ben and Fon were moved to silence, awed by the setting, as once had been the people of earlier times who sensed the holiness of the place and chose to build their temples there.

Fon seemed unusually quiet until she turned to Ben and said she was very thirsty. As he had left his water bottle in the pick-up, they wandered back the way they had come and stopped to buy a cold drink from a boy carrying an ice box. Resting in the shade of a tree, Ben noticed a winding path running into the undergrowth which led to some wreckage, possibly a plane in military camouflage, a few hundred yards away. He decided to take a look. It was an army helicopter, the fuselage split wide open. He could not recognise the type, but noticed manufacturers' writing in Russian and 'Do Not Step' signs in English. As the cause of the crash was a mystery, he urged Fon to ask the boy if he knew anything about it. The story was simple. 'Helicopter have monks inside, fly over the temple and go higher than the Buddha. So helicopter fall down, have accident.'

Back at the car park, Fon and Ben met up with the others, some of whom had not even left the shopping area, preferring not to climb to the temple in the heat. The next move was to sit down and eat at one of the many open-air eating places. Everyone was laughing and joking, a day out for the ladies being a rare and special event, all instigated by Ben's visit to Fon's home.

After the meal the pick-up took them back to the village. As it was going on to Nang Rong, Fon, Jinda and Ben stayed aboard and went back to the hotel, arriving there in the early evening. Jinda wanted to stay in the room, but Fon was full of energy and was determined to take Ben to sing karaoke. Only a short walk across the street, the karaoke bar was clean and modern but very dark. One of the many hostesses directed them to a table and took orders for drinks. A girl at another table was singing a Thai pop song, the video with the lyrics showing a half-naked model seductively rolling around on a beach. Ben's eyes almost popped out of his head but Fon did not even seem to notice.

Fon was keen to sing and asked for the list of song titles when the drinks arrived. She wrote down her requests and two tracks later, the microphone was brought to her as her first choice came on the screen. Holding the cordless microphone horizontally in front of her face and looking intently at the video screen, she sang with pleasure and absorption. Ben could now stare at her profile, listening to the disembodied voice coming from the speakers, hardly believing it could be hers. The style of the song was high-pitched and unfamiliar to him, but Fon was clearly an accomplished singer and everyone in the bar clapped when she finished.

As they were leaving the karaoke bar something crossed Ben's mind.

'Fon, there's far more hostesses in here than they need to serve drinks. I don't get it.'

'Why you not understand? What you think, Ben?'

'That's what I'm asking.'

'Man sit with lady, sing karaoke, pay bar, go hotel together.'

'What! Even in a small town like this? They use our hotel for sex?'

'Maybe they do.'

'God, so people seeing you with me think you're one of them?'

'Yes. No good for me,' she said solemnly.

That night alone in his double bed, the room took on a new meaning for Ben. It was just a cheap knocking shop across the road from the karaoke bar. What struck him most forcibly was that the sex industry inevitably stigmatised Thai women who like Fon, knew how to behave. Just by being seen with a foreigner, she would inevitably be taken for a whore.

25

Other than the shenanigans with Fon at the hotel later that night, the trip to the waterfall was the most memorable event of Ben's last full day in the North East. As it was very hot, Fon had arranged for a pick-up to take the three of them to a waterfall to eat, swim and cool down. Jinda had the only swimming costume, so Fon took with her the length of green cloth she used as a sarong just in case she could not resist going in.

There was confusion when the driver was unsure of the route and they found themselves bumping down remote tracks, asking village people where the best place for swimming was. When eventually they arrived at a waterfall that seemed to satisfy the two sisters, they piled out of the pickup.

It was a weekday and the food and nick-nack stalls were almost totally deserted. Though still only mid-morning, Fon and Jinda went over to one of the food stalls and spent ages talking intently with the woman in charge. They then all walked on down the track and came to the river above the falls. The waterfall itself was not much more than a series of rapids but had formed a pool deep enough to swim in. It was unspoiled and intimate and they had it entirely to themselves.

Ben hardly managed to keep up with the girls as they scrambled across the rocks towards the pool. He watched them nimbly crossing a tree trunk over a drop to the shingle beach below and followed with some trepidation, trying not to look down.

On seeing the water, Fon was now determined to swim and ordered Ben to turn the other way while she changed under the trees. When he was allowed to look round, he gazed in adoration as she stood there, her eyes shining at him, gift wrapped in his all-time favourite, a sarong. Both for aesthetics and accessibility he could think of nothing more seductive than a sarong, loosely tucked in above the bust and likely to fall off at any moment. The fantasy was even more distracting as there was no pantyline visible through the tight fabric; he had no idea what if anything she was wearing underneath.

Without wasting time, the two girls plunged into the water and started splashing around, shrieking like kids. Already in swimming shorts, Ben slipped off his tee shirt and went in after them. Fon was in flirtatious mood but was keeping her distance, playing with Jinda, while Ben shamelessly showed off his crawl and jumped from the rocks into the pool. He longed for a watery wrestle but as always it was one long waiting game.

As he floated lazily on his back, he saw a boy coming down the path towards them carrying a basket.

'Who's this?' he asked Fon.

'Bring food.'

'Is it for us?'

'Special fish for you, Ben,' she said.

And for Ben it was the best, not just the food but everything that went with it; the tropical heat, the sounds of the river and jungle and most of all because he was with Fon.

The boy laid out the dishes on the rocks next to the water, the dappled light falling through the trees, a feast of freshly cooked food produced as if from nowhere. Squatting next to Ben, Fon ate hungrily, her knees held tightly together by the sarong, which against all odds stayed wrapped around her. He was captivated, her body golden and glistening, the wet cloth clinging to every contour.

When they had finished eating, they sat under the trees for a time before Jinda went back in the water, followed closely by Fon. Ben did not want to go in again so soon as his shorts were now dry and because of the half hour rule about not swimming after a big meal. But Fon had other ideas and called to him from the pool.

'Ben, why you not swim? Come swim with me, Ben.'

'Not yet, I'm too full,' he shouted back.

Fon said nothing in reply but standing in the middle of the pool, the water up to her waist, she turned away towards the waterfall and very deliberately untucked her sarong. Looking back at Ben over one shoulder and with the sarong in both hands, like a cormorant drying its wings, she stretched it out at arms length behind her back, revealing her body to the rocks across the pool. Screened as she was by the sarong, Ben had no idea if she was decent in strapless bra and pants or totally naked.

'Ben, swim with me … swim with me now,' came her siren call.

Ben needed no further bidding. He bounded across the rocks and within seconds was swimming towards her as she hastily refastened the sarong and plunged further into the pool. There then followed an energetic chase punctuated with squeals when he learned how difficult it is to keep hold of a determined and slippery woman in deep water. When Fon finally escaped him and hid behind her sister, his blood was up, his hopes very much aroused.

On the way home in the back of the pick-up, Jinda was tired and lay on her back full length on the seat. Sitting behind Ben on the other seat, Fon settled snugly against him without a word and rested her head on his lap. She was at risk of rolling off the narrow seat and the sun was falling across her face so he tried to make her comfortable, supporting her with his arm and shielding her eyes with his towel. It was an intimate moment as if between old friends and he was now longing for more.

When they got back to the village, wind-blown and weary, Fon went to make a telephone call before talking at length with Jinda and their mother.

'That all sounded a bit serious,' said Ben when they had finished.

'Jinda go back Koh Samet,' said Fon without explanation.

'When? What for?'

'Now, tonight,' she said.

Ben never learned why Jinda had to leave so soon, but that was not his first concern. More important, he and Fon were to be left alone together. Maybe now, at last, he was in with a chance.

'So what are we going to do tonight?' he asked her.

'Stay hotel. Jinda go bus Rayong,' said Fon.

'One room or two?' screamed Ben silently, his mouth tightly shut.

Early that evening, Jinda said goodbye to her mother and they waited beside the road for the bus into town. Back at the hotel, Ben sat with the sisters in their room while Jinda started packing her bag. He tried asking Fon what bus Jinda was going to catch but he did not get a clear answer. They then went to the market and ate at a noodle stall in the street before returning to the hotel.

Time drifted on and Jinda went into the washroom to take a shower, leaving Ben and Fon together, listening to the noise of sluicing water. Utterly frustrated by the long stand-off, it was now at last time for him to make his move. Quietly he sidled up behind Fon, slipped his arms round her neat little waist and held her tightly to him. There was a sharp intake of breath.

'No Ben, not here,' she protested in a low voice, pulling away and motioning frantically that Jinda could hear them. He reluctantly let her go but felt cheated when, flashing a grin, she threw herself full-length across the bed, her legs spread wide apart. Unable to resist the tightly rounded back pockets of her jeans, he gave chase, leaping onto the bed and pinning her down with all his weight. Astonished she was so strong as she struggled to escape, he was enjoying a sensuous wrestle when the sounds of showering suddenly stopped.

'Ben, Jinda finish already … can hear us,' hissed Fon breathlessly, rolling out from under him just in time.

When Jinda came out of the shower, she glanced round with amusement at the flushed faces and bright eyes; it was obvious what had been going on. For Ben it had been a tantalising little taster, but it was all over far too quickly.

As Jinda was dressing and doing her make-up, he had a moment of panic; Fon was stuffing her clothes into her bag.

'Whatever are you doing?' he asked her.

'Doing my bag,' she said.

'You're not going too?'

'No … put bag in your room. When Jinda go, one room enough.'

Once again trumpets sounded in Ben's head. With Jinda gone, could this be it, sharing a room with Fon? He made sure his tongue wasn't hanging out and tried to keep calm.

When Fon had left her things on his bed, the two girls paid for their room and they all sauntered out into the street. A short way towards the bus station they parted, Jinda giving them a little wave as if polishing a plate glass window. As she disappeared in the direction of the bus depot, Fon turned and strode purposefully across the road towards an internet shop.

'Go internet,' she said, as she opened the door and went inside.

'Whatever for?' asked Ben in surprise.

'Video games,' she replied, sitting down at one of the few computers not surrounded by a huddle of small boys.

Ben liked the thought of air conditioning but not of video games. To his dismay, Fon was an addict and sat and played happily for ages. Eventually she began to lose interest.

'We go sing-a-song. You like?' she asked him.

'Go where?'

'Sing-a-song,' she said. It could not be karaoke as they had done that already, so Ben guessed it must be some kind of nightclub. It would be fun to see a local club, though he did not want to be out late that night as he had other things on his mind.

They left the internet shop and went outside onto the dark streets of the town. Around the corner some old men in baggy shorts were huddled half asleep on the cramped back seat of their *samlors*, old-fashioned tricycles one evolutionary step up from the rickshaw. Fon and Ben climbed into one of them and they slowly moved off, sinewy brown legs laboriously turning the pedals. Down the next street they gathered speed and soon reached the other side of town where they were dropped in an unpaved car park outside a low building. Loud music was coming from a shabby looking nightclub decorated with strings of twinkling white light bulbs.

A hostess led them into the dimly lit club, half bar, half auditorium, capable of seating perhaps a hundred people. It was almost empty except for a few customers sitting at tables and tarty-looking hostesses hovering in corners. Three girls on stage were making love to a microphone, singing loudly to the empty room.

'God, they look awful,' said Ben as he sat down and ordered

drinks.

'You no like? Not sexy?'

'No, I do not like … they're gross.'

The singers were young and fleshy, their faces powdered to an artificial pallor. They wore short frilly skirts in reds and purples and cream tights which Ben thought deprived their legs of any allure.

When some men wandered in, he noticed that one of them came down from the stage and sat chatting at their table. Then he realised that the only women in the place were singers or hostesses.

'Fon, what is this place?' he asked her abruptly.

'Sing-a-song.'

'Yes, I know it's sing-a-song. They sell beer and sing … but what else?'

'What you think?'

'You mean they sell sex?'

'Go together, hotel,' said Fon looking down at her feet.

'Christ almighty. Do Thai men all do this?'

'Don't you, Ben?' she said with half a smile.

'Fon, please! No I do not.'

'Never?' she probed playfully. 'Never have sex?'

'With someone I love who feels the same for me, yes of course. But taking a woman for money … not in a million years.'

It was getting late when they headed back to the hotel, squeezed cosily into the back of the *samlor*, Ben with his arm around Fon. Passing the hotel reception desk, he now understood how she must feel about the knowing look the girls gave them as they went to his room. Following her inside and closing the door behind them, he tried not to feel too triumphal.

But once in the room, Ben thought Fon seemed tired and subdued. She did not immediately fall into his arms but rummaged distractedly in her bag, then went into the washroom to brush her teeth, as if playing for time. When she came out again, she said nothing and went and sat on the bed as far as possible from him, her eyes down. Before he could say anything, she looked up, her face severe and unsmiling.

'Okay Ben, I go now,' she said. 'Go back Mama's house.'

Ben was devastated.

'Why Fon? But what about me?' he blurted out in dismay.

'You stay here … hotel better.'

'No Fon, please! I'm not going to be left on my own …'

'Small town … everyone see me here,' she cut in. 'Men come hotel, bring girl … but not same me. Cannot stay room with you!'

Ben's jaw fell open but no words came. Distressed and angry, he did not know whether to plead or cajole. But her claim to respectability was unanswerable and he quickly realised that trying to make her change her mind would be futile and unfair. He watched aghast and could do nothing to stop her when she got up, strode to the door and made a quick getaway.

As the door slammed behind her, he sat down on the bed in a state of shock. Within seconds his great expectations had turned to total farce. But now Fon had gone and all he could do was to lick his wounds and try to sleep.

In the shower he began to ask himself what he was doing here anyway, alone in a small town miles from anywhere stuck in this grotty hotel. The place made his flesh creep, it was so seedy. The washroom door refused to shut as it was rotten, a leaking pipe had made the wall mouldy and everything smelt damp and disgusting. Coming out of the shower again he banged his head on the low concrete lintel, but that was not what hurt most of all.

Sleep proved impossible and he lay face down on the greying bed sheet before trying to read in the feeble light of the bedside lamp. After he had been reading for some time, half falling asleep, he was startled by a loud banging on the door. Now wide awake, he jumped off the bed and threw the door open. To his astonishment, Fon pushed past him into the room, her face dark and furious as he had never seen it before.

'Thought you were going to your mum's,' said Ben coldly.

'Wait long time … no have bus,' she replied, refusing to look at him.

'So what d'you want now?'

'Take shower. Then go stay with friend,' she said brusquely.

'What friend? Girl or a boy?' he demanded.

Fon flashed him a furious glance.

'Girl … but why you want to know?'

Softening a little, Ben then tried to take her in his arms but she thrust him away.

'You *farang* … same animal!' she shouted indignantly.

'No, Fon, that's not fair … it's not like that at all.'

'You not touch me then,' she said, grabbing a towel and retreating into the shower.

He tried to talk to her over the top of the partition wall but there was no answer, only the sound of cascading water. After an age she came out again, the towel wrapped round her and silently defied him not to look while she dressed. She seemed seriously fired up about something so he sensed he should back off and let her be for a bit. If he could manage to keep quiet, she might calm down.

But Ben's heart was too full for him to say nothing at all, so as she finished dressing he begged her not to be so cold and unfeeling. Then, when she spat back something he couldn't understand, his anger and hurt began to spill over. He did not mean it aggressively when he took her wrist and pulled her towards him, but she resisted him ferociously and broke his grip. Shouting something in Thai, she stormed out of the room, loudly slamming the door behind her.

Too stunned to follow, Ben slumped onto the bed and put his head in his hands with a feeling of déjà vu and despair. Girlfriends could be challenging, but this time it was all totally beyond him. Thoroughly drained, he was not too sorry things must finally be over for the night, perhaps even forever. When he found himself staring at Fon's bag, tossed into the corner of the room, he began to feel a little more in control. At least she would have to come back for it the next day.

His eyes were far too tired to read any more, so he switched off the light and tried to sleep. But the night was long and wakeful, his head churning with all that had happened. Fon's volatile behaviour was so totally incomprehensible; she had welcomed him to her home and they'd had a lot of fun together, but after being so warm and flirtatious, she'd suddenly dumped on him and pushed off to stay with a friend. Why had it gone so terribly wrong?

The next morning far too early a loud knocking woke him out of a deep and dreamless sleep. He fell out of bed in a daze and opened the door to find Fon standing there, smiling and unrepentant. She walked past him into the room without a moment's hesitation.

'Sleep good?' she asked him sweetly.

'No, like shit,' said Ben. 'And you? Where the hell did you go?'

'Sleep okay,' she replied. 'Go small hotel ... one hundred baht.'

'But you said you were going to a friend's place.'

'Not meet friend,' she said meekly.

As she sat beside him on the bed, her story slowly began to come out.

'After I go away first time, not look bus to Mama's house. Stay internet shop long time, play video game.'

'Whatever d'you do that for?' he asked, appalled.

'Cannot trust ... I not believe,' she said quietly.

'Fon, you can trust me, you really can,' he implored, almost tearful.

'But last night when I shower, you not understand, you angry me ... so cannot stay. Then I walk long time ... come back here very late, sit outside room, thinking strong. Maybe I knock door, stay with you ... but no, impossible, cannot.'

'Why ever not, Fon? Of course you could've come in,' said Ben, tantalised.

'Too dangerous ... maybe change my life,' she said almost inaudibly. 'So, what I do? Go find small hotel.'

'Fon that's terrible ... you locked outside and me longing for you to be with me.' The thought was unbearable.

As they sat side by side on the edge of the bed, Ben put his arms around her and hugged her. This time she did not push him away but looked up at him and smiled.

'Last night, cannot decide. Maybe I wrong ... maybe big mistake,' she said.

They moved closer together and Ben said nothing in reply.

Their final day together in the village slipped by easily with walks into the rice fields digging up crabs and with final visits to neighbours.

The last little intimacy came when Fon pulled out the family photographs to share with Ben. It was a battered and much-loved collection of faded photos of high days and holidays. One picture of Fon in her early teens with a group of village girls caught his eye.

'That's a pretty kid next to you. Who's she then?' The girl had an angelic face and unusually fair skin.

'My friend … same age me,' said Fon.

'So where did she end up?'

'She go Bangkok, work restaurant. Her Mama sell her when she fourteen.'

'Sell her?' said Ben, perplexed.

'Yes, they give Mama ten thousand baht. Girl, she have to turn back ten thousand baht working in Bangkok.'

'That's a hell of a lot to repay out of low wages, isn't it?' he asked.

'Too much,' said Fon quietly. 'So they make her sell sex.'

Ben could hardly believe what he was hearing.

'Christ, so young. She should've refused and gone home.'

'Cannot! She not yet turn back money … and no have money for bus.' Fon paused, her face dark. 'And if she make trouble, they beat her … then she end up dead!'

Ben looked at the optimistic face of the child gazing out of the photo, her arms around her friends' shoulders, unaware of what lay ahead. He was lost for words.

The photos put away, Fon sat on the floor talking with her mother, knowing they would not see each other again for many months. And for the last time Ben savoured the cheeping of baby ducks and chickens and the cacophony of cockerels, geese and pigs, as he petted the muzzle of the Brahman calf that had taken to him like a dog. They ate a final meal sitting round together on the floor and then the time came to take the overnight bus back to the island.

Parting was a muted affair, Fon's mother coming outside to see them off and standing around with infinite patience as they gathered their things and boarded the pick-up Fon had chartered into Buriram.

There were no hugs and kisses, no heartfelt goodbyes between mother and daughter. Fon and Ben just got into the cab of the pick-up, shut the door and rode away.

'Mama cry inside,' Fon explained, 'but no problem … not like I die. She think of me, wait me come back again, maybe six months, maybe one year. Always the same when you leave village … not see Mama Papa, long time.'

Ben sat squashed in the middle between Fon and the driver, his arm around Fon's shoulder because there was nowhere else to put it and because they both wanted it there. As the driver did not understand English, they could talk freely about their friendship from the very beginning. They talked of eating and dancing together on the beach and about all the things they had done together around the village. And for Ben, the slow bouncy ride back to Buriram became one of the best moments of the trip as Fon came close to expressing her feelings for him and to saying he was special.

There was a peaceful glow as they settled into their seats on the overnight bus, relaxed and happy again and confident of their growing friendship. They managed to sleep a little and the journey through the night passed quickly, but as the morning light appeared, they both came down to earth. In the cold light of day, where could it all go from here?

Ben knew that Fon would now return to her work and responsibilities, he to travelling on alone before flying home to the beginning of the rest of his life. Sitting so close to her, he was afraid his breath smelt bad and he felt too bleary to look her in the face. Staring fixedly out of the bus window, she too seemed to be hit with the same hopelessness. There was little they could say as the bus brought them back to reality, but at last Fon broke the silence.

'What you thinking, Ben?'

'Thinking about everything,' said Ben.

'About everything?'

'Yes … about you, Fon. About us.'

'Same me, Ben. Me and you … like beautiful dream. *Bpen pai mai dai*. Impossible.'

26

Once on the ferry and no longer confined together on the bus, Ben began to feel a little less dejected. Enjoying the beauty of the islands around Koh Samet and the chain of mountains in the haze towards Cambodia it was hard to be self-obsessed. He noticed too that Fon was regaining something of her usual sparkle. She was going back to her life on the island, to see Joy and all her friends and to the hard discipline of work and responsibility. For him, on holiday with the world at his feet, there was opportunity and choices but none of the certainty of routine and, for the moment, nothing except loneliness and drift.

They went and stood together on the bow in the cool of the breeze passing over the boat. The silence between them was interrupted by Fon's quiet voice.

'Ben, how long you stay Koh Samet?'

'Don't know.'

'Where you go next?'

'No idea,' he said miserably.

'Why not, Ben? You lucky, have holiday ... can enjoy.'

'It's not that easy, Fon. I don't know what to do with myself ... and you're a big part of the problem.'

'Problem? You have problem?'

The foredeck where they were standing was crowded with German tourists in expensive leisure gear, accompanied by their Thai tour guide. They were a boisterous group, enjoying the view as the boat ran along the island's coast with its necklace of white beaches. One of them, a big man in his forties was standing at the rail taking video shots and talking loudly with his friends. Ben's feeling that he was taking a fancy to Fon was confirmed when he stopped filming and came and spoke to her in heavily accented English.

'Which one Pineapple Beach?' he asked, smiling broadly.

'Ao Sapporot too far ... cannot see,' she said, pointing ahead.

'So you live on the island, uh?'

'Yes, Ao Sapporot ... Pineapple Beach. Same you?'

'We're booked into Montego Resort. Any good?'

'Yes, good ... and good you stay same place me!' said Fon, smiling her most dazzling smile. The man was captivated, Ben mortified.

'You like Thai massage?' she asked the man.

'Depends who with.'

'With me?' she purred.

'Ya, good! When can we start?' he said, rubbing his hands.

'Today, anytime. Make booking.'

'So who's this,' he asked her, indicating Ben. 'This your boyfriend?'

'This Ben ... my friend.'

Ben knew Fon was only trawling for work but her charm, so easy and endearing, was totally wasted on this anonymous jerk. He tried not to feel betrayed but with little success.

As Fon went on chatting, Ben found himself talking to the Germans' Thai tour guide.

'She your girlfriend?' the guide asked him.

'Yes,' said Ben.

'Are you married?'

'No,' said Ben.

'You going to get married?'

'No,' said Ben in a subdued voice.

Fon was now surrounded by a circle of admiring males, while the one with the video camera drifted across to where Ben was still standing at the bow.

'That your girl?' the man asked Ben.

'Yes,' said Ben assertively.

'Where you been?'

'To her village ... holiday with her family.'

The man looked impressed.

'Wouldn't mind one myself. It's so cheap here. Get a girl and settle down ... made for life!' He gave Ben a lascivious smirk.

The beach, the huts and bars on Ao Sapporot were all familiar to Ben but their novelty was almost gone. Though beach life was much the same as before, it was also very different because the friends with whom he had spent most of his time had now moved on. Maca and Chuck were gone and so of course was Emma; she was now somewhere in Cambodia, perhaps with a boyfriend from Chiang Mai.

Things with Fon were different too; something had changed. He now saw little of her; a glimpse in the distance perhaps as she walked along the beach with Gaeo or a smile in passing on the beach. But she was too busy to spend any time with him and it seemed impossible for them ever to be alone together.

It was a weekend in the high season and with the contacts she had made on the ferry, she was much in demand. The first evening back on the island she told Ben she had already managed five hours of massage. After the overnight journey she was exhausted but now had to cook and put Joy to bed. Ben understood her situation, but this made the adjustment no less difficult. Having been so close to her for that precious time together, here on the island he could hardly be with her at all.

The following morning, Ben sat on the beach near where Fon was working, hoping for a massage. Eventually he dared ask if he could be next, but his moment did not come until evening when the sun was falling and the mosquitoes were rampant. So he could talk to her face to face, he insisted on starting the massage lying on his back, though he had little idea what he was going to say.

'Fon, it's good being alone with you for a bit,' he began.

'Sorry, Ben ... no have time for you now.'

'No, of course not, no problem ... well, it is a problem, but anyway ...'

'Ben, you no have friends. Where you go now?'

'I just don't know, Fon.' It seemed a feeble answer.

'I thinking Ben ... about you and me. Mai *sanuk* ... too seeliat.'

'Too what?'

'Seeliat, seeliat.'

He watched her fingers pressing deep into his thigh.

'Oh yes, too serious. No, not fun ... not fun at all.'

'Ben, I think better you go.'

'Go? You mean leave Koh Samet?' He could hardly believe what he was hearing.

'Yes, go.'

'Where to?' he whispered.

'Anywhere. Not stay here.'

Though Ben knew she was right, her directness came as an awful shock; it was a bit like the trauma of Emma all over again. Alone with Fon and with the intimacy of the massage, he found it hard to suppress the quaver in his voice.

'Suppose I could join Maca and Chuck on Koh Chang,' he said despondently.

'You go tomorrow?'

'So soon? Well yes, okay, I'll get the boat tomorrow morning.'

The massive bulk of Koh Chang, elephant island, the second largest in Thailand, reared up out of the sea as the smoky little ferry boat drew closer. From his seat in the bow, Ben could make out the coconut and banana plantations which ran from the shore up into the jungle-clad mountains behind.

A row of pick-ups standing on the dark red laterite of the vehicle park, their drivers lounging around touting for fares, greeted the arriving travellers. The first ones quickly filled up with passengers and left and when Ben found himself about to be crammed inside the last to go, he decided instead to ride shotgun on the wide metal step at the back. The step was heaped with sacks of fresh fish and ice but he could just about find a foothold.

The overloaded pick-up moved off and began to career wildly along the narrow concrete road at the foot of the mountains. With the wind in his face and clinging on precariously, he began to feel that life was worth living again. New perspectives appeared around each corner. Plantations followed scrub and jungle, then a village and a Chinese temple, and to his right the sea and the distant hills of the mainland.

Soon the pick-up was beginning to climb, to struggle and slow, its exhaust farting and burbling beneath his feet. Grinding down through the gears, the driver swerved through the potholes and round steep hairpin bends, threatening to throw him under the wheels of the more powerful truck that snarled impatiently behind.

He stared up at the mountains as they climbed to where the narrow ribbon of road cut into the vertical side of the rock face. Then as the road reached its highest point, he caught his first glimpse along the island, a chain of bays, headlands and peaks softened by a gentle evening light that merged the colours together in a warm glow. All this and the rush of hot air, richly scented of earth and foliage, the tallest trees and densest jungle he had ever seen and the sweat and exertion of not quite falling off the back of the pick-up brought his usual optimism flooding back.

The pain of the last few days on Koh Samet was already beginning to subside and he was suffering fewer flashbacks to his parting with Fon. Saying goodbye had been a highly-charged moment, but there on the beach with the world watching, there could be no contact. Little was said as he boarded the boat except, 'I'll try to phone you Fon or fax maybe,' and, 'Fon, it's been great.'

The minibus he took to Koh Chang had been claustrophobic and packed full of tourists, including some unsavoury-looking European men, one of them pawing the Thai girl sitting next to him and swilling beer all the way. The journey seemed long and Ben had too much time to think about everything that had happened on the roller-coaster ride of the week that had just gone by.

Now as the pick-up began to wind down through the mountains towards White Sand Beach, he was feeling more positive. The excitement of moving on and the beauty of his surroundings were doing him good.

The island was a National Park and as tourism had arrived decades later than on many Thai islands, he was hoping Koh Chang would be pristine and unspoiled. But as the pick-up reached the bottom of the hill and cruised along through the coconut palms behind the beach, he was dismayed by the messy developments on either side of the road. There were huts and bungalows everywhere, mini-marts, noodle stalls, obtrusive signs, motorbikes for hire and all the disorder of Thailand in pursuit of the tourist dollar.

He stayed aboard to the far end of the beach and got down where he hoped Maca and Chuck were staying. Leaving his backpack in the thatched reception hut he went to have a look around and as he walked up the path he saw a familiar figure. Sure enough it was Maca.

'G'dye. How ya goin', Ben?'

'Hi, Maca ... thought I'd find you here.'

'Good on yuh, mate. Enjoy yourself with Fon then? Hot nights huh?'

Ben went back down to the reception desk and was lucky to get the last of the huts, two along from Maca and Chuck. On the low cliffs looking west out to sea, they stood on springy turf under coconut palms and were surrounded by hibiscus and bougainvillaea bushes in riotous flower.

He opened the door of the hut and looked around his new home. The walls were of woven bamboo matting nailed onto the wooden frame of the hut, the floor of black palm wood tilting crazily away to the left. At the back was the usual washroom with a squat loo, a tap and bin of water. The double mattress on the floor filled the room and there was no fan and not a stick of furniture.

It soon became obvious to Ben that he was not going to be lonely; Maca and Chuck gave him an immediate entrée into a busy social scene. After he had dumped his things beside the mattress, Maca took him to meet a group of friends sitting on mats in front of one of the huts, watching the sunset.

'This is me old mate Ben ... pommie bastard but a good'un,' Maca announced loudly.

'Hi, Ben ... Stewart Robertson. Welcome to Koh Chang.' Ben found his hand being crushed by a large and bespectacled Scot. 'How d'ye like a dram of Sang Som?'

'Thanks. Thai rum isn't it?'

'It's rum alright! You'll want to soften it with some Coke.'

A large bottle of cola brought his generous tot up to the brim of the glass.

'And this is Darren, another Pom ... seriously into wine and women,' said Maca, introducing him to a fit-looking boy-band sort of a guy.

'Wine, women and Sang Som,' quipped Darren in a strong regional accent, moving up so Ben could find space on the mat.

'And we call this one Dutch,' Maca went on. 'He's from Holland!'

'Hello Ben, I'm Gerrit ... you Brits can't pronounce it properly, so I'm "Dutch" to my friends.' In his early thirties, clean cut and confident, he thrust out his hand.

Then there was an Irish couple from Dublin, he a bright-eyed leprechaun, she petite and pretty, and finally a Norwegian couple in their final week before returning home to their jobs as teachers. With all these conspicuous pairings around him Ben felt a little solitary, but the Sang Som was having its effect and, when a spliff came round, his release from reality was complete. The sun was a red ball falling into the sea and Ben was in Eden, though like Adam he was alone. He drew heavily on the spliff and passed it on.

'It's good ganja, that. Enjoy, man,' said Chuck, taking it from him.

Ben lay back and listened to the traveller chat around him and gave in to the warm glow of the sunset, the alcohol and skunk. Making any effort at being sociable was now out of the question. He was floating along on a tide of delirium, the muscles in his cheeks involuntarily contracting into a foolish grin that fortunately was hidden by the gathering darkness.

He found himself talking to Stewart who was from somewhere in the industrial lowlands of Scotland.

'So, Ben, what d'ye do for a living when you're not travelling?'

'Just graduated ... running away from work really.'

'Keep running, mun.'

'How about yourself?'

'Steel-worker by trade ... welder and that. Done a bit of everything though, prison officer, security, taxi driver. But this is where it's at.'

'Got nothing to keep you at home then?'

'No. No kids ... just a divorce. Wasn't easy but there you go.'

'So why d'you like Thailand?'

'Well, Scotland for starters ... cold as a witch's tit. Who wouldn't leave?!'

'But why here?'

'Usual things. Food, scenery, prices ... not to mention the girls.'

'You go for them then?'

'Went crazy over a Thai girl once ... thun as a wuppet she was. Fragile like glass,' he said, enraptured. 'But I try to hold back ... when I first got here I was like a dog with two dicks.' He polished his glasses which were beginning to steam up.

'So how long are you here for?' asked Ben.

'Six months or until the money runs out.'

'Then back to work?'

'Don't mention work,' said Stewart. 'Shrinks me goolies to think of it.'

'My worry too ... I want to find something with real job satisfaction,' said Ben.

'Job satisfaction?' roared Stewart. 'Haven't a scooby doo what yer fuckin' talking about. Well ... maybe a beer taster in a Thai brothel!'

It was now almost dark and Dutch was getting hungry.

'Anyone coming down to Odin's?'

'What's Odin's?' asked Ben.

'Odin's Pleasure Dome,' said Dutch. 'It's the best place to eat on Koh Chang ... run by a ladyboy. Great food and Odin's something special.'

Ben stumbled off into the darkness to get his money from his hut. He was convinced he was still sober but there was something wrong with his legs which weren't responding properly to the usual commands. Unlocking his padlocked door proved impossible so he climbed in through the veranda window, to be faced with blackness of an intensity he had never before experienced. Somehow he found his wallet and fell out of the window giggling just as Darren was going past. The two of them walked down the grassy slope together and followed the others to the beach.

Odin's restaurant stood on the edge of the sand facing out to sea. The first thing Ben saw were the words "Odin's Pleasure Dome" and the stylised design of a Norse god boldly painted on the gable end. Curious as always, he went inside and had a quick look round while the others found a table on the terrace. Furnished with heavy varnished wood, there was a bar bedecked with bottles and to the rear some soft seating and shelves of used paperbacks.

As he was coming out again he was confronted by a tall, slim Thai waitress almost blocking his way. In slinky white trousers and blue tank top, she had a red scarf round her head in pirate-style and was liberally garnished with jewellery, bangles and beads. Ben thought her a little strange, though the real give-away was when she opened her mouth.

'Hello! Do I know you?' she said in a husky voice, batting dark eyelashes at him.

'No,' said Ben in alarm.

'So I haven't had the pleasure. Pity!' she said, stroking back a stray quiff of hair and shifting from one hip to the other. 'My name Odin. Welcome to my Pleasure Dome!'

Ben could not help liking the gentle eyes of this very feminine ladyboy.

'And I'm Ben,' he said, backing away a pace or two.

'You like to try my special fruit shake, Ben? Here, take this one,' said Odin, handing him a purple plastic mug with a head of frothy pinkness spilling down its sides. 'I make it for the cow with that beautiful man over there … but better she wait!'

Ben drew on the straw thirstily while Odin watched for his reaction.

'It's amazing. Whatever's in it?' he said.

'My secret! I knew it'd work fast on you.'

With Odin giving him the eye, Ben was now struggling for something to say.

'So why Odin?' he asked.

'Because that's my name of course … and because I'm the goddess of wisdom, poetry and war.' Ben was finding it hard to suppress a laugh. 'But tonight Ben, I give you special dish … not on the menu. Bring your table fie minute.'

'Whatever is it?' he asked.

'Baby octopus,' lisped Odin. 'Smell so bad ... but taste so lovely.'

Soon their table on the terrace was laden with water bottles and fruit shakes, with Chang beers standing in growing pools of condensation and with spirit lamps for sparkling eyes. Finding space for the food was going to be difficult, but anything was possible. Following his taster of baby octopus, Ben then became engrossed in one of his greatest ever sensual experiences, Odin's red curry.

When he managed to take breath, he asked Dutch what he knew about their host.

'Odin's educated I think ... and really quite shy,' said Dutch. 'Doesn't talk a lot about himself, but I guess he's from a well-to-do family and had to make a life for himself. The Thais tolerate ladyboys if they make them laugh, but they don't allow them much dignity. Coming out must be a big step.'

'I'd love to know more about him.'

'He closes down for the rainy season and goes off to Europe and America. As he likes Holland, we have lots to talk about.'

'So what about you?' Ben asked Dutch. 'Heard you speaking Thai just now.'

'I'm an English teacher ... freelance. Been in Bangkok six years.'

'And in that time you've learned Thai?'

'Yes. It's not an easy language because of the tones. Took me four or five years, but now I can make myself understood.'

'I like the idea of settling in Thailand too ... been thinking about it recently.'

'A girl, I suppose,' said Dutch knowingly.

'How did you guess?'

'It's not always the best of reasons, Ben. Things can change overnight and then you're in trouble.'

But it was not the moment for serious talk; the sky was laden with stars and Ben's belly with euphoria. When Dutch suggested they all go on to a bar further along the beach, he was not in a fit state to resist and readily succumbed to the temptation.

27

The bar Dutch wanted to go to was about ten minutes walk along White Sand Beach where the dry sand above the tide mark was at its widest. Everyone who had eaten at Odin's ambled along the beach to the encampment of mats and cushions spread out on the sand in front of the bar, where the *farang* tribes were comfortably reclining. Ben sat down on one of the mats with Maca and Chuck and his new friends and ordered a round of beers.

Curious to know more about Darren, he tried the usual opener.

'How long've you been travelling, Darren?'

'Six months this trip … about two to go.'

'And where've you been?'

'Thailand and Lao,' he said. 'But Ben, you don't look like no traveller.'

'Just finished uni … thinking about careers. So, what about your work?'

'Construction worker and that.'

'And do you like it?' asked Ben.

Darren looked at him as if he was mad.

'Yeah right! Work sucks!'

'Don't fancy a career then?'

'It'd do my head in. Look mate, me brother's getting educated … works all the time and never goes out. If he gets to be a college lecturer, he'll earn half what I do, so what's the point?' Darren lolled contentedly on his pile of cushions. 'It's just plain stoopid!'

'So where else have you been?' asked Ben, trying a safer line.

'Australia. Got a working visa … bars, fruit picking, that sort of stuff.'

'And where did you go in Australia?'

'Everywhere worth goin'. Like Byron Bay for the surfin' and Nimbin for the dope.'

'God's own country,' interjected Maca. 'Makes me homesick … well, almost!'

'So, Maca, where you from in Oz?' asked Darren.

'Cobram, Victoria … back of beyond. But good.'

'But if Australia's so good, why did you leave?' Ben was curious to know more about him.

'Don't have any roots there anymore.'

'Why not?'

'When I left school, did a course in electrical engineering, then went fruit picking on the Murray River. Hard work … but no sweat! Oranges the best … get skin allergies from peaches, strawberries break yer back and raspberries you get scratched. Winter go north to Queensland for tropical fruit … summer, vegetables in Tasmania. So that's how I started travelling.'

'How long on the road?'

'About eight years,' said Maca.

Ben was highly impressed.

'In Khao San, Chuck said you'd been travelling in Africa, Maca. Where did you go?' he asked.

'London to the Cape was the big one.' Maca drew on the spliff Chuck passed him and they all listened as he told the story in his unhurried way.

'Was working in London. Teamed up with four of me mates and we were given this 1985 Ford Sierra Estate. Could just about get in with all our stuff on the roof. Drove down Morocco through Marrakesh to Goulimine where the glass beads come from. Then along the beach in Mauritania through to Senegal and way inland to Mali. Bamako, Djenne, Mopti … those mud mosques blow you away. South to Ghana … loved the Ghanaians. Togo and Benin were the smallest … no Vegemite, but beaut' French wine and women with breasts like mangoes. Flogged on through Nigeria ... wild place that. Had big hassles crossing into Cameroon where we cooled off for a bit in Mamfé, Zaire in the middle of the punch-up with Kabila, then crossed Angola to Zimbabwe and on sealed roads all the way to Cape Town.'

'But that's impossible in an old Sierra,' said Dutch. 'You must've been mad.'

'It helped,' said Maca.

'But how d'you keep an overloaded heap going on dirt roads?'

'Roads? What roads? No mate, lots of the time we didn't keep going. Car was rusty ... Andy went through the floor in the middle of the Sahara. And we had to get things welded time and again. Suspension broke and was flailing around ... tied it up with wire until we could find a blacksmith. Radiator leaking ... stopped every few miles to fill it up, then the engine overheats and seizes up. Got second-hand engines twice ... about fifteen US dollars, bought and fitted. Then we found a wreck out in the desert with this beaut' radiator. Got it out, but it was too big, so we had to have the engine bay cut to fit it in. Then the engine was over-cooling as there was no thermostat. Steering hardly worked, tyres were worn out and we kept having flats. And a truck ran up the back of us in Ghana. Pain in the ass ... but in the end it came good.'

'Crazy,' said Ben.

'Fun,' said Maca.

'Getting visas and taking a car across borders can be tricky too,' said Dutch. 'And what about bribes?'

'Bribery bigtime. "*Donnez-moi cadeau*, gimme dashie" every inch of the way. And yeah, visas were hell. Big problems with car insurance and customs bonds too. But we got good at forging things ... amazing what you can do in a desert copy shop. Our visas for Nigeria went out of date as we were running late so we had to doctor'em. They were dead suspicious but we got away with it.'

'And you kept out of prison?'

'We came close!'

'Sounds like hell. So why do it?' said Ben.

'Why climb Everest? Because Africa's there too ... and because it's hard. You see a lot of stuff and learn about yourselves.'

'And you all stuck it to the bitter end?' asked Dutch.

'Yup, we all made it to the Cape.'

'That's an achievement! When the going got tough, any of you could've got going.'

'There were some tense moments ... but it was good when we got there.' Maca put his beer bottle to his lips and tipped it slowly back.

'Makes it hard to settle down again, I guess,' said Dutch.

'Sure does! So we did it again a year later in a better car, a Peugeot 504. But we hit political problems in Algeria ... had to sell the 504 and come home,' said Maca.

'Bet Asia seems easy in comparison.'

'Like paradise! Pass us that spliff, mate ... I'm talking too much.'

'So Maca, you're a hard-nosed achiever when it comes to travelling then,' said Ben.

'Cheers, mate! Well, some of the time anyway.' Maca gazed round at his friends with a foolish grin.

Ben was intrigued by this new perspective on serious travelling. Although most backpackers in Thailand were just taking an extended holiday, he wondered if Indo-China might be a bit more challenging.

'So what about Lao and Cambodia?' he asked. 'They've not been open to travellers long.'

'Yeah, Lao's real primitive,' said Darren. 'Me and a mate went up to Chiang Khong, crossed the Mekong to Lao and got a boat downriver to Luang Prabang.'

'What did you do in Luang Prabang then? Temples and stuff isn't it?'

'Yeah, 'fraid so. Beer Lao's good though. Spent our time in this bar ... cheapest piss-up ever. When our visas ran out, we still had four bottles of Lao whisky and a bag of stuff to finish. Couldn't take it with us so we blew it all overnight!'

'Right then Darren, so that was your cultural tour of Lao!' teased Stewart. 'But what beats me is how you drink and smoke so much as well as being a fitness fanatic. You like to trash yeself, mun ... running up and down the beach in the sun, doing press-ups like a demented lizard.'

'Gotta keep fit. The girlies like it ... and it helps with the folks. They think I'm too clean-living to take drugs.'

'But they must know you hit the bottle a wee bit.'

'They're not well-pleased. Me and me brother get rat-arsed at least once a week and Dad goes ballistic. Sometimes we go on a bender the whole weekend ... crawl back to work Tuesday or Wednesday.'

'You'll die young, mun,' said Stewart.

'Been lucky so far ... like the time Dad phoned me from work. I'm just waking up and can't figure out what he's talking about ... keeps asking me if I'm okay. Anyway I'd broken me nose and come in half comatose. Mum cleaned me up and in the morning I couldn't remember a thing. Friends said I was tanked up something wicked, and these blokes were battering my face against a telephone box. It was a good night, that one.'

'If that's what you like doing!' said Dutch.

'And Glastonbury's wild!' Darren went on. 'Last year, I got six hours sleep in five days. Was out of me head and lost a day ... completely lost it, dunno what happened to it. When I came round I was still dancing.'

'What were you on?'

'Anything. You can get the lot these days. Tried this heroin in Lao, but don't bother ... it's overrated rubbish.'

'Risky too.'

'Risky? So? Like at Glastonbury, there were these two blokes died from impurities in the "E"s. They put it over the loudspeaker to stop us taking any more but I'd already had three. Yeah, we were taking three at a time!'

'And you've never been nicked?'

'No. But me mate was about to be busted and he had eight on him, so he swallows the lot of 'em. Crazy it was!'

'And you feel okay on your alco-marathon?' asked Stewart.

'Well, it's better'n being bored. Hits you sometimes though ... after Glastonbury, didn't go back to work for a week and a half.'

'Better get wasted here then while you're not working, mun.'

'I do mate. Like the Full Moon Party on Koh Pha Ngan ... slept for days after that.'

'So how was the Full Moon Party?' Ben had read about it in the

Lonely Planet.

'The best. Great beach, booze and boogie. Moon comes up over the sea and you just dance. Pick your music at the different places ... cheesy stuff at the Cactus Club, house, trance, garage, techno, wherever. And there's thousands of party-people drinking and popping all night. When the sun comes up you keep dancing, then you go on to the Backyard in the evening. It never stops ... dance 'til you drop.' Darren fingered the silver medallion around his neck, remembering the good times. 'Yeah, I'm not ready to slow down yet ... gotta see the world first.'

'But do you really see anything travelling, Darren, or do you just pass through?' asked Dutch.

'Piss through, more like,' said Darren. 'Main thing's havin' a good time.'

'Isn't there more to life than just having a good time though?' persisted Dutch.

'Like what? Like I see my mates settling down? Got this friend aged twenty two ... his girlfriend's pregnant and she's dead lazy so she jumps at the chance to stop work. We're in the pub and he says he's getting married, but he couldn't look me in the eye 'cause he knows what I think about getting tied down ... mortgage, kids and stuff. I wasn't going to congratulate him for being so stupid.'

'And what about your family? People usually do what their parents did.'

'No way! Got so many brothers and sisters, I haven't even counted'em.'

'One day your girlfriend'll get pregnant,' said Dutch, 'and that'll be it.'

'Girlfriend? What girlfriend? Don't bother with that anymore.'

'Self-sufficient, are we then?' teased Stewart.

'Sod off, Stewpot! No, it's no big deal ... sex and that. Don't need a girlfriend. There's loads of girls here ... travellers, I mean, and it just kinda happens. You know ... sharing a room with a girl to save money. Then it's inevitable like.'

'Always?'

'Well, sometimes. But they're all up for it!'

'All of'em?'

'Well, the ones I like anyway … and some of the others too. There was this girl I met in a bar in Samui and she says to come to her hut, so I says okay. She goes back to wait for me, but I get chatting to this bloke and forgot … went on to another bar and kept drinking! Thank God she was leaving next day.'

'So where are you going when you move on from here, Darren?' asked Ben, picking idly at an insect that had flown too close to the oil lamp.

'We're so near, it's gotta be Cambodia. Get a bus from Trat to Hat Lek, cross the border and then there's a fast boat to Sinkynoonkville or whatever it's called.'

'Sihanoukville,' prompted Maca. 'Named after Prince Sihanouk.'

'Then to Phnom Penh … see the Killing Fields. And to Angkor Wat. There's this old temple … everyone goes.'

'Okay, Darren, do it and enjoy, but you've got to be careful in Cambodia,' said Dutch. 'Met a guy who was held up at gunpoint in Phnom Penh. And my guesthouse there was offering free laundry and free ganja, and there's bang lassi on the menu. It's a wild place.'

'What are we waiting for then? Let's go,' said Ben.

'Yes, but don't treat Cambodia as a rich kids' playground,' said Dutch.

'They're so poor and they've suffered a lot … everyone's got their own horror story if you talk to them. And I'm not sure we always deserve the amazing welcome we get.'

'So be good and watch your back, Darren,' said Maca, 'or you're dead meat, mate.' He lay back and looked at the stars.

Over the next two weeks, this was to be Ben's pattern of life; a sunset vigil at one of the huts and eating at Odin's, followed by travellers' tales at a bar along the beach, before collapsing half-dressed onto his mattress in the early hours and sleeping late into the heat of the next day. Though the nightlife was good, the daytimes were sometimes solitary and he could not always forget that he was alone.

After the trip to the North East with Fon, it was hard being apart, made much worse as it was so difficult to keep in contact with her. There were many problems with calling Gaeo's mobile and as Fon did not read English, he became obsessed with finding someone to write a postcard to her in Thai. At first he could not think who could do it for him, but then he had a brainwave. He immediately bought a postcard and envelope and walked to Odin's place. It was mid-afternoon and the Pleasure Dome was almost empty of customers. Odin, in a little white jacket, his long hair in bunches, Bavarian-style, was re-arranging the tables in the restaurant. When Ben anxiously asked him if he would write the postcard, his reply was enigmatic.

'I finish cooking ... fie minute,' he said and disappeared through the kitchen door.

After ten minutes he came back jacket-less, showing off a skimpy top and new hair ribbons. He sat down and looked Ben in the eye.

'So,' he demanded, 'you have Thai girlfriend?'

'Yes, she's called Fon and she's a stunner.'

'Oh Ben! Ben! Such a waste!' Odin smiled sadly up at him through long lashes.

With a Buona Vista Social Club CD thumping loudly from massive speakers behind them, Ben was now sitting opposite Odin at one of the tables, close enough to see the pink glitter on his cheeks. This was utterly surreal; he was about to share his most intimate feelings with a Thai guy done up as a German tart.

'Well, Odin, it's one of those things I ought to walk away from, but I can't. I'm sure you know what I mean.'

'Ben dear, I do, I do,' purred Odin, staring back unblinkingly. 'So you think you love her?'

'Of course I love her ... it's a really big thing for me.'

'Ooh yes ... I'm sure it's really big! But tell me this, Ben ... you think with your head or you think with your dick?'

Ben was flummoxed for a moment.

'Well ... more with my heart, I guess.'

'Mmm! Most unusual,' murmured Odin. 'Anyway, what you want

me to say to the lady?'

Ben now fervently wished he had jotted something down to work from.

'Right then ... what shall we put? It's not easy ... cross-cultural and all that,' he said.

'No Ben, you playing this game not me.' Odin wagged a long, bony finger at him.

'Well, let's start with the island. You know, something like, "Dear Fon, Koh Chang's so beautiful. All mountains, jungle, waterfalls, white sand. Miss you like crazy and wish you were here." You can jazz it up a bit if you like.'

Odin's biro snaked across the card in sinuous Thai script.

"Fon darling, this is the perfect place for lovers like me to do just what I please. There's sun, sea and shells and every passion here on Koh Chang."

'Yes,' said Odin, 'I think she like that.'

'Then,' said Ben, 'I want to tell her how I feel about her.'

'Okay, you tell me. How you feel?'

This was the critical moment. So that he could be heard above the music, Ben leaned closer across the table and declared his love to Odin. '"I want to tell you how much I love you and that I want you above all others."'

Odin silently said a thousand things with a scintilla of a shrug, then without a word glanced down and penned his interpretation in Thai.

"All I want now is to have sex with you. Other women no longer satisfy me and I need you most of all."

'So, so romantic!' said Odin. 'What next, Ben *tirak*?'

Ben was now getting into the swing of things.

'"Fon, I can't live without you and long to have you here with me right now."'

This time Odin did not start writing but sat bolt upright frowning

264

darkly.

'Problem, Ben, problem,' he said, brandishing his pen with a limp wrist.

'What problem?' asked Ben, slightly exasperated.

'You say too much. She Thai lady! So she turn you down ... want more money,' insisted Odin in piping tones.

'But it's got nothing to do with money,' said Ben appalled. 'I've just got to tell her how strong my feelings are.'

'No, Ben! You do that, you lose the game. Trust me, I know ... it happen to me.'

'Okay, you can put in the local subtleties then ... but you'd better get it right!' begged Ben.

Without a moment's hesitation Odin was again writing furiously.

"At first it was not true when I said I loved you. But now I miss you, and if you come and stay with me on Koh Chang, I'll love you all night."

'Very good,' said Odin. 'Now she really understand you ... *jing jing.*'

'Please God,' said Ben devoutly.

'So, Ben, how to finish it off? Something sweet, something original.'

Ben prayed for inspiration.

'What about this?' he began haltingly. '"Fon, I know you were alarmed when I told you I loved you, but I hope you don't mind ... I hope you don't mind, if I put down in words, how wonderful life is when you're in the world."'

'Good Ben, good. You think of that yourself?'

As Odin finished writing the card, Ben avoided his question.

'All done then?' he asked. 'Sure you've got it right, Odin?'

'Have ... hundred percent. Hope you get the lady, Ben. Ooh, I do hope so!'

'Yeah thanks ... but you realise I'm not just into shagging Thai girls. It really goes deeper than that.'

'Oh, yes, yes!' said Odin sweetly, 'I'm sure it goes very deep.' He rested his chin on his hands and gazed at Ben, the glitter twinkling on his cheeks.

'And please end it with, "All my love, Ben".'

'Can post it for you too, if you like,' added Odin.

'Oh wow, Odin, thanks … you're a real regular guy. You will post it soon?'

'Trust me Ben, you know you can trust me.'

28

Though Ben found enough to do on Koh Chang during the daytime, it was not always easy to be in a place of overwhelming beauty feeling unsettled when everyone around him seemed to be having the time of their lives. He had many good experiences; taking a hired motorcycle to the fishing village on stilts, climbing a rocky watercourse to the waterfalls and best of all swimming with the turtle.

But life had its limitations. As walking even short distances brought on a sweat, he spent his days between his hut, Odin's restaurant and the bars further along the beach, not a mile away. He thought that by now he should be getting more used to sodden fabric on clammy skin and to his underpants damply clinging to the interstices. But even allowing for the heat and the discomfort of cheap living, it was strange to feel low when the light was so brilliant and the surroundings spectacular. His problem was that he could not stop thinking about Fon.

It troubled him that she gave him so many conflicting signals and kept her cards so close to her chest. Although she played her hand with flair, he knew she had few strong cards, her only trump being her looks and personality. This she used to great effect, keeping her distance at times and at others offering him small tokens of affection. She kept him guessing and he had to be satisfied with a smile or a touch on the arm, flirtations that she lavished freely on her customers on the beach. While she dominated him with her consummate charm, he had little idea what emotional hold if any he had over her.

She often kept him waiting, though he was well aware that she too would have to wait for him; he would fly away soon and she could not follow. He knew a lot about her life and had been to her home, but it was far more difficult for her to size him up; he might be just another hedonist hoping for a casual fling. He knew she was vulnerable but still he wanted much more commitment from her.

His own obsession with Fon struck him as being very different to her cool detachment. He remembered how on Koh Samet he had trailed after her, while at times she seemed almost indifferent to him. Perhaps for a Thai woman, he conjectured, a relationship is more a practical matter than a surrender to natural passions; Fon always seemed to say that to fall in love was self-indulgent and dangerous. Whatever the explanation, Ben feared she did not have any strong feelings for him and all he could do was to wallow in painful introspection.

During the long hot days, his next nagging doubt was whether he was just crudely infatuated with an exceptionally lovely girl. He was wildly attracted to Fon, no question, but he tried to persuade himself that the seat of his obsession was not primarily below the belt. Though he knew he was caught between the head, the heart and a hard place, he was convinced his compulsion was liking and love more than lust. He liked Fon's strength and her dignified struggle for her family; his heart made decisions for him and governed his life; and his involuntary member firmly pointed the way ever onwards and upwards. Last, though not least, this was surely not the root cause of his emotional turmoil.

There was too much that Ben still did not understand about Fon and he knew that language was a part of the problem. In an idle moment, he pulled out the Thai language tapes he had bought in Sukhumvit Road, but he found it surprisingly difficult to learn from them. Sitting on his veranda with his Walkman, the tapes drove him mad. He was irrationally irritated by phrases such as, 'I am buying the dog,' and 'Excuse me, I think that is my hat'. Did he really need to know the word for desert or alligator when Thailand has neither deserts nor alligators?

Most difficult of all was the five tones used in Thai. The tape told him that the word '*glai*' can mean either near or far depending on its tone, while the word '*ma*' said with different tones and vowel lengths has seven different meanings. Although he thought he could distinguish the different tones on the tape and repeat them reasonably well, remembering the tone of all the vowels in every single word seemed utterly impossible.

Continuity on the tapes was provided by an exaggerated American voice and he winced as he listened.

For those who love the animal world, here are the Thai words for our animal friends:

Cat	*Miaow* 'That sounds right,' thought Ben.
Darg	*Ma*
Horse	*Ma* 'Surely *ma* was dog.'
Pig	*Moo* '*Moo* should be cow.'
Snake	*Ngoo*
Cow	*Mooer* 'Spot on!'
Elephant	*Chang* 'That's beer.'
Lion	*Singh toh* 'And that's beer too.'

Then came an impossible list of verbs.

To follow through all the way	*Talord*
To cover an entire area, accomplish thoroughly	*Tua teung*
To succeed in filling up a set, complete	*Krop*
To accomplish a temporary or indefinite task	*Set*
To finish a prescribed task with definite limits	*Jop*

Ben fast-forwarded the tape and dejectedly pressed the 'play' button again.

Listen and repeat the following adverbs:	
With pleasurable absorption	*Ploen*
With unbearable difficulty	*Yak*
Busily, with unpleasant absorption	*Yung*
Boringly	*Beua*

Ben was finding that learning Thai was unbearable, difficult, unpleasant and boring. Defeated, he switched off the tape, leaned back in his chair and stared out to sea. How else could he attack the language problem?

Then he thought of Odin. Surely Odin should be able to help, and perhaps also tell him some of the secrets of the Thai love affair. As it was late afternoon, this was not a bad time to go and find him.

When he got to the restaurant, Odin for once was not working but was lounging in a soft chair slowly stroking a white cat. As he approached, the cat leaped off Odin's lap and shot off into the kitchen.

'Eadie, you not like Ben? He very handsome,' simpered Odin to the departing cat. 'So Ben, you forget your lust for that girl yet?'

'I still love her if that's what you mean.'

'You not come because you care about me then?'

'No, sorry Odin, I need your help learning Thai.'

'Yes, and I know why! You men!' sighed Odin.

Ben ignored his sulk.

'For starters I want to be able to say basic stuff like hello, goodbye, yes, no, please and thank you. Then maybe verbs and tenses.'

'No, Ben, Thai language not have tenses.'

'But how can you get by without tenses?' asked Ben in surprise.

'We say "already" or "later", then we understand. No problem ninety percent.'

'Well, that makes life easier. So what about yes and no?'

'Words for yes and no, Thai language not have.'

'But you must have words for yes and no.'

'Not have. If I say, "Ben, do you love me?", you say "love". "Can you sleep with me, Ben?", you say "can".'

'Bizarre. And what about please?'

'Thai people not say please.'

'Then how do you ask for something politely?'

'By saying *krap*.'

'Crap? Polite? So what does crap mean?'

'In Thai language crab's *bpoo*,' said Odin.

'I know crap's poo, but I still don't get it,' said Ben, thoroughly confused.

'Ben, listen to Odin. Thank you's *korp khun*, so to say thank you politely you say *korp khun krap*.'

'Weird.'

'Men say *korp khun krap*, but lady say *korp khun ka*. Odin lady,' he said with a pout, 'so always say *korp khun ka*.'

Odin got up and put a new CD on the machine. The music had a catchy theme picked out by a moody bass guitar.

'What is it?' asked Ben.

'Air … Moon Safari. You like?'

'Very much,' said Ben.

'So seductive, my lovely,' whispered Odin, sitting down on the bench a little too close for comfort.

'And there was something else I wanted to ask you,' said Ben, trying not to be put off, 'something we talked about when you wrote the postcard. Do Thai women fall in love emotionally, same as Westerners? You know, like me … love-sick and all that.'

'Same same movies?'

'Well yes … I suppose.'

'Titanic, Moulin Rouge?'

'Wasn't exactly what I was thinking of.' He sensed Odin was sending him up.

'Ben sweetie, Titanic so sad … but oh Leonardo, why did you go with that fat slut Winslet?'

'You mean Leonardo De Caprio? Don't say you *like* him, Odin? He's just a sad teenage pin-up.'

'Oh Ben, I do, I do … even more than David.'

'David who?' Ben was even more puzzled.

'You know, Ben … David, the big butch statue in Florence, the one by Mike Angelo. David who took off his G-string and slew Goliath.'

'Oh, that David! Been relegated then, has he?'

'Yes … so now De Caprio's my number one!'

Mildly irritated, Ben shifted away along the bench.

'No, seriously Odin, what do you think about Thai women and love?'

'Ben, I tell you, Thai women all bitches. *Gohok, gohok!* Lies, all lies! Jerk your kite string till you're desperate, then bleed you dry, down to your last baht.'

'All of them?'

'All of them … except my mother.' Odin lovingly kissed his palm and touched it to his cheek.

'Odin, you can't really think that.'

'Ben, dear, I do, I do … but enough serious. Tomorrow Odin and Ben go dive boat.'

'Dive boat? Where to?'

'Dive school have big boat … we go swim. You have Speedo trunks? Better than shorts.'

'Sounds great,' said Ben. 'Can I borrow a mask and flippers?'

'Can, no problem. See you tomorrow, Ben. *Korp khun ka.*'

Odin's final vowel sound was long and languid, its falling tone slipping slowly from his lips.

The dive boat left the beach at ten the next morning. Ben paid for a non-diving place and watched the serious work of the divers with wetsuits and scuba gear going on around him. He was happy to save his baht and to enjoy the innocent beauty of snorkelling without the incidental distraction of trying not to die deep under water.

Odin arrived at the last possible moment in white singlet and blue sarong, his hair piled up and pinned on top. With him was a roly-poly lady friend from London who climbed aboard the boat with difficulty and sat with Odin immediately behind Ben where they chatted intently. They made a quirky pair, two girlies intent on a good day out, she plump and female in a flowery bikini, he, as always, slinky, slim and ambiguous.

Odin opened his bag and pulled out a shiny pink G-string.

'I buy New York … Forty Second Street. Real silk and only twenty dollar,' he cooed.

'Ooh nice! Let me feel.'

When the boat got to the first dive site, it became clear to Ben that neither of the two was going to be an active snorkeller. He doubted Odin could pull the mask strap over his head without spoiling his hair, and once launched into the sea, the ample fertility goddess would never be got back on board again. But Odin did briefly go into the water. He smiled winningly at Ben as he removed his sarong to reveal not Speedos but y-fronts and climbed carefully down the ladder into the sea, clinging all the time to the side of the boat. When he emerged, it became clear that cheap copy y-fronts are transparent when wet, and that he had not yet had the operation.

On the other side of the boat, the boatboy was feeding bread to a seething mass of fish. Ben pulled on a mask and flippers, fell backwards over the side into the water and swam into the shoal which continued to do battle for the bread. There were hundreds of stripy black and white fish, elegant white pomfret, long sinister pipe fish, colourful parrot fish, and in shallower water when he stood on the sand to rest, a vicious little fish that repeatedly came at him and bit him on the legs. Once he saw a stingray and later glimpsed a small shark slinking darkly away behind the rocks.

The coral was alive and flourishing, with overhanging plates of crimson and blue, staghorn with bright yellow growths, brain coral, corals like glass paperweights and a soft brown coral flowing like a head of hair in which orange and cream-striped clown fish were hiding. He saw spiky sea urchins with evil eyes, clams with blue lips that closed tight as he cruised by, fields of cabbages, billowing seaweeds and always the surge and bubble of the sea where the rocks broke the surface.

At the second dive site, Ben found himself swimming in pale green water high above a sandy bottom. Staring down into nothingness, he spotted what he had been told to look for, an indistinct oval shape just moving far below. It was a turtle. As it would have to come up to breathe, he waited for it to surface. When at last it came up directly beneath him, he was amazed just how big it was.

The next time it came up, the turtle was in no hurry to go back to the bottom. As he swam alongside it, Ben could hardly believe he was not dreaming, he was so close to this bizarre creature. He could see it looking at him, a survivor from another age, seemingly awkward yet so elegant and agile at sea.

From time to time his turtle raised her head, quickly gulping air before dipping down again. Once Ben held onto her shell and was briefly pulled along before she sensed the drag and dived a little to shake him off. It was an unreal experience; the greenback's bulk, the tiny fish swimming just beneath her belly and the sense of communion as she breathed the same air as he, each of them looking curiously at the other. Now he could say he had ridden on the back of a turtle.

He was not sure why he felt this must be a female. He had read about turtles in Thailand; how they return from thousands of miles to the beach where they were hatched to lay another generation of eggs, and how they lay in huge numbers because of the high mortality of the tiny hatchlings. He had seen pictures of the female, grotesque and ungainly struggling up the beach at night beyond the high tide mark to dig a hole into which to deposit her eggs. Out of her natural element, her eyes stream with tears, as if mourning the fate of the children she will never see.

As he got back to the boat, exhausted from the long swim, he called out to Odin.

'Saw this amazing turtle ... rode on its back.'

'On its back? Turtle not scared?'

'No, it didn't seem scared at all.'

'Lucky! With Odin on its back, it be terrified.'

At the sunset gathering that night, because of what happens to wet y-fronts, Ben was able to report that Odin had a small tattoo on his left buttock. As he could not describe it in detail, there was ribald speculation about its design and about how exactly he knew it was there. The night was long and alcoholic and Ben had more than a skinful which he feared he would regret the following day.

In the night his stomach rebelled. Staggering out of his hut, he watered the nearby lemongrass and was lucky not to have to see Odin's green curry again. Thrashing around unable to sleep, his heart pounding wildly, the damp bedsheet became a crumpled heap beneath him, the bare mattress apparently impregnated with sand. Worst of all, he could not get Fon out of his head. She haunted him pitilessly in his whirling pit of stupefaction and excess.

29

Ben woke to the blinding light of the morning and the dank smell of the mattress, feeling like death warmed up. Seriously dehydrated both by his epic intake of alcohol and from torrential sweating, he swore he would never hit the bottle like that again. It was a brutal lesson that a hangover in the heat is by far the worst; the tropical version takes some beating. Somehow he now had to face the day.

He thought of getting some ice to wrap in a towel for his head but he felt too awful to move. Then he drank a litre of water and felt even worse. From bitter experience he knew he would have to eat something to restore his low blood-sugar level, so finally he staggered down to the restaurant and ordered black coffee and a fruit muesli. It was the perfect remedy. Cool, sweet and refreshing, the glass bowl was brimming with chunks of papaya, pineapple and banana, sprinkled with oat flakes and crushed ice and with a sticky pink yoghurt poured on top.

As he ate, he began to hope for the first time that, if he could crash out for at least a week, he might not die. Going slowly back up the grassy slope to the huts, he glanced in through Darren's open door. Darren was unconscious on his mattress fully dressed, half lying on his Lonely Planet guide to Thailand, alongside him a packet of Marlboro Lights and a plastic bag spilling ganja. It had been a memorable blow-out.

But tormented by thoughts of Fon, Ben knew that sleeping off his hangover was not an option. He desperately needed to do something to keep in touch with her, to write, phone or send a fax. Even a nominal gesture would help. Writing a letter probably meant using Odin's personal translation service again, so he decided first to send a short fax in English. Declarations of undying love would not go down well with Fon and anyone in the resort office in Ban Phe could take his message off the fax machine and read it. So he wrote briefly promising to call her on Gaeo's mobile after she finished work the next evening at six and saying he would soon come back to see her before flying home to England.

Carrying the precious paper, his head pounding, he endured the sweaty walk along the beach to the office behind the mini-mart where there was a fax machine. It was easy to find but there was nobody there. He asked in the mini-mart when the office would be open but the boy hardly looked up.

'She go out. No problem ... you come back later.'

Ben swore under his breath.

He stumped back to his hut and sat and seethed on the veranda, the sweat pouring off him. In the early afternoon he walked along the beach again and to his relief the girl was there. She was all apologies and the fax was quickly sent on its way.

He was relieved to have done something to make contact with Fon but for the rest of the day he would still have to suffer for his night of heavy drinking. Even worse, he now had to wait as the earth turned full circle beneath him before he could phone her the next evening. Sober and alone that night he watched the sun slip into the sea in a blaze of colour. When it rose above the mountains the next morning, throwing shafts of light through the coconut palms onto his hut, he was still dead to the world. It was going to be a long and sultry day.

Just before six that evening Ben went down to the reception desk and asked to make the call to Fon. His mouth was dry and his heart thumping as the girl handed him the mobile phone. He dialled Gaeo's number and let the phone ring out, trying with difficulty to keep an image of Fon in his mind's eye. There was no reply and he had a sudden foreboding that this was not going to work. He was about to ring off when a male voice abruptly answered the call. He asked to speak to Fon, but the man did not understand, so he asked again more loudly, the sweat trickling down his spine. There was a brief hiatus when he could hear only background noises and then to his joy a female voice came on the line.

'Hello, that Ben?' she said.

'Yes, Fon? Fon, you okay?'

'Not Fon ... this Gaeo.'

'So where's Fon? I faxed to say I'd call at six.'

'Fon not here.'

'Oh God ... I must speak to her.'

'I see her before but she not come back yet.'

Ben was distraught.

'Look Gaeo, can you ask Fon to call me? Say in two hours time, at eight o'clock. Oh, and if she can't get me, can she call tomorrow at six in the evening?'

'Yes, okay, no problem.'

He gave Gaeo the mobile number, thanked her effusively and rang off, desperately hoping she had understood.

At ten to eight he returned and sat flicking distractedly through a dog-eared German fashion magazine, waiting for the phone at the reception desk to ring, his stomach in knots. He kept glancing anxiously towards the surly girl slumped over the desk; little did she know what he was going through. Eight o'clock came and went and there was no incoming call. At twenty past he gave up in disgust.

'Shit, if she can't be bothered to phone, what the hell can I do?' he fumed. He thought of calling Gaeo again but bottled out. If Fon was there, she would have phoned and if not there was no point trying again. Now he faced another day's wait for her to call after work the next evening. He was afraid the uncertainty would kill him.

Ben didn't feel like facing the crowd down at Odin's so he sat and ate fried rice alone on the terrace nearby. As he walked back up the slope, the late night party was already in session by the huts. Stewart saw him slipping past and called him over.

'Ben, where you been, mun? Come and join us.'

'Okay, Stew-pot, but don't tempt me with the hooch this time.'

'Burning the Bob Marley then? Darren's just skinning up.'

Ben subsided onto the mat with a sense of relief. It was impossible to feel depressed with such a good crowd of people around him.

He had been with them for only a few moments and had just poured a drink when a small figure appeared out of the darkness and came and sat down next to him.

'Hi, I'm Penny,' she said in a strong Australian accent. She was petite, barefoot and tanned, in loose pants and a skimpy top which showed off a taut stomach and tummy button. What Ben found so attractive was not just the smiling face, nor the snub nose, pink and peeling, but her gamine cuteness. Her dark hair, cut short and standing on end, willed his fingers to touch and explore. In the semi-darkness he found Penny most appealing.

'Hi,' said Ben. 'Travelling alone?'

'It's what I like best.'

'Me too. How long've you been away?'

'Nine months already ... can't believe it,' she laughed.

'And where've you been?'

'Indo mainly. Lombok, Bali, Java, then Lao and Cambodia. Been brilliant!'

'You don't look big enough for all that.'

'Didn't think so either a few months ago.' She gave Ben a winning smile.

'The best things come in small packages,' Ben beamed back at her.

'Small's still beautiful.'

'Thanks. I don't take up much space!' Penny paused for a moment. 'Like tonight ... all the huts are taken so I've nowhere to sleep. A few months ago I'd've been scared silly but now, no worries ... of course the ganja helps.' She drew deeply on the joint Darren had just passed her.

'Yeah, no sweat ... something'll turn up for tonight,' muttered Ben, missing his chance.

Penny slowly released the smoke from her nostrils and moving closer, held the spliff to his lips. As the smoke filled his lungs and caught at his throat he came perilously close to spluttering. Feeling seriously uncool and swallowing hard, he and Penny were drawn back into the mainstream chit chat around them.

Maca was now pouring more rum and opening a bottle of

Red Bull.

'This Thai stuff's supposed to be stronger than the Red Bull back home,' he said.

'I read somewhere an Austrian guy got the recipe from tuk tuk drivers in Bangkok,' said Stewart. 'Sold it worldwide.'

'Amazing to be able to market such a disgusting drink,' said Dutch.

'Get real, man. It's not the taste ...' drawled Chuck derisively, knocking back his cocktail of Red Bull, rum and cola.

'So what's the music?' asked Ben.

Dutch had a tape recorder on the grass beside him on which a haunting male voice and acoustic guitar were playing.

'Don't you know Nick Drake?' Nobody did. 'Wrote his own stuff in the late sixties, but it didn't sell and he died of a broken heart ... now he's a cult figure.'

'It's really something,' said Ben.

'This album's called "Five Leaves Left" from the reminder in the Rizla packets.'

'Yeah man ... great traveller music.' Chuck lay back on the mat, soaking it all up as Darren took advantage of the lull.

'Here Dutch, you're a teacher,' he challenged. 'Can you teach me to speak English proper then?'

'Very funny, Darren ... not a chance. Anyway I usually teach women.'

'Randy bugger! So you get to sleep with 'em, huh?'

'No, never. Thai women are very proper and I'd ruin my business if I did.'

'But you must have a wild time in Bangkok, speaking the language and that.'

'No I don't. There's bar girls of course but that's Russian roulette, and regular Thai women aren't usually available except for marriage.'

'Get real! In the discos they're seriously up for it ... gagging if you ask me.'

'That's discos! The conventional Thai woman's expected to be home before dark to look after her parents ... lose her reputation and she won't make a good marriage.'

'Bit different to us,' Penny broke in. 'I know which I prefer.'

'So it's near impossible for me to go out with a girl from a good family,' Dutch went on. 'The parents control her contacts with men and don't want her going with a *farang* ... unless they're poor and want the free ride.'

'Seems Thai women get a bum deal,' said Penny insistently. 'Can't have a good time without being called a slag. And they do all the work while the men sit around on their backsides.'

That was Aussie feminism thought Ben, but he said nothing. Penny was cuddled up close to him, was fit and feisty and could easily be forgiven.

'Anyway,' said Dutch, 'I'm not here for the girls. Holland's cold and efficient but the Thais've got the balance right. Life here's always *sanuk*.'

'*Sanuk*?' said Ben. 'You mean making everything fun.'

'That's right ... so even when life's a grind, the Thais keep smiling. They think the *farang* are a miserable lot who have to get drunk to enjoy themselves.'

'Dutch, that's tight mate, I mean ... what's wrong with getting pissed. When you're not working, you gotta have a good time,' said Darren.

'Yes, but for ordinary Thais life's all work, so it's work that has to be fun.'

Ben's thoughts turned to Fon. He remembered her once saying, 'Not have holiday, so work's my holiday'. Every day on the beach, grinding from massage to massage in the heat, she was always showing joy in the simple things, laughing and joking and giving pleasure. That was one of the things he liked so much about her.

'*Sanuk* means you've got to be harmonious too,' said Dutch. 'The Thais hate us confronting them or making them lose face.'

'Isn't that kind of fake?' said Ben. 'Superficial friendliness doesn't mean friendship ... and it makes it more difficult to know what's going on underneath.'

'Maybe, but I'm sure it's why tourists love Thailand ... the Thais are so gentle, even with horrible foreigners. Though we'll spoil them forever if we're too aggressive.'

'Yes, I hate seeing tourists whinging at the Thais,' said Penny. 'But if I was Thai, I'd resent the *farang* anyway for having so much money to throw around.' She drew on the soggy butt-end of a spliff that Ben had passed her and tossed it into the darkness.

'But I work bloody hard for my dosh!' protested Darren. 'Though I couldn't work all the time like them do ... gotta chill out and go clubbing.'

'So why do you need a regular blow-out then?' asked Dutch.

'Because work's dead boring. I'd go ballistic if I couldn't get wasted.'

'So we're all bored at work and have to get paralytic, is that it?' laughed Dutch. 'Instant gratification through clubbing!'

'Look mate, you need an adrenaline rush kind of ... it's a must-have.'

'But why can't we enjoy life, even at work?'

'Like I said, work sucks,' said Darren with finality. 'That's why I come to Thailand.'

'Well I tell you, I'm never going to do boring work just for the money. I'd rather die,' said Penny with passion.

There was silence as the different attitudes to work and the disturbing idea of fitting fun into the working day slowly sank in. Then Stewart shifted the debate up a gear or two.

'Well folks, I'm over thirty,' he said, 'and here's what I think about the boredom crisis. Back home we've never had an all-out war ... just the Falklands, the Gulf and Bosnia. So we're all bored and need an artificial high in between earning our pension contributions and paying the mortgage ... a bit of controlled risk, like soft adventure holidays, skydiving, whitewater rafting and stuff.'

'But we're travellers, not tourists,' interrupted Darren. 'Travellin's a way of life.'

'Get real, Darren! Travelling's just a privilege for rich *farang* with nothing better to do,' said Dutch, to a storm of protest, before he began stirring at a much bigger hornet's nest.

'And if you're bored because you haven't had a decent war,' he said facetiously, 'why not go and start one. Look at George Bush ... revelling in warlike rhetoric and playing to his electorate. It's what the Americans love … violence and conflict.'

Ben was thinking of Penny; make love not war was his motto for that night.

'And when they hit the World Trade Centre,' added Chuck, 'it was a great distraction for a weak president with problems at home. Bush was bound to make a meal of it.'

'But September eleven was an outrage! It changed the world,' said Ben waking up.

'Yeah, it's war! Gotta get the bastards!' hooted Darren.

'And maybe kill thousands of innocent bystanders?' said Stewart. 'The arms industry and the military need wars, but they're not bothered about "collateral damage". Only American lives matter.'

'Our wars are usually about domestic politics anyway,' said Chuck despairingly. 'Bush calls it a "war against terrorism" so he can dispense with due process … but then when we hold suspects in Cuba he says the rules of war don't apply either. Wouldn't bother me if I didn't love my country … but the terrorists are undermining our principles.'

'Bush is crazy shouting war,' said Dutch, holding his head in his hands.

'Call it a campaign against terrorism but not a war. Is the threat really so bad that we're on a war footing? Terrorists destabilise by spreading terror, so why make everyone panic?'

'Exactly … if the world changed, it was Bush making threats and alienating world opinion that did the real damage,' said Chuck. 'And anyway, why act like it was something new? Twenty years ago hundreds of our marines were killed in Lebanon. They've busted our embassies in East Africa killing hundreds more and they attacked the USS Cole in Yemen. And it wasn't even the first attack on the twin towers … a few years ago they bombed the basement, trying to topple one of the towers into the other. After a nifty practice session, why be surprised when they do it again?'

'Okay,' said Maca, 'it's a security operation then, not a war at all. But let's hope Bush isn't crazy enough to invade Iraq … the UN'll never back it. Though if the Americans do go in, you bet Bush'll focus on getting Saddam and kicking ass ... he'll forget he's got to win the peace and find an exit strategy too. War's always bloody chaos ... remember Vietnam.'

'It's kinda ironic talking about a *war* on terrorism,' said Chuck. 'At the time of Vietnam we illegally bombed Lao and Cambodia from bases in Thailand ... more bombs were dropped on those poor bastards than both sides dropped in the whole of World War Two. The bombing of Lao and Cambodia was kept secret, even from the American people ... Henry Kissinger couldn't call it war, only a sideshow, because they were both neutral countries. And Kissinger got given the Nobel peace prize!'

'Is that really true?' asked Ben dubiously from out of the darkness.

'Yes, and I've seen some of the wreckage,' replied Chuck with rare passion. 'Last year I was in northern Lao at a village miles upriver and I couldn't believe all the American cluster bomb casings still lying about the place ... the women were using'em to grow herbs in. And the school bell was an American shell.'

'State terrorism!' said Maca. 'American jet fighters used to shoot up their buffaloes to deny'em food. Hardly endearing ... no wonder the Laos looked to the communists for help.'

'It was a remote mountain village I was in,' Chuck went on with a catch in his voice, 'but I guess we thought the peasants there were better dead than red. So our planes put rockets into the cave where the women and children were hiding and killed the lot of 'em. When I saw the place, it hit home to me what we'd done. Same in Vietnam ... and I guess in Afghanistan right now.'

'And maybe soon in Iraq,' added Maca. 'They always think you can resolve things with violence ... they're trigger happy enough to invade.'

'Yeah man, so let me tell you this then,' said Chuck, sitting bolt upright on the mat, beer bottle in hand. 'Would you believe ... the US military's bombed twenty one countries since World War Two! Twenty one! September eleven was real bad but if you compare the headcount with the numbers we've killed, it looks minor. Bothers me too when all that bombing's done not by a suicidal bunch of extremists but by a superstate ... and in my name as an American citizen.'

Ben was intrigued by Chuck's strong views about his own country;

he was usually so quiet and unassuming, and he was patriotic too.

'So Chuck, why are you saying America got it all wrong after September eleven?' he asked.

'Don't forget, Ben ... it was a horrific atrocity!' Chuck replied. 'And though I guess we're used to handing it out and seeing death on TV, this was our first experience of the American heartland getting hit. Wars somewhere else from thirty thousand feet are fine, but Bin Laden really shook us up. So someone's gonna pay. When the American people are insulted, Mister President's gotta avenge'em ... even if it's indiscriminate.'

'So when Bush comes to shove, he's got to keep up his reputation as world bully,' quipped Stewart noisily. 'The revenge of George Doubleyuh!'

'It's pure Hollywood,' shouted Maca excitedly, the spliff glowing in his hand. '"Wanted dead or alive ... this is a crusade against evil and you folks are either for us or agin' us," says Bush. Dead scary! No surprise if Saddam wanted to arm himself. Who's the rogue state with the weapons of mass destruction anyway?'

'And "Ground Zero" and "Operation Infinite Justice" are straight off a second-rate screenplay!' groaned Chuck. 'There's this big family feud you see ... Poppa Bush didn't get the bad guy so now it's all down to boy George to nail Saddam!'

'But George has lost the plot ... and the bad guy's even got five o'clock shadow and a silly moustache!' Stewart hooted with delight. 'Though Maca, this is no "B" grade movie mun, it's a box office blockbuster ... look how Bush's ratings rocketed. And remember how real life reflects the movies. Ronald Reagan started as a screen cowboy and now he's been voted the best modern President ever ... even with alzheimers. It beggars belief!' He stood up and hurled a stone into the darkness towards the edge of the cliff.

'Pick a famous actor who's stupid and they can probably get him elected. Maybe it's Arnie's turn next,' joked Maca loudly.

'Problem is,' said Chuck, 'we're always so simplistic in our foreign policy. Americans don't travel abroad, so we're inward-looking and can't appreciate other cultures. No surprise we always get it wrong ... like when we support a compliant regime, it's the kiss of death for them. Every time we intervene, it's counter-productive. So when I'm travelling, I try to see how the local culture's different to mine.'

'America's got a culture!' quipped Stewart. 'Like what? You mean militant materialism and Mickey Mouse? Or like the American dream ... the survival of the fittest in the world's biggest candy store! American nightmare I'd call it.'

'The key cultural difference is this,' said Dutch, lolling against the veranda post but still deadly serious. 'Asian values are collective ... the family, the village and so on. But in the West it's all about self and individual rights ... maybe that's why western nations behave as we do. But we aren't colonials any more and it's time we respected other cultures.

'We do respect them, Dutch,' Ben protested. 'Course we do.'

'No we don't. The West dominates world trade and overwhelms smaller countries with its economic clout. America's been almost a quarter of the world economy during the twentieth century and its wealth and culture are so attractive. Like in the Cold War it was dead easy for the US to buy Thailand to stop it going communist. Look how the Thais fell for the consumer society.'

'Yeah, and Bin Laden hates American influence in Saudi,' said Maca. 'I saw that problem when I worked in Jiddah.'

'Exactly. What Islam fears is being subverted by materialism. They can't buy into the western goodies without getting contaminated by the corrosive values,' argued Dutch.

'So Uncle Sam's invading the globe with burgers, Budweiser and Britney. Irresistible!' said Stewart.

'Nice one, Stew,' crowed Darren over the laughter before Stewart had his final say.

'And they want to impose the American dream on everyone else ... liberty and democracy American style. Some model for the world to follow! Bush got fewer votes than Gore and only got in as President when his brother fixed it for him. And what a choice for the American people that was ... Gore and Bush, bore and gush! No wonder they couldn't decide. And when you think about the presidents they get ... Kennedy,

Johnson, Nixon, Clinton ... half of 'em were sex maniacs or shits, and most of the others ... Ford, Reagan, George Doubleyuh ... just plain stoopid!'

Sitting silently with Penny, Ben decided it was time to balance the debate a bit.

'This liberal stuff's all very well but September eleven was an outrage. Tony Blair knows Saddam's got weapons of mass destruction, so the free world's got to defend itself and strike first.'

'Yes Ben, but terror's an ideological struggle which Bush just doesn't begin to understand,' said Dutch passionately. 'He's totally out of his depth, so he did exactly what Bin Laden wanted ... to overreact and be belligerent. Then world opinion polarises and America makes more enemies, more extremists and more potential terrorists. You lose sympathy if you threaten everyone and bomb poverty-stricken Muslims. Yes, we have to do everything possible to protect ourselves, but that's about security. Shouting war does the opposite ... it creates instability and fear and sets the world against us.'

'Funny thing,' said Stewart, 'Vietnam was exactly the same ... they got obsessed with dropping bombs on an abstraction. Then it was "communism" ... now it's "terrorism". Trouble is, you can bomb the jungle and you can bomb the desert, you can kill as many people as you like, but you can never capture their minds.' He looked round for a response, impressed by his own ramblings.

'Very clever, Stewart, but the West's got modern weapons to defend itself with,' said Ben angrily. 'So why shouldn't we use them.'

'Like these new precision bombs that never kill civilians, you mean? So we tell the satellites to look for a beardie with a turban hiding in a cave, then send off a smart bomb with "Bin Laden" written on it. Is that what we do?'

'No way,' said Maca. 'Looking for Bin Laden's like a needle in a haystack.'

'Some needle! And first they've gotta find the fucking haystack!' bellowed Stewart. His noisy one-liner brought a ripple of amusement, though Chuck ignored the laughter.

'When I'm in Lao or Cambodia I see poverty everywhere ... in

Thailand too sometimes,' he said in a low voice. 'And I tell it you straight, the West's got too much of the cookies. Look at us sitting here knocking back the hooch ... we've got it made.'

'It's like we're from another planet,' said Dutch, 'and most travellers don't begin to see what's going on around them.'

'One B2 bomber costs six billion dollars,' persisted Chuck. 'Think what that'd do for poverty in Phnom Penh. Or what they'd save cancelling a B2 mission from Missouri to pulverise mud huts in Afghanistan. We could win over the world if we'd share a bit more ... we don't need bombs.'

'Okay then,' joked Stewart, 'so I'll get a poster printed and put it in the Oval Office. It's of Ronald McDonald with a speech bubble saying, "Mr President, never forget, *the hamburger's mightier than the sword*!" Think about it mun.' He took a swig of his Sang Som and lay back theatrically on the floor, exhausted from the strain of so much mental activity.

Hazy brains tried to absorb Stewart's conversation-stopper. In the silence that followed, Maca got up and said he was about to turn in for the night. He came across to where Ben and Penny were sitting huddled together in the darkness.

'Ben mate, Penny's from the lucky country and she's homeless tonight. Yours is the only hut with one body in it, so d'you think maybe ...?'

'Yeah okay, why not,' said Ben, trying not to sound as if he'd just won the lottery.

'Thanks Ben,' said Penny, squeezing his hand and not letting go. He realised he was grinning foolishly again, the muscles in his cheeks in involuntary spasm.

Not long after, as he lay on his double mattress listening to the sounds of showering a few feet away through the thin partition, Ben had visions of Penny's body, naked and slim, the cold water coursing down her sharp little breasts and into the cleft of her bum. He could see the fingers caressing soap across her slender topography, finding their way into the secret valleys, towelling the golden skin and tying on a short cotton sarong.

It was perfectly normal for travellers to share a room with the opposite sex, he told himself and it meant nothing. But then he vaguely remembered something Darren had said about what happens when you share a hut with a girl. And he began to wonder whether he was only canned on skunk or whether he was pissed as well. Not that it mattered much, so long as he managed not make a total fool of himself that night.

30

Shortly before six the next evening Ben was again sitting on the rattan sofa in the reception hut, thumbing through the same battered fashion magazine as he waited anxiously for Fon to call. At two minutes to six the mobile phone at the desk rang. He jumped to his feet but it was not for him. He waited a small eternity until six fifteen when it rang again. The unsmiling girl answered it and handed it him.

'Hi, Fon?'

'No, this Gaeo. How you, Ben?'

'I'm okay but ...'

'Koh Chang good? Expensive?'

'Gaeo ... where's Fon?'

'She with me now.'

Ben was overjoyed, but to his dismay the new voice that came on was weak and strangled and he could hardly recognise it as Fon.

'Fon? Is that you?'

'Hello Ben.'

'You okay, Fon?'

'Very tired ... work, work every day. Many people.'

'But that's good.'

'Yes, good money.'

'So I'll see you when I get back to Koh Samet in a few days, like I said in my fax.' There was a moment's pause. 'Fon? Can you hear me? The line's terrible.'

'No Ben, you not come Koh Samet ... please, you not come back.'

'Fon! Why ever not? You don't want to see me again?' Ben was thunderstruck.

'And you not call Gaeo's mobile,' she said in a choked voice.

'You won't even talk to me?!'

'This her husband's phone. Big problem!' he could just hear her saying.

'But why can't I see you? Fon!' he wailed.

'Ben, you not understand? Two together here ... no possible.'

To Ben's horror the line then began to break up and Fon's voice faded away to nothing.

In a daze he handed back the mobile, walked out of the building and headed for the beach. Feeling shocked and numb, he stood looking out to sea and tried to take in what had just happened. If Fon had finally finished with him, then why, why, why? Was it the card Odin had written for him? Because she could not be seen on the beach with a *farang*? Because she would not risk her heart? Or was the boyfriend back on the scene?

He knew there were a thousand things working against their friendship but only the fear of harming her reputation stopped him packing up and heading back to Koh Samet immediately. As the horizon blurred with tears he began to think the unthinkable, that perhaps this affair had been too painful and ending it might be a relief.

But now he did not know how he was going to get through the next few days. He desperately needed to talk things through with somebody, but with whom? Penny had gone off to stay on a quieter beach where there were empty huts, though she was about the last person he could confide in. Odin might understand the tensions with Fon, but he too was hardly an impartial observer. Stewart was a mature sort of guy and was probably the best choice. But most of all he thought of Emma. Ironically it was she, his best pal, who would be able to make sense of it all.

Though in the end Ben did not bring himself to confide in any of his friends, he did somehow manage to survive the trauma of Fon's rejection. He read and swam and socialised much as usual, and he took a wheezy wooden boat for a day trip to Koh Wai and Koh Rang, two tiny islands with coral beaches just a few hours away. Sitting on the roof as the boat wallowed back through the swell with the mountains of Koh Chang sprawled across the ocean before him, he decided this must be one of the most beautiful places in the world and that he should not be too heartbroken for long.

Back at his hut, satisfied and sweaty from his day in the islands, he was about to shower when the surly receptionist appeared at the door.

'You have phone … lady ask for Ben,' she said.

Ben's pulse raced wildly.

'When?'

'She call yesterday.'

Ben was outraged.

'And it's taken you a whole day to tell me! Who was it?'

The girl's face darkened.

'Not give her name,' she replied.

'So what am I supposed to do then?'

'She phone again twenty minutes ago … say she call in twenty minutes.'

'But that's right now for God's sake!'

Ben shot out of the hut, the girl slowly following him down to the reception desk with a studied air of detachment. She looked away and said nothing as he paced around like a caged lion waiting for the call. Then the phone rang and it was Fon.

'Hi, Fon, I can't believe it.'

'Ben, I phone yesterday. Why you not call me?'

'Because they didn't bloody tell me you'd phoned.'

The receptionist glowered at him.

'Ben you angry me?' said Fon, sounding worried.

'Course not! And I can hear you this time, the line's so good. Where are you?'

'Ban Phe … phone box.'

'What are you doing there?'

'Go bank, send money Mama. Ben you okay?'

'I am now. Fon, you nearly killed me.'

'How I kill you?'

'Telling me I couldn't come back like that.'

'Nearly kill me too,' she said.

Ben's heart leaped with joy.

'But Fon, you don't want to see me?'

'Want very much ... but cannot.' This was just amazing.

'Why ever not?' he said.

'You not understand? Not listen before?'

'Tell me again then,' said Ben in suspense.

'When we go beach together, a hundred eyes follow us ... think I sell sex.'

'God, it disgusts me ... why can't they just leave us alone?' he complained indignantly.

'Ben, I boring ... want go holiday,' said Fon, laughing down the phone.

'Oh, Fon, I wish. And I wish you really loved me.'

'Ben I do! Love you thirty percent already!' she said to more laughter.

'Can't you make it forty percent?' Ben was thinking hard. 'Suppose I come to Koh Samet and nobody knows I'm there?' he said.

'Then no problem.'

'If I get a ferry to one of the other beaches and get a hut ...?'

'Then I come see you.'

'Possible?'

'Yes, possible. But how I find you there?'

'When I've checked in, I'll send a message somehow.'

'So Ben, when you come?' asked Fon.

'Tomorrow ... why not!'

'Tomorrow, okay, okay. Sorry Ben ... money finish.'

Ben tried to say something more, but it was too late and the phone went dead.

It had all been so quick, a breathtaking turnaround, with Fon's voice clear and strong, so different to the tragic tone of the earlier call to Gaeo's mobile. But yes, she had said he could come back to Koh Samet, which now meant packing up and leaving early the next morning. Walking back to his hut, it struck him that a day is a long time in a Thai love affair.

Now he would have to face what travellers never get used to doing, severing the intense friendships he had so relied upon in the past few weeks. He felt he had known Maca and Chuck for ages, Stewart was the salt of the earth, Dutch a decent and impressive guy and everyone had a soft spot for Darren. In their place he would be left with a short list of email addresses.

Eating at Odin's that night was the same as usual but with a sense of nostalgia, coupled with the excitement of moving on. As always nothing at Odin's was ordinary. The food was a triumph, the atmosphere electric and the men's lavatory a monument of bad taste. Filled with pot plants, it was a shrine to the male form, the walls liberally plastered with pictures of multinational beefcake torn from magazines.

The evening was finally rounded off with a moment of farce when a fisherman came up the beach with a massive fish for the restaurant.

'What a size!' said Stewart. 'How the hell do you land and kill a thing like that?'

'Have gun … shoot'em in the head,' said the fisherman.

After they had all eaten, there was now one last favour Ben wanted from Odin. As he paid the bill, he asked him if he could write a brief note in Thai to Fon.

'Last time you make her angry,' whined Odin. 'Say all the wrong things.'

'You mean all the things you said!' grumbled Ben. 'No, this time it's very simple. I just want you to tell her to meet me tomorrow night by the jetty on Ao Hin Kong as soon as it gets dark.'

'Ooh, Ben, you so romantic. Can I put in some extra bits?'

Leaving Odin's for the last time, Ben and his mates walked slowly along the beach back to the huts where they settled down around a circle of candles on Chuck's veranda for a few bottles and the ritual of a final smoke. For some reason the mood was a little sombre, perhaps a sense that the party was almost over and that the group was about to break up.

Ben had been wondering what life must be like for the Thais living in the islands and wanted to know what Dutch and Maca thought.

'You know, I find it hard to believe Koh Chang's not just some Shangri-La adrift in the ocean,' he said. 'It's another world.'

'Nothing could be further from the truth,' said Maca. 'Thailand's linked into the world economy and feels every hiccup ... even places like this get hit by a downturn.'

'Yes, globalisation's a big thing at the moment,' said Dutch. 'They went for an export-led economy which was a gamble, and they've still not recovered from the 1997 collapse ... bad debts and unfinished buildings everywhere.'

'So what now for Thailand?' asked Ben.

'Unpredictable ... people are questioning the basic assumptions. They want the modern lifestyle but there's always a price to be paid,' said Dutch.

'Seems they want it all and they want it now,' replied Ben gloomily.

'And they're dumping their culture in the process,' added Maca.

'Maybe that's what urbanisation's all about,' said Dutch. 'Bangkok's a bit like Europe in the industrial revolution ... about eight million people, many of them from upcountry, and they all want the best the city can offer ... housing, medicine, education and so on.'

'But don't the rural migrants just lose their old way of life and become the new urban poor,' suggested Ben, pouring another tot of Sang Som.

''Fraid so,' said Dutch. 'That's what gets me. In the nineteenth century Thailand avoided being colonised. King Mongkut was forced to cede Lao and part of Cambodia to the French but he played them off against the British and stayed independent while everywhere else was overrun.'

'Yes, and look at the bloody mess the French made of Indo-China,' interjected Maca.

'King Mongkut and King Chulalongkorn took the best systems and technology from the West, but continued to value their own traditions,' Dutch went on. 'There was no internet then, so it was easier ... but now it seems the Thais are desperate to be colonised economically and culturally. So everything's in the melting pot.'

There was a pause as they all tried to absorb the enormity of what Dutch had just said.

'Wasn't the Vietnam war a big turning point?' said Stewart. 'Thailand was the threatened domino and was flooded with aid from the West.'

'Dead right,' said Dutch. 'American influence was immense ... they even had the use of military bases here. And the GIs were randy so the Thais sold them their women, maybe the soul of the Thai people too ... the nicest people money can buy.'

'Sold for a serving of KFC,' said Stewart, staring into the candles.

'So if they're dumping their culture, what is it exactly?' asked Ben.

'There's many influences,' said Dutch, 'mainly central and northern Thai, with Lao and Khmer rural tradition in the North East and Islam in the south, plus the commercial dynamic of the immigrant Chinese ... not to mention India and Buddhism. Maybe that's why it's so full of contradictions... like with the sex trade. Buddhism condemns sexual misconduct and Thai women are modest and shy, but commercial sex is still rampant ... perhaps because they're so tolerant and non-judgmental.'

'Amazing thing I saw in the Bangkok Post,' said Maca. 'A middle-aged senator was accused of paying for sex with under-aged girls ... but a Health Ministry spokeswomen said it wouldn't be fair to hold him solely responsible.'

'Why ever not?' said Chuck. 'That goes beyond tolerance.'

'She said society should understand him ... men used to take minor wives and concubines, but now they go to prostitutes instead.'

'That can't be the official line!'

'No, I'm sure it isn't, but it's still weird saying something like that, specially a woman,' said Maca, shaking his head.

'Another thing,' Dutch went on, 'Thai kick boxing seems so at odds with their gentleness. And they've let their crafts and architecture be overwhelmed by the plastic, concrete and vulgar. Like traditional dress ... the sarong's so attractive, but they all want to look flash in jeans which are hot and uncomfortable.'

'Listen to this old guy,' mocked Darren.

'I agree with Dutch,' said Ben. 'Thai girls look great in a sarong.'

'In Bali,' said Maca, 'they make brilliant use of traditional building materials but here it's all ugly concrete boxes.' He leaned back against the wall of his bamboo hut.

'I don't want to sound an old fart,' said Dutch, 'but the Thais have sold themselves for an inferior popular culture and tacky bad taste. Take the nightclubs. They're black holes with bad music which is unbelievably loud. The kids stand around trying to look cool, and the live acts on the stage are awful ... some guy who looks like a fifties teddy boy, wearing dark glasses so he can't see. And a skinny girl in a backless bikini made of pink feathers ... probably can't sing either.'

'Take it easy, granddad!' jeered Darren, flexing his biceps.

'And there's a great musical tradition in the North East,' Dutch continued, ignoring him, 'political songs that really say something, but western music's more fashionable so that's it ... no contest.'

'In Bangkok I went to this place called RCA, Royal City Avenue. It's a street with nightclubs,' said Maca. 'When you go down there you're nearly blown away by the noise even when you're outside. I'm no granddad but I think it's gross ... a load of kids posturing and trying to be funky. Don't get me wrong, there's a great world culture of music and dance but they've got to pick the best and value their own.'

Everyone agreed it was time to open another bottle and, with discussion of Thai culture exhausted, Ben now had the chance to change the subject.

'For me,' he said, 'the worst thing's the way Thai women are up for sale. Sex tourism stinks. What's the world's perception of the Thai girl now? Elegant in a sarong or legs apart stuffing things up herself in a go-go bar?'

'Trouble is,' said Dutch, 'how do you stop it? Money from commercial sex flows back to the rural areas and there's so many vested interests, including the police who take their cut. The government cracks down on the girlie bars from time to time on grounds of social order, but it's difficult to dismantle so big an industry, even if they have the will to do it. But yes, prostitution corrupts society, just like gambling, guns and drugs.'

'It's not just for tourists though,' added Ben. 'Sex is for sale everywhere in Thailand. I don't understand why it's such a big thing.'

'There's enough for fifty PhDs on that one,' said Dutch. 'But like it said in the Bangkok Post, Thailand has a tradition of men taking concubines ... of sex being an economic relationship. Today, with so many migrant workers, contraception allowing casual contact and poor women needing a fast buck, hey presto, you've got prostitution.'

'Yeah, if nice girls are virgins and men are promiscuous, there'll be women who'll sell their ass,' agreed Maca.

'What amazes me though is how past governments seem to have connived at international sex tourism. It brings in the money but look what it does for Thailand's reputation,' said Ben. 'It's Thailand's shame.'

'You're right,' said Chuck, 'but governments do desperate things. The Philippine government's been exporting women for years as domestic servants. They're open to abuse, but remittances by overseas workers are the country's biggest foreign exchange earner. Money talks, man, so forget the abuse!'

'Hey guys, this has got a wee bit serious,' said Stewart. 'How about some more Sang Som?

'Yes, I need to release my seriousness a bit,' said Ben stretching his legs. But relaxed as he felt, there was still one more thing he wanted to talk about.

'So what about the environment?' he said to nobody in particular. 'Koh Chang's a National Park, but it's one big building site. With the new road down the west, resorts are going up everywhere.'

'Only the jungle's protected,' said Maca. 'Old coconut and rubber plantations can be developed, so if you want to throw up some huts there's nothing to stop you ... at least that's what Odin told me. What d'you think, Dutch?'

'It's Thailand's big problem ... like tourism in Spain in the sixties. No controls on development means oversupply, cheap prices and environmental damage. Tourism's booming at the moment, but busts always follow, especially when the place goes out of fashion.'

'The government's got some big scheme to turn Koh Chang into a high-class resort area with loads of new infrastructure,' added Maca. 'Okay maybe if they restrict informal development, but I'll believe that when I see it.' He subsided into a pessimistic silence.

'I met a girl who went to the floating market near Bangkok. Thought it disgusting ... hundreds of tour buses crowded into one village and no traditional life anywhere, just a few boats selling the usual tacky handicrafts,' said Chuck. 'If you ask me, the Thais are really going to have to look out. There's more and more competition from Lao and Cambodia and just wait till tourism really takes off in Burma. Thailand's still a great place but we won't keep coming if they ruin it.'

The next day after an early start and a tedious bus ride back to Ban Phe, Ben waited for a ferry to Na Dan, the fishing village on Koh Samet. They told him it would leave as soon as there were twenty people ready to go, so tired, hot and hungry he did not dare order any food in case a flush of people arrived and he had no time to eat it. The only other person waiting for the boat was a grim-faced American with impenetrable shades and a granite jaw. Restlessly pacing up and down, chewing gum, he insisted on telling Ben about all the best beaches he should visit in Thailand.

'How do you know Thailand so well?' asked Ben.

'Bin coming here twice a year last ten years.'

'On holiday?' asked Ben, sensing a sex tourist.

'No, on business.'

'What business are you in?'

'Orchids,' he said, chewing hard.

An hour later after landing at Na Dan and sharing a pick-up along the dusty track with the American, Ben checked into a hut at the Hat Yao Resort. His first thought was how to get Odin's message delivered to Fon so they could meet at sundown. The best idea was one of the vendors who walk the coast path and within minutes a sarong seller was on his way to Ao Sapporot clutching the note for Fon in his hand.

Relieved this was done, Ben went back to his hut and collapsed onto his bed and slept. When he woke, the sun was already low in the sky behind the island. He put on trousers as protection against mosquitoes and started off along the coast path. The walk was not as long as he remembered and he soon got to Ao Hin Kong, a quiet beach with a wooden jetty jutting out into the sea. By the jetty stood a wild mango tree, a magnificent specimen, its gnarled trunk wrapped in lengths of fabric, at its foot a shrine to the many spirits that dwelt in its branches.

He walked to the far end of the jetty from where he could see the full length of the beach and sat and studied the crazy assortment of palm trunks driven into the sand and the narrow walkway of irregular planks. It was the perfect place to wait for the sunset and for Fon. Somehow he felt sure that this time nothing could go wrong.

It was almost dark by the time he saw a small figure appear at the end of the bay. He watched her as she reached the tree, stopping for a moment, before walking at a measured pace towards the jetty. Half way along it, she broke into a run, the boards rattling and bouncing under her feet. She did not slow down but hurled herself at him, her small body hitting him with all its force. Ben held tightly onto her as she clung to him, her feet clear of the ground, joking and laughing and nuzzling her face into his neck. It was far more than he had dared hope for.

They sat together on the jetty in the gathering darkness facing out to sea, Fon between his knees lying back against him, he wrapping his arms around her in undisputed possession determined never to let go of her again. He felt an overwhelming joy as deep as his despair had been when she told him she could not see him again. There were many things he wanted her to explain to him but somehow the setbacks became unimportant as they were with each other now, bonded together by closeness and touch. They did not need to talk much, and talking's not easy when mouths are so engrossed.

For Ben the moment was a sensuous experience to rival even Odin's curries; the waves hissing restlessly up the beach a few feet beneath them, the blackness of the night punctuated by the lights of the fishing boats and pricked by the stars, the salty tang of the sea, the warm scent of Fon's body and the taste of tongues on white ivory.

But then after only a few minutes together, Fon suddenly sat up.

'Must go back,' she said.

'Why? So soon? Fon, I've only just got here.'

'Cannot stay. Joy miss me.'

'When'll I see you again?' he begged her.

'Tomorrow.'

'But when? I'll die if I have to sit around waiting for you.'

'No Ben, you not die.'

And then she was gone, walking away fast along the jetty, leaving him gazing after her as she disappeared into the darkness.

Back at Hat Yao that night, Ben sat alone on the beach, relieved and overjoyed but tantalised. As he ate, an old man in black pyjamas hobbled up to his table.

'You no have lady tonight?' he asked Ben.

'Not here, no.'

'Sorry … I hope you no sad.'

'I'm okay, I think,' said Ben.

'You like, I sing for you,' said the old man, taking a bamboo flute from his pocket. He played a lilting tune and then sang.

When he had finished, he slowly explained the song.

'This very sad story … love story. Beautiful girl, she have boyfriend in village where she born. Then she go work Bangkok, meet new boyfriend. Boyfriend have money, have motorbike … so she marry him. Then she go back village, New Year. She see old boyfriend, tell him she marry already. He very sorry … he very sad. This song very beautiful … same life. Life sometime sad, sometime beautiful. You think so?'

Ben silently nodded his head in agreement.

31

There was a storm in the night and through pleasant dreams Ben was aware of the rain beating on the roof of his hut. He woke early and lay listening to the shriek of the insects, the croaking of the bullfrogs and the more distant sound of the breakers coming ashore onto the beach.

He took a shower and started to sort out the mess from emptying his rucksack the night before. His sarong was damp and smelly so he decided to hang it over the plastic chair on the veranda to air. As he went outside in his boxer shorts his eyes fell on the pool of rain water on the seat of the chair, the moment somehow frozen in time by the impact of what happened next. For there on the steps glimpsed out of the corner of his eye was a slim figure in a blue tie-die shirt, her hair piled up on top, silent and still, watching in amusement as she caught him in a very domestic moment.

Fon launched herself at him, a gust of femininity and fragrance, smelling freshly-washed of shampoo and soap and glowing a little from the walk along the shore. She flung her arms round his neck and kissed him on the cheek, radiant and happy. They retreated into the hut, where she hardly resisted when he dragged her down onto the bed. Cuddled up together, their limbs intertwined, they lay and talked.

'No idea you'd be here so early, Fon. Thought I was in for another awful wait,' said Ben.

'Get up five o'clock, cook food for the monks,' she said, showing him the saffron-coloured string tied around her wrist as a mark of merit.

'So now another day of massage?'

'Fon, always work. And you Ben, where you go?'

'Nowhere … just waiting here for you.' He planted a lingering kiss on her lips.

'So Koh Chang funny?' she asked when he released her.

'You mean fun? Yes, it was brilliant.'

'You have girlfriend, Koh Chang?' she demanded bluntly.

'Yes, I did,' he said. 'You of course!'

'*Pak waan*. You sweet mouth, Ben.'

There was more kissing, but Fon had something important to say.

'Ben, I thinking strong. Last night, see you short time then go back. Now you wait while I work all day. No good for you … maybe find you with rope round your head!' With a shriek, she passed her hand across her throat to suggest suicide by a despairing lover.

'No, I won't kill myself … not if you still like me, Fon.'

'Love you little bit more each time … now maybe forty percent!'

There was laughter as Ben wrestled her onto the mattress again and stopped her talking, but she broke away from him and sat up.

'Ben, I thinking … this my life. Sometime they speak me no good, but no problem.'

'What d'you mean, Fon?'

'I mean, better you come Ao Sapporot, then can see me every day.'

Ben could hardly believe what he was hearing.

'Me stay at Ao Sapporot? But what'll people say?'

'If people speak me no good, if they fight me … I fight back!'

'But this is a big thing for you isn't it, you being seen with me?' he asked anxiously.

'What can I do? If my heart strong, have to follow my heart.'

The impact of what she was saying was hardly sinking in when she jumped up from the bed and dragged Ben to his feet.

'*Hiu khao* … very hungry. We go eat,' she said.

'Okay. Well, I'm too gobsmacked to feel hungry, but yes, why not.'

Sitting in the restaurant overlooking the beach, they watched the workers raking up the leaves and flotsam that the storm had brought in, Ben turning things over in his mind. This seemed to be another huge leap forward. He was no longer a pariah to be kept hidden from sight at a distant beach. It meant that Fon was prepared to let her relationship with him be openly recognised. It was a public declaration, a decision of significance for her and perhaps for him too.

They ordered breakfast from a sleepy girl who gave them curious glances.

'She think I stay with you last night,' said Fon.

'I wish,' replied Ben dreamily.

'Think I stay with you ... sell sex.'

After breakfast they went back to the hut to be alone together for a few moments. It was eight thirty when Fon finally looked at her watch and said she must go; she would be missed if she was not on the beach starting work at the usual time. Ben thought of checking out of his hut immediately and walking to Ao Sapporot with her but decided to follow on later in the morning as if he had just arrived on the island.

He stood on the veranda and watched as Fon walked briskly away through the trees with a bounce in her step, her hair now loose and flowing. Just at the last moment before disappearing from view behind a hut, she turned, saw him gazing after her and blew him a kiss with both hands. Like the moment earlier when he first caught sight of her on the veranda steps, the distant kiss became fixed in his memory with photographic clarity. The bad moments in his Thai love affair had been terrible but the good ones made up for them a million times over.

That afternoon, Ben found himself back at Ao Sapporot staying in the same place he had been with Emma a few weeks earlier. There were many local people who recognised him and gave him a welcome, sometimes perhaps with a knowing look; he could not be sure.

Life on the beach went on much as before, Fon working the height of the tourist season for every baht she could earn, he leading the life of a traveller in a land which for the *farang* flows with milk and honey. When she stopped briefly for a break they could spend a little time together, and there was a daily massage when they always talked intensively for the whole hour. Fon kept well clear of Ben's room, just as he knew he could not be seen near hers nor show her any physical affection in public. But what was now very different for Ben was the fact that their friendship was secure and that even if Fon could not be with him all of the time, he was sure she wanted to be.

Several times they ate together at night with Jinda and Joy. Somehow there was always lots to talk about, Fon using her small store of English to great effect. Ben now knew her village, her mother and sister and about her dream to send Joy to the private school she had shown him on the mainland. But it frustrated him that she understood so little of his life in England. It was impossible for her to imagine his upbringing in Haywards Heath, his world of school and university and the pressures of planning a career. Because of the language gap he could explain very little and when he tried, he used words and concepts that were beyond her.

As he sat on the beach and daydreamed, he again wondered how Fon would adapt if he could take her to England. But there were so many obstacles. He knew that because of their reputation, Thai women were often refused visas, a masseuse perhaps being the least likely person to get one. Nor could he afford the enormous cost of an extra air ticket and of looking after her in England. It was she who was the only one with an income and she would lose that as soon as she left the island.

He tried to imagine her on the cold streets of England, deprived of her family, of Thai television and music and her beloved som tam. It was all so difficult and needed more time and thought, though he was not going to let anything spoil the last few days they still had together.

As the day came closer when he was to meet Emma at the airport for the flight home, Ben wanted to make the most of every possible moment with Fon. One evening as it was getting dark after a late massage, he asked her if they could go and eat together.

'Okay, we find Goong,' she said. 'Remember my friend Goong, massage lady? Her auntie have new baby.'

Fon set off along the beach at speed, Ben following happily in her wake. An evening alone with her would have been better but this was a good second best.

'You like pork balls?' she demanded. 'Banana roti, okay?' she said, stopping to buy cooked foods at stalls along the sand.

At the far end of the beach he followed her into the trees where they came to some low huts on the fringe of the jungle. The first hut, roughly built of wood with a tin roof, had a low veranda on which an elderly couple were squatting, the old man with a faded sarong round his waist, the woman holding a new baby. Fon stooped low under the overhang of the roof and sat down with them.

Ben could see the aunt's resemblance to Goong, her smile as wide as the face, the eyes that crinkled up and disappeared into the smile and the button nose and protruding ears. She and the old man, both of them lined by years of work in the rice fields, were, Ben guessed, probably the proud grandparents of the child.

'Ben,' said Fon, 'this Mama, Papa and this their baby girl.'

Ben just did not know what to say. The night of passion here in this hovel when the baby had been conceived was simply unimaginable. He would have cast the woman as one of the Three Witches and the man as Time the Reaper rather than as parents of a tiny child.

The food Fon had brought was pooled with what Goong's auntie had already cooked and they were soon joined by Goong and by a wizened old woman with bright and lively eyes. As they sat talking under the overhang of the roof, to everyone's amusement Ben was given the baby to hold. She clung blindly to him, mouthing around for a nipple.

'Want milk,' said Fon. 'Better try Mama!'

'But what are they all laughing about?' Ben asked her.

'Mama she say, now Ben can have baby too ... half Thai, half *farang*.'

Her answer left him thinking hard.

Sitting cross-legged on the floor, they ate the rich assortment of dishes with their fingers, the joking and bantering now centred around the old woman.

'What's the story this time?' Ben asked Fon.

'Old lady not have husband, very scared alone at night. Sometime bad devil come and sit on her bed ... she 'fraid devil bite off her big toe.'

Fon did her best impression of a devil that bites off old ladies' toes and everyone erupted in laughter.

The old woman then shuffled off without saying a word but soon came back and proudly showed Ben some photos of a stylish young woman standing by a fountain in a park.

'This my daughter ... stay university Bangkok. Before maybe, I want she marry you, Ben, but now cannot, no possible.' She gave a knowing look towards Fon who remained impassive. Ben had no idea what to make of all these assumptions about their relationship.

Unable to follow the chatter going on around him, Ben's thoughts then turned to the attractive daughter in the old woman's photos. If she could afford to study in Bangkok, perhaps there was some hope for the baby girl, even though born into poverty. The old couple must have left their Isaan rice farm to work on the island and if their child could now do well enough at school, she might be able to earn a better wage somewhere in town. But he was not entirely convinced this apparent progress would necessarily benefit them all in the long run. He still clung to the romantic ideal of a sustainable lifestyle among the rice fields in preference to the pressures and pollution of Bangkok. Nothing seemed worse to him than urban poverty.

When they had cleared the plates, the old folks got up, taking the baby inside the hut and left Ben with Fon and Goong on the veranda.

'Can buy Mekhong ... small bottle, Ben?' asked Fon.

'Yes, why not. Some whisky would be great.'

'Give money then ... get better price than you.'

Fon disappeared with Ben's wallet to buy the whisky, leaving him wondering how he would pass the time with Goong. But Goong had a favour to ask and produced a postcard of Koh Samet.

'This postcard for Luigi ... live Milano. Massage with me many times.'

'He's gone back home now though?'

'Two months ago. But he write me, say he miss me ... so Ben, please you write postcard.'

Ben was just finishing an innocent little message to Luigi when Fon got back with the whisky.

'Goong! Why send card to Luigi? Luigi, Luigi, you go with Luigi!' she teased. Goong fell over backwards and covered her face in confusion.

'No,' said Goong indignantly. 'Not have sex with him, never.'

'You virgin, so want sex!' Fon ducked as Goong swung at her and the two of them rolled across the floor in fits of laughter.

When the fooling was over, Goong wanted to correct an impression.

'Ben, this postcard not serious. Luigi just friend. But can *farang* lady sleep with boyfriend before she marry?' she asked him with a serious face.

'Yes, sometimes they do, but not always,' said Ben cautiously.

'No good if lady like too much sex.'

'Well,' he said, 'what's important is to love someone. We only sleep together when it's special. Though it seems to me Thai men with money can get it whenever they want.'

'Men can, women cannot,' said Goong emphatically.

'But why the double standard now women can go on the pill?'

Goong did not reply but sat and looked at her feet for a moment before glancing up and bowling a fast one.

'You have many ladies, Ben?' she demanded with a mischievous twinkle. Fon, who had been unusually quiet, joined in the uproar. The whisky was having its effect.

It had been a good evening but in the last moments before he was to leave Koh Samet and go home, Ben needed to be alone with Fon. Remembering the night out dancing at the Meridian bar with Jinda and Goong, he wanted to do it all over again, but this time without the others. The following day he put the idea to Fon who looked doubtful, so it came as a surprise when some time later she suddenly declared, 'Ben, we go dancing tonight, Meridian. Just you and me.'

'Nothing I'd like more,' he said, 'well, almost nothing.'

'But first I eat with Joy … she want me same Mama,' she said.

They met on the beach quite late and Ben was blown away by how she looked. Fon's little black dress was about the sexiest thing he had ever seen. It was short with a high collar, on the right bust a pocket, the left cut away to reveal a bare shoulder. He could not take his eyes off her and she was to be his alone for the whole evening.

'Meridian bar too far … lady not walk,' she said twirling around on tiptoes to signify her status and elegance, 'so we go *sorngthaew*.'

She deserved a limousine no less, but they roused a sleeping driver from the seat of his battered pick-up, climbed into the back and jolted away up the track. It was a rough and dusty ride, the vehicle dipping and bumping over the rutted surface, the dry jungle lit by the one headlight that was still working. When they first heard the thump of the music as they neared the bar, Ben could see the sparkle of anticipation in Fon's eyes.

As before, the open air bar was alive with people, serious hedonists drinking and dancing and chilling out in the heat. The music quickly drew them onto the dance floor and they danced as they had never danced before, for the first time as a couple. They found that they danced well together, as if they had long been practising for this very moment. For Ben this was what he had so many times dreamed of, but it was far better in reality. He marvelled at his partner, at how she danced so easily in her slip-on shoes with so natural a sense of rhythm and with such poise and dignity.

They stopped for drinks and sat down at the table again, Ben now soaked with sweat, but when a favourite track came on, they were back on the floor again, re-energised by the music.

An English girl dancing alone came drifting by them.

'Are you together … you two?' she asked Ben over the music.

'Yes,' he replied.

'You've come here to be with her?'

'You bet I have,' he said, taking pride in being seen with Fon.

It struck him as strange that for her it was the opposite; he was a probable cause of embarrassment and disgrace.

At two in the morning when the bar closed, they took a pick-up back to Ao Sapporot, exhilarated but ready to drop. Ben expected Fon to go straight home but there was an unusual look in her eye, sombre, reflective.

'Come, Ben, sit,' she said.

They sat side by side under the trees at the top of the beach looking at the stark white lights of the squid boats out at sea. Fon did not say much but there was an intensity to her mood that Ben had not seen before and did not quite understand. She had a faraway look on her face, half happy, half tragic, very different to that early morning on the bus returning from the North East when the good times together had so suddenly come to an end. If she was now no longer thinking that things were impossible between them, perhaps dealing with a glimmer of hope was proving even more difficult for her.

'Ben, when you come back Koh Samet next time?' she asked him. It was the same question she had asked before, but this time it had much more significance.

'I'm not sure, Fon. But really, I don't know how I can bear to be away from you at all ... it's intolerable.'

'So why you go then?' she asked innocently.

'Because I've no choice. I can't change my flight and I'm running out of money ... and there's the Thai visa problem too. I've got to go home and get myself sorted out.' He knew it was a feeble answer and was relieved when she accepted it without question.

'Sometimes I dream get passport, go England,' said Fon with a sudden glow of happiness. 'I dream, I dream, Ben, you and me.'

'Yes, my dream too. But anything's possible if you want it enough.'

'You mean life can give you what you want?' she asked doubtfully.

'Yes, but it doesn't just happen on its own. You've got to go for it.'

'Maybe, Ben ... maybe it can for *farang*.'

Sitting in the moonlight leaning forward and staring intently into the darkness, they briefly came together. Ben held Fon for a moment until she stood up and said she must go home and get some sleep. Then it was over, his last but one evening on the island.

32

After the night out at the disco, Ben found time fast accelerating towards the moment he would have to board the ferry and head back home, leaving Fon adrift on her tiny island. It would be like falling off the precipice at the end of the world. Now in his last full day, the thought of leaving her was too awful to contemplate and he tried to banish it from his mind. Being with Fon was a bond that seemed impossible to break and somehow the parting seemed distant and remote. It helped that she was still in high spirits, though she was busy all day and the sun was already setting when his final massage began.

In flirtatious mood, she kept repeating a line from a song as she worked.

'*Hua Hin bpen tin mee hoy*,' she sang.

'What are you singing?'

'Thai love song.'

'So what's it about then?'

'It say beach Hua Hin have many shell.'

'What's that got to do with a love story?' asked Ben intrigued.

'Song say *farang* wait on beach for shell.'

'*Farang* wait for shell? What does that mean?'

'Open shell, inside same lady. *Farang* look for lady on beach,' she giggled coyly.

'That's a bit direct, isn't it?'

He was again struck by the earthiness of the rural Thais.

'*Farang* all the same,' she said. 'Same you … want to go with lady.'

'No, it's only you I want, Fon … and that's because I love you,' he said with added conviction as she firmly massaged his shoulders.

'You say *farang* marry for love,' said Fon giving his neck an extra hard squeeze. 'So better I marry *farang*!'

'Well, at least we do try to be faithful.'

'Okay then Ben, tomorrow before you go, we marry ... yes?' She dissolved into peals of laughter, leaving him feeling slightly uncomfortable.

As the massage ended, Ben now wanted to plan the rest of their last evening together.

'We'll eat together tonight then, just you and me?' he asked her.

'Yes, no problem.'

'Let's go to the beach we ate at before.'

'Okay,' said Fon packing up her things.

'I'll go change and wait for you here,' he said. 'Be quick, we've so little time.'

Ben had a shower and put on cotton trousers and his last clean shirt and sat on the beach and waited. When Fon at last appeared, he realised why she had taken so long. She was carefully made up, looking a little severe in a dark sarong and a tight black sleeveless blouse, her hair formally piled up on top. Her face was impassive and unsmiling, the earlier lightness now gone. As they walked over the headland and along the coast path, she was the first to speak.

'Tomorrow you go what boat, Ben?'

'Eleven thirty. Gives time to say goodbye and get the Bangkok bus.'

'And when you fly England?'

'The day after tomorrow late at night.'

Fon said nothing in reply.

As they ordered food at their favourite beach and began to eat, the sombre mood lifted a little, but Ben was disturbed that there were so many things unresolved between them. So much still needed to be said.

'It's going to be awful leaving you tomorrow,' he began. 'I hate goodbyes.'

'No problem Ben, you come back when you get money. I wait you here.'

He was wondering how she was so sure he would return when she asked him a difficult question.

'Your girlfriend … you seeing her again?'

'No,' said Ben, feeling a bit guilty but figuring she would not answer his awkward questions either. He wanted to ask about the boyfriend she had talked about when they first met, but knew he would not get a proper answer. Instead he raised something else that had been bothering him.

'Fon, you told me not to come back to Ao Sapporot, but you changed your mind. Have there been any problems for you?'

'People say, "Fon, when you marry Ben?"'

'They've got a nerve. Why can't we just be boyfriend and girlfriend?'

'Because if we not married, then I go with *farang* for money.'

'Oh God, Fon, not that again.'

'And they say to Joy, "You like, now you have Papa *farang*?" So Joy, she say, "Yes, I like."'

Ben stopped eating and sat bolt upright.

'Why can't people leave you alone, Fon?' he said angrily. 'You work your butt off all the time and you'd never be bought by anyone.'

'Yes, my life's my work,' she said. 'When cannot work, maybe shave my head, go monastery.'

To Ben's relief she hooted with laughter.

'Yes, but Fon, I want you to have a life, to make something of yourself right now.'

'What life? Which dream?'

'Fon, I just can't bear the thought of leaving you behind.'

'So I get passport? Go England?' she said, her smile vanishing.

'It's not that easy to get a visa … you know what they think about Thai women. But Fon, trust me, please … you've got to trust me.'

'You have good heart, Ben. I do trust you, *jing jing*.'

Walking back to Ao Sapporot after the meal, they left the path and walked to the rocks overlooking the beach where once before they had almost kissed. This time the moon was full and there was no restraint. They held each other tightly, Fon straining upwards, her arms around Ben's neck. After a time they hid together in the rocks, Fon sitting between his knees, cradled back against him. Twisting round, she pulled him towards her and clung to him, her breath coming in short gasps. When at last they disengaged, she lay in his arms looking up at him.

Ben knew that whatever was to be said between them had to be said now. This was probably their last chance.

'I keep telling you how I feel about you, Fon,' he began, 'but you told me you'll only say when your heart's sure as a rock. I go home tomorrow and I have to know.'

'Last time say I love you forty percent ... now go up litty bit!' she said, trying to lighten things with a laugh.

'Fon, seriously, I can't go away not knowing.'

'Okay, Ben, I love you ninety five percent ... maybe ninety nine!'

She gave him a roguish smile.

'Fon, you're playing with me again.'

'No, Ben, not playing. How I ask you come here with me if not serious?'

'So are you sure of your feelings then?'

'Sure. Since you come back Koh Samet, I know my heart.'

'Yes Fon, but what do you feel? You've got to tell me,' he demanded impatiently.

'Ben, I tell you. Now I know my heart same rock.'

When Ben finally got back to his hut late that last night, there were still ten hours before he was to be parted from Fon. On waking the next morning, he had only four and a half hours left before the eleven thirty ferry was due to leave. Nearing the end of the world, he could not yet see the edge of the precipice, though he knew it was coming very close.

He slowly packed his things, paid the bill for his hut and went down for breakfast. He could hardly eat. When Fon did not appear, he decided to wait for her on the fallen tree trunk and within minutes saw her coming along the beach. She was in dark slacks and a grey top and could only manage a shadow of her usual smile.

'Where were you?' said Ben.

'Have booking nine o'clock and start massage. When I not see you, give Gaeo to finish, then come looking.'

'You okay?'

'Have to be, Ben.'

He felt sick, his heart thumping, his mouth dry.

'What are you going to do now?' he asked her.

'Help you do your bag.'

'You mean in my room?' She had never come near his hut before.

'Yes, why not?' she said.

As they walked, they passed some cleaners admiring a new motorcycle and Fon stopped to talk to them, leaving Ben to go ahead on his own. He was just finishing brushing his teeth at the sink when she appeared round the door, smiling and animated. She came up behind him, slipped her arms round his waist and pressed herself up against him. He turned to face her and they held each other for the last time, unselfconsciously admiring themselves in the mirror.

'We look good together, you and me,' he said.

'Yes … beautiful dream!'

'I can't bear it … this time it'll really kill me,' he sighed.

'Up to you, Ben. I have to be strong for Joy,' said Fon coolly.

Then Ben tried to kiss her, but she resisted him.

'No, Ben, not here. I shy,' she said.

'But nobody can see us,' he protested.

'Not now … too hot inside.'

Hearing the cleaners coming to make up the hut for the next guests, she slipped away from him and went to the door.

Now it was finally all over. Ben could do nothing to step back from the void that was opening up in front of him. Stuffing his spongebag into the top of his rucksack he lifted it over one shoulder and followed Fon out onto the veranda and down the steps.

'So what now?' he asked her.

'Have booking manicure, ten thirty,' she said.

He was dismayed at first but then relieved; at least it would help fill the awful final hour. There was nowhere they could go to be alone, there was nothing more that could be said or done.

Fon found her customer, a pleasant middle-aged woman sitting in a deckchair by the beach restaurant. She collected her box from under a tree, knelt down on the sand beside the deckchair and began the manicure. Ben sat at a table nearby and watched, going through the motions of reading the novel he had tucked down the pocket of his pack. Time was inexorable as with total concentration Fon trimmed the woman's finger nails, clipping and filing and applying crimson nail varnish. Lost in her work she did not once glance up, even though Ben was sitting so close by. It was as if he had already gone, the leave-taking over.

He was disturbed by her detachment, though her ashen face gave her away. For a few moments she chatted happily with the woman as she worked, then asked him to get her a bottle of drinking water. As he walked to the bar, Gaeo came up to say goodbye and squeezed his arm affectionately. Blinking back tears he just managed to blurt out, 'Look after Fon for me,' before stumbling on, head down.

When a vendor came by selling fruit, Fon wanted a coconut with a straw. Ben got it for her and bought some bananas for the long journey. He wandered off to check that his rucksack was still where he had left it, but still Fon did not look up. It was now almost time to go as the boat boys were launching the shuttle boat. This was the moment he most dreaded.

When the manicure was finished, he rejoined her and for a few moments they were alone together, sitting on her blue sheet on the sand. She was silent, her eyes down, and then in the dying seconds she spoke.

'Ben, your nails … can cut them for you,' she said, taking his hand in hers and cutting them for him; far too short for his liking, though he was past caring.

He stared at her intently for the last time. Looking so tragic, she somehow seemed even smaller than before. He desperately wanted to say something significant, something memorable, but nothing came.

'Thanks Fon,' was all he could say as she put her nail clippers away.

'Okay Ben, manicure free today, but next time you pay!' She looked up and gave him a wan smile.

By now the small boat had already left the beach loaded with tourists on its first trip to where the ferry was moored in the bay.

'Look,' said Ben, 'the boat's gone. But no problem, I'll just have to stay.'

'And I can get passport … go England,' said Fon.

It was a valiant effort but it did not help and Ben now wanted it to be over. The real goodbye had been in his room in front of the mirror an hour or so earlier. This was just prolonging the agony.

When he realised the boat had returned to the beach, he glanced uselessly at his watch. They both got up and stood side by side under the trees looking out to sea at the ferry that would take him away. But they were still briefly together; it was not yet quite over. Their fingers became intertwined, a gentle squeeze, a sidelong glance, all the world oblivious to them. Then he let go of her hand and shouldered his rucksack.

Fon said, 'See you, Ben.' And, in a choked voice, Ben said, 'Yes, see you, Fon,' and stumbled off down the beach under the weight of his pack. Fon did not follow but stood rooted to the spot as if in shock.

Ben was the last onto the boat and remained standing so Fon could see him as the boat pushed out through the waves. Halfway to the ferry he saw that Fon had left the trees and was running down to the water's edge. She blew him a kiss of farewell with both hands as she had done a few glorious days before, but this time she did it twice and once more again. He could see her dancing up to her knees in the waves, trying to throw off the bleakness of the moment. He raised a hand in reply.

When the boat came alongside the ferry, he went up to the top deck and stood in the stern and stared back at the distant shore. He could see that Fon had been joined by Gaeo; they seemed to be standing together talking. He tried waving with both arms but there was no response. Then the big diesel engine started up and the men cast off the mooring lines. As the ferry moved steadily out to sea, he stood leaning over the rail, his eyes straining towards the tiny figures on the beach. Just before it rounded the headland and the bay disappeared from view, he thought he saw them separate and go in different directions along the beach for another day's work.

Ben sat in a corner at the stern to avoid anyone staring at him and tried to stay composed. But something more precious than he had ever possessed was being ripped out of him as their two worlds were torn apart. Briefly he held back the tears but then the white sand and jet skis, the brightly coloured umbrellas and holiday bungalows along the shore misted over and became a distant blur.

But life had to go on. After a depressing bus ride back to Bangkok sitting too close to the smell of the toilet cubicle and with the air conditioning hardly working, Ben took a taxi from the Eastern Bus Terminus to the Georgia Hotel off Sukhumvit Road. Now early evening, he checked into a top floor room and took a shower. It was a pity he had no clean clothes to change into; he would just have to make sure nobody came too close.

The familiar old-world atmosphere of the hotel was a calming influence, distancing him a little from the traumas of the day, and he found himself thinking of Emma. He went downstairs to check his email and was pleased to find a brief message from her saying she was arriving in Bangkok at the Southern Bus Terminus the following evening. She was planning to go direct to the airport after some final shopping and would be there at least three hours before the flight was due to leave late that night. It crossed his mind that if he got to the airport when the flight desk opened, perhaps they could check in together.

As he slowly rejoined the world of the living, he began to grasp that tomorrow was the first day of Songkhran, the Thai New Year festival, and that he would have the whole day free before flying out that night. Maca had told him about Songkhran and how the Thais go crazy, thronging the streets and chucking water at each other. As the hot season was over and it was now the very hot season, this seemed a thoroughly good idea and, despite everything, he was not going to miss out on it.

A long night's sleep, misery and the swimming pool got him through to noon of his very last day when he had to settle up and check out of his hotel room. He put on his oldest shorts and a faded shirt which he could dump when they were wet and chalky later that afternoon. He stuffed the clothes he was going to wear on the flight into a plastic bag and left his rucksack with the receptionist. As he was paying his bill, he met a French couple who asked him how to get to Khao San Road. This was always the liveliest and wettest place in town where most of the young people of Bangkok would already be throwing water and smearing white stuff on each others' faces, so Ben suggested they share a taxi.

On the way there the taxi was sprayed by kids with hoses and by marauding pick-ups packed with excited teenagers armed with water guns. In the taxi they were safe and dry but passengers in tuk tuks were at risk of a dousing. Nearing Khao San Road the traffic locked solid and Ben and the French couple decided to get out and walk. Saying goodbye to them, he pressed ahead on his own. Now the streets were overwhelmed by tens of thousands of young Thais aimlessly milling around. They were mostly male, in shorts and tee shirts, all comprehensively soaked and covered in white paste. The roads, pavements, parked cars, phone boxes and buildings were awash with water and liberally smeared in white. It was mayhem, a seething, excited mob out to have fun and to get very wet and white.

Ben found the crowds becoming denser as he came within a few hundred yards of Khao San Road and, with the revellers packed shoulder to shoulder, he could hardly move. His six foot height was an advantage as he was able to tower over most of the Thais, though a foreigner was a conspicuous and interesting target. Water fell in torrents from above and came horizontally from windows, from balconies, from parked trucks, from everywhere. He was by now totally sodden, but it was so hot that the showers were very welcome.

Nor could he avoid being smeared with liquid chalk. As he made his way through the crush, the gentle faces of the boys and girls gazed up at him, wished him 'Happy New Year', and caressed his cheeks with a handful of white paste from their plastic pots. He soon got the idea that as they came within range he too could dip his hand into their pots and plaster a little revenge on their cheeks. Nobody resisted or ducked away; they all took it on the chin. Khao San Road was an aggression-free zone.

The road was now jammed solid with sodden grey ghosts. At one bottleneck caused by a parked truck, the street was even more crowded and the pressure increased to the point that toes were getting trodden on.

Ben was quite glad Emma was not there as she hated crowds. He decided to cut through one of the side alleys to the lanes at the back and found a beer garden where he sat and had a drink, the chalk drying and cracking on his cheeks. Then he fought his way back to Rajadamnoen Avenue to find transport to Sukhumvit Road, but it looked a forlorn hope. Both sides of the carriageway were closed off and there were thousands of young Thais cruising around flinging water, flirting with the girls and showing off to their friends. It was a happy disaster area of water and whiteness.

By a small miracle an empty tuk tuk came by, so Ben flagged it down and climbed onto the open seat. The driver was in manic mood and the noisy little monster stormed away through the milling crowds, swerving round the Democracy Monument and braking hard at the first traffic jam. Just as it stopped, one of the cruising pick-ups loaded with wild-eyed warriors and water guns drew alongside. They whooped with joy when they saw the *farang* in the back of the tuk tuk. Ben was a sitting duck, but it was so hot he could take to yet another drenching like a duck to water.

Songkhran, a new year, a promise of new beginnings, had given him a few hours when he had almost managed to forget about Fon. It was boarding the airport bus from Sukhumvit Road that brought home to him the awful finality of leaving Thailand and the girl he loved, to fly back to London and whatever his future might bring.

33

The taxi that took Emma from her final shopping in Siam Square to Bangkok's Don Muang airport was old and smelly. It took an age to find its way through the traffic jams and then hurtled along the elevated expressway, the driver juggling with the wheel to keep it in a straight line. She watched the interminable cityscape for the last time, psyching herself up to re-enter the real world of jobs and responsibility and thinking about Ben. She was not at all sure how she felt about seeing him again; much water had flowed under many bridges since she walked out on him on Koh Samet.

Since breaking free and being apart for a time, her new-found freedom to explore fresh relationships had proved to be totally liberating. She had made friends of many kinds who took her seriously and showed interest in everything she had to say. Now she was confident she would no longer be overwhelmed by his irrepressible personality and almost wanted him to be there at the check-in desk, if only to show off her own transformation. To her surprise, she had done extraordinarily well travelling alone.

Saying a silent goodbye to the heat and humidity of Thailand, she pushed her baggage trolley through the automatic door into the air-conditioned chill of the airport. It was an immediate return to the bleak anonymity of the industrial society, a world of plate glass, stainless steel and plastic. Even the Thai airport staff seemed distant, depressed by the impersonal departures hall and the endless stream of foreign faces.

Her backpack had grown heavy with presents in the last few hours but it was still too early to check it onto the flight. After an uncomfortable night on the bus coming back from the southern islands, she now dreaded the dreary wait in the airport and the long flight home. It could help to pass the time if Ben turned up soon, though it might go very badly. He had not replied to her last email and, if he was still seething from his dumping and the disaster at the Regal, he could refuse to have anything to do with her. But she was hoping diplomatic relations would be restored; apart from anything else, she was curious to hear about his time in Thailand as a single man.

Still more than three hours before the flight departure time, she was sitting on a hard plastic seat reading a novel when she heard a familiar voice behind her.

'Hey Emm, there you are. Fantastic!'

'Hi Ben, I wasn't sure you'd show up,' she said a little awkwardly.

They did one of those cheek to cheek kisses that usually mean nothing, but which for Emma had the association of past intimacy; Ben was still an attractive guy.

'Emm, you look amazing ... never seen you looking so good,' he said smiling broadly.

'You too, you devil.'

'How d'you take off so much weight with all that food out there?'

'Swimming and the outdoor stuff, I suppose. Just seemed to drop off me.'

'Grown out those highlights too. Dark hair's still the best.'

'I'd noticed you liked black hair!'

Ben ignored her gentle taunt.

'Let's get a drink then, while we wait for check in,' he said.

Emma was relieved Ben had bounced back so easily since the split-up, though she hoped being given the push had not been entirely painless for him. She let him open the cross-examination.

'So what've you been up to, Emm? How was Chiang Mai?' he asked as they sat down and ordered coffees.

'Really great. The mountains always were my first choice,' she said pointedly.

'Tell me more then,' said Ben. 'I'm not prying.'

'Well, there were lots of us coming and going, meeting new people all the time ... Swedes, Dutch, Canadians. Stayed in this amazing guesthouse inside the moat just off Moolmuang Road. This Thai guy called Eddie's rebuilt an old teak house, planted palms and things around the rooms and furnished it all with antiques. It's the sort of place you can't sit and have a drink without chatting to everyone.'

'Sounds great. It was sociable like that on Koh Chang.'

'You went to Koh Chang? Everyone says it's excellent.'

'Brilliant. So what did you get up to in Chiang Mai?'

'You know, the usual things ... going to temples, eating, drinking, music. There's some great places ... like the roof-top bar by the Tha Pae Gate. And we fell in love with this Thai singer called Nong at one of the restaurants ... sang to an acoustic guitar. Don Maclean, Cat Stevens, Beatles ... that sort of stuff. We were his fan club for a few days.'

She casually leaned across and tried Ben's cappuccino.

'Do any trekking?' he said, ignoring the familiarity.

'We did a three day trek near Pai. Two day ones, you're on the road half the time.'

'It's a bit packaged isn't it though, the trekking?'

'Suppose so, but it's still worth it. You see places you'd never get to on your own and the scenery's mind-blowing.'

'Do you actually get into the hilltribes?'

'Of course ... had one freezing night in a village, miles from anywhere.'

'But wasn't it a bit touristy? Souvenirs for sale and stuff?'

'Not at all. In fact they almost totally ignored us ... didn't even sell us food.'

'And did you see anything of their way of life?'

'Yes, lots. And Gin, our guide was great ... dead keen to tell us all about them.'

'Which tribe was it?' he asked as he watched the people going by with loaded luggage trolleys.

'Lisu. Gin said they'd moved from southern China to Burma a few generations ago and crossed into Thailand in the early seventies. They're refugees really. Some of them don't have Thai identity cards so they can't register their kids for education ... can't even get a motorbike licence.

Seems it's a big problem up there.'

'And how do they live?'

'In bamboo huts on the hillside … it's pretty basic. And they raise chickens and pigs and clear the jungle for slash and burn agriculture. We saw a small field of opium poppies … they grow some for "medicinal" purposes. Then there's upland rice … and ginger which is good money but depletes the soil. They have to rest the land for three or four years and they clear it again by burning it off, which the authorities don't like. And we saw them bringing bat guano down from the limestone caves in the mountains for fertiliser.'

'So you saw a hell of a lot then.' Ben looked quite envious.

'Yes, but what fascinated me most was their belief in spirits which seems to hold the place together. We couldn't go into their huts because our spirits might come in with us. And they'd had a run of accidents and fires and stuff in the last few years so they'd moved the whole village just to escape the evil spirits. We saw the remains of the old village not far away. Loads of good timber was left behind because if you take it with you, the spirits'll come too.'

'And after the night in the village?'

'We walked for about five hours. Went down to a river and spent the night in huts, then the next day, elephant rides and bamboo rafting. That bit was tourist stuff, though the mountains and jungle are still the real thing.'

'And after Chiang Mai?' asked Ben artlessly.

'Well, you know what happened after Chiang Mai, don't you, Ben.'

'You mean you cocking it up and not finding me at the Regal when I was there all the time?'

'It wasn't my fault if the receptionist was incompetent,' said Emma.

'Bloody was! It was horrible for me, you not showing up.'

'But I asked at reception and they told me you weren't there. Not fun for me either.'

'Bet you were pleased you missed me though,' he moaned.

'Come on Ben, give us a break!' she said, exasperated.

As they were talking, she looked up at the departures screen above their heads and saw that their flight was now listed for check in. The moment of tension was immediately forgotten and Ben got up and followed close behind as she walked briskly to the check-in desk, wheeling their bags on the trolley.

'Passport and ticket Ben, and put the stuff on the scales,' she said as they reached the desk.

'Anything you say m'lady,' teased Ben.

'Can we have two seats together please,' she asked the check-in clerk, 'preferably with a window and near the back.'

'Why at the back?' he asked her.

'You get a better view from behind the wing and if the plane crashes you're the last to crash.'

The next long wait was in the departures lounge where Ben browsed in Asia Books while Emma struggled with her novel. When he sat down again, they continued the debriefing where they had left off.

'So after Chiang Mai, Cambodia was it?' he asked her.

'Yes, Angkor Wat was something ... the biggest ancient temple complex in the world. It really made up for the road from Poipet to Siem Reap. Six hours like sardines in the back of an open pick-up ... heat and dust, sore bum, broken back and nowhere to put your legs. Don't know how we survived.'

'That travel agent girl in Khao San warned us, didn't she.'

'Yes, but it was worth it ... Khmer temples everywhere, and the countryside's so beautiful. Siem Reap's attractive in a dusty sort of way with a river and bullock carts ... the cartwheels have seventeen spokes, same as on the temple carvings. But now they're going for tourism in a big way and it's all changing too fast.'

'How's Cambodia compared to Thailand?' he asked her.

'It's dirt poor ... decades behind. Sitting in a French bistro with a line of amputees on the pavement looking in at us eating nouvelle cuisine for a quid or two really got to me. Though I wouldn't have missed going to Angkor with my mates for anything.'

'Better than being with me?' he said playfully.

'Shut up, Ben!' she said with a smile, pulling in her legs to let some people go by.

'So where did you go then, Emm?'

'After Angkor, south to Samui and Koh Pha Ngan. I loved the islands.'

'Go with the same people?'

'No, not all of them.'

'You there for the Full Moon Party?'

'Just got back ... that's why I'm so knackered.' She pulled a wry face.

'Hideous or what?'

'Well, if you like Ibiza and the other big scenes, it was amazing ... but better because it's on a brilliant beach. I wasn't wowed by it that much ... but yeah, I enjoyed it. Some of the party posers got to me though ... all pumped up and preening and carrying these little plastic buckets.'

'For making sandcastles?'

'No sweetie!' she said derisively. 'Buckets with drinking straws sticking out of 'em ... usually a set of Red Bull, Sang Som and cola. Pretty lethal ... but fun! The music's good too and for company you've got about seven thousand sweaty people to choose from.'

'So who did you choose then?' quizzed Ben, half-seriously.

'Wouldn't you like to know!' she said, watching carefully for his reaction.

'Not that bothered,' he replied, pausing for effect. 'I've got good memories of that full moon too.'

Emma looked at him hard, but it was too risky asking questions as any personal revelations would have to be reciprocated.

'Hat Rin's incredible in the moonlight, but the Full Moon Party's a bit over the top,' she said, sticking to safer ground. 'Incredible how they keep the booze flowing.'

'It's big money keeping that number of people pissed all night.'

'Tell you what really bugs me though,' she added. 'It's one thing the Thais having a good time and trashing their own place, but we ought to feel guilty doing it for them.'

She leaned back and yawned. It had been a long wait and the screen was still showing their flight as checking in.

'So it was pretty good then. Thailand was okay after all?'

asked Ben.

'I adore it … but I feel bad about what mass tourism's doing. You know, the sex trade, uncontrolled development on the beaches and so on.'

'Like on Koh Chang … it's an environmental disaster waiting to happen.'

'And my travelling was a bit superficial too. I'm not sure I even began to scratch the surface. You meet other travellers which is great but you can't even come close to the Thais. I love them to bits but it's so difficult to get to know them.'

Feeling suddenly unsettled, Ben wandered over to a window and stared out at the aircraft parked on the apron. Emma's comment about the Thais had brought back the pain of parting in all its fury. Not so far away, Fon would now be asleep in her hut with Joy and he was about to board a plane and fly to the other side of the world.

His thoughts were interrupted by Emma coming across and wanting to talk.

'So you made lots of friends after I went?' she asked him.

'Sure did, especially on Koh Chang,' he said as they sat down again.

'Where else did you go then?'

'Went to the North East.'

'Why the North East?' she probed.

'To get away from the tourists and see a bit of the real Thailand.'

'How did you manage that?'

'Stayed with a rice-farming family in the middle of nowhere near Buriram.'

'And who were they?' she persisted.

'Thai friends who asked me to go,' he said evasively, glancing around the lounge.

'Yes, but who? Spill the beans, Ben.'

'Two sisters from Koh Samet … took me to see their mum.'

'Did I meet them?'

'No, not really,' he said, staring vacantly at the people sitting opposite.

'Hang on, you don't mean that masseur? Fon was it?'

He hesitated before answering.

'Yes ... but so what? Her sister Jinda came too.'

'Ben, I had a feeling you were going to go crazy about Fon. I know you too well.'

'Sod off Emm. I haven't asked what you've been up to.'

'And I haven't asked you either. But I hope to God you knew what you were doing and haven't messed her about.'

'What d'you mean? Course I didn't mess her about,' he said edgily.

'You know exactly what I mean, you donut. If she took you to meet her family, it must've been a big thing for her.'

'No, it wasn't like that at all. She's serious and independent and not into boyfriends. And anyway she's got her dead sister's child to look after.'

They were interrupted for a moment by a couple wanting the seats next to them.

'So what did the sister die of?' Emma asked, refusing to be distracted.

'No idea.'

'And do you know why Fon took the child? When we had our bust-up you told me she had a boyfriend somewhere.'

'What are you getting at?' he said, leaning forward and staring at the floor.

'Nothing ... but can you take everything she says at face value? She probably tells you what she thinks you want to hear.'

'I'm sure I can trust her,' he said sharply, shifting uncomfortably in his seat.

'But can she trust *you*, Ben? Knowing you, you probably raised her hopes and promised the earth. You don't know you're doing it, but you come on so strong.'

'Course I didn't! And she's quite capable of looking after herself anyway,' he said irritably.

'But you're so unequal, Ben. The thought of marrying a rich foreigner must be irresistible, even for the most independent Thai woman. Especially as she's got a child to think of.'

'Come on, Emm! Marriage? Do you really think I'd rush into something with a girl off the beach who hardly speaks English. Anyway there's not a chance of me staying in Thailand or making a living here … even if I wanted to.'

'And what would mummy think if you brought home a Thai masseur?' she taunted him.

'No way! It'd never work in England,' he said, glaring back at her, unable to believe he was saying all this.

'So Ben, the whole affair was a non-starter from the beginning, wasn't it,' said Emma, rubbing it in. 'But I bet Fon doesn't look at a quick fling in the way you do. I dread to think of her falling for you and waiting on the island for you to come back and rescue her.'

'No Emm, you've got it all wrong,' said Ben looking rattled.

'Have I? I hope so for Fon's sake.'

The screen was now listing Qantas flight QF301 as ready for boarding, so they gathered their things and walked to the boarding gate, Ben silent and miserable.

Sitting together on the plane for the long flight home, they were plied with surprisingly good food and a generous flow of Australian wine. Feeling mellow and sleepy, both their tongues began to loosen.

'So our Thailand trip didn't exactly turn out as we expected, did it,' said Ben.

'In Bangkok I wished I'd never come. Once I'd dumped you, it was okay though,' said Emma with a twinkle.

'I love you too, Emm! Bet you went wild on your own.'

'Well, it's my life, but if you really want to know, I didn't go to Chiang Mai with a bloke … I went with two. Though now there's nothing ongoing as they say.'

'You went off me bigtime, didn't you,' he said resentfully. 'Can't think why.'

'Because you really pissed me off, Ben Farnsworth. You and your talk about having a cultural experience when you were only there for the beer. All you wanted was to skate over the surface and use the place as an adventure playground, just like the typical traveller.'

'Well, I saw more than you did. I went out and helped with the rice harvest in the North East and met the locals.'

'And got into their knickers! That's one way in I suppose.'

'No, seriously, Emm. I learned a lot … I mean about the gap between us and the rest of the world,' he said earnestly. 'Think of the rice farmers next time you chuck rice in the bin. We're seriously rich compared to them.'

'Suppose I was only a tourist,' admitted Emma, 'so maybe you didn't do too badly.'

'You should've stuck with me then,' he grinned.

'No, Ben, splitting up was the right thing. It gave us the chance to be ourselves for a change.'

She stared out at the light on the wing tip flashing in the darkness.

'But Emm, it was a real shock when you dumped me … couldn't see what I'd done wrong,' he said quietly.

'You mean all those naughty things that made me cross!' she said icily. 'Like you leering at the strippers, just gagging to fuck them? I wasn't jealous, but you were so pathetic, Ben. And you walked all over me.'

'No, I never!' he said without much conviction.

'You damned well did! You took me for granted, you didn't listen to me, didn't give me any space … and, worst of all, you told me I was fat. You managed to make me feel bad about myself in just about every way possible.'

'That's really rubbish.'

' … and just when I was having an all-time low.'

'Were you, Emm? Why?' he said, sounding surprised.

'Think it was a touch of DAG syndrome. You know … depression after graduating. So I tried binge eating and travelling with you instead. Stupid or what!'

'Thanks Emm! Anyway, it was the same for me … I'd just graduated too.'

'Yes, but you've always got your family backing you up and you never have any doubts about yourself. You were just so bloody irritating, Ben, I could've killed you.'

'Still homicidal are we then?' he joked.

'Not now … well, not quite as bad. Maybe I don't care any more.' She downed the rest of her red wine and looked around for the stewardess.

'Well, I'm sorry I wasn't the perfect man, but at least I didn't go with any of the bar girls ... not once.'

'I wouldn't be sitting anywhere near you if I thought you had!' she said forcefully.

'And, Emm, I'm sorry I got up your nose in Bangkok, because now the commercial sex scene really turns me off. Selling the Thai girl to promote tourism makes me puke.'

'You always were a bit slow off the mark. In Spain when I wouldn't go to the bullfight you thought I was being a wimp. Same as the bullfighting, just by sitting in the bars and buying beer you sustain the trade in women.'

'Suppose it does ...'

'And for God's sake Ben, stop calling them Thai girls ... they're not girls, they're women.'

'Okay, Emm, it's a fair cop!' he said with a smile, though he knew she had a point.

'And it's what you were saying about the wealth gap too,' Emma went on. 'It's so difficult not to exploit ordinary Thai people in whatever we do.'

'You don't have to remind me,' he said.

'Don't I?' she demanded. 'It's why I worry about you being so close with Fon.'

Emma expected him to reply but he just sat looking glum before changing the subject.

'So we're the wealthy ones eh, Emm? Going to pay off the overdrafts are we then?'

'Dunno about you, but I am. Didn't tell you ... I think I've got a job.'

'Wicked! Tell me more,' he said, looking pleased.

'You remember I had an interview with Consageo?'

'Who?'

'Used to be Consolidated Biscuit ... head office in Swindon. I applied for their management training scheme more than six months ago and they kept my application on file. Just got an email from Mum saying they're making me an offer.'

'Fancy you beating me to a job, Emm. Now I'll really have to pull my finger out.'

'Typical! That was vintage Farnsworth,' she said sourly.

'Sorry Emm … and sorry about all the other stuff in Bangkok too. Got kind of over-excited I guess. Hope I've matured a bit since the slap in the face.'

'Well, there was plenty of room for improvement, wasn't there.'

'Thanks Emm, thanks a million!'

He settled back in his seat and pulled the blanket up around his neck.

Neither of them slept very much and, as the plane crossed Europe, Emma was aware that Ben was awake.

'Three years at uni together seemed a lifetime, didn't it,' she whispered, 'but it's funny how little you really know each other.'

'Emm, I thought I could read you like a book.'

'No, Ben … you didn't see the changes coming.'

'And maybe there are some things about your partner you can never discover,' he said.

'Like what?'

'Like whether you were upset when you missed me at the Regal.'

'Or whether you slept with Fon,' she retorted.

'Not that again! Does it really matter that much?'

'Yes Ben, it does. If it matters to Fon, it matters one hell of a lot.'

Flying west across the world, the night seemed an eternity. Emma envied Ben being met at Heathrow by his mother and was dreading the wait at the bleak coach station with its surly attendants and the depressing bus ride back to Swindon. Thailand had done her good, but life had been on hold for long enough and now she was ready to deal with whatever it threw at her, with or without Ben for company.

Nearing Heathrow, the aircraft left the sunny uplands above the clouds and descended through the gloom for a long approach to the runway. Sitting by the window, Emma could see nothing but greyness. It was a heavy landing in high wind, the plane coming down with a crash, causing one of the overhead lockers to fly open. As they taxied towards the terminal building, she stared out at the rain-swept runway and leaden sky. Thailand seemed somehow irrelevant, already a distant memory.

Epilogue

Three weeks after his return, Ben received a letter from Fon. He found it disturbing to have in his hand the small pink sheet of lined paper closely written in Thai script and to be totally unable to extract any meaning from it. The letter sat in his drawer for almost a week until he went up to London for a job interview with a firm of solicitors in the City. After the interview was over he found a Thai restaurant and a waiter told him what it said.

Fon started by saying she hoped he was okay and that the journey home had passed off safely. Joy was well, but she had heard that her Mama had been ill and she was worried about her. The beach was still crowded with tourists and she was busy with her work every day. She said that on Ben's birthday, the seventeenth, she had remembered him by getting up early, cooking for the monks and praying for him in the temple; giving alms and making merit is so much better than squandering money on parties.

The letter then ended on an emotional note, Fon saying she was sorry she had been unable to look at him the day he left the island for the last time. If she had met his eye, she could not have contained her tears. Finally she said she missed him desperately and hoped he would write soon.

Confused and upset, Ben did not ask the waiter to write a reply. Instead he went home to collect his thoughts and a few days later when he had a free moment, he wrote a letter to Fon in English. As a friend would have to read it for her, he could not say anything too personal.

He told her he was well and hoped her mother's health was improving. He said he too missed her very much and that he had a wonderful memory of their time together in Thailand which would stay with him for the rest of his life. And he broke the good news that he was to be sponsored by one of the big London law firms to study law at college for two years before starting a two year training contract with them. It was an excellent firm which paid well and he would be able to clear his debts almost immediately. He thought of telling her that the firm had an office in Bangkok but for some reason decided not to mention it just yet. He asked her to say hello to Joy and Gaeo for him and finished by saying he hoped she would write again when there was any news from the island.

He did not post the letter for a couple of days but took it to the Post Office when he went in to renew his mother's car tax. The counter clerk was brisk and efficient. As she weighed the letter and took his money, she chatted about the dreadful weather they were having before finally dropping it into a sack of airmail packets on the floor behind her.